HIS KISS WAS WONDERFUL. . . .

Her whole body felt hot, as if he'd lit a fire inside her that danced beneath her skin and made her burn in places that were as shocking as they were secret.

Nicholas groaned his torment. A ragged sob escaped him. Never in his life had he desired a woman as he did Sophie; never had he felt such urgency, such unbridled need. There was no coyness in her passion, no self-consciousness or calculation. She gave it freely and joyously, with a generosity that was as innocent as it was brazen. Driven beyond all thought by her responsiveness, Nicholas deepened the kiss.

Sighing her rapture, Sophie melted against him. Oh, those sensations . . . the ecstasy! They kindled within her the strangest and most bewildering desires, ones that made her moan and flush and quiver all over. She sighed again and clung to him tighter. Ecstasy, yes . . . sheer ecstasy.

FOR ALL ETERNITY

Heather Cullman

A TOPAZ BOOK

TOPAZ
Published by the Penguin Group
Penguin Putnam Inc., 375 Hudson Street,
New York, New York 10014, U.S.A.
Penguin Books Ltd, 27 Wrights Lane,
London W8 5TZ, England
Penguin Books Australia Ltd,
Ringwood,
Victoria, Australia
Penguin Books Canada Ltd, 10 Alcorn Avenue,
Toronto, Ontario, Canada M4V 3B2
Penguin Books (N.Z.) Ltd, 182–190 Wairau Road,
Auckland 10, New Zealand

Penguin Books Ltd, Registered Offices:
Harmondsworth, Middlesex, England

First published by Topaz, an imprint of Dutton NAL,
a member of Penguin Putnam Inc.

First Printing, December, 1998
10 9 8 7 6 5 4 3 2 1

 REGISTERED TRADEMARK—MARCA REGISTRADA

Printed in the United States of America

For sweet T.K.,
My little lost kitty boy.

I hope that wherever you are
has milky treats and hammy-cheesy bagels.
We love and miss you,
and pray that you are safe.

Chapter 1

London, 1807

The drawing room was hot, insufferably so, the air scented with a headache-inducing fusion of beeswax, potpourri, and the cloying mélange of perfumes that wafted from the fashionable crowd. Yet, despite the stifling atmosphere, there was nowhere else Sophie Barrington would rather be at that moment than there, at Lady Stuckely's exclusive *soirée*.

"Lumpish," murmured someone at her left. Recognizing the voice as belonging to her best friend, Lydia Kemp, she glanced to her side to find the girl stationed there. "Lumpish," Lydia repeated, indicating a newly arrived gentleman with a nod of her green and gold turbaned head.

Raising her fan to hide her scrutiny, Sophie swept his length with her critical gaze, shuddering when she came to his spindly, white silk encased legs. "And will you look at those calves," she whispered. "Dreadful!"

"Mmm, yes. Dreadful," her companion concurred, "though not half as dreadful as his thighs. How he can stand with those twiggy thighs, I'll never know."

Sophie cringed at Lydia's indelicate observation. Not, of course, that she, herself, hadn't noticed the man's deficiency in that particular area. It was just that she knew better than to remark upon it, especially in public where they might be overheard and branded as brass-faced romps.

Though she knew her words were in vain, for outspokenness was as much a part of her friend as her dark, gypsy wild hair and catlike green eyes, she felt it her duty to chide her. "Really, Lydia. You know as well as I that it is exceedingly ill-bred to remark upon such things."

As she always did when called to task for her frankness, Lydia merely shrugged. "If being honest is ill-bred, then I suppose I'm the most ill-bred chit in all of England. And since we've established me as such"—she stared pointedly at Lord Motcombe, one of Sophie's most ardent admirers—"I see no reason to refrain from stating that I've never seen a worse cut suit of clothes than the one Lord Motcombe is wearing this evening."

While thighs and related nether regions were subjects to be whispered about only in girlish confidence, everything else about gentlemen was open to comment. And having voiced her perfunctory protest to Lydia for breaching that rule, Sophie felt free to resume their game and do just that. "Oh, I don't think the fault is so much that of his tailor, but of his lordship's figure," she said, regarding his narrow chest and sloping shoulders with disfavor. "One can only improve so much with padding, you know."

At that moment their victim glanced up from the platter of oysters he studied and spied them looking at him. Instantly his expression of bored petulance transformed into the one of fawning ingratiation that Sophie always found so odious.

She groaned. Any moment now he would saunter over, and they would be stuck listening to his inane prattle. Apparently Lydia found that prospect as torturous as she did, for she looped her arm through Sophie's and pulled her into the crush of people at their right. Nodding and smiling as they went, Sophie allowed her friend to escort her to a small clearing next to the fireplace.

Like everything else in the room—the friezes of gilt plasterwork dragons, the painted glass lanterns and gaudy Chinese wallpaper—the red-and-black-pagoda-shaped monstrosity of a fireplace reflected their hostess's zeal for everything Oriental. After sharing several disparaging observations about that fact, the two women turned their attention back to the crowd.

"Fine eyes, bulging belly," Lydia pronounced of Lord Swale, resuming their game from their new vantage point. Appraising the gentlemen was their favorite pastime, one they'd invented while watching the passersby from their boarding school window in Bath.

Easily falling back into the spirit of their wicked sport, Sophie declared of Mr. Trent, "Good figure, face like a ferret."

Lydia nodded. "And whatever do you suppose you call that stuff on his head? It's altogether too limp to be called hair."

Sophie tittered and homed in on Lord Walsingham, who had the misfortune to stroll by at that moment. "Well enough looking, but hardly exceptional. Certainly not handsome enough for a husband."

"I should say not," Lydia agreed, then turned her attention to his lordship's companion. "Fine thighs. Too bad he's bran-faced."

Sophie was about to take her to task again for her thigh remark when Lord Quentin Somerville swaggered into view. Just the sight of him was enough to make the words die on her lips. With his romantic tousle of mahogany curls, his extraordinary violet eyes and elegant build, he embodied the word magnificent.

"Perfect," Lydia declared, breaking their awed silence. "Flawlessly beautiful. Too bad he's only a second son, eh?"

"Tragic when you consider his brother's looks," Sophie replied on a sigh. "How a man as handsome as Lord Quentin can have such an ugly brother, I'll never understand."

"Lord Lyndhurst? Ugly?" Lydia stared at her with mock consternation. "My dearest Sophie, are you quite certain that your eyesight is up to snuff?"

Though they had been in accord in their assessment of every other man they had seen during the Season, Lyndhurst remained their one bone of contention. And as happened three out of every five times the subject of his lordship came up, Lydia was now tossing that bone between them like the proverbial gauntlet.

A gauntlet which Sophie readily snatched up. "I can assure you that there is nothing wrong with my eyes," she countered, emphasizing the word "my" in a manner that pointedly questioned her friend's vision.

Lydia made a derisive noise. "In that case, it seems that I have clearly overestimated your taste in men."

"No. You've underestimated it if you think that I could ever be swayed to favor that unsightly creature. Unlike yourself, I have standards for men. And those standards include a handsome face to go with his title."

"The rest of the ton seem to think Lyndhurst comely enough," Lydia retorted in a superior tone. "As you well know, there are at least a dozen other eligible titles on the market, even a duke, and he is still considered to be the catch of the Season."

Sophie sniffed. "Lord Murdock would be considered the catch of the Season if his pockets were as plump as Lyndhurst's." Not only was Lord Murdock the biggest wastrel in London, his dissolute behavior had all but banned him from polite society.

"Perhaps by those whose only concern is marrying a fortune," Lydia shot back. "Lyndhurst, on the other hand, is a true gallant and counted desirable by those in the very top-of-the-tree. No one, not even you, can dispute the fineness of his character."

"Oh, his character is fine . . . fine to the point of crushing dullness. Indeed, there's not a finer or more boring man in London." Her voice perfectly reflecting her contempt, Sophie mimicked, "Yes, Miss Barrington. No, Miss Barrington. As you wish, Miss Barrington." Resuming her normal tone, she finished, "He's so stiff and proper. Never once have I heard anything remotely witty cross that man's lips."

"My brothers tell me that he's counted quite the wit at their club," Lydia returned slyly. "I've also overheard them discussing his—um—prowess with the ladies. From what they say, the entire *demi-rep* set are all but pulling out each other's hair in their zeal to be his mistress . . . and not because he's so rich."

"Lydia! It is—"

"Ill-bred to speak of such things," her friend finished for her. "Perhaps. But it proves that he isn't dull, eh? My guess is that his lordship would be quite amusing once one got to know him." She paused to slant her companion a look of pure devilry. "A rich, amusing earl with excellent thighs. What more could a girl ask?"

Sophie let the thigh reference pass unchastened, too vexed by Lydia's blind adulation of his tedious lordship to concern herself with propriety. Struggling hard to mask her growing annoyance, she rebutted in what she hoped was a cool tone, "Even if he is by chance as witty as you claim, there is still the matter of his unfortunate appearance."

"Is there indeed?" Lydia looked positively smug. "According to gossip, the only thing the other ladies of the ton find unfortunate about Lyndhurst's appearance is that he makes it far too infrequently to suit them."

Sophie sniffed at that. "In my opinion he makes it far too often. Why, I can't so much as turn around that he isn't there, towering over me like some great"—she made a fluttering hand gesture as she sought the right word—"Goliath." She settled on this analogy, though it hardly seemed adequate to describe his ungainly size. At well over six feet tall with broad shoulders and a muscular build, he dwarfed every other man at any given gathering.

With a derisive noise that echoed her, Lydia retorted, "Well, I haven't noticed you exactly discouraging his attentions. Indeed, you've been seen together so often of late that he is expected to make an offer any day now. My brothers tell me that the betting book at White's has him wed to you by Christmas."

Sophie couldn't have been more shocked had Lydia informed her that Napoleon now served ices at Gunter's. "Why—why—that's preposterous!" she sputtered. "Never, in any way, have I indicated that I would welcome an offer from him. As I've told you a hundred times before, I receive him only because my aunt and cousin insist that I do so."

"Receiving him is one thing, but going driving with

him three afternoons a week is quite another. And let's not forget all the times you've allowed him to escort you to the theater—six isn't it?—as well as all the other outings you've attended together. It seems to me that you've given him plenty of reason to assume that you would favor his suit."

As much as she hated to do so, Sophie grudgingly granted Lydia that point. Because Cousin Edgar, her guardian since her uncle's death five years earlier, had mandated that she accept Lyndhurst's invitations, she had spent an inordinate amount of time with him. And though she'd never flirted with him or offered him anything beyond the required courtesies, she could see now how her constant acceptance of his company might have given him the wrong impression.

She sighed. Ah, well. She'd just have to set him straight the next time she was forced to endure his company. In truth, it was something she should have done weeks ago, for in that time she had grown to love another and now intended to marry him.

Him. Lord Oxley. Her Julian.

As she always did when she thought of her beloved, Sophie smiled. He was everything she'd ever dreamed of in a husband and—oh!—so much more. Not only was he witty, charming, and titled, he was divinely handsome. Perfection, itself!

If only her aunt and cousin would open their eyes and see how truly exceptional he was.

Slowly her smile faded. Though they allowed him to call—the more titled men to court her, the more desirable she'd be to the ton, her aunt said—they had made it clear that under no circumstances was he to be considered as a potential husband.

"He isn't at all suited to you," they had informed her when she'd questioned their edict. And though she'd argued in his favor, they had remained adamant, at last silencing her by threatening to forbid him to call again should she persist in her green-girl infatuation.

Of course she had bitten her tongue and never pressed the matter again. What choice did she have? Aside from the precious moments they managed to steal together at social functions, her beloved's brief calls were all they had. Besides, she was confident that if her aunt and cousin spent time in his company, they would come to see him as she did and allow her to marry him.

And since she would thus be wedding Julian, she would be doing Lyndhurst a kindness by dashing his hopes, hence saving him the humiliation of having his suit rejected.

"Sophie. Do stop woolgathering." It was Lydia, and by the annoyance in her voice, it was clear that this wasn't the first attempt she'd made to gain her attention.

Sophie gave her friend an apologetic smile. "I'm sorry. I was just considering what you said about Lord Lyndhurst."

"And?"

"And I can tell you most assuredly that a proposal will never cross his lips. At least not one intended for me."

"Did you ever see a more frumpish creature than Lady Byrde?" Aunt Heloise twittered, her dark eyes gleaming in the dim lamplight of the Town coach. "Even rusticating in Cumberland as she does, you would think she would know that it is exceedingly dèmodè to powder one's hair."

Sophie nodded, only half listening to her aunt's usual post-*soirée* character assassinations. On most occasions she relished Heloise's scandalmongering and matched her tittle for tattle until they had shredded the reputations of all those unfortunate enough to have caught their notice that evening. Tonight, however, she had more momentous matters weighing on her mind, namely Lord Lyndhurst.

Nodding again at whatever her aunt had just said, she sank back into her seat, praying that the shadows would mask her agitation. Lord Lyndhurst. That wretch! Not only was he big and ugly and boring, this evening he had proved to be insufferably presumptuous as well.

Shortly after she and Lydia had turned their discussion from him and his rumored proposal to the more agreeable topic of their latest gown purchases, his tedious lordship had arrived at the *soirée*. As was his tiresome habit, he immediately sought her out and spent the entire evening rooted by her side.

Though she usually ignored his smothering presence—well, at least as much as she could within the bounds of civility—tonight she forced herself to note his actions, hoping upon hope to find something to prove the proposal rumors false.

What she saw only validated them. Why, you would think they were one step from the altar the way he hovered over her and tried to monopolize her attention. Worse yet, where she'd thought his hovering a bid to bask in the glory of her success, she now saw that it served to guard her against the addresses of her other, more desirable suitors. With the slightest frown or a few clipped, albeit polite, words the horrid man effectively discouraged all who sought to woo her.

All except her darling Julian, that is, who boldly ignored his glowering presence and spirited her off for a stolen kiss.

A soft sigh of frustration escaped her. It was galling, that's what Lyndhurst's possessiveness was. Galling.

And she refused to tolerate it a day longer. When he called on the morrow, as he'd so pompously announced he would do, she would tell him in no uncertain terms what she thought of him and his high-handed presumption. By the time she was done, his overblown pride would be so tattered that it would be the last she ever saw of him. And good riddance!

She paused a beat from her gloating vision of a humbled Lord Lyndhurst to consider what her aunt and cousin would say when he ceased to call. For some unfathomable reason they favored the man and would no doubt demand to know why he no longer haunted their drawing room.

Ah, well. She would just have to convince them that he had lost interest in her. Men did lose interest in women she'd heard, though, of course, it had never happened to her. She was the Toast of the Season, and all the gentlemen were in love with her.

It was remembering her success that made her smile with sudden inspiration. Because she was so celebrated, she would tell her aunt and cousin that Lyndhurst had finally come to his senses and acknowledged himself unworthy of her. Anyone with half a wit could see the truth in that.

And if they somehow discovered that she'd dismissed him?

That thought sobered her instantly. As punishment they might forbid Julian to call. Worse yet, they could banish her to her father's West Riding estate, as they so often threatened to do. Then, what was she to do?

For one miserable moment her confidence wavered. But she remembered Julian's kiss that evening, and her resolve hardened.

Fine. If they forbade him to call, she would tryst with him in secret. And if they tried to send her away? Well, then they would flee to Gretna Green. Once they were wed, her aunt and cousin would have no choice but to accept him.

Enraptured by the thought of elopement, Sophie closed her eyes and pictured her beloved. Oh, but he was handsome. Handsomer even than Quentin Somerville, though she knew there were those who would debate her bias. As for his brother . . .

Unbidden, the image of Lord Lyndhurst intruded into her mind. She shuddered. No one, not even Lydia, could dispute the fact that Julian was far and away better-looking than him. Where Lyndhurst's hair was dun-brown, Julian's fashionably coiffed mane was a rich, gleaming gold. Julian's eyes were the clear azure of the August sky, where Lyndhurst's . . .

A frown knit her brow. What color were his eyes, anyway? In truth, she'd never been able to see past the hideous scar on his cheek to note their hue. Come to think of it, she'd never really looked at his features, either. Not that they mattered. For even if they matched the perfection of those of his brother, they would be rendered ugly by his marred cheek.

"Sophie, dear?" Her aunt's voice pulled her from her reflections, delivering her from the frightful vision of Lyndhurst's disfigured countenance. "Are you suffering from a touch of dyspepsia?"

"Dyspepsia?" She opened her eyes.

Her aunt, who sat on the opposite seat next to her cousin, leaned forward, frowning her concern. "Perhaps it was the oysters," she said. "They sometimes cause dyspepsia, you know."

"They do?" Sophie stared at her aunt blankly, then the meaning of her words soaked in and she shook her head. "Oh. No. It wasn't the oysters . . . or anything else. I'm fine. Whatever makes you ask?"

"It's just that you had the oddest expression on your face just now. Didn't she have an odd expression on her face, Eddie?" Heloise asked, deferring as she often did to her son.

Edgar spared Sophie the briefest of glances, then shrugged and resumed staring out the window. "She looks fine to me."

"She does now, but her expression was markedly distressed only moments ago." Heloise pursed her rosebud lips, clearly displeased by his indifference. "As her guardian, you really should note these things and inquire after her health."

He made an impatient noise. "Fine." Pinning Sophie with his glittering onyx gaze, he ground out, "Are you well, cousin?"

Where her Uncle John, her guardian from the time of her parents death in a carriage accident when she was eight up until his own demise five years earlier, had been a comfortable sort of man, there was something about her cousin that unsettled her. What that something was, she couldn't say.

Perhaps it was his habit of watching her, his expression shrewd and calculating, as if he measured her for some secret purpose. Or the way his smile never seemed to reach his eyes. Maybe it was simply the fact that he was thirty-two years old and seemed to have forgotten what it was like to be seventeen. Whatever it was, it disturbed her.

Like it was doing now. Tensing as she always did beneath his regard, she murmured, "I'm quite well. Thank you for asking," praying that her reply would satisfy him and that he would turn his attention elsewhere.

Apparently someone above was listening, for he nod-ded once and resumed his observation of the world be-yond his window.

"I, for one," Heloise shot her son's averted profile an exasperated look, "am glad to hear that. It wouldn't do at all for you to be indisposed. Especially tomorrow. It's a day you shall no doubt wish to remember and cherish for the rest of your life."

"It is?" Sophie frowned. All she had planned for to-morrow was taking tea with Lady Kneller and attending the Seabright's rout, neither of which promised to be particularly memorable.

Just as she was about to say as much, Heloise poked her son in the ribs with her fan, chirping, "Shall we tell her the marvelous news, Eddie? Or shall we let it be a surprise?"

He flinched at her jabbing assault. "By all means tell her so she can properly primp. We want her in looks tomorrow."

"Our Sophie is always lovely, which is why she's had such a splendid offer." Looking ready to burst with ex-citement, Heloise took her dumbfounded niece's hand in hers, gushing, "It's true, dear. You've had a fine offer. Your cousin received a letter this very afternoon phrased in the most flattering of terms. He spoke with the gentle-man this evening and gave him permission to call on you tomorrow morning."

When Sophie merely stared at her, too dismayed to respond, she prompted, "Well? Isn't that the most mar-velous news?"

Marvelous? A giant hand seemed to tighten around her chest, squeezing the breath from her lungs. The only suitor she wished a proposal from was Julian, and she knew for a fact that this one wasn't from him. Her aunt would be locking her in her room instead of beaming like she'd just landed a prince if such were the case. No. It could be from only one man.

Lyndhurst.

Her stomach gave a sickening lurch, roiling as if she'd indeed eaten a bad oyster; a sensation that intensified to a gripping nausea as her cousin slowly turned his head and fixed her with his unnerving stare. After subjecting her to what felt like an eternity of scrutiny, he more barked than said, "Well, girl? Aren't you even interested to learn your future husband's name?"

"No, no, Eddie!" her aunt chimed in, playfully stabbing him with her fan again. "Let her have the fun of guessing. Not, of course, that it will be an easy game." She flashed her niece a proud smile. "Not with our Sophie's legions of suitors. Why, it could be any one of a dozen gentlemen. Even—"

"It's Lyndhurst," her cousin interjected flatly. "And you will accept him."

Accept him, indeed! Of all the high-handed, unreasonable—Sophie opened her mouth to voice her protest, but the words strangled on her outrage and all that came out was a squawk.

"You will also make him wish to be wed as soon as possible," he continued, pointedly ignoring her unintelligible outburst. "Perhaps if you kiss and tease him a bit, you might even rouse him to whisk you away to Gretna Green."

For a long moment she merely gaped at him, her mouth working soundlessly as she fought to vent her fury. Then something inside her exploded, and she erupted forth, "How dare you! How dare you demand that I marry that horrid man. You know I detest him!"

Edgar released a harsh grate of laughter. "I dare, dear Cuz, because he's worth over seventy thousand a year and is heir to the Marquess of Hereford."

"Bicksford," Heloise corrected him. "I do believe Lady Seabright said that his father is the Marquess of Bicksford. Or was it Hartsford?" She shook her head and sighed. "I don't know where my mind is these days. I simply cannot seem to keep the titles and names of the ton straight. I do, however, remember quite distinctly that his family seat is in Somerset and—"

He cut her off with a wave of his hand. "Hereford. Bicksford. The name is of no import, only the fortune attached to it."

"But what of the man himself? What of my feelings toward him?" Sophie demanded, barely able to believe her ears. Why, they were talking of selling her like silver at a debtor's auction.

Edgar spared her an impatient look. "What of your feelings?"

She flailed her arms in exasperation. "Don't you think it even the least bit important that I love the man I marry?"

"No." It was more a snort than a reply.

"Well, I do."

Another snort. "And what, pray tell, does a green chit like you know of love?"

"Obviously more than you do," she retorted with a sniff.

His eyes narrowed. "Oh? And I suppose that you're going to tell me that there is someone you love?"

She met his gaze defiantly. "As a matter of fact, there is."

"Oh, my. Sophie . . . dear," Heloise wheezed, short of breath as she always grew when anxious. "You haven't done anything . . . ruinous . . . have you?"

"Calm down, Mother. Of course she hasn't." Edgar shifted his gaze from his rebellious cousin to the now panting Heloise. "She hasn't been out of our sight long enough to do more than steal a kiss or two." Turning his attention back to Sophie, he drawled, "Now, Cuz. Shall I guess with whom you shared those kisses?"

She shrugged. "Why bother with games? I've made no secret of my feelings for Lord Oxley."

"Oxley. Bah!" He spat the words as if the taste of them offended him. "A mere viscount with only ten thousand a year. He might do well enough for a vicar's daughter or a chit with no expectations. But you, my dear, can and will look much higher."

"And by higher you mean Lyndhurst, I suppose?" she sneered.

"Indeed I do. Why settle for a viscount when you can have a future marquess? And a rich one at that?"

"Because I don't love Lyndhurst, and I would rather be the viscountess of a man I love than the marchioness of one I abhor."

Edgar's eyes narrowed further until they were little

more than glittering slits. "And how, pray tell, do you intend to rub along on his paltry ten thousand a year? You've spent close to that amount on frippery and gew-gaws this year alone."

"You seem to be forgetting the fortune my father left me," she smugly pointed out. "Combine that with Julian's ten thousand and we shall get on quite splendidly, I assure you."

"Edgar," Heloise puffed. "I really think you should tell—"

"Let me handle this, Mother. It's your overindulgence that has made her so willful. Besides"—his thin lips twisted into a cynical smile—"as you're so fond of point-ing out, I am her guardian. As such, it is my duty to see that she makes the best possible match. And I've de-cided that that match is Lyndhurst."

"And if I refuse to marry him?" Sophie flung back.

"Then you shall be hauled off to King's Bench prison, where the best offer you're likely to receive will be one of whoredom."

Sophie gasped, momentarily taken aback. Then she saw the words for what they were: a vain attempt to bend her to his will, and she laughed. "What utter rub-bish! You can't send me to prison for refusing to marry Lyndhurst!"

"No. But your creditors can send you there for being unable to settle your accounts," he grimly retorted.

"But of course I can settle them. You know I can," she exclaimed, ignoring the implication of his words. "You yourself have put it about time and again that I have sixty-eight thousand pounds, plus a fine income from my father's estate."

Edgar looked away, rubbing his temples as if they sud-denly ached. Closing his eyes, he gritted out, "The estate was sold three years ago, and your sixty-eight thousand pounds are gone."

"What! But that can't be!" she cried, desperately tell-ing herself that it was another ruse. "You told the entire ton—"

"Lies to buy you *entrée* into society. With your charm

and beauty, I was certain that you would land a rich husband and save us all from debtors prison."

"And you have. You've landed Lyndhurst," her aunt piped in, giving Sophie's hand a squeeze. "Marry him, and you shall never have to worry about funds again. None of us will."

Sophie tore her hand from her aunt's, glancing wildly from her to Edgar and then back again. "But my fortune . . . how . . ."

Edgar and Heloise stared at each other, as if trying to fob the duty of explaining off on the other. Then her aunt sighed and turned back to Sophie. Her voice hitching with breathlessness, she began, "It's all the fault of your Uncle John, God rest his soul, and his fondness for gambling hells."

"Are you saying that he gambled away my entire fortune?" Sophie exclaimed, unable to believe her kindly uncle capable of such villainy.

Her aunt shook her head so hard that motes of jet down floated from the plumes in her hair. "Oh, no. No! He never touched a shilling of your inheritance. Your sixty-eight thousand was fully intact when he died. Indeed, he even managed to save an additional twelve hundred pounds from the annual income you received from your father's estate."

"Then, how . . . but . . . I-I don't understand," she choked out, beyond bewilderment.

Heloise shot her son a beseeching look. When it was clear that no help was forthcoming, she sighed again and replied, "Well, you see, dear. After he died, we discovered that he'd left some rather, um, astonishing debts. Indeed, he'd even given a note of mortgage on Marwood Manor."

Sophie felt as if someone had punched her in the belly. "He lost Marwood?" she whispered, remembering the stories her mother had told her of her happy childhood at the estate, as well as her own jolly memories of the place. That her own children would never float toy boats upon the garden pond or play hide-and-seek in the maze of hidden passages brought tears to her eyes.

Her aunt nodded solemnly. "The man holding the

note seized it two months after your uncle's death." She wrinkled her nose. "And a more distasteful person I've never seen. Anyway"—she shook her head as if to dispel the thoughts of Marwood's unsavory new owner—"without the income from the estate, we hadn't a prayer of repaying the rest of the debts. So you see, Eddie had no choice but to borrow the funds from your inheritance to discharge them."

"And exactly how much did he 'borrow'?" Sophie inquired, not even trying to mask her bitterness.

"Forty-two thousand," Edgar snapped. "And as your new guardian, it was all quite right and legal that I do so."

"But how can it be legal? I was told that the income from my father's estate was to be used to keep me, and that the sixty-eight thousand we realized from the sale of his business interests was to be my dowry."

Edgar's lips flattened into a harsh line. "Oh, it was perfectly legal, I assure you. You see, Cuz, while it's true that your father's will bequested everything to you, your inheritance was entrusted to my father, your guardian. Therefore, it was up to him to determine how best to administer your monies, and he decided upon the plan you just described."

"And an excellent plan it was," Heloise commented with a nod.

Ignoring her annotation, he proceeded, "When he died, your guardianship naturally fell to me, as did the right to govern your funds. And I decided that the best use for them was to discharge my father's debt so we could continue to provide you with a home."

"B-but what of my remaining twenty-seven thousand pounds? What of my father's estate?" Sophie choked out, not certain if she should scream or weep.

It was Heloise's turn to explain. "You see, dear. About three years ago, Eddie met a man who offered him a chance to invest in a shipping venture to China. He said that he could more than triple his investment. Thinking it a way to pay back the monies he'd borrowed from you, plus make a handsome profit for himself, he invested the remainder of your fortune."

"And?" Sophie prompted, though she already knew that she wasn't going to like the outcome of the tale.

Her aunt looked away. "The man turned out to be a fraud."

"And so you lost everything. My dowry. My father's estate."

"No. Not the estate," Edgar quickly interjected. "That I sold to keep us for the last three years, and to finance your launch into society. At least we had enough to pay for part of it. As for the balance, well, once I'd purchased us the illusion of wealth, the tradesmen were eager enough to extend credit."

"Credit you expected to hoodwink my husband into paying," Sophie spat.

Heloise made a clucking noise and patted her knee. "Really, dear. You mustn't think too unkindly of Eddie. He only did what he had to do to insure your future. And it will be insured if you marry Lyndhurst."

"Will it indeed? And what happens when he discovers our deception?" she demanded. "Even I know that settlements must be made and dowries paid before the wedding can take place."

Edgar eyed her coldly. "I've already told him that our solicitor's son was wounded in Alexandria and that he has gone there to bring him home. Naturally, he's not expected back for several months." He laughed. "By the time his lordship learns that there is no solicitor, you'll have eloped with him and he shall have had his wedding night. A man with Lyndhurst's pride isn't going to risk letting it be known that he was played for a fool."

"Perhaps not," Sophie whispered brokenly, suddenly more tired than she'd ever been in her life. "But he shall no doubt hate me and strive to make my life miserable."

"Cuz . . ." Edgar looked almost regretful as he reached over to take her hands. She jerked them away and crossed her arms over her chest, glaring at him in a way that clearly conveyed the hurt and betrayal she was helpless to voice. He dropped his hands to his lap with a sigh. "See here, Sophie. I realize that things will be difficult for you at first. And I'm sorry for that. I truly am. However, I feel certain that he'll come around and forgive you once you present him with an heir."

"And if I fail to conceive before he learns the truth? What then? I doubt he'll seek the bed of a woman he loathes." Was that really her voice, so weak and raw?

"Well, then we shall just have to hope that his lust is stronger than his pride."

Sophie shuddered at the thought of suffering Lyndhurst's lust. Yet what choice did she have?

Lyndhurst or prison.

A sob of defeat tore from her chest. What choice indeed?

Chapter 2

"My lord?"

Nicholas Somerville, the Earl of Lyndhurst, tossed aside his ruined neck cloth and turned from the mirror to inspect the Hessians his valet offered for his approval. Narrowing his eyes critically, he scrutinized their gleaming contours, searching for the slightest blemish. When he found none, he nodded once and returned to the exacting task of donning his neck cloth.

Unlike most mornings, when he tied it with mindless ease, this morning the starched length of cloth refused to be drawn into a symmetrical knot, resulting in the growing pile of rumpled muslin at his feet. Not, of course, that he could compare this morning to those which had come before it. No. Today was different. Special.

Today he was to propose to the incomparable Miss Barrington.

And that meant that every detail of both his person and attire must be perfect. Thus resolved, he picked up a fresh neck cloth and resumed his quest for a flawless knot.

"My lord? Will this do?"

Nicholas's fingers slipped, crushing the stiff fabric between them. Cursing his clumsiness, he glanced to where his valet stood holding the modishly embroidered red waistcoat his brother, Quentin, had given him for his birthday.

For a brief moment he considered the garment, wondering if the ever-fashionable Miss Barrington might favor it. Then he shook his head and returned his attention to his neck cloth. "Perhaps something a little less, um, colorful might be more appropriate to the occasion, George," he said, eyeing his spoiled neckwear with frustration. "We wouldn't want Miss Barrington to think me suddenly possessed of foppish tendencies, would we?"

George chuckled. "You could rouge your cheeks and wear a dozen patches, my lord, and no one would think you anything but a gallant. You are too fine a man to ever be considered less."

It was Nicholas's turn to laugh. "Spoken like a good and loyal servant. Remind me to raise your wages."

"You are ever generous, my lord," the man countered, moving to the wardrobe at the opposite end of the room. "And if I might be so bold as to comment, Miss Barrington is a most fortunate young lady to be engaged to you."

Nicholas sobered instantly. "She hasn't accepted me yet."

"But she will. You're counted among the finest gentlemen in England. How can she refuse you?"

How indeed? Nicholas mused, ripping off the ruined neck cloth and tossing it onto the discard pile. The name he offered her was old and respected, the attending title one of power. As for his fortune, well, it ranked among the mightiest in England. Possessed as he was of all those attributes, he could have his pick of the Season's finest marriage market offerings.

And he'd selected Miss Barrington.

Smiling his bemusement at his choice, he plucked a new neck cloth from the stack before him, and arranged it around his collar. Beautiful, *young* Sophia Barrington. She wasn't at all what he'd had in mind when he'd decided to take a bride. Indeed, she was the exact opposite of the sort of woman he'd envisioned.

Having turned twenty-eight the past January, he'd at last given into his mother's badgering and agreed to take a wife. Not, of course, that his mother had truly had anything to do with the decision, though he chose to let her believe that she had. No, the truth was that he'd promised himself long ago that if he hadn't fallen in love by the age of twenty-eight, that he would come to London and simply pick a suitable miss.

His faint smile broadened into a wide grin. Miss wasn't exactly the word for the sort of bride he'd sought. Miss denoted a young girl fresh from the schoolroom, and what he'd wanted was a woman with maturity; one who'd not only be a good, loving mother to his children, but who would be wise enough to partner him in the overseeing of his estates.

As a means to that end he'd decided to select his wife from the females who had been out for several Seasons, a woman of say, twenty-two or twenty-three, who had outgrown the silliness that seemed to possess the younger set these days.

What he'd sought was a *sensible* wife.

Who he intended to marry was a seventeen-year-old girl with a head full of balderdash and the beauty of a goddess. An odd choice indeed for a man who chose his mistresses for their wits rather than their looks.

He paused mid-knot to wonder at his own madness. Exactly what had wrought his curious turn of mind, he couldn't say. All he knew for certain was that he'd somehow gotten caught up in the fierce race to court Miss Barrington, and was now driven to the point of obsession to win the prize: her hand in marriage.

Perhaps it was his competitive nature that urged him to behave so. Or maybe the reason stemmed from the sense of entitlement that had been instilled in him since birth. He was, after all, the heir to the rich and powerful Marquess of Beresford, and as such was used to having the best of everything. Therefore, wasn't it only natural that he should desire to have the finest of the Season's bridal offerings?

Sighing confoundedly, he looped the fabric in his hand and threaded the opposite end through it. Maybe, just maybe, it was neither of those reasons. Maybe he'd simply succumbed to what was being called "Barrington Fever," the besotting delirium that had smitten every male in the ton between the ages of twelve and one hundred. Whatever it was, he wanted Miss Barrington.

And he fully intended to have her.

Tugging the now completed knot a fraction to the left, he considered the girl herself. While it was true that he didn't love her, he liked her well enough. She was agreeable. And charming. And gay. Yes, she was exceedingly gay. So what if her conversation was limited to mindless pleasantries? He'd accepted long ago that she was one of those beautiful yet none too witty creatures men married for show rather than stimulating discourse. And oh! What a show she made!

With her mane of golden curls, her soft gray eyes and lithe figure, she was the sort of woman every man desired and other women envied. No doubt she would give him beautiful children—the getting of which would afford him the greatest of pleasure.

As always happened when he thought of loving Miss Barrington, his groin flamed with sudden heat, making him crush the knot he was adjusting. Oh! Dangerous thoughts, these. Ones that he was constantly forced to guard against while in her presence, what with the snug fit of breeches these days.

He made a face at himself in the mirror. Ah, well. He'd just have to take care and concentrate on her other—safer—assets until after they were married. Commanding himself to do just that, he removed the neck cloth he'd spoiled in his lust and reached for yet another, the eighth of the morning.

Her other assets. Hmm. Well, with her easy charm and flawless manners, she would make a perfect hostess when he chose to entertain. And speaking of entertaining, she had a distinct advantage in that she was accepted into the best of circles . . .

Despite the unfortunate fact that her father had been in trade. A cloth merchant, if he recalled correctly.

A faint frown creased his brow at that recollection. How her mother, the daughter of an earl and the greatest beauty of her day, could have made such a *mesalliance,* he couldn't fathom. True. Walter Barrington was reputed to have been a most dashing man, not to mention wealthy, but he was still a commoner and therefore unsuitable . . .

As would be his daughter had she not been all but

raised by her mother's brother and his wife, the Earl and Countess of Marwood. Fortunately for Miss Barrington, the ton had forgiven her humble paternity and accepted her as the Marwood daughter.

Not, of course, that the earl had been the most respectable peer of the realm. Not with his regrettable fondness for gambling hells. Yet he was nobility, and as such had raised his niece in the ways of the ton. His son Edgar had seen to the finishing of her education by sending her to Lady Beal's exclusive school in Bath.

Nicholas's fingers worked away on his neck cloth as he considered the latest Earl of Marwood. There was something not quite right about the man, though he was powerless to say exactly what that something was. It was more a feeling than anything his lordship had ever said or done.

Nicholas sighed. Ah, well. What did it matter? He was marrying Miss Barrington, not Marwood. And considering his lordship's fondness for Town, they would no doubt see little enough of him once they removed to the country, which was where he intended them to spend the bulk of their time.

Satisfied with that conclusion, he refocused on the problem of his neck cloth. To his amazement, he found that he'd tied it and perfectly at that.

"My lord? Is this more appropriate?" George stood behind him, reflected in the mirror, holding up a blue-and-gold-striped waistcoat.

Without turning, Nicholas nodded and raised his arms so that the valet could dress him.

When the last gold button was secured and his shirt frills adjusted, he sat on the edge of his dressing-table chair and allowed the servant to draw on his boots. That done, he picked up his watch and bejeweled family crest fob.

As he rose to attach it, his valet moved behind him, studying him through squinted eyes. After a moment the man blinked and said, "I say, my lord. Your Egyptian brown coat, the double-breasted one, would be quite dashing with that waistcoat."

Nicholas paused in his task to consider. "I do believe you're right," he countered with a nod.

"And your new hat, my lord, the one with the curled brim. You should wear it. It's exceedingly nobby, you know."

"By all means, I must be nobby," Nicholas agreed, hiding his smile at his valet's modish vocabulary.

"Oh. And yellow gloves, my lord."

"Yellow gloves it is."

When Nicholas was at last dressed and had been pronounced, "Complete to a shade," by George, he summoned a footman and commanded, "Please have Mrs. Herbert meet me in the foyer with that basket of strawberries I had sent down from Hawksbury. And have Wykes bring around the carriage."

It was time to claim his bride.

"Lord Lyndhurst has arrived," Heloise announced, bustling into Sophie's dressing room. "And just look what he brought you." She presented a beribboned basket. "Strawberries! He had them sent all the way from his estate, Hensbury, just—" She broke off abruptly, a frown knitting her brow. "Or did he say Birdbury?"

She considered for a moment, then made a dismissive hand motion. "Oh, well. It matters naught. What is of importance is that he had this lovely fruit sent down because he knows of your fondness for it. Such a kind, considerate man! He shall no doubt be the most doting of husbands."

Until he finds out about our deception, Sophie ached to counter. But of course she couldn't, not in the presence of her lady's maid. As anyone with a single grain of sense knew, servants gossiped, and one must always guard their tongue against speaking of private or ruinous matters in their presence. One must also take pains to foster the illusion of well-being, even if one's world was crumbling around them.

Miserably forcing herself to adhere to that last rule, she glanced from the berries to the mirror before her, smiling as her gaze met the reflected one of the servant arranging her hair.

Because of the taboo against her expressing her true feelings for Lyndhurst, her maid, Mademoiselle De Laclos, had automatically assumed her to be thrilled by the prospect of his proposal. Thus, the woman had spent the entire morning rambling on about his lordship's sterling qualities. Indeed, so passionate was her admiration of him, that Sophie wondered if she didn't perhaps harbor tender feelings for him herself.

Bridling her urge to sniff at that thought, she returned her gaze to the basket, trying to look suitably pleased by the gift. If only mademoiselle would hurry up and finish her hair. Between the woman's incessant chatter and having her scalp jabbed with hairpins, she had the beginnings of a headache . . . a headache that threatened to blossom into a full-blown megrim at her aunt's vocal raptures over his lordship's gift.

"Oh! Such lovely, darling berries," Heloise enthused. "Just look at how perfect they are . . . so plump and luscious. I'll wager that there is nothing like them to be found in all of London." Grinning as if it were she, instead of her niece, who had received the gift, she held a berry temptingly to Sophie's lips.

Sophie recoiled back, shaking her head. Had they been from anyone else, she'd have taken it without hesitation and would no doubt have devoured the entire basket of fruit before tea. Seeing as they were from Lyndhurst . . .

Lyndhurst or prison.

The looming threat of King's Bench prison was enough to make her feign a smile and say, "Thank you, Auntie. But I'm not very hungry right now. I shall enjoy the berries later when I have more of an appetite."

Mademoiselle made a soft clucking noise behind her teeth. "But of course zhee young miss has no hunger. She has zhee nerves, no?" she said, apparently mistaking Sophie's lack of appetite for maidenly anxiety. "And no wonder. Eet isn't every day zhat a girl receives a proposal from a *magnifique* man like Lord Lyndhurst? *N'est-ce pas?*"

Sophie gave her a strained smile, which the woman took for an affirmative answer. "Ah, well. Not to worry.

His lordship will take one look at you zhees morning and eet will be him who has zhee nerves. Miss Barrington looks *vraiment belle* this morning. *Oui?*" She looked to Heloise for confirmation.

Her aunt nodded. "You do look lovely, dear," she verified, setting the basket on the dressing table next to the untouched box of bonbons Lyndhurst had sent the day before. After pausing to watch mademoiselle wind a ribbon through Sophie's coiffure, she wandered across the room to examine the primrose and lilac round dress that had been selected for her niece to wear.

The next few minutes passed in silence: mademoiselle deciding whether to knot or bow the ribbon, Heloise debating if Sophie should wear pearl or hoop earrings, and Sophie wondering if she had pin money enough to buy passage to France.

Just as Sophie came to the dismal conclusion that her funds might take her as far as Dover, mademoiselle stepped back crying, *"Voilà!"* gesturing grandly at her masterpiece of hair and satin.

And it was a masterpiece. Leaving a single curl at either side of her brow, she had drawn Sophie's hair back from a center part and pinned it up on her crown in a cluster of perfect ringlets. The lilac ribbon, which had been used as a band around her head, terminated in a bow that rested above her left temple.

Even Sophie, as dispirited as she was, had to admit that the effect was fetching. Too bad the effect was to be wasted on Lyndhurst.

"Excellent!" Heloise exclaimed, leaving off rummaging through Sophie's jewelry chest to take a closer look. "You've truly outdone yourself today, mademoiselle."

Not given to false modesty, the maid nodded. *"Oui.* I have. I now have only to dress miss in zhat charming gown and add zhee jewelry, and—*voila!*— she is ready to accept his lordship."

Sophie made a face at the reminder of the horrid duty that awaited her. Never, not even with all the primping in the world, would she ever be ready for Lyndhurst and his cursed proposal.

Unfortunately for her, neither of the other two women

missed her sudden grimace of distaste. However, before
her maid could comment upon it, and by the look on
her face she was clearly about to do so, Heloise said,
"You may go now, mademoiselle. I wish to speak to my
niece in private."

"But zhee gown, madam! Eet has Spanish sleeves.
Spanish sleeves must be arranged just so to be
effective."

"I am perfectly capable of arranging sleeves," her aunt
countered, her voice ringing with a note of finality.
When the maid still hesitated, she clapped her hands.
"Chop! Chop, now, mademoiselle! There are delicate
matters I must discuss with the girl before she goes
down, and we mustn't keep his lordship waiting any
longer than necessary."

"Delicate?" A look of sudden dawning crossed the
French woman's face. "Ah! Zhee bridal talk, *oui*?"

"Bridal talk?" Heloise looked momentarily nonplussed. Then she flushed a dull shade of red. "Ur, yes.
That talk, yes."

Mademoiselle chuckled and shot Sophie a knowing
look. "You listen to your aunt, *oui*? She will tell you all
about marriage so you won't be frightened."

Sophie nodded, more wretched than ever at that prospect. Excellent. Just what she wanted to do, listen while
her aunt told her of the horrors awaiting her in Lyndhurst's bed. Filled though she was with repugnance, she
still remembered herself enough to say to the departing
maid, "Thank you, mademoiselle. His lordship shall no
doubt be quite pleased with your efforts."

It was no lie, she thought, studying her reflection in
the mirror. Despite the fact that she hadn't slept a wink
all night, she looked as fresh and rested as if she had
just spent a quiet fortnight in the country. And a blessing
it was, too. If she were out of looks, his lordship might
have second thoughts about marrying her. Then she
would end up in prison, where she'd heard a girl's
beauty faded in less than a day.

Shuddering at the horror of such a tragedy, she rose
and stepped into the gown Heloise held. With no reason
to continue her pretense of either cheer or goodwill

toward her aunt in the absence of her maid, she settled into a brooding silence.

She had just sunk into a dark yet satisfying fantasy in which she feigned death to escape Lyndhurst, when her aunt grasped her arm and towed her to the cheval mirror.

"See, dear?" she said. "That gown is just the thing for a girl to wear for a proposal. Charming yet sophisticated; youthful but womanly enough that you look of an age for marriage."

Sophie gazed at her reflection, though for the first time in her life she had no interest in her appearance. The gown in question was a new one, one which had arrived only two days earlier. Though she had been thrilled with it then—how could she not with its scalloped ruff and slashed Spanish sleeves?—today she saw it as a depressing symbol of her need to marry Lyndhurst.

"Poor dear," her aunt murmured, awkwardly patting her arm. "I know this is a blue day for you, and I'm sorry. Truly I am. If there were something I could do, you know I would do it."

When Sophie didn't reply but continued to stare stonily into the mirror, Heloise tried again. "Please believe me when I say that I never wanted anything but the best for you. I—I—" Her voice quivered, then choked completely as if she fought tears.

Sophie stole a glance out of the corner of her eye in time to see a fat tear roll down her aunt's cheek. That rivulet of distress paired with Heloise's woebegone expression instantly crushed her resolve to never forgive her.

Ah, well. In all fairness her current fix was Edgar's doing, not her aunt's. Why, the poor dear probably hadn't known a thing about it until it was too late.

Having thus absolved the other woman's guilt, Sophie turned and gathered her in her arms for a hug. "There, now, Auntie. Don't cry," she crooned. "There is nothing to forgive. Truly. You didn't lose my fortune, Edgar did." Him, she would never forgive.

Heloise clung to her as if she were the last hope of

redemption on Judgment Day. "You mustn't be too hard
on Eddie, dear," she said, punctuating the word dear
with a loud sniffle. "He feels as badly about all this as
I do."

Sophie just bet he did. Especially in light of his parting
remark the previous night: "You do anything to jeopar-
dize your marriage to Lyndhurst, girl, and I swear that
I shall take my mother and flee to America, leaving you
behind to pay the piper." By his harsh tone, it was clear
that it wasn't an idle threat.

Still rankled by his words, she opened her mouth to
dispute his alleged remorse. One look at Heloise, however, and she closed it again. Her aunt was peering at
her so earnestly, with such naked faith in her son's goodness, that she hadn't the heart to crush her motherly
illusions. So she bit her tongue and murmured instead,
"What is done is done, and there's nothing we can do
about it now. I must marry Lyndhurst, and that is that."

"Yes, you must marry him," Heloise conceded. "But
your marriage doesn't have to be intolerable, you
know."

Sophie eyed her skeptically. "Oh?"

Her aunt nodded and pulled from her embrace.
Frowning at Sophie's sleeves, which were now quite
crushed, she elaborated, "Lyndhurst is very wealthy, and
he clearly adores you. That means that his pockets shall
no doubt be open to you. Why, just imagine the fun
you'll have spending his money."

"True. But I can't shop all the time," she pointed out,
lifting her arm to allow her aunt to puff her undersleeve
through the slashed outer one. "I shall eventually have
to go home to his lordship and suffer his tedious
company."

"Not if you attend entertainments every evening. Most
married couples I know never so much as glimpse at
each other while at *soirées* and balls. Best of all, as a
married woman you shall be free to speak, flirt, and
dance with whomever you please."

Sophie considered her aunt's words for a moment,
then nodded as she recalled how married men seemed

to all but disappear the instant they arrived at any function. The idea had promise . . .

Unless, of course, Lyndhurst was one of those men who shunned the gaiety of the ton the second they left the altar. When she voiced her concern on that account, her aunt merely chuckled and circled behind her to tame her other sleeve.

"Then, you must invite guests to dine with you every evening," she advised.

"And if he turns out to be one of those tiresome creatures who insists on rusticating at some remote estate?"

"There are always house parties. Why, Lady Barberry has them so frequently that she hasn't been without at least five guests for over fifteen years now."

"That takes care of the problem of the days and evenings," Sophie murmured, bowing her head to hide her sudden blush. "But what am I to do about afterward, when—" She swallowed hard, fighting her rising terror at the thought of what came next. "When he insists on coming to my bed." The sentence came out as little more than a panicked squeak.

Heloise left off her fussing to wrap a consoling arm around her distressed niece's waist. "You must do what other women in your situation do," she replied in a soothing tone. "You must think of something else . . . something pleasant. Like all the new gowns you can buy with your husband's money."

"I doubt I shall be able to concentrate on gowns during . . . *those* acts," she whispered brokenly, remembering Lydia's youngest brother's whispered accounts of the ways between men and women. Why, just the thought of reciting lewd verses while tickling Lyndhurst's bare backside with a feather . . .

Her knees buckled in horror at the thought of what that tickling led to, and she would have crumpled to the floor had Heloise not grasped her beneath her arm. Helping her to a chair, her aunt feebly suggested, "If you can't think about gowns, perhaps it might help if you pretend that he's someone else. Someone you desire. Oxley, perhaps?"

"There is no way I could ever imagine Lyndhurst to be Oxley. Lyndhurst is so . . . well . . . big!"

"It might work if you close your eyes." When Sophie remained unconvinced, Heloise sighed and said, "Well, if Lyndhurst is like most men, it shouldn't take him more than a moment or two to spend his desire. Then you shall be left in peace. Once you give him an heir or two, he will no doubt lose interest in you altogether and take to spending his lusts on his mistress."

"If the marriage lasts long enough for him to get me with child," Sophie reminded her, voicing the most troubling of her concerns. "What if I don't conceive right away, and Lyndhurst's pride isn't what we suppose? He could dissolve our marriage, you know. Then what is to become of us? Everyone knows that the courts favor men of wealth and power, like Lyndhurst."

Her aunt's expression grew grim. "Then, you must try extra hard to get in the family way from the very beginning."

"You mean . . ." Sophie broke off, too appalled to voice what she was certain her aunt was suggesting.

Heloise nodded at her unspoken query. "Yes. You must engage in relations frequently, before he learns the truth. You're young and healthy. You should have no problem getting with child if you but try."

At Sophie's mew of distress, her aunt kneeled before her and took both her hands in hers. "I know the prospect of all that trying is troubling, but I see no other choice. Truly I don't. Besides, it should be tolerable enough if you remember my advice."

"Yes," Sophie responded in a toneless voice. "Close my eyes and think pleasant thoughts."

Chapter 3

The moment she was dreading had arrived.

"Smile, dear," Heloise chided, pausing before the closed drawing room door.

Sophie tightened her lips, commanding the corners to curl up. When she'd feigned joy to the best of her present ability, she looked to her aunt for approval.

Heloise eyed her efforts critically, then shook her head. "No. No. That shan't do at all. You look like you're suffering a bilious complaint. You're supposed to be happy, not ill."

"But I am ill," she grumbled. And it was true. Her head ached, and her stomach churned so fiercely that all she wanted to do was lie in a darkened room with a cool cloth on her forehead.

Her aunt made a soft tsking sound. "A slight touch of vapors. Nothing more. Perfectly normal under the circumstances."

"This is hardly what I would call normal circumstances," she muttered, feeling sicker by the moment.

"No. Which is why you must put on a cheerful face." Her aunt demonstrated what she meant by grinning like a lunatic in the throes of a pleasurable dementia. Patting Sophie's chin to encourage her to follow suit, she coaxed, "We can't have his lordship seeing you out of sorts, now, can we? He might have second thoughts and decide to seek a more amiable bride."

Sophie sighed and tried hard to adopt a like expression. Her aunt was right, of course. She really must make more of an effort to look thrilled by his lordship's proposal. How else was she to convince him of her desire for a hasty marriage?

After a moment of toiling toward that end, when she was certain her smile could get no more radiant, she asked, "Better?"

Heloise cocked her head to one side, studying her. "Hmm. A bit, though you're still hardly what I'd call radiant."

She parted her lips to display some teeth. "How is this?"

It was her aunt's turn to sigh. "If that's the best you can manage, I suppose it will have to do. Hopefully his lordship will attribute your brittleness to maidenly reserve." With that less than encouraging verdict, she opened the door and all but shoved her reluctant niece into the room.

Lyndhurst, who sat military straight on the edge of a chair, jumped to his feet the instant they appeared and sketched a courtly bow. "Lady Marwood. Miss Barrington."

Heloise nodded in acknowledgment, while Sophie stood powerless to do more than display a fraction more tooth.

For several interminable moments the parties gazed from one to the other, waiting for the other to proceed. Then, in a frantic burst of pleasantries, both Lyndhurst and Heloise began to speak at once. With Heloise blushing and Lyndhurst clearing his throat, they abruptly fell silent again.

After a few beats in which neither ventured to speak again, his lordship nodded. "Please, Lady Marwood. Do go first."

She nodded back. "I was saying that I believe you came to see my niece, and that you wish to speak with her alone."

"Indeed I did," he replied with a smile.

Not that Sophie actually saw his expression. She was staring at the knot of his neck cloth, avoiding, as she always did, the trial of looking at his scar. She just assumed that he smiled by the warmth of his voice.

"Well, then"—Heloise jabbed Sophie in the back with

her fan to urge her forward—"I shall bid you a good day."

Sophie opened her mouth to protest the poke, but mercifully caught herself in time. Sealing her lips with another strained smile, she obeyed her aunt's prodding and advanced forward. Remembering her manners, she offered her hand to Lyndhurst.

In a flash he loomed before her, taking it in his. Behind her she heard the door slam as her aunt exited. Lucky Heloise, she thought enviously. What she wouldn't give to escape his lordship's tedious presence as well. With much effort she stifled her urge to sigh. Hopefully this proposal business wouldn't take long.

And even if it did, it was better than the alternative.

Remembering that alternative was enough to prompt her to glance at the man before her. If she was to avoid prison, she must remember to pretend that she fancied him and behave accordingly. That meant casting him an adoring gaze or two.

As she attempted to do exactly that, he kissed her hand and all she saw was the back of his head. For several beats she stared at the hair that grew there, shocked to discover that it was quite nice. Lovely, in truth, with its lustrous burnished brown waves. In the next instant he straightened up again, and all favorable thoughts vanished as she found herself faced with his scar.

Though she wanted nothing more than to look away, she commanded herself to hold steady, suddenly determined to see beyond his disfigurement. If she was to be his wife, she must know the shape of his nose and lips, learn the curve of his brow and the color of his eyes. Who knows? She might find something besides just his hair to like.

Thus resolved, she tried to force her gaze a few inches higher to peer into his eyes. But, alas, it was no use. As always happened, it remained morbidly fixated on the long white line that ran from cheekbone to jaw.

As she stared in grim fascination, she heard him say, "You're looking exceedingly lovely this morning, Miss Barrington."

She started at the sound of his voice and self-consciously dropped her gaze to the floor. Confound it! She had to be more careful. It wouldn't do at all for him to catch her gaping at his scar like it was a hanging spectacle at Newgate Prison. Especially since there was always the danger of her forgetting herself and grimacing her revulsion.

Feeling her face flame at the thought of such a fiasco, she replied by well-bred rote, "You're looking well, too, my lord."

His hand covered the back of the one he still held, sandwiching it between both of his. "I assume you know the purpose of my visit?"

She nodded slowly. Here it came.

"Excellent. Then, you have had time to consider my offer. Before I ask for your answer, however, there are a few matters I feel we should discuss. Shall we sit?"

Oh, botheration! She should have guessed that he would insist on prolonging this miserable business. Seeing no other choice but to grant him the time, she dipped her head in assent and allowed him to lead her to the tête-à-tête by the window.

When they were settled, he again took her hands in his and began, "First off, I want you to know that above all else, I desire to make you my wife."

She nodded, settling her gaze modestly—and safely—on his fashionable yellow gloves.

There was a beat of silence, as if he were deciding how to proceed, then he cleared his throat and said, "You are young, Miss Barrington. Exceedingly so. And because of your extreme youth, I feel it my duty to explain to you what awaits you as my wife. Marriage is, after all, not something to be entered into lightly or with ignorance."

Her duties as his wife? Her stomach gave a sickening lurch. Oh, dear! He wasn't going to talk about dirty verses and feathers, was he? Worse yet, maybe he was going to inform her that he was one of those beastly men who Lydia's brother had said liked to stand on their heads—naked—while their wives teased them all over with a daisy. It was all she could do to suppress her shudder at the thought of suffering such a trial.

"As my bride," he continued, "you will, of course, gain the title of countess. Later on, and I pray that it is many years from now, you shall become a marchioness."

Countess? Marchioness? She looked up abruptly and smiled a genuine smile in her relief. That part of marriage she could stomach. Easily.

He smiled in return. "I'm glad to see that that prospect pleases you."

"Yes," she murmured, bowing her head again before her gaze could rivet onto his scar.

"As you most certainly know by now, my title comes with an enviable position in society. Indeed, there isn't a door in England that will be closed to you, should you wish to enter. There is also the advantage of my wealth, which is such that I can promise you that neither you nor our children shall ever want for anything."

She nodded. She had to admit that his offer was handsome.

If only he had the face to match.

He squeezed her hands. "You also have my pledge that I shall be the most generous of husbands. The allowance I shall allot you will make it possible for you to buy out every shop in the Arcade, should that be your desire. In short, you can expect the best of everything, as will befit your new position."

The best of everything? Very handsome indeed. If he was as wealthy as all that, perhaps her lack of dowry and debts might not matter much . . . especially if she could convince him that her deceit was a result of her desperate infatuation with him. Hmm. Perhaps Edgar's plan might succeed after all.

"Last, but most certainly not least," he enumerated, "you shall have my everlasting devotion. I promise to treat you with nothing but the utmost respect and kindness."

Devotion? That word was like a pin to her ballooning confidence. Surely he felt more for her than mere devotion? By the fervor of his courtship, she'd assumed that he was in love with her. Madly so. If she was wrong . . .

She gave her head a mental shake, pushing away the ridiculous notion. Of course he loved her. How could he not? She was the Toast of the Town, and all the gentlemen desired her.

"Miss Barrington?" Clearly he had just said something of importance, and she had missed it.

"I'm sorry. This is all so . . . overwhelming," she stammered, forcing herself to look at him and smile. "You were saying?"

He touched her cheek, and she had to steel herself to keep from flinching away. "It's quite all right, my dear. I realize that the notion of becoming a wife is somewhat intimidating for one so young."

"Somewhat, yes," she agreed, tearing her gaze from his cheek. Blast. She was staring again.

"In that case, I hope you won't be unduly alarmed when I tell you that there are as many duties as benefits that attend the title of Countess of Lyndhurst."

"Of course not, my lord. My aunt taught me that with any title comes responsibility."

"Very wise of her," he returned solemnly. "And did she by chance tell you what those responsibilities were?"

Sophie nodded. "She said that I must always guard my manners so as not to sully my husband's name. I am also to keep abreast as to what the ton finds amusing, so that I can entertain in a manner worthy of my position. It is also my duty to manage the servants and make certain that the household runs smoothly."

"Households," he corrected her. "You shall have three at first, six when you become marchioness."

"Three?" she echoed, praying that his palace-like residence on Pall Mall numbered among them.

"Three," he confirmed. "There is Ebbatson Hall in Durham, Newlyn Manor in Herefordshire, and Grafford Keep in Leichester. We shall spend most of our time at Newlyn, though we shall visit my other estates for two months each out of every year. As my wife, it will be your duty to see to the cottagers. That includes directing the charities, ministering to the sick, and organizing the village festivities—such as the annual Harvest feast."

It was all Sophie could do not to gasp her dismay. Not

only was she to rusticate, she was expected to fete the local peasants. It was simply too much!

Her face must have reflected her thoughts, for he dryly observed, "I take it that you find those duties distasteful?"

Though she wasn't normally given to cursing, Sophie cursed herself then for her carelessness. Damn! Damn! Damn! She must learn to school her expression before she ruined everything. Desperate to rectify her faux pas, she stammered out, "Not distasteful, my lord, but . . . um . . . perplexing. You see, I know little of country affairs."

There was a pause of silence, during which she feared the worse. Then he chuckled and said, "Of course you don't, my dear. I didn't expect that you would. It is one of the many things I shall teach you once we are married."

"You may be assured that I shall follow your instruction to the best of my ability," she vowed, almost sagging in her relief.

"That is all I shall ever ask of you. Now, having told you that, I believe it is time for me to frame my question." Clasping both her hands between his as if they prayed, he asked, "Miss Barrington, will you do me the honor of becoming my wife?"

At last. Tugging her mouth back into what was by now a well-rehearsed smile, Sophie looked up and said with as much pleasure as she could muster, "You do me great honor, my lord. Yes, I will marry you." Despite her efforts, the words came out wooden.

Apparently only the meaning of those words mattered to him, for he smiled as if she'd just granted him the world. Lifting her left hand to reverently kiss her ring finger, he murmured, "You've made me the happiest of men, my dearest Sophie, and I promise that you shall never regret your decision." Lowering her hand to clasp it to his heart, he inquired, "I may call you Sophie now that we're engaged, mightn't I?"

"Of course, my lord."

"Nicholas," he corrected her. "You must call me Nicholas."

"Nicholas." Oh. So that was his name. She'd never so much as wondered what it was. Before she could ponder the matter further, his palm cupped her chin and raised her bowed head.

Drawing her face close to his, he whispered, "I believe that it is traditional for us to seal our engagement with a kiss." Without awaiting her response, he pressed his lips to hers. As he did so, the scar came into clear, sharp focus.

Sophie screwed her eyes shut. Tightly. Think pleasant thoughts. Think pleasant thoughts, she frantically chanted to herself. Pretend that he's Julian.

Yet, try as she might, it was impossible for her to imagine that it was her beloved who kissed her. Where Julian's lips were soft and cool, Lyndhurst's were hard and hot, claiming hers with a hunger that she found terrifying.

Oh, heavens! He must be a daisy man after all. Or worse yet, a custard man. Lydia's brother had told them of men who made their wives sit naked on their equally bare laps, licking custard from a cup held pressed between their breasts. Just the thought of being subjected to such an indignity made her want to die.

Mercifully the kiss was a brief one, and was over almost as soon as it began.

"Now," he murmured, pulling back with a grin. "The only thing left to do is to choose our wedding date. I was thinking of sometime around Christmas, say, the twenty-second of December?"

"I, uh," she stammered, distracted by the horrible suspicion that he might be a custard man. The twenty-second of December? Hmm. Why not? She opened her mouth to give her consent, then her mind cleared and she remembered that time was of the essence. Praying that he wouldn't think her brazen and thus withdraw his offer, yet seeing no other option, she coyly ducked her head and whispered, "I'm not so certain I want to wait so long."

Silence.

Just when she was starting to dread the worse, he

chuckled. "In truth, my dear. After kissing you, I'm not so certain I can wait that long, either."

A custard man. He was definitely a custard man.

His hand cupped her chin again. "Just say the word, sweet Sophie, and I shall obtain a special license. We can be married within the fortnight."

"And that word is?" she sweetly inquired.

He kissed her. This kiss was a gentle one, filled with all the tenderness and reverence a girl could wish for from her groom. To Sophie's surprise, it wasn't nearly as awful as the first. Not when she didn't think of daisies or custard.

Like his first one, this kiss too ended quickly. Yet this time he didn't pull away, but instead leaned his forehead against hers to stare into her eyes.

Brown, she noted. His eyes were a rich, warm brown, rimmed with a most enviable fringe of lashes. In truth, they were quite beautiful.

If only they weren't set in a ruined face.

"The word?" he finally murmured, tracing the line of her jaw with his thumb. "It was the unspoken promise of your kiss."

It was over.

At last.

And Sophie had never been more wretched in her life. Not only was she to be Lyndhurst's bride at the end of the month, the headache that had plagued her all morning had exploded into an excruciating megrim, making her pray for a quick and merciful death.

Unwittingly heightening her misery was her aunt, who hovered over her sickbed, chattering like a magpie enthralled by a particularly tasty worm. "I must say that Eddie is quite pleased with the way you handled Lyndhurst," she said in a head-splitting chirp. "Why, his lordship all but demanded that you be married within the fortnight. If you ask me, such eagerness bodes well for our scheme. Indeed, my guess is that our troubles are over."

Yours, maybe. But mine are just beginning, Sophie thought grimly. In just two weeks time she would be the

Countess of Lyndhurst. That meant that she must begin the nightmarish ordeal of trying to get with child. And to do so she must—

Shuddering convulsively, she pushed the swirling montage of feathers, daisies, and custard from her mind.

Heloise made a clucking noise. "Poor dear. Are you cold?"

Sophie opened her eyes to reply, only to moan and squeeze them shut again in the next instant. Though the drapes were drawn, the midday sun blazed around the edges, stabbing through her eyes and into her brain like stakes of red-hot steel.

Apparently her aunt took her moan for an affirmative response, for she said, "Yes. It is a bit chilly in here. I shall summon a footman to lay a fire."

Alarmed by the prospect of more light from a fire, Sophie started to shake her head. The first motion, however, sent paralyzing pain stabbing through her temples, and she was forced to lie still, croaking instead, "No. Not cold, just ill. Terribly ill. My head . . ." she broke off with an agonized groan and laid her hand on her brow to illustrate her complaint.

Heloise countered with another series of her mother-hen clucks. "I know, sweeting. I know it hurts." There was a splash, then she gently pushed Sophie's hand from her forehead and replaced it with a cool, vinegar-soaked cloth. "Mademoiselle has gone to the stillroom to prepare her special megrim infusion for you. She should be back in a moment or two."

Sophie made a face. Vile stuff! Still, her maid's concoction did ease her megrims, usually within a half hour, so she would gladly swallow it without protesting its foul taste.

As if on cue there was a scratch at the door, followed by the faint creak of well-oiled hinges. A beat later she heard the swish of her aunt's skirt as she crossed the room. Though Sophie recognized the voice of the new arrival as that of her maid, the woman spoke too low for her to decipher her words.

After a few moments, during which her aunt replied in an equally hushed tone, the door closed with a soft slam. A brief time later the cloth was lifted from her head. "Here's your infusion, dear. You need to sit up to drink it." It was Heloise.

When she had propped Sophie up on four plump cushions, her aunt held a cup of steaming liquid to her lips, crooning, "Drink it slowly, now. Just one tiny sip at a time. It won't do you a bit of good if it comes back up again." Obediently, she did as instructed, holding her breath against the foul aroma.

For a long while they remained like that: Heloise coaxing Sophie to drink, and Sophie docilely complying. When the cup was at last empty and Sophie lay back down with a fresh cloth on her head, her aunt bid her to sleep and slipped from the room.

Sleep, yes. I shall lose myself in my dreams . . . escape my troubles, Sophie thought. As she teetered on the brink, ready to embrace the sweet oblivion of slumber, her mind flashed on Julian and what he might think when he heard of her engagement.

Oh! Awful, selfish girl! she reproached herself, vaulting back to the grimness of reality. So consumed was she with self-pity, that she hadn't stopped to consider him. Now that she did, she wanted to weep with despair.

Her poor, poor darling. Surely he wouldn't think that she willingly married Lyndhurst, would he?

Of course not, she told herself firmly. He had only to reread any one of the dozen notes she'd written him to know just how much she adored him. No. He could never believe she'd played him false. Unless . . .

Unless in his hurt he chose to push aside the evidence of her love and judge her a heartless jilt.

A cold rush of panic washed through her at that thought. It could happen, especially in light of the fact that he'd had his heart broken by such a woman just last Season.

Her panic deepened as she remembered his agonized tone as he confessed the affair. He'd told her of it the day he declared his love, saying that he wanted her to understand the depth of his feelings that he would risk as he did being hurt again. And he had been hurt. So badly, in fact, that he broke down halfway through his tale, weeping and begging her to never forsake him. She meant everything to him, he sobbed, more than life itself. Moved to tears herself, she'd taken him in her arms and sworn her undying love.

Remembering the tender scene made her eyes well up all over again. Oh! She simply had to see her beloved and reassure him of the steadfastness of her vows . . . before he heard of her engagement and suffered more pain. Once she expressed her anguish at her upcoming marriage, he would . . .

Why, he would refuse to let her wed Lyndhurst. Sophie clasped her hands in a sudden burst of excitement. Hadn't he told her time and again that he adored her beyond everything, that he would do anything for their love? That being as it was, he would probably insist that they elope to Gretna Green.

For one fleeting yet marvelous moment, she envisioned their flight across the border, thrilling at the romance of the adventure. Then she remembered her debts, and the dream vanished. Whatever would he say when she told him of them?

Briefly she pondered the problem, then dismissed it with a smile. The way he worshiped her, he'd never let a thing like money stand in the way of their happiness. Besides, her debt wasn't so very large. Edgar had said that it was only fifteen thousand pounds. Well, fifteen thousand, two hundred and sixty-three to be exact. Not an impossible sum by any means. No doubt Julian could discharge it readily enough. If not the full amount, surely enough to satisfy her creditors until he could pay the balance from his ten thousand a year.

And if clearing her debt left them unable to afford the pleasures of Town? She pushed the cloth from her brow and sat up, her headache vanishing with her renewed optimism. With Julian by her side, she would gladly rusticate in the country . . . forever if necessary. No doubt he shared her feelings.

Her only problem now was seeing him before he heard of her upcoming marriage. And she must see him. A note simply wouldn't do. She could never adequately plea her case or convey the true depth of her feelings for him in writing.

Bending her knees to her chest to rest her chin upon them, Sophie contemplated her problem. Waiting to see him at the Seabright's rout tonight was out of the question. By then the news would be all over England, and he would most certainly be too devastated to attend.

Absently she rubbed the bridge of her nose, searching for another option. Well, there was always Hyde Park. Like all young bucks, he rode along Rotten Row every afternoon at five o' clock. Perhaps she could speak to him there.

She considered the plan for a moment, then flopped back onto her pillows with a sigh of frustration. No. That would never do. Even if it weren't too late by then, they would never be able to steal a word in private. Not with the way mademoiselle and her aunt's groom shadowed her every move.

That left only one alternative, the shocking and scandalous one she'd hoped to avoid: She must go to Julian's quarters now, this morning, before he ventured forth for the day and heard the news. It was really the only hope she had.

Unnerved by the prospect, she rolled over and hid her face in her pillow. Did she dare do something so very bold? If she were seen, it would mean instant ruin. Visiting a gentleman at his bachelor quarters was an unforgivable sin in the eyes of the ton, one almost akin to murder.

Visiting a bachelor, yes. But there was no sin in a wife attending her husband at his home.

Sophie's smile returned in a flash. And she would be a wife. Indeed, by the time news of her indiscretion got out, if indeed anyone even noted it, she'd be a married woman. Married to the man whose quarters she'd visited.

She'd be Viscountess Oxley.

She rolled onto her back with a sigh and said the name out loud, savoring the feel of it on her tongue. Even if the dragons from Almack's were to witness her banging at his door, her position in the ton would be secure once they revealed their elopement. Indeed, their daring would probably make them the most celebrated and romantic couple in all of London.

Her decision thus rationalized, Sophie tossed aside the covers and slipped from the bed. It wasn't until she'd donned her gown and struggled to button it that she bothered to consider Lyndhurst and how her actions might affect him.

He'd be crushed, of course. Like every bachelor in the ton, he adored her and was desperate to marry her. Unlike those men, however, he had an arrogant, overblown sense of pride . . .

. . . A cold, aristocratic pride that could very well turn vengeful if stung.

Her hands stilled on her buttons. Dear heavens! What if he directed his ire at Julian and called him out? While dueling was illegal, she'd heard that it still took place, usually over matters of the heart such as this.

For one awful instant she pictured Julian and Lyndhurst in the pale haze of dawn, leveling pistols at each other's head. Then she remembered Lyndhurst's sterling character and laughed. What a chucklehead she was! Why, his dull and ever decorous lordship was the last man in London who would ever engage in anything as dangerous or litigious as dueling.

Shaking her head at her own foolishness, she buttoned the last of the buttons. No. Though the affair would undoubtedly wound his lordship's pride, he would recover in time. Indeed, by next Season he should be improved enough to return to London and find a new bride. If he were as sharp-witted as his reputation claimed him to be, he'd have learned from his experience with her and pursue someone more suited to him— say, a plain woman with excellent breeding and no looks to speak of.

In the long run he'd be happier with such a wife. And who knows? He might someday come to see her jilting him as the blessing it was and deign to forgive her, though in truth she didn't care.

She'd have her Julian, and that is all that mattered.

Chapter 4

"Yes?"

Sophie returned the majordomo's haughty stare, momentarily taken aback. Wherever was Julian? She'd expected him to answer her knock. Indeed, she was counting on it. So much so, that she'd spent the whole miserable hackney ride here dreaming of the moment when he opened the door and saw her standing there.

And—oh! What a splendid dream it was. She'd grown positively giddy just imagining it. Especially the part where he crushed her into his embrace and welcomed her with a tender yet eager kiss. And . . .

"Miss?" When Sophie merely stared at him, mute in her disappointment, he made an impatient noise. "Your business, miss? I haven't all day."

Her business? She blinked. Yes. Of course. What a ninnyhammer she was to be thrown off by a minor hindrance like this. Why, she had only to ask to see Julian for him to come and enact her dream exactly as she'd envisioned it. Her wits thus restored, she nodded and said, "Miss Sophie Barrington to see Viscount Oxley on a private matter of the utmost importance."

"A private matter, is it?" He pursed his lips and swept her length with a critical gaze. Unlike the gentlemen of the ton, who grew calf-eyed at the sight of her, he was utterly unimpressed, glancing away without pausing so much as a beat to admire her numerous feminine charms. Rolling his eyes toward the heavens, he muttered, "They're always private matters with his lordship."

Sophie ignored his remark, too affronted by his rude dismissal of her person to ponder its meaning. Insolent old wigsby! As if she cared what he thought. He was clearly too moss-grown to appreciate an Incomparable when he saw one. Promising herself to dismiss him the instant she became Viscountess Oxley, she coolly demanded, "Tell his lordship I'm here. Now."

"Your card?"

Gracing him with her most withering look, she yanked open her ridicule and extracted one of her gilt-edged calling cards. As she offered it to him, she mentally revised, *No. I'll not wait until Julian and I are married to dismiss the old crosspatch; I shall insist that it be done now, this very hour.*

With disapproval tainting every line of his furrowed face, the man seized her card between two fingers, holding it suspended by the corner as if it were a soiled chamber pot rag. After a moment during which he perused it from arm's length, he intoned, "I shall see if his lordship is receiving." Without sparing her so much as a parting glance, he closed the door, leaving her standing on the stoop like a tradesman with unsolicited goods.

Sophie glared at the brass knocker, more outraged than she'd ever been in her life. Rude old crank! How dare he treat her so! First he detains her on the stoop, interrogating her as if she were a pickpocket on trial. And now this! It was too much! It really was. Especially after all she'd suffered to get here.

And she had suffered—dreadfully!—being forced as she was to take her first, and hopefully last, public conveyance. Why, if she'd even suspected how poorly hackney coaches were sprung, much less how vile they smelled—

She stamped her foot in impotent rage. Enough was enough!

In that brief instant she seriously considered marching down the stairs and, yes, hailing the first hackney she saw. Then, in a flash of reason, she remembered why she was there and all thought of retreat fled.

She was there to marry Julian.

And wasn't spending the rest of her life with him worth tolerating an hour or so of travail?

Sighing her resignation, she peered around her to assure herself that she remained free from prying eyes. Just because her scheme wasn't going exactly as she'd planned was no reason to abandon it. Besides, she'd been a fool to believe that Julian would answer his own door. He was a viscount, after all. Of course he'd have a majordomo . . .

A majordomo who she was beginning to think had ignored her request. She was about to knock again when the door swung open. Certain it was Julian, she smiled and took a step forward, preparing to fly into his embrace.

To her disenchantment it was the majordomo, and if such a thing were possible, he looked even more censorious than before. Stepping aside to wave her into his inner sanctum, he rasped, "His lordship will receive you now."

The first thing Sophie noted when she stepped into the foyer was that it was lacking in decoration. Conspicuously so.

At odds with every other foyer she'd seen during the Season, the pearl-gray walls of this one were void of a single picture, mural, or wall hanging. More curious yet, there were no hall chairs, or even the requisite side table with its silver calling-card tray. Why, there wasn't so much as a carpet in sight.

Obeying the majordomo's command that she follow him, Sophie climbed the stairs and trailed him down the second-floor corridor, mentally noting the touches she would add when she became Viscountess Oxley. She was just imagining the barren hallway graced with a Grecian urn and a nymph statue, when her guide stopped before a partially open door.

Sprawled in a chair just inside was Julian. Garbed as he was in a sky-blue dressing gown with his golden hair in a decidedly unartistic tousle, he appeared to have only just risen from bed.

Sophie shoved the door the rest of the way open. "Julian?"

The instant he saw her, he sprang to his feet, extending his arms in welcome. "Sophie, dearest. What a lovely surprise."

Ignoring the impropriety of his unclothed state, she flew into his waiting arms and gladly claimed his ready kiss. "Oh, Julian. I just had to see you," she sobbed, letting all her pent-up grief flow forth. "The most dreadful thing has happened!"

He drew back a fraction to peer anxiously at her face. "Why, dearest. Whatever has happened?"

She released a shuddering sob and shook her head, suddenly too overwrought to reply.

He made a clucking noise, not unlike those Aunt Heloise favored. "Surely things cannot be so very dreadful as that? Indeed, I am certain that I shall be able to set them right if you'll but tell me what they are."

Desperate to confide her troubles to him, to let him lift the heavy burden from her shoulders and take it upon his own, infinitely broader ones, she tried to speak. Yet, despite her valiant efforts, the words strangled in her misery-clogged throat and all that came out was a smothered squawk.

"Come, come, now, my sweet. You know that I'd do anything for you," he murmured, capturing her tearful gaze with his warm blue one. "Truly I would. But I shan't be able to help you if you don't tell me what's wrong."

So lit with love were both his eyes and voice, that the throttling tension in her throat eased enough for her to blurt, "It's . . . it's that ugly . . . boring! . . . Lord Lyndhurst. My aunt and cousin insist that I wed him. We're to be married in two weeks time. Two weeks!" she repeated, her voice raising with hysteria.

"Sh-h-h. There, now, love," he crooned, patting her back as if she were an infant with stomach gas. "The situation is hardly as terrible as all that."

"Not terrible? It's worse than terrible! It's . . . it's . . ." She shook her head as she grappled for a phrase powerful enough to express her repugnance for the marriage. "It's intolerable! More than flesh and blood can bear," she finally wailed. "I'm to be wed to a man whose face

I can't abide. Why, when I think of the torment of having to spend the rest of my life looking at that hideous scar . . ." she broke off, shuddering with revulsion.

There was a low chuckle from somewhere to her right, then, "I always thought that scar rather frightful myself, though I daresay you're the first chit I've ever found discerning enough to agree." Another chuckle. "Or could it be that you're simply the only one bold enough to voice her honest opinion?"

Sophie gasped and sprang from Julian's embrace, gaping in horror in the direction from which the voice had come.

There, a mere four feet away, lounging on a faded red sofa with a glass of what appeared to be brandy in his hand, was Lord Quentin Somerville. Lyndhurst's brother.

She could have died on the spot. "Oh . . . oh!" she sputtered at a loss to do or say more.

He laughed and straightened up. Tossing the remainder of his drink down his throat, he drawled, "Never fear, Miss Barrington. I can assure you that your less than flattering assessment of my brother has given me no offense whatsoever. In case you haven't heard, his lordship and I aren't exactly on the best of terms."

Grinning the grin that had melted a hundred hearts that Season alone, he flung his empty glass onto the cluttered tea table before him and stretched with feline-like languor. "I must say, Oxley," he groaned, running his fingers through his mussed mane of curls, "this sofa is a devilish uncomfortable place to spend the night."

Julian returned his grin. "Frizell tried to tow you up to bed, but you would have nothing to do with the notion. Said something about needing to go to Harriet's house."

Quentin grimaced as if suddenly pained. "Harriet, yes. Come to think of it, I did promise to pay her a visit last night. She shall no doubt be cross as crabs that I failed to show." He seemed to ponder his pickle with Harriet for a moment, then shrugged and rose rather stiffly to his feet. Even in his disheveled state, he somehow managed to look impossibly handsome and elegant.

"Ah, well," he muttered, picking up the wadded coat that had served as his pillow. "A trinket from Rundel & Bridge's should coax her out of her pet quickly enough." He sketched a bow to Sophie. "If you'll excuse me, Miss Barrington. I shall leave you lovebirds to plot how to save you from marital hell with my brother."

As the door closed behind him, Sophie transferred her dismayed gaze from his retreating back to Julian's still smiling face. "I—I thought we were alone. I"—she made a helpless hand motion, feeling sicker by the second— "I never imagined there would be anyone else here at this time of the morning."

He looked rather surprised by her comment. "You didn't know that Somerville lives here?"

Tongue-tied with humiliation, she shook her head.

"Well, he does. As do Hucknell and Dumont."

"Four of you live here?" she squeaked. Visiting the quarters of one bachelor was scandalous, visiting the quarters of four was social suicide. Why, if anyone so much as suspected that she'd been here, she'd be irredeemably ruined. Even marriage to Julian might not save her from being exiled from the ton.

Apparently her expression reflected her alarm, for Julian made another Heloise-like clucking noise and drew her back into his embrace. "Don't fret, dearest," he crooned, nuzzling his face close to her ear. "Somerville is a good sort of fellow and shan't mention your visit here. Not if I swear him to silence."

She hid her face in the folds of his dressing gown, wishing that the earth would open up and swallow her. "Oh! I've never been so embarrassed in my life. What his lordship must think of me."

Julian chuckled and kissed her ear. "Quent thinks you're the most charming and beautiful girl in the world, as do I."

"But the way I was carrying on . . . the awful things I said about his brother . . ."

"As he told you, there is no love lost between them. He thinks Lyndhurst an arrogant, pompous ass, an assessment with which I heartily agree. No doubt his respect for you has risen a notch or two for being sharp-witted enough to look beyond his brother's wealth and title to see the man he is."

Not at all reassured, she anxiously clutched at his dressing gown, wading the silken fabric in her clenching hands. "Oh, but this is dreadful," she exclaimed. "What a peagoose I am. I should never have come here. I should have . . ."

"Of course you should have come here," he interjected.

"But . . ."

"Look at me, Sophie." His voice was gentle, yet firm in its command.

Reluctantly she did as he directed.

Cupping her chin in his palm, he drew her face close to his, murmuring, "I love you, Sophie, and I want you always to turn to me in times of trouble. You know I'll do anything for you." He dipped his head and dropped a light kiss on her lips. "Anything."

She melted against him, moved by his words. For a long while she remained like that, content to pillow her face against his chest, comforted by the steady beat of his heart. When at last her distress was soothed, she propped her chin on his shoulder and stared adoringly at his handsome face. Loving him more than she'd ever dreamed possible, she whispered, "I knew I could trust you to help me. I knew it."

He smiled gently. "Always, dearest. I shall always help you, no matter how dire your problem."

"I can't imagine any problem being more dire than this one." She clutched at his robe again, though this time without her earlier desperation. "Oh, Julian! Whatever are we to do? Edgar says that I must marry Lyndhurst. He made me accept his proposal this very morning."

Julian's smile faded abruptly, and his expression grew solemn. Inching his face nearer to hers, he murmured, "Do you love me, Sophie? Truly and deeply?"

"You know I do," she swore.

"Enough that you could spend the rest of your life with me?"

Joy, fierce and pure, exploded through her chest at

the meaning behind his words. As she'd hoped, he was
going to marry her to save her from Lyndhurst. Thrilled
beyond rapture, she whispered, "Yes, Julian. Yes! I love
you with all my heart. Haven't I told you so a dozen
times?"

"I just wanted to be certain of your feelings."

She threw her arms around his neck and pulled his
face down to hers. "I have never loved another, and I
never shall. You are the only man in the world for me."
She sealed the declaration with a passionate kiss.

He groaned and squeezed her close. "And you, my
dearest, are the only woman for me." He returned her
kiss in kind. "Marry me, Sophie. Today. We shall flee
to Gretna Green and save you from Lyndhurst." He
kissed her again. "Say yes. Say you'll be mine."

It was all she could do not to squeal in her delight.
Her fondest dream was about to come true. She would
be Viscountess Oxley. Wrapping her arms around his
waist to give him an ecstatic hug, she cried, "Yes. Oh,
yes! Let us go now! This very instant!"

He chuckled. "I can hardly go to Gretna Green in just
my dressing gown, though"—his grin grew wicked—"my
lack of attire might come in handy afterward."

Afterward. Sophie ducked her head, flushing at the
thought of what followed the ceremony. Odd, but she'd
never thought past the altar with Julian, where that was
all she thought about when with Lyndhurst. Now that
she did think about it, she wondered what sort of man
he was.

Somehow she couldn't imagine her beloved as a daisy
or custard man. No. Or even a feather man for that
matter. H-m-m. She hastened to recall Lydia's brother's
marriage-bed accounts. Ah, yes. He was probably a bonbon and poetry man . . . the sort who fed a woman
sweets while wooing her with romantic verses.

Tingling with excitement at that thought, she stole a
glance at his face. He was smiling down at her, looking
every inch the loving groom-to-be. Yes. He was definitely a bonbon and poetry man. Shyly, she returned
his smile.

He growled in response and crushed her against him

so completely that she felt every contour of his body through the thin fabric of his dressing gown. "Dear God, Sophie. You don't know how I've dreamed of this moment," he groaned. "You're so beautiful, so very desirable. You could have any man in the ton—one far richer and with a much more important title than mine. I hardly feel worthy of you."

"Of course you're worthy. There's not a worthier man in the entire ton," she assured him, smoothing a lock of hair from his brow. She liked the feel of the wifely motion and repeated it, thrilling at the thought of doing it every morning for the rest of her life. "As for wealth and title, I would rather live a modest life as your viscountess than a lavish one as Lyndhurst's marchioness. Your love is all the riches I desire."

"Modest life?" He chuckled, a low, indulgent sound, as though she were a child who'd just said something particularly foolish. "My dearest Sophie. Though we shan't live as opulently as you would with Lyndhurst, our existence shall hardly be modest. Between my ten thousand a year and your fortune, we shall rub along quite famously."

Sophie froze for a beat, then looked away from his smiling face, her happiness dimmed at the mention of her fortune. Of course she had to tell him it was lost. And she fully intended to do so. It was just that she'd hoped to break the dismal news later, after she'd had an hour or so to bask in the euphoria of her upcoming nuptials.

"Dearest? Did I say something to distress you?"

"No. It's just . . ." she trailed off, suddenly apprehensive. What if he refused to take a debt-ridden bride, despite their love? Men were ruled more by their heads than their hearts, she'd heard, though she'd personally seen no evidence to that fact.

"Sophie?" He grasped her chin and tipped her face back up to his. After scrutinizing it for a moment, he frowned and murmured, "I was right. You are troubled. You're not having second thoughts about marrying me are you?"

"Oh, no! Never!" she exclaimed, aghast that he would even ask such a question.

"Then what? What plagues you? You know you can trust me."

He looked so earnest, so genuinely sincere in his desire to help her, that her apprehension evaporated. Of course he wouldn't put money before their love. He simply wasn't that sort of a man. What a hen-wit she was to even imagine such a thing. Smiling with renewed confidence, she met his gaze and replied. "There's something I must mention about my fortune."

He returned her smile, clearly relieved. "If you're worried that your cousin will deny us your dowry for defying him, I can assure you that he can't. We shall drag him before a magistrate should he try."

"No, it's—it's not that. It's just that—well"—she swallowed hard, then softly confessed—"there is no dowry."

He recoiled as if she'd slapped him. "What?"

"There is no dowry," she repeated, this time more loudly. At the sight of his slack-jawed astonishment, she hastened to add, "I did have one—all that my cousin claimed—but he lost it."

Julian's eyes widened to the point of bulging. "All of it?"

She nodded. "Worse yet, we have debts. The debts are why I'm to marry Lyndhurst."

He couldn't have looked more stunned had she confessed to being a highway robber. "Lyndhurst knows about your dowry?" he expelled, incredulously.

"No. Oh, no! He knows nothing about any of this. No one in the ton does. Even I was ignorant of it until last night." She shook her head, still a bit dumbfounded by the news herself. "I've been the pawn in Edgar's scheme to save us from debtors prison."

"Scheme?" He pulled from her embrace, scowling.

Certain he frowned at Edgar using her so, she briefly outlined the plan. When she was finished, Julian released a harsh snort of laughter and ground out, "In other words, you were going to dupe Lyndhurst. How very amusing that would have been, the high and mighty Earl of Lyndhurst played for a fool. That would have brought him down a notch or two, I daresay."

Sophie stared at him, utterly taken aback. This wasn't how he was supposed to respond. He was supposed to tell her that he'd pay her debts and that they would live happily ever after. Desperate to hold on to her dream, she wrapped her arms around his waist and murmured, "None of that is either here nor there now. All that matters is us being together."

He grasped her upper arms and pushed her away. Holding her at arm's length, he growled, "It is very much here and now. It just so happens that I, too, am financially embarrassed."

Sophie shook her head over and over again, unable to fathom the sudden harshness of his face. "We'll scratch by somehow," she reassured him, certain that his expression stemmed from shock. "With careful management of your income, we should be able to discharge our debts in a few years' time. Of course, that means we shall probably have to live on your estate."

He stared at her as if she'd lost her wits, then snorted and released her arms with a shove. "I don't want to scratch by, and I most certainly have no intention of rusticating in Lincolnshire for the next few years."

"What does it matter where we live or how modestly as long as we're together?" she appealed, unwilling to believe that he meant his words. "Our love will see us through."

"Love?" He released a bitter grate of laughter. "Love had nothing to do with my desire to marry you."

"But you said that you loved me," she cried. "You vowed that you'd do anything for that love."

"Pretty words, nothing more. The same empty ones every man uses to hook a rich wife." He folded his arms over his chest and eyed her with visible scorn. "If you actually believed the flowery phrases men whispered in your ear all Season, then you're a bigger fool than I imagined."

Sophie returned his gaze, tears welling up in her eyes. "You don't love me?" she choked out, feeling as if her heart were being ripped from her chest.

"You might be a fool, but at least you learn quickly," he snapped. "No. I don't love you. I never did, though had you the dowry you claimed, I'd have gladly wed you. You are, after all, a most beautiful woman, and I desired you from the moment I saw you."

He cocked his head to one side then, viewing her thoughtfully. "In truth, I desire you still. Hmm. Perhaps I can help you after all. Yes"—he nodded—"I believe I can. You have only to agree to be my mistress, and I shall arrange it so that your creditors will never find you."

She gasped her indignation. "Your mistress? Why . . . why . . . that's . . ."

"Most generous of me," he interjected, reaching out to trail a finger down the slope of her breast "Just think, my dear. Not only will you be spared the horrors of prison, you shall have the pleasure of my intimate attentions. Since you profess to love me so, that prospect should please you immensely."

Sophie slapped away his hand, more affronted than she'd ever been in her life. "How dare you insult me in such a manner."

He laughed. "Come, come, now, dearest. Don't think of it as an insult, but as a rescue."

"I would rather marry Lyndhurst than enter into such a—a—an indecent arrangement," she flung back, and it was true.

"Perhaps, but I'm afraid that marriage to Lyndhurst is an option you no longer possess."

"Of course it is. I'm officially engaged to him. By this evening everyone in London will know of our betrothal."

"By this evening everyone in London will know of your visit here, and of your uncle's hoax. I can assure you that neither the ton nor Lyndhurst will look kindly upon being played for a fool."

She gaped at him, stunned by his threat. "You wouldn't!"

"Indeed I would. You see, my dear. Though I shan't marry you, I do want you in my bed. Very much so."

He smiled with a ruthlessness she'd never have believed he possessed. "And what I want, I always get."

Hating him with every fiber of her being, she spat, "Not this time. I shall deny your allegations with every breath in my body. It shall be your word against mine."

"Yours against mine and Somerville's," he reminded her. "No doubt I shall be able to persuade Hucknell and Dumont to take my part as well. That's four against one."

"You're despicable," she hissed, impotent to do more. "I can't imagine how I could ever have thought you kind and noble."

"I've already told you how: You're a fool."

Wishing that looks could kill, she fixed him with her most murderous glare and shot back, "I may be a fool, but I'm not a harlot. You shall never have me for your mistress. Never!"

He smirked. "Watch me."

Chapter 5

It had been a most satisfying day indeed.

Having spent the entire afternoon writing his parents and relatives of his upcoming marriage, Nicholas now traveled the short distance to his club to trumpet his triumph to his fellow clubmen. It was a moment to which he'd looked forward almost from the instant he clapped eyes on Miss Barrington, a victory that would make him the envy of every bachelor in the ton.

He smiled at that last as his carriage pulled to a stop in front of White's. Unlike his parents, who would be thrilled by the news of his engagement, his peers would greet them with hisses and groans of disappointment. As they always did in such situations, they would then proceed to call him every insulting name in the book—jokingly, of course!—after which they would clap him on the back and toast his happiness until they were all quite foxed.

It would be the perfect ending to a perfect day.

Ready to burst with excitement, Nicholas peered out the window and tried to gauge the crowd at the club. By the number of men loitering on the walkway and the long queue of coaches lining the street, it was clear that there was a crush inside.

His smile broadened into a grin. Excellent! The more in attendance, the more to hear his splendid news. His excitement mounting another degree, he stepped from the coach. The instant his feet touched the ground, the men on the walkway fell silent and eyed him in the

queerest of manners. Several of them even raised their
quizzing glasses.

Taken aback, Nicholas froze mid-step. Whatever possessed them? He hadn't seen them stare at him in such
a—critical?—yes, critical fashion since his scapegrace
brother had gotten foxed and ridden down Park Lane
with his bare buttocks hanging out—

His brother! Of course. He almost groaned aloud. As
cup-shot as Quentin was at the Stuckely's *soirée* last
night, he wouldn't be at all surprised to learn that he
had done something utterly disgraceful. And as they
were wont to do, his peers no doubt blamed him for not
keeping a tighter rein on the scoundrel.

Promising to find his madcap sibling and take him to
task for whatever he'd done this time, Nicholas strode
forward, nodding cordially as he went. At his approach
several of the men nudged their neighbor and exchanged
wide-eyed looks that were nothing short of incredulous.

Wondering at the punishment for murdering one's
own brother, he mounted the stairs and stepped through
the punctually opened front door. It was only after he'd
handed his hat and walking stick to the waiting footman,
and the servant had walked away that he allowed himself
to sigh his exasperation. Quentin was clearly in the basket this time.

Dreading yet determined to learn the scope of his
brother's infamy, he stalked down the hall, his steps faltering as he neared the salon where he and his peers
assembled nightly. After pausing to brace himself for
what would no doubt prove an arduous ordeal, he
squared his shoulders and entered the room. As he did
so the men nearest the door fell silent, all gaping at him
as if stunned.

Forcing himself to smile, Nicholas nodded politely and
glanced down the line of dumbstruck faces, seeking an
ally among them. Frensham . . . Rivell . . .
Clendon . . . Randolph . . .

Randolph, yes. His old school chum from Cambridge.
Recalling that his lordship was always flush with the latest gossip, compliments of his prattlebox wife, Sarah, he

approached the man, murmuring, "Randolph. Good to see you."

By the pained look on his lordship's narrow face, you'd have thought that he'd slugged him in the belly rather than tendered a greeting. After several beats during which his mouth opened and closed like a ground mackerel, Randolph gathered his wits and croaked, "Uh, Lyndhurst . . . uh . . . fancy seeing you here."

Nicholas felt as gut-punched as his friend looked, though he tried hard not to show it. How very unlike the imperturbable Randolph to act so—so, well, perturbed. Whatever Quentin had done, it must be wicked beyond imagining.

Wishing his brother were there so he could wring his worthless neck, he coolly pointed out, "In case it's escaped your notice, I've been here every evening at precisely this time since the start of the Season."

"True, but we all thought that . . . a-hem! . . . well, with Miss Barrington . . ." He broke off, eyebrows raised in a confidential manner, clearly assuming that Nicholas knew exactly what he meant.

Miss Barrington? Nicholas frowned, momentarily nonplussed. Then enlightenment dawned, and it was all he could do to refrain from laughing out loud.

Ah. But of course. Sophie's cousin must have been there earlier and delivered the news of his engagement. That meant that this queerness was most probably some sort of joke aimed at punishing him for snatching up the Season's prize.

His suspicions were further confirmed when he noted that the room was now completely silent and that the other men inched forward, visibly straining to catch his response. Judging it high time to call their bluff, he said loud enough to be heard by all, "I hardly see how my engagement to Miss Barrington would curtail my visits here. Indeed, you should have guessed that I would come to share the grand news." There. That should end their ruse.

They merely gawked at him.

Wondering exactly what they wanted him to say or do, he grinned and tried again. "Yes, gentlemen. I'm afraid it's true. Miss Barrington accepted my proposal this very morning. We're to be wed in two weeks' time."

Several jaws dropped, and in every direction he looked he was greeted with a confounding mélange of expressions that ranged from pity to outright contempt. He even heard what sounded suspiciously like a snicker. In the next instant everyone started to whisper at once, their indecipherable exchanges buzzing around him like agitated bees. After several moments one of the gentlemen, Lord Bowton if he remembered correctly, stepped forward, and they hushed.

"Um . . . Lyndhurst," he began, gazing at his companions as if seeking their sanction. When they nodded, he nervously looked at Nicholas and continued, "It appears that you haven't heard—"

"Lyndhurst! Thank God!" someone interjected. "I went to your house, but your man told me you'd just left for here. I almost killed myself in my rush to catch you."

Recognizing the voice as that of his best friend, Freddie Priscott, Earl of Huntley, Nicholas turned. By the flush of his face and the way his black hair stood willy-nilly atop his head, it was evident that he hadn't lied about the madness of his dash. Peering at Nicholas as if he'd suffered a death in the family, he murmured, "Good God, man. I'm so sorry. Are you quite all right?"

Frustrated to the point of anger, Nicholas gritted out, "Huntley, will you please be so good as to tell me what the hell is going on around here?'

"You haven't heard?" His friend more gasped than said the words.

"Apparently not," he retorted as the buzz about him started anew.

"The devil you say! I thought everyone had heard."

"Everyone but me it seems," he snapped. "And I do wish you would enlighten me."

Motioning with his head for him to follow, Freddie led Nicholas down the hall to the less crowded library. Mercifully, the occupants of the cozy book-lined room were too engrossed in their newspapers to spare them more than a preoccupied nod.

After settling in facing wing chairs and ordering a bottle of the club's finest brandy, Freddie turned his attention to Nicholas, his expression contrite. "I'm sorry, Lyndhurst. I should have come around to your house the instant I heard the gossip and made certain that you'd heard as well. It's just that"—he shook his head—"I assumed Quentin would tell you."

"Quentin?" Nicholas made a derisive noise. "Just as I suspected, this has something to do with him. As for him telling me anything"—he shrugged one shoulder—"you know well enough that we're scarcely on speaking terms."

"Yes. But being as the gossip is of a scandalous nature and involves you, I was certain he'd delight in telling you himself."

"Not if by refraining from doing so he could make me look a fool, which, as you saw, he did quite admirably." Nicholas made an impatient hand motion. "But enough about my plaguesome brother. Tell me of this scandal in which I'm purportedly involved."

Freddie nodded somberly. "As you wish. But before I begin, I think it only fair to warn you that Oxley, Hucknell, and Dumont were here with Quentin, all bandying about the same tale and attesting to its truth."

"But of course. The Hell-born Four are as thick as thieves." Emitting a contemptuous snort for emphasis, Nicholas crossed his arms over his chest and nodded for his friend to spill the bag. When he didn't immediately comply, he prodded, "Well?"

Freddie returned his gaze for a moment, then ducked his head as if suddenly too embarrassed to look at him. "Ah, yes. Of course. It's about—um—Miss Barrington."

"I gathered as much," he retorted dryly. "Please do go on."

"Well, uh—" Freddie started to pick at his coat buttons, a sure sign that what he was about to say was very dreadful indeed. "Uh, by all accounts, Miss Barrington—um—visited them at their bachelor quarters this morning. Seems she's madly in love with Oxley and went to beg him to flee with her to Gretna Green. Your brother claims to have witnessed the entire scene. More shocking yet, they all maintain that Oxley was wearing nothing but his—ahem!—dressing gown during the whole interview."

Nicholas frowned, unable to credit what he was hearing. Miss Barrington was a lady to the first degree. As such she was far too genteel to even consider indulging in such ill-bred behavior. Add that to the fact that she was utterly without guile, and one could only conclude that had she some attachment to Oxley, she'd have told him so when he proposed and thus rejected his suit. Therefore, it must be a lie—a vicious, slanderous lie fostered by his brother to ruin what should be the happiest day of his life.

When he said as much, Freddie sighed and pulled on his top button so hard that it was a miracle it didn't pop off. "She accepted you because she's desperate for funds. The lot of them are. It seems that Marwood lost Miss Barrington's much touted fortune several years ago, leaving them all but penniless."

"Nonsense!" Nicholas more roared than said the word in his disbelief. Several of the other gentlemen lowered their papers to scowl at him, but he was beyond caring. "If such a thing were true, it would most certainly have been the talk of the ton. And I can recall hearing no such tattle. Indeed, aside from the former Lord Marwood's weakness for gambling hells, I've never heard so much as a whisper of scandal regarding Miss Barrington or her relatives."

Freddie shrugged. "How they managed to keep the matter hushed, we shall probably never know. What I do know, however, is that they concealed their ruin so as to introduce Miss Barrington on the Marriage Mart as the heiress she once was. With her charm and beauty they were certain she would make a plum match, thus ending their monetary woes. Miss Barrington herself is said to have confessed the scheme to Oxley."

"But that's absurd!" Nicholas exclaimed. "Even a fool would see that such a hoax could never succeed."

"Well, desperation often breeds fools," Freddie returned philosophically. "Yet, fools or not, what better or quicker way to get funds than to lure the wealthiest bachelor in Town, namely you, into a hasty marriage?"

A hasty marriage. To gain funds. And here he had spent the entire day believing that it was his kiss that had spurred Miss Barrington's urgency to wed. That it might not be so struck a crushing blow to Nicholas's manly pride.

"As you've probably guessed, they have debts," Freddie continued, his tone growing more somber with each new revelation. "Bad ones. They all went deep into dun territory to keep up appearances. Word is that they are on the very brink of being hauled off to prison."

Numbed by the mounting charges being laid before him, Nicholas watched as his friend twisted a button and then released it to spin like a top. Grasping it again to wind it in the opposite direction, Freddie confided in a low voice, "I, too, dismissed this business as being just more of Quent's trumped up nastiness. In truth, I didn't give it another thought until I stopped by Fribourg & Treyer's this afternoon to buy snuff."

"Oh?"

His gaze still glued to his buttons, Freddie nodded. "While there, I overheard a clerk inform Mr. Fribourg that Marwood is months in arrears on his bill. Though I didn't catch the entire exchange, I did hear that when he went around to collect earlier today, he was met on the stoop by five other creditors, all clamoring for payment. I couldn't help wondering then if there wasn't perhaps some truth to the Hell-born Four's claims."

"It does make one wonder, yes, though I fail to fathom why Miss Barrington would turn to Oxley if matters are so very dire. Besides being worth only ten thousand a year, he, too, is deeply in debt." Nicholas shook his head. "None of it makes a whit of sense. Not when you consider the ease with which she could have escaped her coil by marrying me."

Freddie stared at the gold button in his hand as if suddenly fascinated by its pressed griffin design. "As I said, she fancies herself in love with him. You know how silly chits are when they get all calf-eyed over a man. She no doubt views him as a fairy-tale prince capable of magically rescuing her from her woes."

"Miss Barrington may not be the most wide-awake of

females, but she's no goose," Nicholas countered, refusing to believe he'd so grossly misjudged her. "And a girl would have to be an utter goose to be taken in by Oxley's pretty face and smooth manner."

"Ur—yes. Silly to the extreme." Freddie gave his button a vicious tug. "Any woman corkedbrained enough to put such stock in looks and manner is far too silly to merit the notice of a man such as yourself. Bloody undeserving, if you ask me. Indeed—"

Nicholas's eyes narrowed as Freddie rattled on, suspecting by both his words and fidgeting that his friend hid something. When Freddie actually tore the button he worried completely off his coat, he was certain of it. Determined to learn exactly what that something was, he leaned forward and demanded in a soft voice, "What is it you're not telling me, Huntley?"

Freddie plucked at the threads left behind by the button. "Nothing."

Nicholas was about to pursue the matter further when a footman bearing a bottle of brandy and two glasses came to a stop beside them. When he'd poured them each a healthy ration of the spirit and bowed himself from their presence, Nicholas turned back to his friend and resumed his interrogation.

"How long have we known each other, Huntley?"

Freddie looked up and smiled at the question. "Fifteen years. Since you saved me from that thrashing at Harrow."

"And after all these years, don't you think I can tell when you're hiding something?"

His friend shrugged, but the gesture was far too stiff to project the nonchalance he was obviously trying to convey.

"Well, I can," Nicholas informed him. "And it's evident that you're concealing something, something truly awful by the expression on your face. As my best friend, I do wish you would tell me what that something is. Otherwise, I shall be obliged to ask around and learn it from someone else."

When his friend remained mute, Nicholas made an impatient noise and rose. As he started to move away,

Freddie grasped his arm. "No, wait. I shall tell you. Best you hear it from me."

With a curt nod Nicholas sat back down. After an extended moment of silence, he prompted, "Well?"

Looking infinitely unhappy, Freddie muttered, "According to the Hell-born Four, Miss Barrington found the prospect of marriage to you intolerable. That is why she didn't go through with the scheme."

Intolerable? Him? Nicholas frowned. Though he knew she didn't love him any more than he did her, he considered them companionable enough. Indeed, she'd always appeared content in his company, as he was in hers. Not knowing quite what to make of that latest disclosure, he murmured, "Did she, by chance, say what she finds so intolerable?"

By the expression on Freddie's face, were he a woman he'd have burst into tears. Hanging his head as if confessing to the greatest of sins, he mumbled, "She thinks you're arrogant. And . . . um . . . boring."

Nicholas accepted the charge of arrogance without offense, but boring? Never in his life had anyone accused him of being so. More confounded than ever, he picked up his brandy and took a deep swallow. Him, boring? His brow furrowed as he considered.

Well, perhaps, just perhaps, it was possible that a girl as young and frivolous as Miss Barrington might find him a bit . . . reserved. And perhaps some of their outings may have been a jot too . . . academic . . . for a chit fresh from the schoolroom.

He took another quaff from his glass. Indeed, now that he thought back on some of their outings, he saw that they might not have been completely to her taste. Like, for example, when he'd escorted her to Vauxhall Gardens and insisted they forgo the amusements in favor of him teaching her about the plants. Though she'd been polite, smiling and asking an occasional question, she hadn't looked exactly thrilled.

And then there was that lecture last week by that African explorer. The few times he'd glanced over to see if she was enjoying it as much as he, she'd been staring into the air looking rather stupefied. Assuming the cause to be a lack of comprehension on her part, he'd taken it upon himself to explain afterward everything that had been said.

He tossed back the remainder of his brandy. Come to think of it, she'd looked none too captivated by his explanations, either. Odd that he hadn't noted it then. Hmm. Could he have been blind to other things about her as well?

Like her character?

Sighing over his splintering illusions, Nicholas glanced to where Freddie sat morosely staring into his own glass, and asked, "Is that the whole reason, then? I'm arrogant and boring?"

"Uh, well . . ."

Sighing again, this time with irritation, he muttered, "Just cast it forth, Huntley. How much worse can this get?"

Freddie looked at him then, his expression woeful to the point of grief. "You know, Lyndhurst," he said in a rush, "I never thought Miss Barrington nearly good enough for you. She is, after all, only a cloth merchant's daughter and truly not—"

"What did she say?" Nicholas demanded, in no mood whatsoever to be placated. "If you don't tell me, and tell me now, I shall call on my brother and ask him."

"She, uh—" Freddie's already flushed face darkened to the color of an overcooked pork roast. "She supposedly cannot bear the sight of your . . . um . . . face."

"My face?" Nicholas ejected. Of all the things his friend could have said, this was the last one he'd expected to hear.

Freddie nodded miserably. "It's your—ur—scar. She finds it o-offensive."

His scar? Without thinking, Nicholas reached up and touched his disfigured cheek. That she or anyone found it offensive was a disturbing notion, one that provoked a long dormant niggle of self-consciousness. Could it be true that his face disgusted her?

His mind whirling, he searched for an answer, scrambling to recall an instance in which she might have said or done something to betray such a feeling. Yet, try as he might, he couldn't recollect so much as a second in which her conduct was anything less than perfect. On every occasion she had been charming yet demure, as befitted a girl in her position.

Demure? His eyes narrowed with sudden misgiving. At least he'd always attributed her reluctance to look at his face to demureness. Was it possible that that reluctance stemmed not from modesty, as he'd assumed, but from revulsion of his scar?

The more he considered, the more likely it seemed. Indeed, now that he thought about it, he realized that she never seemed to have any compunction about looking at her other suitors. Especially Oxley. How many times had he come upon them together at balls and such, and seen her staring at his face?

It was remembering those occasions that made the pieces of his puzzled disbelief fall into devastating place. The tale was true. It had to be. It simply made too damn much sense, something that Quentin and his cohorts woefully lacked.

"You know, Lyndhurst. I always thought Miss Barrington a singularly stupid creature," Freddie remarked, clearly trying to hearten him. "That she'd prefer Oxley's priggish looks to your noble ones merely proves me correct."

Slowly Nicholas lifted his gaze from his now empty glass to fix his friend with a cynical stare. "You always thought her lovely and charming. You must have said so a hundred times."

Freddie shrugged. "That's only because you were so set on having her."

"Well, if she's stupid, then I'm a bloody idiot," he shot back. "So idiotic that I attributed her reluctance to look at me to schoolgirl shyness."

"As would I, I assure you. One does expect a Bath Miss to be somewhat reserved around men."

"Maybe. But even the greenest of girls will at least glance at a man when he speaks to her, something that Miss Barrington seldom did."

That any woman could find him so repulsive stung Nicholas to the very core, and he couldn't help wondering how many of the women who claimed to find his scar dashing secretly agreed with Miss Barrington, lying in hopes of gaining his wealth and title. The very notion leveled a serious blow to his confidence.

Always an optimist, Freddie leaned over and clapped him on the shoulder. "We should all be thankful that this happened, eh? Imagine if you'd actually married the girl?"

Nicholas cast him a jaundiced look. "Thankful? For being publicly humiliated?"

"Pshaw! You've been nothing of the sort. No one thinks any less of you for any of this. Indeed, there isn't a man in the ton who wasn't taken in by Miss Barrington, and they all feel just as foolish as you."

"Perhaps. But none were corkbrained enough to actually propose to her."

"They would had they thought there was a chance she might accept." Smiling weakly, Freddie refilled the glass clenched in Nicholas's hand. "Look, Lyndhurst. If it's any consolation, Miss Barrington is ruined. By this time tomorrow the news of her hoax shall have reached the ears of her creditors. Unless she and that aunt and cousin of hers find a way to settle their debts, they will probably be hauled off to prison at the end of the week."

Though Nicholas knew the news was meant as a balm to his wounded pride, it did nothing to reduce the sting. In truth, he didn't believe in the practice of incarcerating debtors, especially women . . . not even one whom he despised as much as he currently did Miss Barrington. To his way of thinking, it made far more sense to allow a person to work off his obligations, a point that he'd been known to expound upon on more than one occasion.

Heaving a weighty sigh, he tossed back the entire contents of his glass in one fiery gulp. Ah, well. It was none of his affair what happened to the chit now.

"Look on the bright side of things. Since Miss Barrington is ruined, you can finish out the Season with the assurance that you shan't be meeting her anywhere,"

Freddie persisted, as if by her mere absence the scandal would magically disappear.

Nicholas eyed his friend in consternation. "You don't honestly think that I shall remain in Town after what has happened, do you?"

"Why ever not? You yourself said that this has been a particularly lively Season. Besides, it's not too late for you to find another bride, if you're still of a mind to do so."

A bride? Nicholas felt physically ill at the notion of courting. What if whomever he chose the next time found his face as hideous as Miss Barrington did? That thought deepened the dull ache in his belly to a torturous wrench.

Shaking his head as much in response to his pain as in reply, he gritted out, "No. I shall spend the remainder of the Season in Scotland. Fishing."

Where no one would have to look at his face.

As Freddie predicted, every tongue within the fashionable district between Grosvenor Square and St. James Street was a-wag over the Barrington-Marwood hoax by the following afternoon. The merchants, upon hearing of the trio's insolvency, merged upon their residence en masse, banging on the door and bellowing for payment. When it became apparent that they would receive neither money nor a response, they retreated one by one, each shouting threats of arrest as he stormed off down the street.

Of course the Marwoods blamed Sophie for their fix, Edgar with a rage that exploded into violence the instant he read Lyndhurst's note accusing them all of fraud and calling off the wedding. Indeed, had Heloise not shielded Sophie from his wrath, he'd have no doubt added murder to his growing list of sins. It was during that volatile outburst, as she lay sobbing in her aunt's arms, that he'd banished her to her chamber, vowing to throttle her should she remain in his sight a second longer.

And she was still there, though many hours had passed.

Her eyes welling with tears for the hundredth time

that day, Sophie rolled over onto her belly and buried her face in her pillow to smother her anguished wails. If she'd only been sensible and married his dreadful lordship, they wouldn't be in this coil . . . this hopeless, tangled coil.

She also wouldn't be suffering the pain of discovering Julian's true character.

As happened every time she thought of Julian, raw, savage grief clawed at her heart. Better she'd wed Lyndhurst and spent her life mourning for Julian's love than to have learned that it had never truly been hers. At least then she'd still have her dreams.

But now she had nothing. Literally. And by this time tomorrow she would be sailing for the wilds of America, fleeing the country like the criminal she was. She'd overheard Edgar and Heloise plotting their escape to the New World when she'd tiptoed past the library earlier that evening.

Mind you, she hadn't meant to eavesdrop. Indeed, had they still had servants she'd never have ventured forth from her exile. But the servants were gone, every last one of them, all having quit the instant they learned of their employer's straitened circumstances. That meant that there was no one to bring her her meals. And since neither Heloise nor Edgar had thought to do so, she'd been forced to forage for herself.

So forage she did, though, in truth, she'd had no real appetite. No. What drove her to the kitchen wasn't hunger, but craving; one for the Shrewsbury cakes the cook had baked the day before. There was always something comforting about their sweet, buttery taste, something that reminded her of her father's laughter and her mother's hugs—of picnics and Christmas and stories by the fire. Their taste took her home again: home, where she'd always been safe, happy, and loved.

Filled with bittersweet longing for those peaceful bygone days, she'd gorged herself on the remainder of the cakes. Full to the point of bursting and exhausted from her emotional turmoil, she'd crept back to her room, where she'd fallen into a restless, dreamless slumber sometime around eleven o'clock.

Lifting her face from her pillow, Sophie wondered what time it was now. As tired as she felt, she couldn't have slept more than an hour or so. That would make it what? Twelve or one? Close to the time her aunt would be coming to bid her to ready herself for the voyage. She'd heard Edgar say that they would leave the house promptly at three to catch the four-fifteen coach to Dover. If it were indeed one o'clock, she had but two hours to prepare. Best she stop moping and start her packing now.

Though she felt boneless from fatigue, Sophie some-how managed to force herself from her bed. After toss-ing on a white cashmere wrap, she lit a candle and dragged herself to her dressing room. For several beats she stood drowsily surveying her surroundings, wonder-ing what to do first. Then she caught sight of her reflec-tion in her dressing table mirror, and her vanity decided for her. Was that really her hair or had a bird nested on her head?

Grimacing at what had mutated from a fashionable crown of curls into a matted horror, Sophie sat before the table. No wonder mademoiselle always insisted she take it down and brush it before bed. It turned impossi-ble when left up.

Wishing that mademoiselle were there to help her now, she dug through the knotty wad and extracted what hairpins remained. She then picked up her brush and launched her attack. She had finished taming the golden chaos and was pinning it up when the hall clock began to chime.

One, two, three . . . four?

With a gasp she dropped her hairpins, scattering them across the table to lay like the wire skeletons of long defeated tin soldiers. The clock was wrong. It had to be! Desperate to confirm the fact, Sophie rushed to her jew-elry case to check the time on her watch.

It was gone. All her jewelry was gone save the paste coronet she had worn to a costume ball at the beginning of the Season.

Certain she'd been robbed by the servants, Sophie dashed to the door and flung herself out into the corridor, frantic to inform Edgar. Her thin white wrap chasing behind her like a ghostly shadow, she ran down the hall at neck-break speed, coming to a sliding stop when she reached her destination.

Her frenzied voice mingling with the bruising whack of her knuckles against the door, she cried, "Edgar!" over and over again.

No response.

Dropping her now numb hand to her side, she leaned over and pressed her ear to the door to listen for signs of life within.

Not so much as a creak or a sigh.

A frisson of foreboding tingled down her spine as she straightened up again. Had he made good his earlier threat to take his mother and flee the country without her? Had the "we" in his plan not included her?

As quickly as the thought entered her mind, she dismissed it. Though he was no doubt angry enough to desert her, Aunt Heloise loved her and would never allow him to do so. And Edgar, despite his tyrannical manner, always yielded when she asserted her matriarchal command. Factoring that with the lateness of the hour, it was reasonable to conclude that the plan had been changed and that he was out somewhere modifying the arrangements. Yet—yet—

Possessed by a sudden chill, Sophie snugged her wrap around her. A change of plans might explain Edgar's absence, but where was her aunt? All the banging and shouting should have drawn her attention. Growing more uneasy by the second, she opened Edgar's door. It took only a single glance to confirm her worst fears.

Every drawer was pulled from its slot, every box and chest stood open, their hastily rifled contents spilling over the sides and across the floor. What little of value there was in the room, the silver candlesticks, the marquetry clock, even the gilt mirror, had been stripped away, probably to pay for passage. The sight left no doubt in her mind as to who had stolen her jewelry.

With mounting horror she backed away from the threshold, moving step by trembling step across the hall until her back butted against the facing wall. For what felt like an eternity in hell, she stood there, paralyzed by panic. Then she turned and numbly stumbled the short distance to her aunt's chamber.

It, too, was ransacked.

A ragged sob of betrayal tore from her throat. Like Julian, it appeared that Heloise, too, had lied about loving her.

"No!" she cried out loud, the word echoing forlornly in the forsaken room. No. Heloise loved her. She knew she did. She would never abandon her, not willingly at least.

Desperately clinging to that belief, Sophie searched the littered chamber, looking for a note, or anything at all, to sanction her faith in her aunt. But there was nothing.

Shattered by disappointment, she wandered from the bedchamber to the dressing room, though deep inside she had little hope of finding anything there, either.

At first glance her pessimism looked to be justified, a justification that deepened as she explored the normally overfilled wardrobe. Aside from a few old gowns, a pair of spoiled red dancing slippers, and two broken fans, it was completely empty.

Her shoulders drooped as she turned away. Ah, well. She hadn't truly expected to find anything there anyway. Dejected nonetheless, she shuffled over to her last bastion of hope: her aunt's dressing table.

Bracing herself for yet more disappointment, Sophie reached for the silver pull on the top drawer. As she did so, the light from the lone lit wall sconce spilled across the tabletop, lifting the shadows to reveal a sheet of unevenly folded vellum. So homogenous in hue was the paper to the ivory marble surface that Sophie counted it a miracle that she'd noticed it at all.

Cautioning herself against hoping too much, she picked it up, her hands quivering with both anticipation and dread as she drew it nearer to the light.

Written in her aunt's delicate, spidery hand was her name.

Her breath stilling in her throat, she slowly unfolded

it. By the uneven scrawl and smeared ink, it was clear that the brief note had been written in a rush.

> *Please forgive me for leaving you so, dear. Were there a choice, I would have taken you with me. Regretfully, our funds are such that doing so is impossible. Therefore, I urge you to go to your father's uncle at the address below. He is said to be a man of some consequence, and you, dear, are his only living relative. No doubt he shall help you. You will find what I pray is enough to take you to him in the top drawer. Please be assured that I love you and will write you in care of your great-uncle as soon as we are settled. Aunt Heloise.*

Further down the page was the name Arthur Bromphrey and an address in Exeter.

Her great-uncle Arthur? Sophie frowned, vaguely remembering meeting him at her parents' funeral. If memory served her correctly, he had been positively ancient back then. So ancient, that it defied logic to imagine him still alive. Did Heloise know for certain that he lived? Or did she direct her to him on nothing more than hope?

Trying without success to stir her optimism, she opened the drawer and stared at the coins within. Be he a certainty or a hope, she had no choice but to go to Exeter. With luck, she would find him alive and be able to persuade him to help her.

And if he were dead?

Well, at least she would be away from London and the immediate threat of arrest.

Chapter 6

"Bath?" Sophie echoed in dismay.

"Bath," the majordomo confirmed with a nod. "Mr. Bomphrey left yesterday and isn't expected back for at least a month. If you would care to leave your card and your business, I shall have him contact you upon his return."

"I'm Miss Sophia Barrington, his great-niece, come all the way from London to see him," she replied, fumbling through her reticule for her card. Upon presenting it to him, she added, "If you please, I would prefer to await his return here."

By the man's sudden frown, it was apparent that he didn't please. "I am afraid that is impossible, Miss Barton," he replied, a sudden and inexplicable chill frosting his previously warm voice.

"Barrington," she corrected, pointing at the card in his hand.

His gaze followed her finger. After a beat he nodded. "Ah, yes. I see. A thousand pardons, Miss Barrington."

She returned his nod, though what she really felt like doing was sag with relief. By his pinched expression, it was clear that he recognized her name and felt exceedingly foolish for almost sending her away. Deciding that she rather liked the man, she hastened to hearten him. "It is quite all right, uh—" she broke off to cast him an inquiring look.

"Beasley, miss."

"Beasley," she repeated with another nod. "Now, if you would please be so kind, Beasley, I am dreadfully weary from my journey and would like to be shown to my chamber."

"I am sorry, miss. Be your name Barrington or Barton, I still cannot allow you in Mr. Bomphrey's home. Not without his orders."

"But that's absurd! I'm his great-niece . . . his only living relative," she protested, instantly reversing her favorable opinion of the servant. "As such, I am certain that he shall be none too pleased to hear that you sent me away."

"If you are indeed who you say, then no, he shan't be pleased. However, as he has made no mention of you or any other family member, I cannot be certain that you are who you claim. Thus, I must bid you a good day."

"But of course I'm his niece," she exclaimed, grasping the edge of the door he sought to close. "Why ever would I say so if it weren't true?"

He released a much put-upon sigh. "I mean no insult, miss, for you look to be"—his gaze swept her travel-rumpled length—"a, uh, decent sort of gel, but Mr. Bomphrey is a wealthy and exceedingly well-known gentleman here in Exeter. As such there have been numerous ladies over the years who have sought to cozy into both his graces and fortune. Indeed, he had two so-called nieces show up just last month. Them, he turned away without so much as a glance."

The servant paused to shake his bald-pated head. "I got the distinct impression then that he had no nieces. Had he, I am certain he'd have at least looked at those gels."

"Not if neither of them were named Sophia Barrington," she retorted, growing curt in her desperation. "Besides, he has one, not two, nieces. And that niece is me"—she thumped her chest to indicate herself—"Miss Sophia Barrington."

"Well, then. If what you say is indeed true, he shall no doubt send for you the instant I present him with your card." With that, he nodded and again tried to close the door.

Sophie tightened her hold on the edge, foiling his attempt. She had to convince him to take her in. She sim-

ply had to! She had nowhere else to go. Panicked almost
to the point of weeping, she argued, "But he won't know
where to find me."

"Then, I suggest you leave your address."

She bowed her head, as much to hide her tears as in
shame at her confession. "I-I have no address to leave.
I thought to be s-staying here."

"Well, you thought wrong. Now, I suggest that you go
and find other accommodations. I believe that Mrs. Wilson on Bear Lane has suitable lodgings to let."

Sophie released her grip on the door to extend her
hand in a gesture of appeal. "Please—"

"Good day, miss." Taking advantage of his opportunity to do so, the butler slammed the door in her face.

For a long moment Sophie stood on the stoop, not
knowing what to do or where to go. Bath. Uncle Arthur
was in Bath. Considering her lack of funds, it might as
well be China. She heaved a dispirited sigh. Had she
known he was there, she could have gotten off the coach
at that stop and saved herself the torment of having to
travel the extra sixty miles here.

Like the hackneys in London, her experience with the
public coaches had proved singularly unpleasant. Not
only was the vehicle smelly and crowded, if it had
springs she hadn't felt any evidence of them. Indeed, she
was certain she was black-and-blue beneath her clothes
from being tossed about over the rutted roads.

Wanting nothing more than to lie in a hot bath and
soothe her aching bones, Sophie picked up her over-
stuffed valise and lugged it down the steps. By the time
she'd hauled it down the long carriage drive and through
the gates onto Northernhay Row, her arm felt quite
ready to fall off.

Miserable and frustrated, she dropped her burden at
the edge of the road and flexed her stiffening elbow.
Ignoring the burning pain emanating from the joint, she
looked first up and then down the deserted lane, trying
to decide which way to go. Well, since she hadn't the
funds to seek her uncle in Bath, or take the recom-
mended lodgings at Mrs. Wilson's house, she had best

go seek what meager quarters her remaining half crown would buy her.

Feeling like the proverbial lost lamb, she hoisted her bag again and trudged toward the crumbling city wall. Uncle Arthur's large yet homey-looking half-timbered manor house stood just outside the wall, and as she knew from her wretched walk there, it was a goodly distance back to the heart of town.

Yet back to town she went, her hopelessness growing with every plodding step. Exactly where she should look for lodgings once there, she couldn't say. All she knew for certain was that it would be dark in an hour or so, and that she would be far safer in town than traveling the desolate road outside.

The sun was just setting as she limped through the ruins of the ancient gateway, irradiating the sky with glimmering streaks of scarlet, pink, and gold. After pausing to remove a stone from her flimsy velvet walking shoes, she veered left down a road marked St. Paul Street, wandering toward what she hoped was the heart of town.

Lined on both sides with uniform rows of brown brick houses, St. Paul proved a pleasant but unremarkable street. It also proved a short one, abruptly ending before a large, rather grand stone building at whose purpose she could only guess.

Aggravated, not for the first time that day, by her atrocious sense of direction, Sophie pivoted on her heels and wearily stalked down the abutting street. Like St. Paul Street, Gandys Lane, too, was edged with houses. These, however, were smaller and markedly older, the sort of dwellings occupied by a class of people a full step below the brown brick crowd.

She was halfway down the lane, being rudely jostled by urchins chasing a ball, when she was struck with a disquieting sense that she'd again taken a wrong turn. Wanting to scream her frustration, she looked around for someone to ask directions. The only person she saw was one of the ballplayers, a runny-nosed creature who stood a few feet away, hitching up his ragged breeches.

When he noticed her watching him, he stuck out his tongue, then dashed off.

Sophie sniffed her affront. Filthy little beggar. Seeing no one else, save an old man conversing with himself, she continued on her way. It wasn't until she neared the end of the lane that she encountered anyone she deemed appropriate to ask.

That anyone consisted of several chattering clusters of people on a common across the street. Judging from the makeshift stalls and the partially laden wagons, carts, and horses, the common served as the marketplace. And today was market day.

Or had been, she amended, watching a gaily painted wagon advertising cheese and other fine comestibles roll from the grassy square. No doubt one of the departing merchants could give her directions. With luck, he might even be able to recommend an inexpensive but genteel inn.

After waiting for a produce cart and two pot-festooned packhorses to pass, Sophie stepped into the street. She was halfway across when there arose a deafening clatter. Startled, she looked up. To her right, careening drunkenly around the corner on its left two wheels, was a wagon. A speeding wagon, to be exact. One bearing down on her at an alarming rate.

Shrieking her terror, she dropped her valise and dashed from the road, blinded as her whole life flashed before her eyes.

Smack! "O-w-w!" Her shins slammed against something hard.

Plat! "Oomph!" She stumbled back and fell upon her already bruised backside. Then everything went black.

For several dazed moments she lay sprawled there, certain she was dead. Then she saw pinpoints of light piercing the dark and realized that her straw hat had fallen over her face. As she yanked the modish confection back atop her head and secured its Paris net ties, she heard the wagon thunder to a stop several yards away.

"Damnation," growled a masculine voice, followed by the sound of someone jumping from the vehicle. There was the stomp of rushing footsteps, then, "Good heavens, miss. Are you quite all right?"

"If you call being scraped and bruised within an inch of one's life all right, then yes, I suppose I am," she snapped, angrily surveying her soiled and torn blue sarcenet pelisse.

"My humblest apologies, miss. I didn't see you until it was too late to stop."

"At the speed you were driving, I can't say I'm surprised." She sniffed and pushed aside her pelisse to examine the striped muslin gown beneath. It, too, was filthy, and one of the costly lace frills trimming the hem was all but ripped off. Excellent. Not only was she as poor as a pauper, she now looked like one.

"You are right, of course. I was going much too fast," the voice acknowledged in a chastened tone. "Indeed, I ought to be thrashed for racing so in town." Abruptly a white-gloved hand appeared before her eyes. "Please do allow me to assist you."

For the first time since her brush with death, Sophie looked at her assailant, her tongue primed with a stinging rebuff . . . a rebuff she forgot to deliver the instant she glimpsed his face. She'd expected to see a rakish man of say, twenty-five or thirty, one with the wild eyes and demented expression of a Whip Club member. But this . . . this . . . boy! Why, despite his impressive height, he couldn't be a day older than herself.

It was while observing his stature that she noted his attire. He wore livery, an exceedingly splendid deep burgundy one, lavishly trimmed with gleaming gold braid. By the quality of both the cloth and trim, he was clearly in the service of nobility.

Sophie frowned as she studied his coat. There was something about that particular shade of burgundy, something she found exceedingly disquieting. Wherever—

"Please, miss. Do allow me to assist you," he repeated. There was something in his voice, an odd, almost breathless quality that made her glance at his face in wonder.

He stared down at her with the same moonstruck look of admiration she'd seen countless times on countless

men's faces during the Season. Smiling timidly, he nodded his white-wigged head at his outstretched hand.
"Please?"

What remained of her anger melted away beneath his
shy adoration. Returning his smile with her forgiving
one, she grasped his hand and accepted his aid. Stoically
trying to ignore the pain in her shins, she let him pull
her to her feet.

Apparently her misery showed on her face, for the
youth frowned and said, "Perhaps you should sit a bit
longer. You did plow into that mounting block rather
hard."

"Mounting block?" she repeated blankly.

He peered down at her face, visibly alarmed. "Ad-
zooks! You don't remember?"

She blinked. "Remember what?"

"That you tripped over the mounting block there."
He jerked his chin to her right.

She blinked again, then looked over to where he indicated. A groan escaped her at the sight of the solid stone
cube. No wonder she hurt as she did. Indeed, considering the force with which she'd hit it, she was lucky her
legs hadn't snapped on impact.

Staring at her as if expecting her to keel over and cock
up her toes at any moment, he murmured, "Perhaps I
should drive you home, miss. You are clearly in no condition to walk."

Home. Sophie bowed her head, wanting to weep at
the reminder that she had no place to go. But of course
she couldn't, not in front of a stranger. It simply wasn't
done. Equally loathe to admit her vagrant state, she
swallowed back her burgeoning tears and somehow managed to say, "Thank you, but that isn't necessary."

"But I insist," he countered, taking her arm.

She pulled it from his grasp. "No. Please. You are most
kind, but I really must decline. Besides, gauging by your
rush, you are evidently overdue for an appointment."

"Oh. That." His broad shoulders drooped as he
glanced at the last of the departing merchants. "I'm not
merely overdue, I look to be far too late." Sighing as if
the world were at an end, he returned his mournful blue

gaze to her. "I was to attend the Mop Fair at the market today and bring back a new maid. But as you can see, it ended long ago."

If possible, his spirits seemed to sink even lower. "This is the first time Mrs. Pixton—uh, she's the housekeeper—entrusted me with an important task. And I failed. Miserably so. It shall be a wonder if I don't lose my position when I return alone. We do so need a maid, what with Carrie up and eloping last week."

On and on he lamented, his words inspiring Sophie to view him with new eyes. Shrewd, speculative ones. He needed a maid. She needed a place to stay until her uncle returned. Was this accident God's answer to her desperate prayers? Hmm. Perhaps, though working as a maid was hardly the deliverance she'd envisioned.

Only half listening as he rambled on about rutted roads and a broken wheel, she considered a servant's lot in life.

From what she'd observed, it didn't seem so dreadful. Indeed, aside from scattering a "yes, my lord" here and a "yes, my lady" there, with a bit of fetch and carry in between, there appeared to be little to it. It was certainly nothing she couldn't endure for a month, especially when one considered her alternatives.

Her mind made up, she opened her mouth to tell him of her decision. Before she could speak, however, she was struck by a most chilling thought: What if she knew her new master and mistress? Considering the lofty circles in which she had moved over the years, it was entirely possible.

Panicked by that thought, Sophie glanced at the footman, who was complaining about the ineptness of some wheelwright. The only way to know for certain if it was safe to take the position was to inquire as to the family's name. Thus, she cut into his moaning barrage asking, "Who is your master?"

He stopped mid-sentence, his mouth hanging open as if stunned by her interruption. "Huh?"

"Who is your master?" she repeated.

His mouth snapped shut and he blushed, as if suddenly aware of his whining. "Uh, the Marquess of Beresford."

Beresford. Hmm. The name sounded vaguely familiar, though she couldn't put a face to it. Deciding that further investigation was in order, she inquired with a casualness she didn't feel, "Why is it that you didn't accompany his lordship to London? It is the Season, you know, and he shall no doubt require your services."

The footman shrugged. "Neither Lord Beresford nor his wife have been to London in years. They don't much fancy it or the ton."

Excellent. That meant there was no chance of them recognizing her face. Wanting to shout her delight, Sophie took the first step toward acquiring the position. "Is his lordship a good master?"

"The best!"

"And what sort of maid does he seek?"

The footman grimaced at her reminder of his failed mission. "We need someone to do odd chores. A maid-of-all-works."

"Does the position require previous service experience?"

He grimaced again. "At this point I'd hire anyone with a wit above a sheep."

Sophie laughed, as much from excitement as at his droll reply. "I can assure you that I possess wits beyond those of a sheep."

"What!" He gaped at her as if she claimed to be the king in women's clothing. "You aren't saying that you want the position?"

"That is exactly what I'm saying."

"Egad! Surely you jest."

It was Sophie's turn to be taken aback. "You think me unworthy of the job?"

"No! I assure you that I meant no such insult." He frantically shook his head. "I just naturally assumed that a fine lady such as yourself must be jesting to suggest taking such a mean position."

Sophie returned his gaze for a beat, then sighed and bowed her head, shamed by the admission she knew she must make. Choking on her pride, she haltingly confessed, "I might be a lady, but I'm afraid I am no longer so very fine. In truth, I have but a half crown to my name. And unless you hire me for the maid position, I shall be sleeping on the street tonight."

"What!" he gasped.

Miserably she shook her head. "I am utterly destitute."

There was a long, heavy silence, then he cleared his throat and said, "Might I ask what happened to put you under the hatches?"

"I suppose you must know if you are to consider hiring me," she murmured, though what she would tell him, she didn't know. All she knew for certain was that the truth was out of the question.

He cleared his throat again. "Miss—"

"Barring—uh—I'm Sophia Barton." Why tempt fate by giving her real name?

He bowed. "A pleasure to make your acquaintance, Miss Barton. And I am Terence Mabbet, fourth footman to the Marquess of Beresford."

She dipped a shallow curtsy in acknowledgment.

Straightening back up to his impressive height, Terence continued, "Though I am but a mere fourth footman, I can assure you that I always adhere to the rules of gentlemanly conduct. One of those rules is that a gentleman must always see to the welfare of a lady in need. That means that it is my duty to give you the position whether you chose to confide in me or not."

Sophie smiled and nodded, though what she really longed to do was hug him. "You are most kind, Mr. Mabbet."

"Terry. All the other servants call me Terry."

"Terry. And you may call me Sophie. All my friends do so."

He grinned. "By gum! We will be friends." Looking beyond thrilled by that prospect, he reached over and once again took her arm. "Now that everything is settled, we should be on our way. It's almost dark, and we have a goodly ride ahead of us."

At her nod of consent he escorted her to the wagon, a glossy burgundy and gold affair with polished brass lamps. He had just lit the lamps and was gathering the reins in preparation to depart, when Sophie remembered her valise.

"Oh no! Wait. My valise. I dropped it when I ran from the road," she cried, desperately peering about her. Though the black leather bag held little of monetary value, it contained the last vestiges of her bygone life and was thus priceless to her.

Gallantly pledging to retrieve her belongings, Terry jumped from the wagon and raced to the site of her near demise. It was but a moment later when he returned, bearing a large, badly scuffed object that bore little resemblance to her once elegant valise.

Visibly abashed, he handed it to her, muttering, "Sorry. I seem to have run it over."

Him and half the merchants in Exeter, she thought, staring at her crushed bag with dismay. No doubt her bonnets were flattened beyond repair. As for her mother's ivory hand mirror . . .

Her dejection must have shown on her face, for Terry reached over and gingerly squeezed her arm. "Please forgive me, Sophie. I feel ever so wretched about all this. I do hope I haven't ruined anything of great importance." By his expression you'd have thought that he was responsible for all the plagues in history.

Hating to see him, her rescuing knight, look so, Sophie smiled and hastened to reassure him. "Please don't feel badly, Terry. Of course I forgive you. Save a crushed bonnet or two, I am quite certain that you did no irreparable damage to anything."

"But your bonnets—"

"Their value is nothing when weighed against the kindness you've shown me." And it was true, she realized with sudden dawning. One ounce of kindness in a time of need was worth far more than all the bonnets in London. That revelation stunned her, who valued possessions above all else, to the very core of her materialistic soul.

"Bah! I did nothing that any respectable person wouldn't have done," he retorted, though she could tell from his blush that her praise pleased him. Without further ado he slapped the reins, and they were off.

Chapter 7

Down High Street they dashed, onto Fore Street and over the Exe River bridge. Though Terry kept his recklessness in check, he still drove far too fast for Sophie's peace of mind.

Ah, well, she thought, clinging to the side rail for dear life. At least the seats are well cushioned, and I most certainly can't complain about the springs. Not that she'd have complained at any rate. She was much too grateful simply being in the wagon and headed for sanctuary to find fault with anything.

After traveling a couple of swift but blessedly mishap-free miles, she grew confident enough of his driving to release her grip on the bar. Feeling suddenly safer than she'd felt in what seemed like forever, she relaxed back in her seat and watched the moon rise, smiling as Terry began whistling a jolly tune.

On through the dark they dashed, each night-stained landscape indistinguishable from the last. Rocked by the wagon and lullabied by Terry's whistling, Sophie soon sank into a deep, dreamless slumber. She felt as though she'd just closed her eyes when she was awakened by a sudden jolt.

Blinking away her sleepy fog, she drowsily peered about her. They were in a courtyard of sorts, formed by two jutting wings and what she assumed was the main house, all built from a brick whose hue was obscured by shadow. By the lines of mullion windows, many of which spilled forth a hazy stream of light, she could see that the house stood four stories tall and contained a myriad of rooms.

As she watched two silhouettes pantomime in a second-floor window, she heard a door creak open. In the next instant light flooded from her right, drawing her attention to a short female form holding a lantern.

"It's about bleedin' time you got back, Terry Mabbet," the form bawled. "Her ladyship took sick this afternoon, and with us short 'o help and you off dillydallyin', the Pixie's had ta do the 'xtra fetchin' herself. She's in a fine nettle over it, I can tell you. Says she gonna scold you stone-deaf for bein' gone so long."

"The Pixie?" Sophie looked to Terry for clarification.

"Mrs. Pixton, the housekeeper." His face paled as he uttered the name.

"Well?" the form demanded. "What've you to say for yourself?"

"Not that it's any of your business, Fancy Jenkins, but it took longer than expected to find a suitable maid," he retorted, his confident tone at startling odds with his frightened face. "Good help is hard to find, you know."

"She'd better be the bleedin' best maid the Pixie ever saw if you're to keep your hearin'."

Terry shot Sophie a rather anxious look. "Er . . . I assure you she is."

The form emitted a loud sniff. "Well, come along with you then. The longer you dawdle, the harder it'll go for you."

After handing the reins to a boy who seemed to appear out of nowhere, Terry jumped from the wagon, then assisted Sophie down. By the way his hands trembled as he took her arm, she could tell that he was terrified by the prospect of facing the housekeeper.

Sorry for his trouble and wanting to do something to help, she murmured, "Perhaps it would be for the best if we tell Mrs. Pixton that the wheel broke on the way back here, and that it took us a goodly time to find a wheelwright to fix it."

Looking as if he were next in line for execution, Terry shook his head. "It broke on the way to Exeter, not the other way around. The Pixie will see through me for sure if I try to tell her otherwise. She always knows when someone is fibbing."

"You don't have to fib. Simply say that a broken wheel delayed you, and leave it at that. Since you returned with me, she shall no doubt assume that you attended the fair, thus concluding that it broke on the way back here."

"And I shall be out of the briers on all accounts without uttering a single fib," he finished for her.

She nodded.

He grinned. "Clever girl. I can see that I truly did bring back the finest maid in all of England."

"Unless you wanna get sacked, you'd best come along and 'xplain your tardiness to the Pixie," the form snapped.

"Ah, well," she whispered, casting Terry a reassuring look. "Might as well face the dragon now and be done with it."

He nodded his agreement, and together they followed the form through the door. Just within lay a shadowy flight of stone stairs, down which the form vanished. Guessing that the kitchen lay below, Sophie trailed down behind Terry, who took the steps two at a time.

It was indeed the kitchen, and a very grand one at that. By its dimensions and the impressive array of amenities, it appeared that the house had seen some grand entertainments. Judging from the number of people toiling away, it was apparent that those entertainments still occurred from time to time.

"The Pixie's in the stillroom. She said you was ta go there the minute you returned," said a voice from their left.

Recognizing the shrewish tone as that belonging to the lantern-bearing form, Sophie looked over to put a face to the voice. From her domineering ways, she expected to see a woman somewhere on the ripe side of thirty. Like Terry, however, the form's age proved a surprise. Why, she couldn't have been much past twenty.

She was also very pretty, Sophie noted, viewing her with the critical eyes one female employs to assess another. With her lush figure, wide blue-green eyes, and the auburn hair she spied peeking from beneath her cap, the woman no doubt commanded a great deal of male attention.

She also noticed that the woman returned her scrutiny in kind. By her fierce scowl she apparently had little liking for what she saw. When Sophie smiled, hoping to disarm her obvious hostility with friendliness, she sniffed and tossed Terry a disdainful look. "I hope to heaven that this ain't the new maid."

"Indeed she is," Terry replied, giving Sophie a small push forward. "Fancy Jenkins, please meet Sophie Barton. Sophie, this is Fancy, one of our three chambermaids."

"It's a pleasure to make your acquaintance," Sophie murmured, punctuating the pleasantry with a cordial nod.

Fancy sniffed again. "Mrs. Pixton ain't gonna be pleasured to meet you, Miss Hoity-Toity. Bet you ain't never wringed a chicken's neck in your whole uppish life."

"W-wring a ch-chicken's neck?" Sophie echoed, growing queasy just saying the words.

Another sniff. "Whadda you think a maid-of-all-work does? Sip tea and play the pianoforte?" Redirecting her displeasure to Terry, Fancy more hissed than said, "I won't be at'll surprised if the Pixie sacks you for this bit of buffle-headedness."

"What buffle-headedness?" a man inquired, coming to a halt beside Fancy. By his livery he, too, appeared to be a footman.

And a fine-looking footman he is, Sophie thought, discreetly appraising his person. What a shame that God has chosen to waste those fine hazel eyes and that handsome, dimpled face on a mere servant.

Fancy's harsh demeanor visibly softened at the sight of the footman, though Sophie doubted if he observed the change. He was far too busy ogling her to notice anyone or anything else.

Fancy, however, noticed him and his interest in Sophie. Elbowing him sharply in the ribs to draw his attention to herself, she said, "I were tellin' this dolt"—she stabbed a finger at Terry—"that he'll probably be sacked

for hirin' her"—she redirected the finger to Sophie—"as
the new maid-of-all-works."

"Indeed?" The footman returned his admiring gaze to
Sophie. "I, for one, must say that I heartily approve of
his choice."

Fancy joined him in staring at Sophie, though in a
manner that was far from admiring. "*Humph!* You'll be
changin' your mind quick 'nough when you find yourself
havin' ta do her chores for her."

"I shall be honored to assist such a lovely lady," he
purred. Sketching a courtly bow to Sophie, he added,
"Allow me to introduce myself. Charles Dibbs, second
footman, at your service, Miss—"

"Barton. Sophie Barton," Terry supplied.

When Charles took her hand and pressed a lingering
kiss to her palm, Fancy yanked Sophie's arm from his
grasp and shoved her against Terry. "The Pixie's waitin'
for you," she snapped. "If you know what's good for
you, you won't keep her waitin' any longer."

"In that case, I shall see you later, pretty Sophie,"
Charles cooed, winking at her as Fancy towed him away.

Taking Sophie's arm again and leading her across the
bustling kitchen, Terry cautioned, "Watch out for Charlie. He's a regular devil with the ladies."

"That Fancy isn't exactly what I'd call an angel, either," she retorted. "I can't say when I've met such a
termagant."

Terry sighed as he guided her through a door opposite
the one they had entered. "Fancy's a bit tart-tongued
and coarse, but she's usually not so very rude. No doubt
she's stinging from the prick of the Pixie's nettle." Starting up the left side of a double wooden stairway, he
added, "Charlie making calf-eyes at you didn't help matters, either. Fancy has designs on him, and most probably feels threatened by your beauty and breeding."

"Well, she can rest easy on that account. I have no
interest whatsoever in Charles. She can have him, and
with my blessing."

"Then, you must strive to convince her of that," he
countered, stepping onto the stair landing. Once again
taking her arm, he steered her down a short, barren

corridor, stopping before the last door on the right. After pausing to straighten his wig and smooth his jacket, he scratched at the dark wood panel.

"Enter!" responded an imperious voice.

"Ready to slay the dragon?" he whispered, grasping the knob. At her nod he opened the door.

Inside, standing behind a scarred wooden table strewn with clay jars, dried plants, and glass vials, was a mite of a woman in a brown-striped gown. A crisp white cap perched atop her graying carrot-colored hair, its starched flounce framing a tiny, sharp-featured face that justified her nickname.

Looking up to reveal shrewd green eyes, she briskly uttered, "Terence. Finally. I was beginning to fear that you'd run off with a milkmaid or some other such youthful nonsense."

Terry sketched a meticulous bow. "Never, Mrs. Pixton. I am always at your service." At his hiss Sophie quickly followed suit and dropped into an elegant curtsy.

"Well, well. And what have we here?" the housekeeper inquired, her gaze critically sweeping Sophie's length.

Terry gave Sophie a gentle push forward. "Mrs. Pixton, let me present Sophie Barton, our new maid."

"Indeed?" Her gaze moved from Sophie's face to narrow on her expensive, if spoiled, garments. Raising one eyebrow, she said, "I think that I would like to interview our new maid in private. You, my boy, are excused for now."

Terry shot Sophie an uneasy look. "But, Mrs. Pixton—"

"Go. I shall speak with you later."

He hesitated for a beat, then bowed and reluctantly did as directed.

As the door closed behind him, the housekeeper bore her gaze onto Sophie's and demanded, "Spill it, girl."

"What?" Sophie stammered, genuinely confused.

"You heard me. I said spill it."

"Spill what? I don't understand."

Hardening her gaze into a penetrating stare, the woman snapped, "See here, girl. I'm not blind, and my eyes tell me that you're quality. I want to know who you are and what game you're playing."

"My name truly is Sophie Barton, and I'm here to work as a maid," she replied, growing uneasy beneath the housekeeper's unblinking scrutiny. No wonder Terry was so distraught at the notion of fibbing to her. She seemed able to look right through a person and into their innermost thoughts.

After several more such moments, ones made all the more disconcerting by the silence, the woman jerked her chin to indicate Sophie's modish pelisse. "If what you say is true, then please enlighten me as to why a lady like yourself would go into service."

When Sophie merely gaped at her, trying to concoct a likely tale, the housekeeper looked up at her face again and brusquely answered for her. "My guess is that you're here to try and trap his lordship's son into marriage."

"Son?" Sophie squeaked. It hadn't occurred to her to ask if the marquess had children. If the son was of marriageable age, as Mrs. Pixton indicated, then he was no doubt in Town for the Season. That meant he knew both the scandal and her identity.

"Yes, son. Young Colin. And if it's him you're after, you may as well leave now. Her ladyship received a letter just this morning saying that he's off to Scotland to fish."

Colin? Sophie furiously searched her mind for a Colin. The only Colins she could recall were Colin Redmond, a viscount of some sixty years, and Lady Burges's four-year-old son. Add that to the fact that the housekeeper had prefaced him as young, and she could probably safely assume that he was part of the smooth-cheeked set who favored brothels and gaming hells over ballrooms.

Putting her mind to rest with that conclusion, she shook her head. "I wasn't aware that the marquess has a son, nor do I care. My only interest is in the position."

"Indeed? Well, then. Shall I hazard another guess as to why you are here?" Her gaze dropped to eye her belly. "Could it be that you're with child and have run away from home to escape disgrace?"

"Of course not!" Sophie exclaimed, outraged that the woman would even think, much less suggest, such an insulting thing. "I can assure you that my morals are above reproach, and shall remain so. I am here because I need employment and nothing else."

"You *need* employment, eh?" The housekeeper viewed her through slitted eyes for a beat, then gave a curt nod. "Yes. I do believe that you truly were driven here by need. Before, however, I consider giving you the position, you must first tell me what trouble brought about your need. And I expect the truth, mind you."

Seeing no other choice, Sophie bowed her head and slowly began to speak. Since telling the truth was out of the question, she made up her tale as she went along. "I need the position because my father lost our home . . . gambling, and I now have no place to go. Since I also lack money, I have no choice but to go into service if I want a roof over my head and food in my stomach." She glanced at the housekeeper to see if she bought her story.

The woman's small, pointy face was completely impassive. "And where was your home?" she prodded.

Where was far, far away? Remembering her geography lessons, Sophie responded, "Durham. My father was a baron there."

"A baron, you say? Hmm. And what of your mother, the baroness?"

A flash of inspiration. "Dead. She died giving birth to me. I was her first and last child. It was her death that drove my father to drink and game."

The housekeeper's eyes began to narrow again, not a good sign. "And where is your father now? Surely he didn't up and leave you?"

"Um . . . yes. He did." It seemed as good an explanation as any.

"And all this happened in Durham?"

"Yes."

"Then, how did you come to be in Exeter?"

How indeed? Seeing no harm in telling a dash of the

truth, albeit a twisted dash, she replied, "I recalled having a . . . an aunt there . . . my mother's older sister. Since I'm her only living relative, I was certain she would take me in. I spent the last of my pin money to go to her."

She paused to heave a long, heavy sigh for effect. "To my despair, I found that she no longer lives in Exeter. It was while I wandered the streets, wondering what to do, that I happened upon the Mop Fair and decided to go into service. When I told Mr. Mabbet of my fix, he took mercy on me and brought me here."

"And so ends the sad tale," the housekeeper concluded. With that cryptic utterance she fell silent, her unnerving stare once again riveted on Sophie's face.

Again Sophie got the unsettling feeling that she read her thoughts, and it was all she could do not to fidget. Just when she was certain she could bear the tension no longer, the housekeeper blinked and barked, "Are you willing to work, and work hard, girl?"

"Yes. Oh, yes!" she exclaimed with a surge of hope.

"And do you promise to follow all my directives?"

"You have only to ask for me to comply."

The housekeeper rubbed her chin as if considering her response, then smiled. "Welcome to Hawksbury Manor, Sophie Barton."

Chapter 8

It took only a day of drudgery for Sophie's feelings of gratitude for Terry to wane.

After a full week, one in which each day was more demeaning than the last, she grimly concluded that their meeting wasn't her prayed-for deliverance, but God's vengeance for every single sin she'd committed in her seventeen years of life.

Casting the heavens—all right, so it was the beamed kitchen ceiling—a look of tragic remorse, she trudged to the servants stairs and dragged herself up the two flights to the first floor.

For a being touted as kind and merciful, He certainly had a wicked talent for punishment, for what could be crueler or cause greater suffering for an Incomparable than to tear her from the heaven of the Haute Ton and cast her into the hell of servitude? And who, but one with a most spiteful bent of mind, would add degradation to hardship by landing that poor girl in the lowliest of low positions in the hierarchy of servitude?

More angered than humbled by her punishment, Sophie stepped up onto the first-floor landing and stopped before the concealed servants door. Sighing as much from outrage as at the ache in her arm, she set down her heavy bucket and flexed her overtaxed elbow.

Never in her life had she imagined there to be a hierarchy among the servants. Why, the very notion of such a thing was beyond absurd. Any fool knew that a servant was a servant, and thus all equal in their inferiority. That the servants at Hawksbury chose to believe otherwise was vexing to the extreme . . . almost as vexing as the manner in which they ordered their preposterous society.

Unlike the ton, whose members were justly ranked according to breeding, appearance, and wealth, one's status downstairs was determined by nothing more discerning than position. Hence, the housekeeper and Dickson, the majordomo, reigned as king and queen; the valet and lady's maid as duke and duchess; and so on down the ranks until you reached a level commiserate in the ton to the by-blow of an Impure: the maid-of-all-works. Her, Sophia Barrington, granddaughter of an earl and the Toast of the ton.

She sniffed at the gross injustice of the system. Any servant with half a wit could see that she was his superior, and thus above him and his silly order. It was galling beyond tolerance how the Hawksbury staff chose to ignore her obvious preeminence.

But tolerate it I must, at least for a month, she reminded herself, shifting her light supply basket from her untaxed left arm to her overtaxed right one. After opening the hidden panel before her, she hoisted the bucket with her left hand and stepped into the dimly lit corridor.

Down the long hallway she plodded, past plants and paintings, sculptures and chairs. When she rounded the West wing corner, she let her nose guide her to her final destination: a dog-fouled carpet near the marchioness's chamber door. As she stopped before it, grimacing at the stench, she found herself wishing that Fancy were there so she could dump it over her head. The spiteful cat was responsible for this mess, and nothing she could say or do would ever convince her likewise.

Snorting her contempt for both the woman and her actions, Sophie kneeled beside the excrement to prepare for her vile task.

No one with an ounce of wits could possibly believe Fancy's tale of the gardener's terrier wandering into the house, not if they considered the lateness of the hour and the fact that all the doors, save the Dickson-guarded front one, were routinely locked at ten. No. Someone had deliberately set the animal loose. Someone who disliked Sophie and knew that the disagreeable chore of cleaning up after him would fall to her.

That person had to be Fancy. No one else bore her such enmity. Besides, this wasn't the first bit of nastiness she'd inflicted on her. Indeed, so often did she sabotage Sophie's labors, then finger her as the culprit of the resulting disaster, that she was beginning to think that the shrew spent every waking hour plotting to make her life miserable.

Sighing her self-pity, Sophie pulled a rumpled sheet of newspaper from the basket and scooped up the bulk of the mess. Ah, well. She only had to endure the jade for three more weeks, a month, at the longest. What were a few more weeks when she'd already endured so much?

Sighing again, she set aside the soiled newspaper, then dug a worn scrub brush, a cracked ball of Ox Gall soap, and a clean rag from the basket. Assuming the wretched mien of a condemned martyr, she wet the soap and rubbed it into the remaining dung. As she did so, she dolefully added the terrier accident to the list of trials she'd suffered since coming to Hawksbury. And, oh! What a list it was, recording the most unimaginable sorts of atrocities.

Take her sleeping arrangements, for example. Had she even suspected that she'd have to share a bed, and a lumpy one at that, she'd have dismissed this maid business the instant it entered her mind . . . especially if she'd known that her bedmate would be a laundry maid named Pansy.

Talk about a trial! The creature was a most tiresome chatterbox. From the moment their heads hit their pillows, it was prattle, rattle, natter all night long, and always on the subject of some farm laborer the chit loved. How she could think her interested in a romance between nobodies, she didn't know. All she knew was that she hadn't had more than four hours of sleep on any given night since coming to Hawksbury.

Shaking her head, Sophie picked up her brush and dipped it into the bucket of water. Of course, in all fairness, she couldn't lay the entire blame for her sleep-

lessness at Pansy's door. Were she allowed to sleep until
a decent hour, say, eleven or twelve, Miss Tittle-Tattle's
gab would be more an annoyance than a trial. Unfortunately, such was not the case, which was a trial unto
itself.

As she scrubbed the soaped area, diligently working
it into a froth, she miserably contemplated the hour at
which she must rise. Five o'clock. She must rise at five.
Why, it was inhumane, that's what it was; inhumane to
require a person to wake so ungodly early. Well, it was
inhumane if the person in question was of quality. It was
quite all right to expect those of the lower classes to rise
before dawn. Such hardship was their lot in life, which
they must accept without question or complaint.

She, on the other hand, was born to live a privileged
life, thus giving her the right to protest every discomfort.
And protest she would, the moment her uncle rescued
her.

Sophie smiled at the thought of that happy day. How
gratifying it would be to finally voice her grievances,
what a relief to vent her outrage at having suffered them.
Most pleasurable of all would be shedding her servants
rags.

Pausing from her scrubbing, she glanced down at her
work clothes, shuddering at the sight of them. Because
she, as maid-of-all-work, had little or no contact with
the family, her attire was selected more for thrift than
appearance. Therefore, instead of getting one of the
crisp, blue-sprigged muslin gowns the house and chambermaids wore, she was issued a limp, linsey-woolsey
skirt and an old-fashioned jacket bodice made of what
felt like burlap.

And, oh! That bodice was awful. Not only was it inex-
pertly dyed a blotchy mustard yellow, it had a waist, a
real one that defined her figure in a most démodé manner. Paired with the faded brown-and-green-print skirt,
she looked as if she'd tumbled from a thirty-year-old rag
barrel. And don't even get her started on her cap!

Groaning aloud at the frightfulness of her attire, Sophie resumed scrubbing. As wonderful as it would be to
voice, vent, and shed, the best part of her uncle's return

would be her release from slavery. Between the scrubbing, dusting, polishing, fetching, and whatever other odious chore anyone thought to fling her way, the business of being a maid was drudgery of the worst kind. One had only to look at her hands to see that it was so.

Giving the carpet a final scrub, she tossed her brush into the bucket and picked up her rag. As she blotted the moisture from the now clean, but wet carpet, she grimly eyed her rough red hands. With luck and at least a month of nights spent sleeping in cosmetic gloves, she might be able to restore them to their former glory.

Maybe. She dropped the rag into her basket and extracted a dry brush. Her strokes long and even, she swept the carpet, carefully smoothing its ruffled nap. That finishing touch done, she straightened up and examined her work.

Unlike the dining room carpet she'd attempted to clean on Thursday, this time she hadn't made the dye bleed. Or the wool pill. Or the edges ravel. Why, if her eyes didn't deceive her, she'd even managed to remove the entire stain.

Leaning down, she sniffed the freshly cleaned area. ammonia and clove . . . Ox Gall soap. M-m-m. Not so much as a lingering trace of dog odor. Perfect.

Curiously pleased by her accomplishment, she straightened back up and repacked her basket. With the basket and bucket in one hand, and the paper full of droppings gingerly clasped between two fingers of the other, she rose. As she did so, she heard the tread of heavy footsteps ascending the nearby family staircase.

Oh, botheration! It had to be Lord Beresford coming to bid his ailing wife good night. Mrs. Pixton had warned her that he might do so, admonishing her to be quick about her task so as not to offend him with the sight of her person.

Fearful of receiving yet another scolding, she backed toward the unlit far wall. As she slipped into the shadows, a dark form came into view.

From her brief glimpses of his lordship, Sophie knew him to be tall and strongly built. But this man! Why, he was huge. A regular giant, rather like—

Lyndhurst. Her heart missed a beat. Dear heavens. Could it indeed be the Earl of Beastliness?

No. Of course not. Whatever would he be doing here? She must be daft from sleeplessness to even conceive such a notion. Nonetheless, she kept a wary eye on the figure as she stepped deeper into the shadows.

H-m-m. How very odd. He wore his greatcoat and hat. However had he gotten past Dickson without relinquishing them? From the bits and scraps she'd overheard in the kitchen, he took the utmost pride in the immediacy with which he appropriated visitors' outdoor garments. It was thinking of the majordomo that prompted her to make another, more disturbing, observation: The man was unescorted.

A niggling sense of disquiet pricked her mind. Whatever was he doing stalking about the family wing at this hour of the night? Even if Dickson was for some reason away from his post, the gentleman should know better than to run tame in someone else's house . . .

Unless he was no gentleman. Her disquiet exploded into a full-blown case of alarm. Oh, heavens! What if he was the maniacal, murderous fiend Lydia's brother had mentioned? The one who broke into country houses and butchered everyone in their beds?

A scream welled up in her throat. It was him. It had to be. Who else would be lurking about the halls at this hour of the night, and in his coat to boot?

As Sophie stood poised to scream, the man bowed his head and removed his tall hat. Candlelight, soft and flickering, washed over his hair. Her scream escaped as a squeak. His hair was a deep, rich lustrous brown burnished with gleaming copper highlights—

Like Lyndhurst's.

Tucking his hat beneath his arm, he reached up and adjusted his neck cloth, lifting his face as he did so—

His scarred face.

Thump! Bang! Slosh! The bucket and basket slipped from her hand, loudly spattering their contents across the parquet floor.

Lyndhurst's head snapped in her direction.

In the next instant the marchioness's chamber door

burst open and out stalked the marquess. "What in Hades is that noise?" he bellowed. "Don't you cabbage-heads know that your mistress—" He stopped abruptly at the sight of Lyndhurst.

Lyndhurst nodded. "Father."

"Colin! My dearest boy!" Crowing his delight, the marquess dashed the short distance to Lyndhurst and swept him into a vigorous embrace. "Ah, Colin. Can't tell you how glad I am to see you. Your mother's been in a stew wondering when you'd arrive."

Colin? Sophie frowned as the marquess gave Lyndhurst another hug. But his name was Nicholas, not—

She almost groaned aloud. But of course. Colin was a nickname for Nicholas. Lyndhurst must be the "young Colin" to whom Mrs. Pixton had referred. Expecting "young Colin" to break from his father and brand her as the felon she was, Sophie shrank against the shadowy wall.

To her bewilderment his first utterance wasn't one of denouncement, but a polite inquiry. "How is Mother this evening?"

Mystified, she hazarded a glance at his face. He gazed at his father, ignoring her as if she were any other servant. Could it be that he hadn't recognized her after all? As she pondered that heartening notion, the marquess chuckled and released him.

Draping his arm around his son's shoulders, he led him toward the marchioness's room, replying, "If you ask her, she shall no doubt profess to be dying." He chuckled again. "I, however, doubt her claim. She was in the best of health until you wrote her of the unfortunate Barrington affair. Two hours after reading your letter she lay upon her bed, moaning some nonsense about dying without holding your children. You know how she desires grandchildren."

Lyndhurst groaned. "After years of suffering her matchmaking and being needled about 'doing my family duty,' how could I not know? She's relentless in her efforts to get me buckled."

"Well, I doubt she shall let up until she's successful," the marquess replied, coming to a stop before his wife's door. "Indeed, I suspect that the Barrington business has driven her to hatch a desperate new matchmaking scheme."

"What!" Lyndhurst more spat than uttered the word.

His father nodded. "Afraid so. How else can you explain the way she fell ill like she did?"

"And why else would she summon me, and only me, to her bedside," Lyndhurst moaned. "If she were truly dying, she'd want Quent by her side as well. How could I have been such a cods-head? I should have thought of that and guessed her illness to be the bait in another of her matrimonial traps."

The marquess patted his arm. "Well, she's caught you, and there's nothing to do for it now but find out what, or more precisely, for whom she's trapped you." Grasping the doorknob, he inquired, "Shall we?" At Lyndhurst's nod he opened the door and disappeared inside.

Lyndhurst, however, remained poised outside. After a beat he slowly turned his head.

Sophie gasped and shrank into the shadows, praying that he hadn't and wouldn't recognize her. The instant she saw his face, she knew that her prayers had again gone unanswered.

He looked wrathful, bitterly so.

She shrank back a fraction more, shaking her head over and over again, mutely begging for the mercy she knew he wouldn't grant.

He tipped his head to the side, as if considering her plea, then smiled. Nodding once he stalked into his mother's room, closing the door behind him.

Sophie shivered, chilled by the ominous message behind his response.

His smile was a threat, his nod a promise.

Bloody hell! What was she doing here?

Finger by clenching finger, Nicholas pried his hand from the doorknob, his composure shattered by his encounter with Sophie. He'd thought to find peace at Hawksbury, to escape the prying eyes of the ton and lick his wounds in private. Instead he'd found *her,* the false-hearted chit who had crushed his confidence and instilled a crippling sense of inadequacy; the same shallow baggage responsible for reawakening his self-consciousness about his scar.

Hating his new vulnerability and her even more for provoking it, he dropped his hand to his side, balling it into a fist in his tension. Well, he'd be damned if he'd allow her to continue hiding there, which was undoubtedly what she did, hide from her creditors. No. He intended to corner her the instant he finished speaking with his mother, and find out exactly how she'd wormed her way into service there. Then he'd . . . he'd . . . well, then he'd decide upon a fitting manner in which to deal with her.

A bitter smile curled his lips at that thought of dealing with her. The most fitting manner of doing so would be to make her pay for her treachery, something that would be ridiculously easy given her current situation. Indeed, by styling herself as a maid and taking refuge in service there, she'd unwittingly given him the upper hand.

His smile broadened into an exceedingly wicked grin as he considered the possibilities of that hand. Oh, but this was rich! By the mere act of accepting a position at Hawksbury, she had agreed to subjugate herself to the Somerville family—the *entire* family. That meant that as the Somerville son and heir, he had every right to command her as he pleased. And as their servant, she had no choice but to obey. Not if she wished to preserve her position . . .

And his silence. Or so he'd allow her to believe. He almost laughed aloud in his sardonic glee. Had the goosecap deigned to listen to his views on debtors and their imprisonment, she'd know that he'd never turn her over to her creditors, not even if she defied him at every turn. Since, however, she'd ignored—

"Colin? Is something amiss with the door?"

Nicholas started, his father's voice jerking him from his vengeful trance. "What? No. Sorry." Blinking twice to fully regain his sense of time and place, he turned, staring at his surroundings as if seeing them for the first time.

Salmon, sienna, and blue-patterned wallpaper graced

the walls, hues that were echoed in the thick Axminster carpet at his feet. To his right arched a richly sculpted fireplace next to two tapestry chairs and a tambour, upon which was stretched a needlework masterpiece in progress. Against the far wall, set beneath a jewellike expanse of mullion windows, was his mother's dainty tulipwood desk, cluttered, as usual, with favored books and lovingly preserved letters.

He blinked again, then smiled. Everything was exactly as it had been since his earliest childhood memories . . .

Everything except Mother, he amended, his heart missing a beat as he focused on the bed to his left. So alarmingly pale was her normally rosy face, that he instantly wondered at his father's wits for questioning the legitimacy of her illness.

As he stood gaping, too appalled to do anything else, she smiled weakly and rasped, "Colin, my dearest son. Do come give your mother a kiss. I have—" She broke off abruptly, her eyes bulging as if in surprise. In the next instant they rolled back in her head, and she succumbed to a frightening fit of chokes and twitches.

Galvanized by fear, Nicholas forcibly uprooted his shock-planted feet and hurried across the room.

"Colin." She sighed, then fell deathly still.

His eyes blurred with tears, he clasped her limp head to his breaking heart, sobbing, "Mother . . . please . . . I love you . . ."

She stirred faintly against his breast. "What a good boy you are to come and be with me in my final days."

"No. No!" He gave her a fierce hug. "I shall suffer no such talk from you. Do you hear? Not a word! You shall be in prime twig in no time at all. Indeed, I shan't be a whit surprised if you're up and ordering us all about by the end of the week." Praying without hope that his words would prove true, he laid her back upon her pillows and kissed her cheeks.

She made a mewling noise and closed her eyes, visibly wearied by the slight exertion. "Promise me something, son."

"Anything," he solemnly vowed.

"Promise me that you shan't grieve when I'm gone. Promise—"

"Mother—"

"No. Let me finish while I am able. I want you to promise to remember me with joy, and know that I leave this world with no regret"—a feeble cough—"save one."

"Which is?"

As she lay limply against her pillows, her mouth waged in trembling battle to reply, he heard his father clear his throat. Reminded anew of his sire's untenable dismissal of his mother's condition, Nicholas more glared than looked to where he lounged in a chair at the opposite side of the bed.

His father widened his eyes and patted his breast.

Nicholas frowned and shook his head, almost certain now that his parent ran dotty.

Returning his frown with one of his own, the marquess thumped his breast again, this time more insistently, then patted his own cheek, finishing his addled charade by discreetly pointing to Nicholas's chest.

Utterly dumbfounded by his queer play of motions, Nicholas glanced down to where his father pointed. Streaking his dark blue greatcoat was a chalky substance. When he glanced back up in question, his father indicated his mother, who now gasped in addition to her lip quivering, then tapped his own cheek again. Rolling his eyes in an expression of repressed hilarity, he mouthed, "Powder."

Powder? Nicholas returned his gaze to his now quivering, gasping, and *twitching* mother, his eyes narrowing with sudden suspicion. Though the bed curtains shielded her face from the nearby candlelight, he could still discern enough of her complexion to note its texture.

It looked grainy . . . and blotchy, a description at odds with the frequently uttered one of "porcelain perfect and fine." And come to think of it, wasn't it just a shade too white? If he remembered correctly from when Quentin had almost died from pneumonia, a gravely ill person's skin ran more akin to ash than snow.

His eyes little more than slits now, Nicholas edged a fraction nearer. Aha! His father was correct, she did wear powder. A barrel of it. Indeed, so thickly applied was the cosmetic that she looked as if someone had rolled biscuits on her face.

Though he knew he should feel relief at the discovery, he didn't. As much as it shamed him to admit it, it merely deepened his alarm. That she would feign a fatal illness to sway him to her purpose could only mean that she planned something to which she knew he'd be vehemently opposed.

Slanting his father a long suffering look, he tensely awaited her to finish her scene and spill the bag. She did so a scant second later.

Her voice barely intelligible for all her forced trembling, she whispered, "My only regret is that I most probably shan't live long enough to see you wed and hold your babes." She uttered the word babes on a long, shuddering moan, one reminiscent of the ghost in the production of *Hamlet* he'd seen three weeks earlier . . . only her moan was much more convincing. It seemed that his mother had missed her true calling in life.

Stifling his urge to laugh, he pointed out, "That is two regrets, not one."

She sighed. "Were you wed, I could die safe in the knowledge that I would someday look down from heaven and see you surrounded by your children . . . my grandchildren." Her voice grew gradually weaker and weaker until the last line was barely audible.

"Well, then, I guess you shall just have to hold on to your last breath a bit longer," he countered unsympathetically.

"If but I could! If but I could!" She moaned again, this time with a resonance that would have carried from the stage to the uppermost galleries of Covent Garden.

He made an exasperated noise. "I would wed tomorrow if I met the right woman today. You know I would. But I shan't do so until I find a suitable bride."

"And what qualities"—a choking gurgle—"make for a suitable bride?"

He didn't have to consider her question to reply. "The woman I marry must be good, kind, loyal, and sensible. Find me a wife like that, and you shall have a grandchild

within a year." Nicholas could have cut out his tongue
the instant he uttered that last line. Oh, bloody—
bloody!—hell. He'd just challenged his mother to find
him a bride.

By the glint in her eye as she stole a peek at him, he
saw that she was fully prepared to meet that challenge.

He groaned inwardly. He was in for it now.

Shutting her eye again, she responded in a reedy
voice, "If that is the sort of wife you seek, then you've
been searching in the wrong place."

"Indeed?" This was from his father, who looked enor-
mously entertained by the whole performance.

She made a great show of nodding, her motion more
a spasm than bob. "The only sort of gels one finds in
Town during the Season are stupid, selfish, greedy little
creatures like that Barrington chit. Lovely, yes. But not
worth a farthing to a man."

His father chuckled. "I seem to recall having met you
in London during the Season, Fanny, my love, and you
haven't a stupid, selfish, or greedy bone in your entire
body."

She lifted her head to shoot him a look that was anything but feeble. "That was thirty years ago, and the
times were entirely different. Gels back then were raised
to be helpmates to their husbands, not—" She broke off
abruptly, her eyes widening as if suddenly remembering
herself. *Thud!* Her head dropped back to the pillows.
Instantly reverting to character, she finished with a
groan, "Witless ornaments."

An amused look passed between Nicholas and his father. "Be that as it may, Mother, I'm no more likely to
meet the right woman here at Hawksbury than in London. Therefore, it appears that I shall be forced to remain unwed until you either die or recover."

"Maybe not. One never knows who might turn up on
their stoop," she rasped.

Nicholas gazed uneasily at his mother, who looked
rather pleased with herself. Loath to ask but compelled
to do so, he gritted out, "Pray do tell what you mean
by that cryptic remark."

She choked a couple of times in response, then heaved

several labored breaths. In a voice as thin as watered gruel, she finally replied, "Please don't hate me, Colin, but I simply shan't be able to rest in peace knowing that you are unwed. Therefore I—"

She broke off in an impressive paroxysm of coughing. After tossing in a few gasps and gargles for enhanced effect, she finished, "I have invited three suitable young ladies to visit separately over the next three weeks. It is my"—*cough! sputter!*—"d-dying wish that you take one of them for your bride."

Nicholas watched his mother's masterful encore of pants and twitches, more filled with horror than if she were indeed suffering death throes.

"You wouldn't . . . wouldn't deny me my . . . dying wish, would you?" she appealed between seizures.

His horror exploded into outrage as she collapsed into a perfect portrait of imminent demise. Like hell he wouldn't deny her! How dare she try to manipulate him like this. He was a grown man, and as such would decide for himself when and whom he would marry. It was high time she realized that and ceased her meddling.

He was about to tell her exactly that and announce his intention to flee to Scotland, when she added, "I promise you that all the gels are fine, well-bred creatures. Unlike that wicked Barrington chit, any one of them shall be honored to be your wife."

Sophie. Nicholas's words froze in his throat. So engrossed in his mother's performance was he, that he'd forgotten all about her. If he fled now, he would lose what most probably was his only chance for vengeance. Yet, if he stayed . . .

He grimaced. Heaven only knew what sort of females his mother sought to fob off on him this time. It was entirely possible that one or all of them were cut from the same shallow cloth as Miss Barrington, and would thus be repulsed by his disfigured cheek. Was revenge worth the risk of suffering more blows to his self-esteem? Then, there was the matter of the scandal—

As if sensing his thoughts, his mother launched into a mock convulsion, then more gasped than said, "You needn't fret on account of the Barrington affair. Since none of the gels were in Town for the Season, all are unaware of your embarrassment. Indeed, all three have yet to come out, which means that they are untarnished by tonnish excess."

Not out yet? A sudden warning shrieked through Nicholas's mind. Not out usually meant that a miss was either overly young or too dreadful to merit the expense of a Season, both exceedingly ghastly prospects. He shuddered. Almost ghastly enough to tempt him to forget his lust for vengeance and seek sanctuary in Scotland.

Struggling to decide, he muttered, "Please do tell me more about these rustic paragons."

The triumph on his mother's face was unmistakable, though she did remember herself enough to hack out a few feeble coughs before replying. "One of the gels is Lady Julianna Howland, the daughter of the late Marquess of Chadwick. She's . . . oh, let me think. Twenty? Yes. Twenty. And most sensible. Indeed, it was she, herself, who decided against a Season, judging London to be a frightfully unhealthy place. Unlike those greedy, pampered creatures at the Marriage Mart, you shall find Lady Julianna perfectly disposed to spending the bulk of the year helping you tend to your estates."

Chadwick? H-m-m. Hadn't there been some recent scandal involving a Chadwick? Nicholas considered for a moment. Ah, but of course. Lord Chadwick was that quiz who'd died in a drunken brawl over a bit of muslin last year. Poor Lady Julianna. She'd probably foregone her Season not from health concerns, but from shame, an emotion with which he was intimately acquainted.

A slight frown worried his brow. Understanding her humiliation as he did, how could he possibly refuse to meet her? If he did so, she might attribute his refusal to her family's disgrace, and thus feel all the more stigmatized. Besides, simply meeting her didn't obligate him to wed her. It required only that he be kind and courtly, and in this instance, demonstrate to her that her sire's foolishness in no way reflected upon her person.

Thus, he nodded and murmured, "She sounds delightful."

"She does?" His father couldn't have sounded more shocked had he consented to wed the girl sight unseen.

"She is delightful," his mother assured him, pointedly ignoring her husband's outburst. "As is Miss Minerva Mayhew, daughter of Viscount Brumbly. You might recall the viscount from the times you accompanied your father fishing in Scotland? His manor neighbors ours."

"Of course he does," his father interjected. "How could one forget salmon-mad Brumbly and his endless fishing inventions?"

How indeed? Nicholas thought, nodding. With his drifting left eye and maniacal zest for anything with fins and a tail, he was a most memorable character.

"Yes, well, of course," his mother more wheezed than said. "As for his daughter, I had the pleasure of meeting her several years back at a fishing party in Cumberland. She was but eleven at the time, but showed much promise."

"And you say that she has yet to come out?" Nicholas prompted, not willing to credit the girl by virtue of promise alone.

"With her mother dead and Brumbly's preoccupation with fishing, the matter has most probably been overlooked." This was from his father.

Nicholas glanced at the other man, who grinned as if he found something exceedingly funny. Worried that that something was Miss Mayhew, he inquired, "And have you met the viscount's daughter as well, Father?"

"No. No. Can't say as I've had the pleasure, though I know plenty about her from Brumbly's rattling. Never misses a chance to boast of her skill with a rod and lure."

A miss who shared his pleasure of fishing? That virtue alone merited her worth a look. He nodded. "She sounds promising."

His mother, who lay gagging like a cat with a hair ball, abruptly ceased her theatrics and smiled. "That brings us to the third and, I might add, best bridal prospect: Lady Helene Stancliffe, daughter of the Duke of Windford. I've been friends with her mother, Suzanne, since girlhood, and have followed Helene's progress through her letters. She is reported to be a most lovely and accomplished creature. The dear child was to have made her bow this Season, but her brother, Reginald, died unexpectedly, and the family is only now out of mourning."

A duke's daughter? Lovely and accomplished? Nicholas fingered his damaged cheek, cringing inwardly. She sounded just the sort of miss to be offended by his scar. The others, well—

"What have you to say, Colin? Am I to rest in peace or not?" his mother prodded in a faltering voice.

Nicholas sighed and dropped his hand from his face to his lap. Though he longed for revenge, would vindication be balm enough to soothe the wounds from its exaction? More importantly, would the pain from those wounds be any worse than that he'd suffer in having to acknowledge himself a coward? And indeed he would be a coward if he fled to Scotland to escape his fear.

Miss Barrington would have made him one.

His hands tightened into angry fists at that thought. No! Damn it, never! She may have crushed his pride, but he would never allow her to unman him. He was Nicholas Somerville, Earl of Lyndhurst and heir to the Marquess of Beresford. He would never allow himself to be bested by a mere cloth merchant's daughter. Never! He would remain at Hawksbury and teach her what it meant to reap what one had sown. And she would find it a very bitter harvest indeed.

A slow smile twisted his lips as he imagined her reaction when she tasted her crop. "I shall meet the misses," he announced.

"Thank you, dear." His mother closed her eyes as if lapsing into a coma. "Because of you, I shall find peace."

If all went as planned, so would he.

Chapter 9

Churr! Churr!—flap!—whoo-s-sh!

Sophie jumped, a scream startling from her lips as a dark shape glided from the trees lining the moonlit lane. Down it swooped, its long black wings flapping wildly as it twisted, then turned and shot straight for her head.

A bat! With a shriek she dropped into a crouch, almost toppling over into a faint as she remembered the tale Lydia's brothers told her about the creatures; one involving a bat becoming entangled in a woman's hair and sucking all the blood from her brain. To die such a gory, gruesome death—

Shuddering, she grasped her mobcap and slumped yet lower, certain that the murderous fiend hovered overhead, poised to attack her scalp. Bracing herself for the worst, she waited . . .

Dreading and . . .

Nothing happened. Blessed stillness reigned above.

She hazarded a glance at the sky. As she did so, another eerie cry rent the air, this one sounding from a distance. An instant later the fiend fluttered across the full moon, its form silhouetted against the pale lunar orb.

It had a birdlike tail. Yes, distinctly birdlike. And that pointy thing was most definitely a beak. As for the contours of its wings, well, didn't they look more hawk than batlike?

Sophie frowned as she sought to recall the drawings she'd seen of bats. When she did, she sighed. Yes. Whatever it was, it most certainly was not a bat. Not with a wingspan like that. Thus assured of her brain's safety, she picked up the valise she'd dropped in her panic and resumed her trudge down the country lane.

Exactly how long or how far she'd traveled, she couldn't say. All she knew for certain was that she had to reach the road to Exeter by dawn. Dawn was when the farmers traveled to town for market, at least that was what she'd heard Cook tell a kitchen maid, and she hoped to wheedle one of them into giving her a ride.

And when she reached Exeter, then want?

She sighed. She didn't know. In truth, she hadn't considered what she'd do or where she'd go from there. All that concerned her now was getting as far away as possible from Hawksbury . . .

And Lyndhurst. Sophie kicked at a tuft of moon-silvered gorse, imagining it to be his lordship's head. Despicable beast! No doubt he'd alerted his parents as to her identity and now searched the house for her with vengeful intent. She couldn't help smiling at the thought of him lumbering through room after room, bellowing like a speared boar each time he failed to find her.

And when he finally ascertained that she'd fled?

She sniffed and shifted her heavy bag from her numb right hand to her left one. Arrogant tyrant that he was, he'd probably drag the other servants from their beds and bully them for information as to her whereabouts. Not that it would do him a whit of good. No one had seen her leave, not even Pansy.

For the tenth time that hour, Sophie thanked God that her bedmate had been off with her suitor when she'd packed her bag and stolen away. Not only had the girl's absence freed her from explanation, it had saved her heaven only knew how much time.

And time was of an essence. So much so, that she'd let her sense of self-preservation overrule her vanity, and had fled the house garbed in her soiled work clothes. Had she paused to make herself presentable, she'd most probably be locked in the cellar now, waiting for Lyndhurst to drag her to London and justice.

Sophie grimaced as she glanced down at her stained and rumpled skirt. Ah, well. So what if she looked like a slattern? At least she was free. If all went as she hoped, she would stay that way. She had only to find a ride to Exeter before his tyrannical lordship finished browbeating the servants. Then—

Thudity-thud! Thudity-thud! She froze, instantly recognizing the low rolling rumble.

Hoofbeat . . . distant hoofbeat on packed soil . . .

Thudity-thud! Thudity-thud! It trembled through the soles of her thin walking shoes, the vibrations growing stronger . . .

And stronger . . . and—

Lyndhurst! She gasped and dropped her valise. What if it was Lyndhurst, hunting her like a blood-frenzied hound? Oh! Oh! She had to hide! Hide, yes. But where?

Wildly she looked around her, her gaze bouncing over the low stone walls and through the starlit mists enveloping the rural realm beyond. To her left lay a wheat field, the tall, moon-blanched grain swaying gently from . . . what? Not so much as a whisper of wind stirred the air. Not even daring to imagine what lurked between those stalks, she shifted her gaze to her right.

Blast! Just her wretched luck. It was a pasture; a particularly flat and open one, enclosed on one side by a hedgerow. She moaned her despair. Doomed. She was doomed to spend the rest of her life rotting away in prison, forsaken and forgotten. Unless—

Her eyes narrowed as she studied the breaks in the hedgerow. Perhaps if she crawled into the thicket and stayed perfectly still, Lyndhurst would ride on by. Then she would be safe . . .

Well, at least safe from Lyndhurst. Sophie shuddered at the thought of what might live in that thicket: hedgerow bogles, deadly little monstrosities with a poisonous bite and a hunger for human flesh. Lydia's brother had told her all about them.

She swallowed hard, though her mouth was as dry as week-old cake, and glanced over the wall. The shadows back there looked deep. Perhaps if she crouched—

A circle of light appeared in the distance, one that grew larger and brighter with every passing second.

Double blast! The despicable man carried a lantern. So much for hiding in the shadows. As tall as Lyndhurst sat in the saddle, the light would spill over the wall and onto her. He'd see her at first glance.

That left her with only one place to hide: the hedge-row. And a choice between two evils: bogles or Lynd-hurst. It took but a second for her to decide.

Over the wall she tumbled, landing in the tall, damp grass on her hands and knees. Pressing as close to the ground as she could, she more slithered than crawled toward the hedgerow. She was almost there when . . . yes, it was Lyndhurst . . . thundered down the road. Praying he'd pass without a glance, she dropped to her belly and lay still.

Ride on. Please ride on without looking this way, she willed, helplessly watching the lamplight pour over the wall and flow nearer. *Please . . . please . . . please.* She screwed her eyes shut, absurdly hoping that by blanking him from her sight she would somehow render herself invisible.

"Oh-ho!" *Jingle!*— A soft nicker, and the hoofbeats ceased.

Dear heavens! Had he seen her? Convulsively, she dug her fingers into the earth, her heart landing in the pit of her stomach with a sickening jolt. Of course he had. Why else would he stop? Any minute now he would jerk her up and carry her off to prison.

And there wasn't a bloody thing she could do to stop him.

For what felt like a millennium she remained frozen, waiting for her world to come to an end. Waiting . . .

And waiting . . .

And waiting. When she could stand the suspense no longer, she opened one eye and lifted her head to see what was happening.

To her bewilderment, he simply sat atop his mammoth stallion, peering at something in the road. As she watched, he leaned over and lowered the lantern to ex-amine that something closer.

Whatever could be find so interesting? she wondered, unnerved by his intense scrutiny. Footprints, perhaps?

In a swirl of shoulder capes, he was off his horse. So

agile, so very fluid was his dismount that it was nothing short of poetic.

Sophie's other eye popped open in her surprise. Had he always moved with such eloquence? Her brow creased as she tried to recall. Come to think of it, she'd never bothered to note the manner in which he moved. Indeed, why would she? His very size marked him as clumsy, and thus not worth observing.

But I was wrong, she grudgingly admitted, watching as he soothed his restless steed. He moves quite well for a giant.

In truth, he moved better than well. His sleek, supple athleticism was as beautiful as it was unexpected. Not, of course, that you'd ever hear her say so. She'd die before she uttered a single word of praise about—

Abruptly he dropped down and disappeared behind the stone wall. Her frown deepened, as did her bewilderment. Whatever was he doing now? Sniffing her scent like a bloodhound?

Rather than ponder the question, Sophie took advantage of his distraction and scurried toward the hedge. She had just reached her destination and was about to crawl into the hole, when she heard a heavy scraping sound behind her. Gasping her alarm, she jerked her head around.

Lyndhurst stood in the center of the road, stuffing a wad of cloth into a lumpy piece of luggage.

Sophie sagged with relief. He'd just been picking up her valise. He—

Her valise! Good heavens. She'd forgotten all about it. Her alarm returned in a heart-faltering rush as she gaped at the bag in his hands. By the way it hung open, with bits of lace and ribbon tumbling out, it was clear that he'd rifled through the contents. No doubt he'd recognized the initials engraved on her silver hairbrush and now knew that she was near.

As if to confirm her frightening deduction, Lyndhurst called her name. He sounded furious. Praying for a chance, any at all to slip into the hedge unnoticed, Sophie rolled into a tight ball, making herself as small as possible.

Again he called her name, then again. Lifting the lantern to widen the circle of light, he stalked toward the wall . . . the one she was behind, naturally. Without breaking his stride, he dropped her valise at the edge of the road, then lifted one long leg and easily vaulted the low barrier.

Nearer and nearer he moved, the warm flood of light broadening with every step he took. When he was but a few yards from where she huddled, he stopped and demanded, "I shall give you to the count of three to cease this foolish game and reveal yourself, Miss Barrington. If you fail to comply, I shall be forced to—"

Rustle! Rustle! The sound came from behind him. He whirled around, sweeping the lantern in a broad arch.

Aha! Her prayed-for chance. Feetfirst. Yes. She'd go into the hedge feetfirst so she could kick the bogles should they attack. Careful, so as not to stir the branches, she eased her legs in.

Nothing attacked. She sighed her relief. It appeared that she'd chosen a bogle-free bush. That fear thus allayed, she slipped in farther. Now she had only to brace her hands just so to propel herself the rest of the way in. Casting an anxious look to where Lyndhurst stood scowling at a hare, the perpetrator of the rustling, she slipped her left hand beneath the small of her back. Lifting her right one, she moved it over . . .

And over . . .

And down . . .

Onto something distinctly alive. Before she could think, much less react, what felt like a hundred tiny teeth sank into her hand.

A bogle! She screamed with all her might, her cries echoed by squeal after unearthly squeal as the beast bit her again and again.

Crash! Lyndhurst dropped the lantern.

"Sophie?" He was on her in a flash, dragging her from the hedge and hauling her to her feet. When she instantly collapsed again, too overwrought to stand, he grasped her arms in a bruising grip and gave her a firm shake. "Good God, woman! Will you cease that infernal yowling and tell me what happened?"

"A bogle!" she wailed. "I was bitten by a bogle!"

There was a pause, as if he were stunned by her dreadful revelation, then he sputtered, "A . . . bogle?"

"Yes. Yes!" She nodded wildly, her frantic gaze searching the shadows at their feet for the deadly creature. "One of the poisonous, flesh-eating kind that lives in hedgerows. And it bit me. O-o-h! I'm doomed—doomed for certain." That last line was uttered on an escalating moan.

As she stood paralyzed by terror, certain that she was only seconds away from death, Lyndhurst expelled a volcanic gasp, followed by a smothered wheeze. Dropping his hands from her arms to clutch at his chest, he burst out—

Laughing?

Her jaw dropped in shock. Why—why—

"A p-poisonous, flesh-eating, hedgerow b-bogle," he howled with hilarity, clenching his ribs as if they ached.

Her shock exploded into outrage. "I don't see anything the least bit amusing about this!" she hissed, glaring up at him.

"A bogle bit you, you say?" He erupted into another explosive series of guffaws. Though the shadows from the hedgerow shrouded his features, his teeth flashed white in the moonlight.

"Yes," she snapped, ignoring the fact that those teeth were perfect. "Are you as deaf as you are boorish? Or just witless?"

"Neither," he gasped between chuckles. "Just amused that a chit your age still believes in fairy tales. Hasn't anyone told you that there are no such things as bogles . . . or pixies . . . or trolls?"

"Oh?" She braced her hands on her hips, eyeing him with violent dislike. "And if there are no such things as bogles, then what, pray tell, attacked me? I can assure you most heartily that it wasn't a badger or a hare."

Another flash of annoyingly straight teeth. "Why don't we look and find out?" Still laughing, Lyndhurst strode over and retrieved the extinguished lantern. After relighting it, he returned to the site of the alleged bogle attack.

"Shall we?" He indicated the hedge with a sweep of his hand. Without awaiting her reply, he began sifting through the shrubbery, pausing now and again to shine the light through its branches.

Still unconvinced as to the mythical nature of bogles, Sophie hung back, watching from what she prayed was a safe distance.

After several moments during which he searched the thicket from top to bottom, he dropped to his knees, crowing, "Aha!" Setting the lantern on the ground next to him, he examined something—what, she couldn't see—then softly commanded, "Come and take a look at your bogle, Miss Barrington."

"What is it?" she asked, reluctant to move nearer. What if it truly was a bogle? Or something just as bad, like a snake or a bat?

He made an impatient noise. "I already told you, your bogle."

"But you said—"

"I said that you are to come here," he interjected brusquely. "Need I remind you that you are a servant to the Somerville family, and thus subject to my commands? If you wish to keep your position, I suggest that you obey me posthaste."

Keep her position? Sophie's jaw dropped as she gaped at him, utterly taken aback. Her belief in bogles aside, did he think her a complete ninny? Keep her position indeed! No doubt his words were a ruse to lure her back to the manor so he could lock her up and send her back to London in chains.

"Sophie?" His irritation was unmistakable.

Squaring her shoulders and lifting her chin, she retorted, "No, I shan't obey you. Why should I? I know perfectly well that you despise me, and that you have no intention of letting me remain at Hawksbury. Contrary to your belief, I'm not an utter goose."

Slowly he rose to his feet, straightening to the uppermost inch of his lofty, and admittedly alarming, height. "Indeed?"

"Indeed," she countered with a sniff. "And I understand with absolute clarity why you hunted me down."

"Oh? Well, then, pray do tell."

"For revenge, of course. You despise me and wish revenge for the way I disgraced you in front of the *ton*. You intend to soothe your pride and even the score by hauling me off to prison."

He acknowledged her response with a curt nod. "You are correct on two counts, Miss Barrington: I do despise you. And yes, I most definitely desire revenge. You are, however, incorrect as to the mode in which I wish to exact it."

She frowned, taken aback by that last. "Are you saying that you shan't drag me back to Town and turn me over to my creditors?"

"That, my dear, is entirely up to you," he replied, stalking toward her.

There was something ominous about the low, purring timbre of his voice, something that sent icy chills up her spine. And when he stopped before her, his eyes glittering in the shadowed murk of his face, it was all she could do not to step away.

Firmly commanding her feet to stay put, she forced her gaze to meet his. "Oh? And exactly what do you mean when you say that it is up to me?" Was that really her voice, so thin and hoarse?

"I mean that you have a choice."

"A . . . choice?"

"Yes. A choice." He inched his face nearer to hers. "You can remain in service at Hawksbury, doing as I command for however long I say, after which time you shall be free to go where you wish. Or I can take you to King's Bench Prison in the morning." His face was so close now, she could see his grim expression . . . and his scar.

Unnerved by both, she ducked her head and shied back a step. "I-If you despise me, w-why do you want me at Hawksbury? I should th-think that you would wish me far from your s-sight," she stammered, hating her voice for faltering so.

There was a tense moment of silence, then he grasped her chin and jerked her face to his again. "Maybe I wish you near so I can torment you with the hideous spectacle of my face," he snarled.

Sophie gasped, shocked to be confronted with her own careless words. How vicious they sounded echoing from his lips, how very cruel she was to have voiced them in the first place.

He snorted and released her chin. "Ah, yes, my dear Miss Barrington. I know all about your horror of my face. How could I not? It's all the talk of the ton. That, and your complaint of my arrogance. Oh, and let us not forget the prime gossip regarding my soporific dullness and my grotesque size."

Sophie bowed her head again, this time from shame rather than to escape the sight of his scar. Not knowing what to say, but compelled to say something, she murmured, "Lyndhurst—"

He cut her off with another snort. "Please don't misunderstand me. I'm not asking you to deny your words, nor do I wish to hear that you've had a change of heart. Indeed, what is the opinion of an ill-bred little goosecap to me? Nothing!" He more spat than said the last word.

"Ill-bred?" Sophie tossed aside her guilt to embrace her affront. "I may be a goosecap at times, but I am most certainly not ill-bred. Lest you've forgotten, my mother was the daughter of an earl."

"And your father was a common cloth merchant," he sneered.

"There was nothing whatsoever common about my father," she shot back, her foot itching to kick him. "He was the noblest, handsomest, most genteel man in all of England. Everyone who knew him says so!"

He made a derisive noise. "If what you say is indeed true, then how did he come to spawn such a vulgar daughter? One can only assume that—"

Wham—th-whap! Her foot relieved its itch against his shin.

"O-w-w! What the—"

"How dare you!" she hissed. "How dare you utter such wretched lies. I am not vulgar, and you know it." When she made to kick him again, he grabbed her arms and hauled her body against his, trapping her flailing foot between his legs as he did so.

Pinning her struggling form firmly against his unyielding one, he gritted out, "Oh? And what would you call a chit who goes to a man's bachelor quarters and begs him to wed her?"

Sophie froze amid pounding his chest, stunned by her pain at his reminder of Julian and his betrayal. Slowly the fight seeped from her body. "I would call that poor chit a girl in love," she whispered, "one too innocent to know the false nature of men."

"And I would call her vulgar for acting upon her *love* in the manner of a whore desperate for a keeper," he flung back.

"Why . . . why . . ." Her fight returned with her anger. "Why, you low-minded cur! It wasn't like that at all. Lord Oxley led me to believe that he loved and wanted to marry me. I was simply following my heart when I went to him." She tipped her head back and fixed him with a look of utter contempt. "Not, of course, that I expect you to understand the purity of what I felt for him. I doubt you've ever felt anything for another person save disdain and a smug sense of superiority."

For a long moment his gleaming gaze bore into hers, then he ejected a scornful noise and looked away. "You haven't a damn clue as to what I or anyone else feels. You're far too vain and selfish to notice anything or anyone else, unless, of course, you see some personal benefit in doing so. Even then—"

"Why you—"

"Enough!" So forceful and decisive was his command, that she instantly obeyed. "I have no intention of standing here all night arguing with you, Miss Barrington. Just make your damn choice and be done with it."

Though Sophie had thought to choose Hawksbury, she was no longer convinced that it would be the better choice. Not after what had just passed between them. That he preferred his own brand of punishment to that which she'd receive in prison spoke volumes of the horrors he had planned for her should she remain. With growing alarm, she wondered if Hawksbury had a torture chamber.

"Well, Miss Barrington?" His grip tightened on her arms as if he expected her to bolt.

With visions of racks and iron maidens dancing in her mind, she croaked, "How can I make a decision when you have yet to tell me what I shall suffer should I remain? Whatever it is, it must be very terrible for you to consider it worse than imprisonment."

He tipped his head down to study her face, a slow and altogether disturbing smile curving his lips. "Ah, but you misunderstand me, Miss Barrington. The revenge I have in mind isn't worse than prison, just more satisfying."

Satisfying? Whatever could he mean by—

Oh, mercy! Her cheeks burned with outrage and embarrassment as she remembered the references to satisfaction Lydia's brother had peppered throughout his explanation of the ways between men and women. Did Lyndhurst wish to keep her as a servant so he could command her to share his bed?

Her visions of torture instruments were promptly supplanted by those of feathers, daisies, and custard. Even more disturbed by the latter, she blurted out, "I shan't share your bed!"

"Share my bed?" After a beat he released a snort of laughter and shoved her away. "My desire is to punish you, not myself, and I can think of no worse punishment for a man than having to bed an ice princess like you. Indeed, my sex would most probably be smite with frostbite should I enter you."

He shook his head, ignoring her squawk of indignation. "Never fear, Miss Barrington. Sharing my bed is the one thing I shall never demand of you. Despite your low opinion of me, there are plenty of women eager to do so. Witty, clever women, I might add, who shan't bore me between the sheets as you undoubtedly would."

"Why—" She stamped her foot. "O-o-o! I'll have you know that dozens of men have expressed desire for me and would be thrilled to have me in their bed." Why she felt compelled to set him straight about the highly indecent and mortifying matter, she didn't know. All she knew was that her pride commanded her to do so.

"Oh, I don't deny that it would be thrilling to see you lying in my bed, clothed in nothing but your glorious hair. For you are a most lovely creature. Beauty, however, isn't everything. Indeed, it is less than nothing when compared to attributes such as goodness, loyalty, and intelligence."

"I'll have you know that I—"

He silenced her with a wave of his hand. "Since your desirability has nothing to do with the matter in question, I see no reason to continue this discussion. As for the sort of satisfaction I seek, it is that which I shall derive from humbling your pride, and crushing your vanity and conceit. So be warned, Miss Barrington, should you choose Hawksbury, be prepared to be taken down a few pegs." He chuckled dryly. "Perhaps you might do better to opt for prison after all."

If he meant his words as a challenge, she was more than primed to accept. Humble her indeed! Ha! It would take more than scrubbing his chamber pot and floors to do that. Indeed, the beast could make her scrub his feet, and she wouldn't feel so much as a tinge of shame. Just resentment, the deep, burning kind, which was exactly what she felt now.

Thus resolved to enter the contest, she snapped, "I shall take Hawksbury and gladly."

"Fine. Then obey my command to view your bogle so that we may return to the house. Oh, and be prepared to tell me how you came to be there on the ride back. I am most curious to learn your logic in choosing Hawksbury as a place of refuge." With that, he stalked back to where the lantern marked the bogle sighting.

For several long moments he stood looking around him, then he exclaimed, "Ah! There you are," and fell to his knees. Indicating with a jerk of his head that she was to approach, he picked something up.

Her fear banished by anger, she lifted her shabby skirt and marched over to him. Bracing herself to see something truly hideous, she glanced at the object cradled in his gloved hands.

It was a ball, one of thick dark fur and wicked-looking quills. Ah. She hadn't been bitten but pricked. No wonder she'd imagined a monster with a hundred teeth. Kneeling down for a closer look, she murmured, "What is it?"

Making soothing noises between his teeth, he eased one hand beneath the ball and tickled it. A few seconds later the ball unrolled and out popped a pointy face with bright eyes. In spite of its oddness, there was something rather charming about the little creature.

"Why, whatever is it?" she inquired, deciding that she quite liked it.

Chuckling, he held the animal up for her inspection and said, "Miss Sophie Barrington, meet Mr. Hedgehog, your deadly bogle."

Chapter 10

"Nigglin' old fury. Made me polish every bleedin' bit of brass in the guest chambers, even the door keys," Fancy groused, stalking into the kitchen. "All this pish, pother, and fuss, and for what, I ask you? Some piddlin' viscount and his whelp! Why, you'd think the friggin' king hisself was comin' to visit the way the Pixie's dingin' on about everything bein' perfect."

John Wilford, the stately first footman, broke from his consultation with the cook to frown at the carping chambermaid. His voice as starchy as it was genteel, he reproved, "We do not utter the word 'frigging' in this household, girl, and most certainly not in association with the king."

She eyed him with unveiled insolence. "Oh? And what call do you got to be tellin' me what I can or can't say? Last I heard the Pixie were in charge down here."

"Indeed she is, and it is her rule that forbids the use of coarse language by servants. Or have you forgotten?" he severely retorted.

Fancy sniffed. "I nivver forgot nothin'. I ain't stupid like some I could name." She paused to shoot a pointed look over to where Sophie scoured the roasting hearth. When Sophie merely continued to work, deeming the barb unworthy of a response, she sniffed again and finished, "Not bein' stupid, I know I don't have to take no heed of you or your—"

"As for the matter of Mrs. Pixton's 'niggling,' as you so inelegantly phrased it," the footman cut in, continuing his admonishment as if she hadn't spoken, "it is her express wish that the staff make a fine impression on the Mayhews. Lest you've forgotten, there is a possibility that the 'whelp' will be the next mistress of Hawksbury. As such, she shall have the power to sack us all should she judge our services inadequate."

Sack us? Ha! I should be so lucky, Sophie thought, scraping at the congealed mutton drippings in the spit trough. But, of course, she hadn't a prayer of being turned out. Not even if she burned down the kitchen, as she'd almost done while trying to light the baking ovens two days earlier. No, she was stuck at Hawksbury until the Beast, as she'd secretly nicknamed Lyndhurst, had tired of tormenting her. And heaven only knew when that would be.

Grimacing as much from dislike for Lyndhurst as at the reek of the rancid fat, she scooped up the last of the drippings and dumped them into the grease pan. After shoving the revolting mess well out of nose range, she picked up a rag and began wiping the last vestiges of slime from the trough.

Though it had been only three days since her midnight clash with Lyndhurst, it was long enough for her to wonder if perhaps prison mightn't have been the better choice. Indeed, compared to life under the Beast's vile rule, the rumored horrors of King's Bench sounded more and more like heaven with every passing day.

Mentally adding a star by Lyndhurst's lengthy entry on her list of Hawksbury trials, Sophie tossed aside her mucky rag and scrutinized her handiwork. True to his word, his despicable lordship humbled her at every turn. Worst of all, he did so without actually doing, or even saying, a thing.

Wishing she could drop what she deemed the spotless trough on his horrid head, Sophie gathered up her cleaning supplies and crawled over the spotless hearth. Dragging her faithful bucket and basket behind her as she went, she squeezed past the equally clean firedogs and spit, and crept into the cavernous fireplace beyond. As she did so, the bedlam of kitchen activity faded to a droning buzz.

After pausing a beat to flex her aching back, she stood

up and peered at the smoke jack in the chimney. Of course it was greasy. Sooty, too. She sighed. No doubt her arms would fall off from fatigue by the time she finished cleaning it.

Blaming its grimy state on Lyndhurst and his request for mutton with red currants the night before, she fished a clean rag from her basket. After dipping it into her bucket of small beer and soap, she began scrubbing the contraption's paddle wheel blades. As she slaved, she cast wary glances out at the hearth, half expecting to see his plaguesome lordship lounging there, staring at her.

That was his mode of punishment, staring. But only when she was engaged in a particularly degrading task. How he knew when and where she was thus occupied, she didn't know. All she knew was that he was always there, stripping away her composure with his gaze.

Of course she tried to ignore him, tried desperately to dismiss his very existence. But, alas, it was no use. Despite her most valiant efforts, she always became flustered and ended up making the most mortifying blunders. And the torment didn't stop there, oh, no!

Instead of wandering off, smirking his satisfaction as one would expect, he watched her frantically flounder about, trying to fix her mistake. Of course she failed at that as well. Indeed, so agitated was she by then that she usually ended up making matters worse. It was only when she'd muddled things past all redemption that he would snort and stalk off. The insufferable cur!

She paused in her scrubbing to glare at the paddles as if they were his lordship. Oh, how she longed to tell him what she thought of him and his infernal staring, to spill forth all the fury and indignation that seethed within her. But she couldn't, she wouldn't! Never. Not if he spent every second of every day for the next hundred years gawking at her. To do so would be to concede victory to his revenge, and she would run queer before granting him such satisfaction.

Her resolve thus reaffirmed, Sophie forcibly banished him from her mind and finished her task. That completed, she turned her attention to the suet-spattered walls around her. Growing more dispirited by the second, she calculated the work before her.

Considering the size of the space and the degree to which it was soiled, she would need at least five bucketfuls of the Pixie's saltpeter, sal soda, and ammonia washing solution to adequately clean it. Factor in five trips outside to empty, rinse, and refill the bucket with fresh water, plus the time it took to measure and mix the cleanser, and it should take her, oh, two and a half, maybe even three hours of filthy, backbreaking work.

She groaned aloud at the prospect. God must think her wicked to the extreme to plague her with the cleaning of a fireplace both vast and greasy enough to lard and roast the Beast himself.

Lard and roast the Beast? She grinned at the fanciful picture of Lyndhurst skewered on the spit with an apple stuffed in his haughty mouth. Giggling her wicked amusement, she crawled from the fireplace, towing her bucket behind her. As she emerged, she was again surrounded by the discordant symphony of kitchen noise, accompanied by a chorus of prattling voices.

Fancy, she noted, had planted herself next to Charles at a long kitchen table, where he and four other footmen sat polishing silver. As for John, he still conversed with Cook, who looked about to erupt at any moment.

Sophie shrugged and stood up. Ah, well. The day wasn't complete unless Cook had a row with someone. Nodding to the other servants as she passed, she hauled her bucket up the stairs and trudged toward the kitchen garden.

Such a lot of unnecessary fetch and carry, she grumbled to herself, weaving her way through the maze of herbs and vegetables. Especially seeing as how the main kitchen had not one, but two sinks with plumbing. However, rules were rules, and heaven help the servant unwise enough to use Cook's precious slate sinks and running water for such a lowly purpose as cleaning.

When she finally reached the far garden wall, she dumped the foul water into a vat reserved for such purposes, then rinsed and refilled the worn wooden bucket at the nearby pump. After lingering a moment to savor the warmth of the early afternoon sun, she reluctantly returned to the kitchen and the dreary task ahead of her. She was halfway down the stairs when she heard John and Cook's discussion explode into a full-blown squabble.

"Frenchy slop? Frenchy slop!" Cook bellowed at the top of her lungs. "And why, pray tell, should I cook that rot when good, solid English fare would serve for the better?"

"I already explained the reason," the footman patiently countered. "The marchioness recalls Miss Mayhew showing a marked preference for this dish the time she dined with her family and thinks to be hospitable by adding it to the welcoming menu."

"What'd have been hospitable would've been to give me the recipe in English," the cook muttered as Sophie entered the kitchen.

John sighed. "I told you that Miss Stewart will be down shortly to translate for you. I can assure you that her French is quite impeccable. She shall—"

"What? Queen High-Horse is gonna favor us with her royal presence? You gotta be waggin'," Fancy exclaimed, casting the footman a spiteful look. "That uppity old hag'd sooner jump off the roof than hobnob with the likes of us. I ain't never seen—"

"Bridle your tongue this instant, Fancy Jenkins," John barked, his face mottling purple. "I shan't hear another word against Miss Stewart. Not a word! Unlike yourself, Miss Stewart is a lady of exceptional refinement. As such, you shall accord her the respect she deserves. If you fail to do so, I shall be forced to take the matter up with Mrs. Pixton."

If looks could kill, Fancy's glare would have dropped him where he stood. "You can talk to the Pixie till you're blue in the face for all I care, and a fat lot of good it'll do you. In case you ain't heard, I'm the best chambermaid at Hawksbury. If you think she's gonna sack me for talkin' about that blind old excuse for a lady's maid, then you're queer in the head."

"She might not sack you, but unless you mend your ways she shall never recommend you for the lady's maid position when Miss Stewart takes her pension. And we all know how you covet the post." This was from Julius, third footman, and a fast friend of John's.

Fancy sniffed. "You don't know nothin' about nothin'."

"Seems to me that if anyone should be a lady's maid, it's our Sophie here," Charles remarked, winking at Sophie as she passed.

She smiled faintly at the footman, who grinned in return.

Fancy squawked and cuffed his ear.

"Well, it's true and you know it, Fancy," he maintained, resentfully rubbing his abused ear. "Sophie's the daughter of a baron, and is a real lady."

Fancy emitted a disdainful noise. "So she says. I, for one, ain't likely to believe it till I see some sort of proof."

"The proof is right before your eyes." Julius nodded to where Sophie searched a cupboard for the saltpeter solution. "You have only to note her pretty ways and hear her fine speech to—"

"Enough! Neither shall be elevated any time soon. I happen to know that Miss Stewart has no intention of taking her pension for at least another year," John barked. "Now, back to work, all of you. That includes you, too, Fancy. Surely you have better things to do than stir up trouble?"

Fancy shrugged. "Not like it's none of your concern or nothin', but I'm waitin' for the Pixie to come down and unlock the stillroom cabinet. I need lavender soap for the whelp's room."

"Then, I shall find her and ask her to come down directly," he snapped. After murmuring something to Cook, who looked more irate than ever, he turned on his heels and marched from the kitchen.

"Pompous old sod," Fancy muttered the instant he was out of earshot. "Everyone knows he's got an itch for Queen High-Horse."

More interested in the gossip than she'd ever have admitted, Sophie took her time in measuring and mixing the cleanser. She'd just poured it into her bucket when someone hissed her name.

Recognizing the voice as belonging to her prattlebox bed partner, Pansy, she looked up and glanced in the direction from which it had come. Being as it wasn't wash day, the laundress had been put to work in the kitchen. Right now she stood at a stout oak table about four feet away, polishing the kitchen knives.

When Sophie raised her brows in inquiry, Pansy pulled a Shrewsbury cake from her apron pocket and waved it temptingly in the air. Sophie eyed it longingly for several seconds, then peered over her shoulder to where Fancy sat enumerating her qualifications as a lady's maid. Seeing her thus occupied and not likely to cause her any immediate grief, she moved over to stand beside Pansy.

" 'Ere. You said they was yer fav-rites," the girl murmured, slipping her the cake.

"Oh, Pansy. Wherever did you get it?" she exclaimed, genuinely pleased. She hadn't had a Shrewsbury cake since leaving London, and not a day had gone by that she hadn't longed for one.

The girl shrugged and picked up a tournè knife. "It were leftover from the family's breakfast. You said you liked 'em, so I asked Cook if I could 'ave it."

That Pansy had remembered her mention of the cakes astonished her; that she had gone to the trouble to procure her one without reason or expectation of anything in return left her feeling oddly humbled. Tucking the cake into her pocket to savor later, Sophie rather shyly murmured, "Thank you. This is indeed a fine treat."

The laundry maid shrugged. "It's jist a Shrewsbury cake. It ain't nothin' much."

"Yes, it is. It's the nicest gift anyone has given me in ever so long," she countered, and she meant it.

Pansy shrugged again, though her cheeks pinked with pleasure. "So. Whadda you think o' this business 'bout John and Miss Stewart?" she mumbled, rubbing the knife briskly against a leather-covered polishing board.

Sophie hid her smile at the girl's embarrassed change of subject. Though she had no particular interest in Miss

Stewart, she was exceedingly fond of John. Unlike many of the servants, who constantly lorded their stations over her, he had never treated her with anything but respect and kindness. Indeed, he'd even aided her with her chores on occasion, though they both knew it was shockingly below his station to do so. Why he extended her such courtesies, she didn't know. All she knew was that she was thankful for his friendship, and that she wished him only the greatest of happiness. It was those wishes that prompted her to inquire, "Is the chitchat true?"

Pansy nodded without looking up from her task. "John's loved Miss Stewart for well on twenty-five years now, tho' she dinna start lovin' 'im back until 'bout two or three years ago."

"Twenty-five years?" she gasped, more startled by the notion of such an ancient lady's maid than by the length of John's courtship. "She's been with the marchioness that long?" When Fancy had called her old, she'd naturally assumed the woman to be about thirty-five, which was definitely on the deep winter side of life for a lady's maid. But if she'd been with her ladyship for twenty-five years, that meant that she must be nigh on—

"No, no. Law, no! She's been with Lady Beresford fer thirty-two years now, ever since 'er ladyship were a bride. 'Course, she's more o' a companion than a maid these days, seein' as 'ow she can't do many o' the duties o' her station anymore. You ain't met 'er yet?"

Sophie shook her head. "I haven't even seen her."

Pansy lifted the gleaming knife for an inspection. "Well, she's been mighty busy since 'er ladyship took sick. I 'ear tell that she's ain't 'ardly left 'er side."

"She sounds to be very devoted to her mistress."

"She is. She's a good-'earted one, Miss Stewart is. Not a bit 'igh-and-mighty like that wicked Fancy Jenkins says. It were 'er praise about the way I press frills that got my wages raised an extra shillin' a year." She nodded her approval at the knife and set it aside. "I, fer one, are glad she finally took notice o' John. 'E's a fine gentleman and makes 'er ever so 'appy."

Sophie watched as the girl picked up a badly stained meat cleaver and scrubbed it with washing soda. "What took her so long to notice him? He's far too handsome a man to simply overlook."

Pansy clucked. "Poor Miss Stewart. She was to marry a sailor, oh, about thirty years ago, but he drowned at sea. Completely broke 'er heart, it did. She pined and pined fer over twenty years. Dinna so much as look at another man all that time."

"And yet John held out hope," Sophie murmured, awed by such steadfast devotion. "He must love her a great deal."

"Aye, 'e does. I 'eard tel that 'e turned down the post o' butler eight years ago so that 'e could stay near 'er. As 'er ladyship's personal footman, 'e spends a goodly time in Miss Stewart's company."

"Well, I do hope their story has a happy ending. It would be beyond sad if things didn't work out after all John's gone through to win her."

"I'm sure they will. I over'eard 'em talkin' about get-tin' married next year and buyin' an inn. She sounded jist as eager—" Pansy broke off, grinning. "Speak o' the devil." She nodded in the direction of the servants stairs.

There, more gliding than walking toward the mut-tering and scowling cook, was a slender woman in a plain dove-colored gown. Though her face was averted, Sophie could tell from the gray in her severely coiffed brown hair that she was indeed past her prime.

Curious to see what it was about her that inspired such dogged devotion in John, she feigned a need for fresh rags and moved to the kitchen cabinet near where Cook stood. As she opened the top door, she covertly studied the approaching lady's maid.

What the footman found so entrancing, she couldn't imagine. With her creased face, thick spectacles, and nondescript features, Miss Stewart fit the word plain to perfection. Indeed, she had to be one of the most unre-markable creatures Sophie had ever seen. And yet . . . yet . . .

She paused amid sorting through the rags, oddly com-pelled to look harder. At second glance there was some-thing rather appealing about her careworn face, something gentle and serene that made her hard to dis-

miss as merely plain. In the next instant she smiled, and
Sophie saw the reason for John's infatuation.

Why, she practically glowed with goodness, radiating
an inner beauty that enchanted the eye, warmed the
soul, and gladdened the heart. Indeed, so lovely was she
that Sophie felt strangely drab in comparison.

"John tells me that I shall have the honor of working
with you this afternoon, Mrs. Higgins," the woman said,
beaming at the cook as if she were indeed blessed with
a notable distinction.

To Sophie's surprise the perpetually dour cook
cracked a smile. "Yes, Miss Stewart. I need you to translate this recipe."

"It shall be my pleasure to do so," the lady's maid
replied, and by her tone it was clear that she meant it.

Visibly charmed, the cook smiled again, this time in a
way that displayed her enormous teeth, and handed over
the recipe.

"H-m-m. Let me see, now." Miss Stewart inched the
paper nearer to her face. After several moments she
removed her spectacles and rubbed her eyes. Blinking
several times, she slipped them back into place. "This
looks to be some sort of fricassèe dish"—she squinted,
visibly straining to see—"uh, yes. Salmon fricassèe."

"Somethin' amiss with your eyes, Miss Stewart?"
Fancy sneered.

"I'm afraid my vision isn't quite what it used to be,"
she murmured, frowning at the recipe.

"Well, then, why don't you ask Miss Hoity-Toity to
help you? Her da's a baron, you know." The chambermaid transferred her spiteful gaze from Miss Stewart to
Sophie. "You do read French, don't you, Miss Hoity-
Toity?" By the smug look on her face, she fully expected
Sophie to plead ignorance of the language, thus toppling
her claim to gentility.

Returning the other woman's look in kind, she countered in her most refined tone, "But of course I do,
Fancy. Fluently. And I shall be most pleased to aid Miss
Stewart. No doubt her eyes are dreadfully weary from
all the sleepless nights she's passed tending the marchioness." She shifted her gaze from the visibly piqued Fancy

to smile at the lady's maid. "I do hope her ladyship is feeling better this morning, Miss Stewart?"

The woman's lips curved into the most lovely smile Sophie had ever seen. "Much better. It is kind of you to inquire, Miss—?"

"Barton. This is our new maid-of-all-work, Sophie Barton," Cook supplied, crooking her finger to indicate that Sophie was to approach.

Obediently she complied, dropping into an elegant curtsy as she stopped before the two women.

"Your father is a baron, dear?" Miss Stewart quizzed, her expression thoughtful.

Sophie nodded. "Yes. But he suffered a reversal of fortunes several weeks back."

"And you were forced to go into service," the woman finished for her. "Poor child. How very dreadful it must be for you."

"Yes," Sophie admitted, her heart swelling at the genuine compassion from the lady's maid.

Miss Stewart smiled again, this time gently. "What other skills do you possess besides speaking French?"

"I'm not so certain that I possess anything that can be properly referred to as skills, though I was educated in Bath."

"Ah, but of course. You were trained in the fine art of being a lady." She seemed to consider that fact for a moment, then inquired, "Tell me, Miss Barton, was it you who mended the marchioness's dressing gown last week?"

"Yes," Sophie admitted, growing suddenly wary. Oh, heavens! Had she somehow bungled the task as she did everything else? She'd thought her needlework excellent, but—

"Then, let me commend you on your skill with a needle. Your stitches are all but invisible, the most delicate ones I've seen."

"Invisible? Ha! They're invisible 'cause she's too bleedin' blind to see them," Fancy muttered.

Pointedly ignoring the chambermaid's rudeness, Miss Stewart continued, "If you perform all facets of your art with such mastery, you shall no doubt rise—"

"Pardon me, Miss Stewart. But the viscount'll be arriving this afternoon, and I need to get started on the—salmon fricassèe, you say?" Cook politely interjected.

"But of course." Handing the recipe to Sophie, the lady's maid murmured, "Miss Barton? If you would be so kind?"

Sophie peered at the paper for a moment, then nodded. "Yes. It is a recipe for salmon fricassèe . . . with dill . . . and, um, a buttery lemon cream sauce." She paused a beat to shoot Fancy a triumphant look, who made an ugly face in return. At Cook's prompting she sat on a three-legged stool by the stove.

As she opened her mouth to read off the required ingredients and measures, the cook turned abruptly and bellowed, "Seeing as how you're in need of something to do, Fancy, you can take Sophie's place and finish scrubbing the roasting hearth."

"You forget that I'm a chambermaid and ain't required to do no kitchen work," Fancy retorted haughtily.

"You're a servant in this house, which means that you're required to do whatever is necessary for the comfort and well-being of your employers," rebutted the voice of Mrs. Pixton.

Hard-pressed not to grin as the housekeeper proceeded to give Fancy a well-deserved dressing down, Sophie turned back to the cook and began her translation.

As for Miss Stewart, she studied Sophie several more moments, then turned away, her lips curled in an enigmatic smile.

Chapter 11

The marquess chuckled and clapped his son on the back. "Eager to meet old Brumbly's paragon, are you?"

"Uh ... paragon ... what?" Nicholas muttered, trying to tear his gaze from the woman on the stairs below him. But, alas, it was no use. Despite his most resolute efforts, he was unable to look away from where Sophie crawled about on her hands and knees, scrubbing pigeon droppings from the sandstone front steps.

His father chuckled again and snapped his fingers before his face, pretending to be a mesmerist awakening him from a trance. "I asked if you were in a stew over meeting Brumbly's girl?"

"A stew? U-m-m—" His voice drifted off as Sophie stretched down to the bottom step, granting him a tantalizing view of her backside. Though he commanded himself to ignore the sight, he couldn't help notice the provocative manner in which her limp skirt defined every contour of her buttocks.

As he stood making his ogling observation, despising himself for doing so, she resumed her scrubbing. Oh, bloody hell! His teeth clenched, as did something in a most troubling place. She was doing it again, wagging her tail in time with her hand motions.

"Ask? Why do I ask?" his father gently prodded.

Nicholas shot him a sheepish glance, wondering if his face was as flushed as it felt. "Um ... yes. Sorry ... ur ... thought I saw something in the distance.'

Another chuckle. "And you wonder why I ask?"

"Pardon?" Damn. How did his gaze get back on Sophie?

This time a sigh. "I ask because you've been standing out here nigh on a quarter hour, gawking up the road like a moon-sick calf."

"Oh . . ." At that moment the provoking chit sat up, flexing her spine and twisting at the waist, clearly trying to ease a kink from her back. There was something about her writhing, an unconscious sensuality, that made Nicholas's own kink tighten a few degrees.

He spat a silent oath at the sensation, one so foul that he'd never have uttered it aloud. What the hell was wrong with him that he should lust so for a woman he loathed? He was a man of principles, for Christ's sake, not some overly libidinous rake. As such, it took more than a pretty face or a fine figure to arouse him. Indeed, he had to at least like a woman as a person in order to experience any degree of sexual interest in her.

Until now, that is. He mentally cursed again.

When he'd selected this, staring, as his mode of revenge, the last thing he'd expected to feel was lust. Anxiety, yes. Self-consciousness, yes. Pain, shame, and a crushing sense of inadequacy—yes, yes, yes. In fact, it was his anticipation of those very emotions that had prompted him to select the punishment he had. He'd thought that by forcing himself to face his feelings, he'd eventually overcome them. And perhaps it might have worked had it not been for his unexpected and perverse lust.

"Colin?" The hand appeared before his eyes again, fingers snapping. "You with me, son?" Unfortunately, it dropped just in time for Nicholas to see Sophie lean over and flash more than a glimpse of her splendid cleavage.

He gritted his teeth, hard-pressed not to squirm as his kink affected his manly anatomy in a most embarrassing way. Certain that he'd moan aloud if he opened his mouth, he pried his gaze from the tempting spectacle and slanted his father what he hoped was a querying glance.

The other man eyed him with exasperated amusement. "I said that the coach won't be arriving for at least another hour. Brumbly's outrider arrived earlier with the news. Didn't you hear?"

Nicholas feigned a smile and croaked, "No, I didn't," all the while struggling to tame his desire.

God, how he hated his arousal, hated it with a fervor that made him long for impotence. He hated the way it felt, throbbing and rampant; he hated how it made him feel, satiric and lewd. Most of all he hated how it called his character to question, forcing him to view it in a harsh new light and wonder if perhaps it weren't as sterling as he had thought.

Tormented almost beyond endurance now, he nodded his accord to whatever his father said. How he longed to abandon his staring revenge and flee his misery. But, of course, he couldn't, no matter how much it pained him to continue. To do so would concede victory to Sophie, and that was something he could never do. Not if he wished to regain his pride.

Nicholas heaved a silent sigh, feeling only a niggle of triumph as Sophie sat back into her bucket of wash water, soaking both her skirt and the freshly cleaned stairs.

As difficult as he found his vengeance, he had to admit that it was effective. By reducing Miss Barrington to a bungling ninny, he stripped her of all pretense and dignity, thus striking at the heart of her hauteur. Once he'd stripped her completely, she should crumble readily enough. How could she not? There would be nothing of any substance left to sustain her. Then he would win. All he had to do was maintain his facade of composure awhile longer.

As he grimly wondered if he were equal to the task, he became aware that his father had ceased speaking and awaited some sort of response. "Yes," he murmured, hoping against hope that he wasn't agreeing to do something excruciating, like squiring Miss Mayhew to the crotchety Widows Gum and Tottle's cottage for tea.

"Exactly what I told him," his father crowed. "Said, 'See here, Ruben, the only help for the gripe is a good bleeding.' "

Bleeding? H-m-m. Nicholas's eyes narrowed as he absently observed Sophie's clumsy attempts to right her mess. Could it be that his own embarrassing condition stemmed not from lust, but from ill humors in his blood? He had, after all, overindulged in brandy the entire week following his disappointment with Sophie. And as every gentleman knew, staying floored for any length of time inevitably led to unpleasant consequences.

Consequences such as the ones he now suffered? He considered for a moment, then sighed. Maybe. But even if drink was responsible for his problem, was opening a vein really the solution? In his experience only one thing cured what ailed him: a woman. Unfortunately, he had no woman at the moment. He'd pensioned off his mistress out of respect for Sophie the day he'd decided to court her. And since he had no stomach for casual relations . . .

"Oh? Then, you think the idea addled?"

The dismay in his father's voice paired with his own wretched thoughts proved an effective antidote for both his visual and mental captivation with Sophie. Hoping to gain a clue as to what it was he was supposed to be considering, he looked at his father and murmured, "I'm not yet of an opinion. Please do elaborate."

Instead his father frowned and laid his palm against his forehead. "Saw you talking to Ruben yesterday. Didn't catch the gripe from him, did you?"

Nicholas frowned. "No. Why?"

"Your face is flushed, and you look deuced uncomfortable."

"Oh. Well, I must be flushed from standing in the sun. As for my expression—" He broke off, momentarily distracted as Sophie stood up and flounced off out of sight. As usual she didn't spare him or his hideous face a single glance. Hating that that fact bothered him, he more growled than uttered, "I look pained because I stubbed my toe this morning, and it still hurts."

"But of course. Of course." His father grinned and clapped him on the back. "No need to fret about your health, eh? Never been sick a day in your life, not since—" The rest of what he said was drowned out by

a most terrible clatter, the clatter of what appeared to
be an out-of-control coach.

Up the drive it careened, its speed so perilous and
reining erratic that Nicholas wondered at the coachman's
sobriety. It wasn't until it halted with an abruptness that
nearly sent the vehicle plowing into the horses, that he
saw the driver and ceased his speculation.

Brumbly. Of course. Dotty, eccentric, Lester Mayhew,
Viscount Brumbly. Nicholas and his father exchanged
amused glances. Leave it to Brumbly to make such a
harrowing entrance.

"Ho there, Beresford! Lyndhurst! Nice day for a
drive, eh?" Brumbly hollered, waving his arms as if they
could possibly overlook him.

The marquess grinned. "Looked more like a race than
a drive to me. Aren't you a bit withered to be a Whip,
man?"

The viscount cackled. "Had no choice but to take the
reins if I wanted to arrive in this century. Old Henry,
here, drives slower than a slug on hot sand." Brumbly
jovially elbowed old Henry, who sat frozen beside him
looking as if he'd just looked death in the face. Judging
from the way the hatless viscount's gingery hair flew
nilly-willy about his head, the poor man no doubt had.

After retrieving a parcel from amid the haphazardly
heaped baggage lashed to the roof behind him, the viscount climbed from the coach. Scurrying toward them
as fast as his bandy legs would carry him, he jabbered,
"Can't wait to show you my latest invention. The 'Sirena,' I call it. Sings to the fish like a siren to a sailor.
Draws them every time." He paused a beat to give each
of his hosts a hearty hug. "You'll be sure to want at
least three."

Grinning like a tickled loon, he opened the moth-
eaten bag and extracted something that looked like a
bagpipe impaled by a long, twisted horn. Making it all
the more curious was the cork dangling by a chain from
what had to be a mouthpiece.

Proudly waving his creation before them, his watery
blue right eye shifting wildly between their faces while

his drifting left one floated off the opposite direction, he crowed, "Well, what do you say? Damn impressive, eh?"

"Er . . . how does it work?" the marquess quizzed, looking as he always did when faced with Brumbly's inventions: bewildered.

"Well you should ask. Well you should ask." The viscount nodded vigorously, which sent his left eye coasting to the corner nearest his nose. The sight was distracting, to say the least.

Smiling in a way that displayed a set of remarkably good teeth, he explained, "First you blow in here," he stuck the mouthpiece between his lips and blew. When the bagpipelike bladder was fully inflated, he removed it from his mouth and plugged the mouthpiece with the cork. Looking giddy enough to giggle like a schoolgirl, he queried, "Ready?" At their nod he squeezed the bladder, producing a noise like a constipated cow with flatulence.

"Ah." His right eye rolled heavenward in ecstasy, while his left one stared at his companions. "Sings like an angel, eh?"

The marquess slanted his son a look of suppressed hilarity. "Impressive," he murmured. "Don't you agree, Colin?"

"Very impressive indeed," Nicholas concurred, ready to choke on his laughter.

The viscount grinned, visibly pleased with himself and their response. "Of course this end"—he thumped the flaring brass horn end— "goes into the water to call the fish." For once, both eyes were trained in the same direction. "Say. You've been going on about the Hawksbury fishing stream for years. What say you to taking the Sirena down there and testing it on Devonshire fish?"

The marquess cleared his throat. "Ah, Brumbly. Aren't you forgetting something?"

The viscount frowned for a beat, then resumed his grin. "By Jove! My tackle. Might as well catch a few while I'm at it."

Nicholas and his father exchanged a look of fond exasperation. "Er, no, Brumbly. I was referring to your daughter. You did remember to bring Minerva, didn't

you?" By his expression it was clear that his father had
his doubts.

"Minerva?" Brumbly looked momentarily nonplussed,
then he slapped his stringy thigh and cackled. "Oh, yes.
Of course. My Mayfly."

"Mayfly?" Nicholas didn't dare to so much as glance
at his father, certain they would both spill their hilarity.
Leave it to Brumbly to nickname his daughter for an
insect that just happened to be common fish food.

"He calls Minerva 'Mayfly' because . . . well, why
don't you tell him yourself, Brumbly?" By his father's
choked tone, it was clear that he was one syllable away
from howling with laughter.

"What?" The viscount's gaze, at least that of his right
eye, shifted from the coach back to his hosts. "Oh, yes.
Mayfly. Call her that because I used to make Mayfly
flies from her hair when she was a babe. Tried it as an
experiment, you see. Was curious to find out whether
fish bite better for human hair or animal fur."

"And the results?" Nicholas squinted at the coach,
attempting to catch a glimpse of the queerly nicknamed
girl. It appeared to be empty. H-m-m. Perhaps Brumbly
had lost her somewhere along the way.

"The fish practically jumped on the hook. Used her
hair until she was about three. Must have changed about
then, because the fish no longer fancied it." He cackled
and jabbed Nicholas in the ribs. "Maybe you and Mayfly
will spawn a fish fly babe, eh?"

Now there was a disturbing notion, one that Nicholas
had no intention of exploring. Clearing his throat uncomfortably, he changed the subject by inquiring, "Are
you certain you didn't leave your daughter at a posting
inn? I don't see her in the coach."

Brumbly seemed to consider the possibility, then
turned to the vehicle bellowing, "Mayfly? You there,
girl?" A second later a head topped by a crooked bonnet
appeared at the window. The viscount waved. "Well,
come along, then, girl. None of your dawdling."

Always mindful of his manners, Nicholas strode down
the steps to greet the girl, pausing on the bottom one to

await a footman to open the door. As he did so, her
head popped down again.

After waiting several moments, during which he didn't
dare speculate upon what she did in the coach, he
frowned and glanced around. There was no one about
save old Henry, who was either dead or frozen from
shock. Apparently the Mayhews either had no footmen,
or they had fallen off their perches during Brumbly's
mad dash.

Or it could be that there was no room for them, he
added, eyeing the fishing gear lashed to every available
surface.

Since the Hawksbury footmen were no doubt scrab-
bling to change from their work clothes into their livery,
what with the guests arriving early, he had no choice but
to act the part himself.

"Miss Mayhew? May I assist you?" he called, fearful
of what he might see should he neglect to warn her.

The only response was an odd scraping sound.

Taking that noise for a yes—after all, he was dealing
with a Mayhew—he more wrestled than folded down the
rusty steps. After mentally preparing himself to be
greeted by oddness, Nicholas opened the door and
peered inside.

There, crawling about the filthy floor, muttering to
herself, was whom he assumed to be Miss Mayhew. The
instant she saw him her face flushed a hectic red, and
she let out a braying laugh. "Dropped my w-worms
w-w-when w-w-e s-stopped," she stuttered, holding up
one of the squirming creatures.

Nicholas eyed the grime beneath her nails, wondering
if she'd dug them up herself. Finding that notion almost
as diverting as the dozen or so fishing flies dangling from
her shabby bonnet, he somehow remembered himself
enough to say, "I see. U-m-m. Perhaps I should send for
a servant to attend them so you can freshen up." The
freshen up part was meant more as a hint than a
solicitude.

She looked as horrified as if he'd suggested setting the
coach on fire with her still in it. "Oh, no. They c-can't
w-w-wait. It's too h-hot in h-here. They s-s-shall die for

c-certain!" She gave her head an emphatic shake, which sent her fly-festooned bonnet toppling from her head.

Her hair, Nicholas noted with distaste, was as much in need of "freshening" as her clothes and hands. Indeed, judging from the greasy clumping of the pale, lank strands, it looked to have been last washed sometime during her father's Mayfly experiment. And they wondered why the fish no longer fancied it?

Refraining from grinning at his sardonic conclusion, he promised in a cordial, albeit tight voice, "If they do die, I shall see that you get new ones. Lovely plump ones."

She shook her head again. "These are lugworms from a s-secret s-s-strand near Formby. B-best b-bait in England there. P-Papa and I s-s-s-stopped on the w-w-way h-here to dig them out of the s-sand. W-we're going to b-b-breed them at our b-bait farm."

"Your . . . er . . . bait farm?"

She nodded as she plucked up another worm and dropped it into a creel full of wet sand. "W-we h-have the finest one in England."

"Indeed?"

Thus prompted, she described her enterprise in detail, her stutter lessening in her rising excitement. As she spoke, Nicholas studied her features.

Eyes, pale blue and watery, but lovely in both size and shape. Nose? Not exactly regrettable, though it was rather short and turned up at the end to be of his taste. Then, there was her mouth.

He narrowed his eyes as he considered it. Nice lips. Yes, very nice indeed, though it was a pity about those protruding front teeth. As for her complexion, well, only one word came to mind: unfortunate. Whatever could she have been thinking to let it get so brown and speckled? He eyed her weak chin for a moment, then blinked and appraised her overall appearance.

While she wasn't what one would call pretty, she wasn't the plainest miss he'd seen, either. No, not the plainest, he mused, taking in her stained gown, just the dirtiest.

She was rattling on about artificial leech habitats when

she abruptly fell silent. Looking as if she'd just hooked a shark, the enormous man-eating kind, she poked the worm nearest her hand. It didn't move. She poked it again.

Once, twice, thrice, her mouth flapped, then she wailed, "It's dead! C-c-c-cooked in the h-h-heat!" Keening as if her heart were broken, she snatched up the stringy corpse and cradled it in her palm. "O-o-o-o! W-what a fine fish it w-w-would've c-c-c-caught."

Not certain whether to console the girl or ignore her outlandish eruption, Nicholas looked helplessly about for Brumbly. He was gone, as was his father. He sighed. Now what?

Deciding it best to get her out of the coach and into someone else's care, he suggested, "Perhaps we should gather up the rest of your, ah, breeding stock before it suffers a similar fate."

She broke off mid-keen. "W-w-we? You w-want to h-h-h-help?"

He graced her with his most charming smile. "But of course. That is what gentlemen do, help ladies."

"W-w-well—" She eyed him critically, as if deciding whether to trust him not to steal a worm or two for himself. After a beat she nodded. "All right. B-but only if you p-promise to b-b-be c-careful. Lugworms are s-s-sensitive c-creatures, you know."

Nicholas cast a long suffering glance skyward. Heaven save him from crazy fisherwomen and matchmaking mothers. When he'd sworn upon his life, she nodded again and stuck her head beneath the seat, calling in what he assumed to be some sort of worm language.

Vowing to make short work of the worm-catching business, he leaned into the coach as far as his body would allow him. Instantly he lunged back out again, gasping for air. What in Hades was that smell? He exhaled forcefully through his nose, trying to expel the lingering foulness.

Fish. Yes. Putrid fish. No doubt the mad pair of anglers had forgotten about a catch stowed somewhere in the vehicle, and it now rotted in the heat. As to why they hadn't smelled it themselves and thus removed it, well, what could he say? They were Mayhews.

Eager to be shot of this particular Mayhew, Nicholas held his breath and manfully charged forward again. Aha! A worm, slithering across the girl's filthy hem. He dived forward to catch it . . . at the same time Miss Mayhew lurched back.

Whap! Her posterior collided with his face.

"Argh!" He tumbled backward—*thump!*—right onto his tailbone. For a long moment he lay sprawled across the bottom steps, too stunned to move.

Miss Mayhew was the rotting fish.

Chapter 12

The Beast had told. She just knew it. Why else did the marchioness demand an audience?

Sophie paused at the end of the hall, her stomach knotting as she gazed to where John stood stationed by her ladyship's door. She wasn't ready. Not yet. She needed a moment, well, maybe two or three, to prepare herself for her coming ordeal.

Unfortunately, John's vision was as strong as Miss Stewart's was weak, and he promptly spied her standing there. Smiling as if hailing a long-lost sister, he gestured for her to approach.

She ducked her head and feigned interest in her gown, pretending not to see him. How could he look so jolly . . . so very friendly? she wondered, plucking at her puffy sleeve. As footman to her ladyship, he surely knew who she was and what she'd done? How could he not? He was as much friend as servant to the marchioness, and thus as privy to her affairs as Miss Stewart.

Sophie shifted her make-believe attention from her sleeve to her scalloped overskirt, her wonderment deepening into confusion as she remembered the equally bewildering conduct of the lady's maid. Why, she'd looked nothing short of gay when she'd waltzed into the kitchen earlier and delivered her mistress's summons. The way she twittered and flushed, you'd have thought she was a schoolgirl.

A schoolgirl bedeviled by the keeping of a very big secret, Sophie amended, thinking of the bright, knowing glances the woman slanted her way. And as if all that weren't enough to throw a body off balance, she had blithely charged her to don her best gown.

Sophie considered her sea-green frock with its puckered bodice and lilac trim for a moment. After much thought she'd opted to wear not her best dress, but her favorite one; the one in which she'd always experienced the best of luck and had had the most excellent times. She'd worn it in hopes that its magic would prevail.

"If I might be so bold, my dear, I must say that you look quite lovely this evening."

She glanced up in surprise to see John standing before her, gazing at her like a proud papa at his daughter's coming-out. Though she was far from in a smiling mood, she appreciated his courtly compliment and thus forced her lips to curve up. "You are most gallant, sir."

Apparently her smile looked as strained as it felt, for he instantly sobered and took her hand in his. "Ah. Plagued by the nerves, are we?"

She bit her trembling lip and nodded.

He gave her hand a fortifying squeeze. "No need for it. Her ladyship is quite tame, I assure you. Hasn't devoured a servant in years." He grinned at his own jest.

Sophie returned his gaze grimly, not at all cheered. Lady Beresford might not deal harshly with servants, but she, regretfully, wasn't a mere servant. She was the girl who had jilted her son; the one responsible for disgracing him in front of the entire ton. And from what she'd heard tell about her ladyship, she was protective to the point of fierceness when it came to her sons. What the woman would do to her for wronging her precious Colin, well, she daren't even imagine.

Her panic mounting by the second, she continued to stare at John's smiling face, her breath hitching in her fear. Oh, what she wouldn't give to be just another servant, one whose only sin against the Somervilles was a badly swept floor or an indifferently scrubbed spoon.

As she stared, his smile faded. Cupping her chin in his palm, he murmured, "Why, Sophie. My dearest girl. You truly are in a fright, aren't you?"

So compassionate, so full of genuine concern were both his voice and face that the fragile wall of her composure shattered and she blurted out, "Oh, John. Whatever shall I do? I'm in such trouble . . . such terrible, wicked trouble."

His eyebrows shot up at her words. "Terrible, wicked trouble? You? I find that rather impossible to believe. Whatever makes you think such a thing?"

Miserably, she shook her head. Though she longed to confide in him and seek his sage advice, she didn't dare. For she knew that despite his paternal fondness for her, his first loyalty lay with the Somervilles. He would hate her if she confessed to harming one of them, and at that moment she very much needed his friendship.

"Come, come, now, girl. Speak up."

"It's just that, well . . ." She shook her head again. "Why else would her ladyship demand to see me unless I've done something dreadful? You know as well as I that she hasn't invited me, a mere maid-of-all-work, upstairs for a friendly tête-à-tête."

He chuckled softly and released her chin. "There are a great many reasons why a mistress might wish to speak with a servant, and not all of them bad. Indeed, I happen to know that you shall find the purpose of this interview pleasant to the extreme."

"But I—" She broke off abruptly, blinking her surprise as his words penetrated her brain. "I shall?" The words came out in a squeak.

He nodded. "Now, stop fretting and come along. We mustn't keep Lady Beresford waiting any longer."

"But—"

He shook his head and took her arm. Too astonished to object, she docilely allowed him to escort her down the hall. It wasn't until they stopped before the marchioness's door that she regained enough of her senses to whisper, "Will you at least give me a hint as to what this is all about?"

The look he cast her mirrored Miss Stewart's mirthful, knowing one. "Her ladyship's business is for me to know and you to discover," he retorted in a singsong voice.

"But—"

He put a finger to her lips to hush her. When she'd

remained silent for several beats, he scratched on the door.

"Enter!"

Sophie frowned. Either the marchioness had a very deep voice, or the respondent was a man. The marquess perhaps?

"Now, then, girl. Don't forget to curtsy. And please do try to smile." With that hasty instruction, John opened the door and announced her.

It was more instinct from years of training than conscious thought that propelled Sophie into the room and down into an elegant curtsy. As she began to rise, taking care to keep her head modestly and correctly bowed, a frail female voice murmured, "Nicely done. Very nicely done. Don't you agree, Colin?"

The Beast. Sophie almost lost her precarious balance.

"M-m-m, yes. Nice," concurred a dry voice she knew so well.

It was all she could do not to look up and shoot him a withering look. No doubt this interview was yet another of his cunningly plotted punishments.

"Do have her move nearer, Miss Stewart. I should like a closer look," the marchioness peevishly directed.

"If you please, Miss Barton?" the lady's maid relayed.

Her gaze still lowered in respect, Sophie rose and did as charged. It wasn't until she'd stopped in the center of the room that she ventured a surreptitious glance before her.

More lounging than sitting in a chair by a tester bed, was Lyndhurst. Sophie couldn't help but to stare through her lashes, astonished to see him, who was always so stiff and formal, in such a casual pose. Hateful cur! He looked as relaxed as she was tense.

He also didn't look so very big and ungainly, she reluctantly noted, not when he sat all loose-limbed like that. In fact, she found the sight of his long, athletic body rather . . . pleasing.

Pleasing? Ha! She must have breathed too much of the Pixie's cleaning solution to be having such outlandish delusions. Delusion or not, the Beast's form intrigued her, and for the first time in their acquaintance she actually observed it.

Up his sprawled legs her gaze moved, up over shapely calves and powerful thighs. So snug were the yellow trousers sheathing them, that they might as well have been bare for all the detail they revealed. Despite herself and her savage reluctance to do so, Sophie found herself admiring that detail.

Strong was the word that came to mind as she stared at those legs: strong, masculine, and perfect in their muscular contours. Rather than casting him in a more favorable light, having to add legs to his growing list of physical attributes merely deepened her dislike.

Wishing him to the devil and herself anywhere else, she attempted to look away. To her exasperation, her gaze defied her will and continued its greedy exploration.

Excellent thighs, yes. A grudging point for Lydia and her skills of observation. An impressive bulge—ur—uh—

Praying her face wasn't as red as it felt, she hastily dragged her attention upward. Hips and belly? She gritted her teeth. Lean and flat, respectively. Perhaps . . .

Her stare intensified as she tried to discern a telltale corset line beneath the thin trouser fabric. After a beat she heaved an inward sigh. Oh, blast! Another credit to his list.

Ah, well. Glumly she raised her gaze to his torso, hoping to see a lumpish waist or sunken chest. Another silent sigh. There was no mistaking it, not with the superb cut of his gold tailcoat, and blue-and-cream-striped waistcoat: His torso was as flawless as the lower half of his body. The wretch!

Beyond annoyance now, she eyed his slim waist, resenting the dramatic and undeniably attractive manner in which it curved into an impressive chest. Knave! As for those shoulders—

Wanting to scream her displeasure she forcefully ripped her gaze from his broad, obviously unpadded, shoulders up to Miss Stewart, who stood behind him.

So? Who cares if his body is perfect? she decided, adding a mental sniff for emphasis. A lot of good it does with that face.

Assuring herself that his ruined face indeed canceled out the splendor of his form, she focused on the lady's maid. As she did so, she became aware that the woman's lips moved and that she peered at her in the oddest of manners. Sophie didn't have to hear her words to know that Miss Stewart spoke to her.

Oh, curses! He'd done it again. Once more the Beast had confused her into embarrassing herself. Wanting nothing more than to wrap her hands around his despicable neck and wring it hard, she murmured, "I'm sorry. Pardon?" She could almost feel him smirk.

"Lady Beresford wishes you to move nearer, to here." Miss Stewart motioned to a place a scant yard from where the scourge of her existence sat.

Though she'd have preferred to remain where she was, Sophie saw no choice but to obey. Not unless, of course, she wished to voice her objections, which would no doubt amuse his odious lordship to no end. And since she'd rather be flayed alive than provide him with yet more entertainment—

She stiffened her spine and strolled forward. As she took her assigned place, she became aware of an all too familiar, all too disconcerting sensation of heat. He was staring. She could feel his eyes upon her, blazing through her flesh and wilting her composure.

For what seemed like forever she stood at attention before the trio, bedeviled by a most vexing urge to fidget. Just when she was certain she could bear the torment no longer, her ladyship coughed and said, "Yes, Miss Stewart. You are quite right. She is indeed a most genteel gel. Pretty, too. Isn't she pretty, Colin?"

Slow fire raked her length. "M-m-m. Yes. Very."

Another soft cough, then, "You are probably wondering why I requested this interview, Miss Barton."

"Yes, my lady." For the first time since entering the chamber, Sophie lifted her lashes and gazed at the marchioness. It was, after all, highly improper to look at an older lady of rank unless spoken to directly. Now that she did look at her, she saw where Lord Quentin got his breathtaking beauty.

Hers was a face of ageless perfection, exquisite in both

contour and feature. Like her son, her ladyship's eyes gleamed a rare shade of pansy, one startlingly more violet than blue. Her hair, though now peppered with gray, held vestiges of a mahogany legacy, the bright heritage of Quentin's much admired curls. After pausing a beat to envy the classic elegance of her nose, Sophie demurely glanced away.

In spite of her ghostly pallor, the Marchioness of Beresford was without a doubt the loveliest woman she'd ever seen. Had she been thirty years younger, Sophie would have thoroughly despised her. Since, however, such was not the case, she felt only wonder, wonder at how such a beauty could have borne a beast like Lyndhurst.

H-m-m. Could it be that she'd suffered a fright while carrying him? She'd heard that a fright could mark an unborn babe in a most hideous manner. She had just concluded that such was the case when her ladyship murmured, "Miss Stewart informs me that you are a gentlewoman, Miss Barton."

"Yes, my lady."

"Your father was a baron, I am told?"

"*Is* a baron," Sophie corrected her, growing uneasy at the line of her questioning. "As far as I know, he is still alive."

"He abandoned her after he lost their estate. Remember, my lady? I told you all about the poor girl's misfortune just this afternoon." A reminder from Miss Stewart.

A faint snort from Lyndhurst.

A choking cough from his mother. "So you did. A tragic tale, most"—another cough—"tragic indeed. A gentlewoman forced to work as a maid. How devastating it must be to suffer such a dreadful reduction in circumstances."

Another snort from the Beast, then, "Ah, well. Matters could be much worse, you know. She could have been unable to pay her debts and ended up in prison. Isn't that so, Miss . . . um . . . Barton?" The heat from his stare intensified. "How very fortunate for you to have escaped such a fate."

"Very fortunate indeed, my lord," she gritted out. Oh, how she longed to kick him!

The marchioness nodded weakly in agreement. "Yes, well, to get back to the purpose of this interview, I—" She broke off abruptly with a frightful gurgling noise, a noise that rapidly evolved into an alarming fit of choking.

Sophie stared at her in horror, at a loss as to what to do or say. Oh, dear! Oh, dear!

To her relief, Miss Stewart sprang into action. In a flash she had her mistress up off the pillows, now patting her back, now pouring some sort of liquid down her throat.

The Beast, she noted with shock, merely folded his arms and tapped his foot, clearly impatient with the whole episode. More disturbed than pleased to be doing so, she added cruel and callous to his list of faults.

When the seizure finally passed and Miss Stewart had laid her mistress back upon her pillows, the marchioness feebly rasped, "You tell her what we require, Claire. I haven't the strength." With that, her head rolled to the side and she lay still as death.

Sophie stared at her for several beats, trying to detect the rise and fall of her chest. When she discerned none, she looked at Miss Stewart in alarm. Miss Stewart returned her gaze with a gentle smile. "No need to look so distressed, dear. Her ladyship shall be fine. She's just exhausted from her illness."

Sophie smiled back in relief.

As for the Beast, he simply grunted as if exasperated by the lot of them.

Either deaf to or simply ignoring his lordship's disdainful noise, Miss Stewart turned her attention to straightening her mistress's covers. Gently tucking them beneath the woman's chin, she said, "What her ladyship wishes me to tell you, Sophie, is that you are to act as Miss Mayhew's abigail during her stay here."

"An abigail? Me?" Sophie pointed to herself, astounded.

Miss Stewart nodded. "With your education and breeding, you shall do quite splendidly."

"But I know nothing about being an abigail," she protested.

"Of course you do. You know what sort of gown is to be worn at what time of day, what hairstyles are fashionable and becoming, and I venture to say, how to apply rouge and such should it be required. Having been raised and educated as you were, you are also qualified to guide the girl in matters of deportment." The woman smiled and nodded. "So you see, you shall be perfect for the post."

Sophie eyed her dubiously, trying to recall her own abigail and her duties. H-m-m. From what she remembered, the woman was nothing more than a glorified nanny with fine manners and a superior eye for fashion. Still doubtful, she murmured, "Is that truly all that is required of me?"

Lyndhurst chuckled. "That and a good hand with a scrub brush."

"Colin!" Her ladyship's eyes popped open, and she glared at him with a vigor surprising for one so dreadfully ill.

He chuckled again. "You're right, Mother. She needs a firm knowledge of delousing as well."

The marchioness scowled and raised her head.

Miss Stewart pushed it back down again. "Your health, my lady. Please do remember your health." After shooting Lyndhurst an admonishing look, she returned her attention to Sophie. "Miss Mayhew requires a bit of guidance in grooming. Just the tiniest bit, mind you. Nothing that you're not equal to, I assure you."

"That must be a relief, seeing as how you have but the tiniest bit of skill, eh, Miss . . . Barton?" the Beast purred, his voice too low for anyone save Sophie to hear.

She gritted her teeth against the tart retort on her tongue. O-o-o! The wretch! She'd show him skill. She'd show him so damn much skill that he'd gag and hopefully die on his disappointment.

Parting her lips into a rather overly toothy smile, she said, "Miss Stewart, you may tell her ladyship that I shall be honored to accept the position."

Chapter 13

The Beast wasn't jesting when he said that she'd need a good hand with a scrub brush and a firm knowledge of delousing. Miss Mayhew was beyond filthy, a veritable walking paradise for hair and body vermin. Why, she'd seen gutter water cleaner than that in the tub following the first of the girl's three successive baths.

Grimacing at the remembrance of that water, brown as muck and afloat with dead lice, Sophie stretched her arm farther from her body, holding her charge's gown as far from her as possible. Like Miss Mayhew's person, it, too, crawled with heaven only knew what.

Wondering how the girl could live with herself, she started up the dark back steps, lifting her candle aloft to light her ascent. But stand herself Miss Mayhew did, and quite cheerfully at that. Indeed, she was actually pleased with the way she smelled, proudly referring to her foul odor as "angling aroma."

Angling aroma, she had stammered out, came from the natural body oil that only one lucky woman out of a million was able to secrete. That oil, when allowed to accumulate for several months, created a scent much like that excreted by mating female fish, thus acting as a powerful aphrodisiac on the males.

According to her aroma blessed charge, male fish, sturgeon and salmon in particular, found her fragrance so enticing that they swam up to the shore and practically hurled themselves at her.

Sophie sighed. Why the viscount allowed his daughter to go about as she did, she couldn't imagine. It wasn't as if he himself were dirty, or that he'd failed to notice her poor hygiene. By the girl's own admission he'd once mistaken her odor for that of a creel full of fish . . . a creel he'd misplaced three days earlier.

Shaking her head in bemusement, she climbed the last three steps to the attic. Could it be that he, like the fish, preferred the reek of "angling aroma" to sweet, ladylike scents like French Violet or Heliotrope?

Unable to believe that anyone, even the rattle-pate viscount, could have such a loathsome predilection, Sophie made her way down the corridor toward the room she shared with Pansy. Were it not for her candle and the light seeping from beneath the closed doors on either side, the hallway would have been blacker than oven soot.

As she walked through the gold-hazed murk, Sophie gave thanks for Mrs. Pixton and her competence. Not only had she concocted a most effective delouser, she had cunningly persuaded the girl to part with her precious "angling aroma," thus allowing for its use.

Unsporting, the Pixie had pronounced Miss Mayhew's odorous fishing advantage. It was extremely unsporting not to mention out-and-out fraud to call herself an angler using such unqualified methods. A true angler depended only on her skill with rod and tackle to hook her catch. Everyone knew it was so. When the housekeeper then slyly expressed doubts that Miss Mayhew possessed such skill, the girl bit at the bait and took the challenge.

From then on Sophie's abigail duties went smoothly enough. Indeed, not only did the girl not object to being bathed thrice, she insisted on adding carnation oil to the final rinse water.

Carnation, she stuttered in a most affronted tone, was a natural fish repellent. By dousing herself with it she put herself at a severe disadvantage, which would serve to prove her angling skills all the more. As Sophie tucked her into bed, vermin-free and smelling like spring, the girl had sleepily vowed to empty the stream of trout on the morrow.

That left but one obstacle to proving her own compe-

tence to the Beast—well, two really, but she'd think of
a way to part Miss Mayhew from her lucky fishing bonnet later—that obstacle was how to rid the girl's only
decent gown of crawlers in time for church.

Washing it, of course, was out of the question. It
would never dry by morning. And since neither she, her
ladyship, nor Miss Stewart were as petite as her charge,
her chances of finding something else for her to wear
were zero to none. That left only one hope: Pansy.

Praying that her roommate wasn't with her suitor and
that her laundry-maid experience included dealing with
a same such problem, Sophie practically flew the rest of
the distance to their chamber. To her considerable relief,
light spilled from beneath their door.

"Pansy. Thank goodness," she exclaimed, barging into
the room.

Pansy, who sat before the shelf that served as their
dressing table, turned from the age-mottled mirror patting the most awful bonnet she'd ever seen. "Well?
Whadda you think?" she chirped, visibly pleased with
the monstrosity.

Sophie eyed the mishmash of flowers, ribbons, and
bedraggled feathers, trying to think of a tactful response.
"Uh . . . with all those colors, I . . . um . . . daresay that
you shall be able to wear it with just about anything. Is
it new?"

The laundress nodded, a move that sent a haphazardly
attached hyacinth tumbling down her back. "It's new to
me, but it ain't exac'ly *new* new, if you get my meanin'."

Sophie didn't get her meaning having worn only *new*
new bonnets. When she said as much, the maid explained, "Well, it's like this: Miss Stewart give me the
fuss 'n flowers fer trimmin', and I found the frame in
the dustbin. I put 'em ta'gather to make this." She indicated the monstrosity. "Been workin' on it fer two
weeks." Grinning as if it were a creation from *La Belle
Assemblèe,* she leaned down and retrieved the fallen
flower. As she did so, two peach roses and a mangled-
looked poppy-anemone fell off.

"Oh, gom!" she muttered, her brown eyes crossing to
watch a feather flutter past her nose. "If this keeps up,

it ain't gonna 'ave a bloom or tribble left fer church."
The instant the words left her mouth, four more
"blooms and tribbles" showered forth.

Sophie didn't miss the dismay on Pansy's face, or the
dejected droop of her shoulders as she removed and examined her molting masterpiece. As she gingerly turned
it over to inspect her stitching, three of her namesake
flowers and a rumpled loop of orange ribbon pulled
away from the pink chip frame.

For a long moment the maid scowled at where the
clump of trim dangled from a thread, then her face
crumpled and she burst into tears. "O-o-oh! 'ateful old
thing! Whadda I want with such a turdy bit o' trash
anyhow? Faw!" Enraged by disappointment, she hurled
the hat to the floor.

Not certain what to do or say, Sophie simply stood
there, awkwardly watching as the girl buried her face in
her hands and wept in earnest. In truth, she'd never seen
anyone cry like that before, not so openly or with such
unbridled anguish. It was, after all, the very height of
vulgarity to demonstrate one's distress in company—
well, beyond a discreet, but attractively shed tear or two,
that is. One most certainly did not wail and snivel, and
make an altogether disagreeable scene.

Oddly enough, she felt neither disdain or offense at
the girl's shameful display, though she knew she should.
What she felt was . . . well, she had no name for the
sensation. All she knew was that she had a most curious
urge to go to the girl and comfort her. It was almost as
if she actually—cared—about Pansy.

Sophie frowned at the preposterous notion. That she
should notice, much less care about, the feelings, of an
inferior was shocking to the extreme. Yet, shocking or
not, there was no other explanation for what she felt.

Not certain what to make of her startling feelings, or
what to do about them, Sophie uncomfortably turned
away and wandered to the chipped green chair by the
bed. After blowing out her candle and setting it aside,
she draped Miss Mayhew's dress over the chair back,
trying to look busy as she decided what to do.

Oh, but she felt helpless. And frustrated . . . so very

frustrated by her ignorance of how to handle the situation. Should she simply ignore Pansy's tears and act as if nothing were amiss? Or should she follow her instinct and offer solace? And if she did opt for the latter, how did one go about consoling a servant?

As she wrestled with the dilemma, growing more uncertain by the second, Pansy heaved a long, ragged sigh and whispered, "I did so wanna look special pretty fer Ezra tomorrow. 'E's to meet me at church and take me walkin' after." Looking as glum as a cleric at a funeral, she leaned over and retrieved her castaway bonnet.

Ah! Ezra Shipley. But of course. Sophie smiled with sudden inspiration. If anything could make Pansy smile, it was prattling about her suitor. Determined to provoke the girl to do just that, she said in a teasing voice. "So, I'm finally going to meet your dashing farmer, am I?"

When Pansy remained mute, staring at the bonnet as if it were the world and she'd just lost it, Sophie began to wonder if there was more to her doldrums than a few fallen flowers. Unable to imagine what sort of troubles might plague a laundress, yet compelled to find out, she went to the girl and knelt beside her three-legged stool. Trying to see her averted face, she murmured, "Is something wrong, Pansy? Something besides your bonnet, I mean?"

So silent and motionless did the maid remain, that for a moment she thought she hadn't heard her. She was about to repeat her question when Pansy turned her head and met her gaze. To Sophie's dismay tears seeped from her red eyes and streaked her pale, freckled cheeks.

Strangely distressed by the sight of those tears, she clutched at the girl's thin arm, begging, "Oh, Pansy. Don't cry. Please don't cry. Whatever is wrong can't be so very awful as all that. Indeed, I doubt it's anything we can't set right if we put our heads together and think."

Pansy's damp eyes widened as if in surprise. "You'd do that? Put yer 'ead with mine and 'elp me?"

She smiled and nodded. "Of course. Didn't I just say so?"

Her response prompted a faint smile in return. "Yer a real chum. Sophie Barton."

It was Sophie's turn to look surprised. Chum? Her? She gazed at her companion's plain, speckled face, utterly confounded. Never once had she stopped to consider the nature of her relationship with Pansy. In truth, she was unaware that they even had one. The girl was simply, well—there—always talking and smiling, always friendly and ready to lend a helping hand to anyone in need.

A warm, cozy glow spread through her at the thought of that hand and all the times it had come to her aid. Pansy was a comfort. Yes, that's what she was, a comfort. Why, just knowing she was there and could be depended upon in times of trouble never failed to fill her with a most soothing sense of security. Indeed, now that she thought about it, she realized that she'd come to view the girl as a guardian angel of sorts.

No sooner had that startling revelation dawned than she was struck by its irony. How singular that she, the granddaughter of an earl, should regard a laundress as her guardian angel. How very shocking that she actually valued her as thus.

Yet value her she did, and for the first time since arriving at Hawksbury, Sophie considered her not Pansy the laundress, but Pansy the person. Someone who she discovered was as admirable as she was generous; someone who she was proud to call friend.

Suddenly shy, Sophie dropped her gaze from her companion's face to stare unseeing at the bonnet in her hands.

Despite her coarse speech, rough manners, and humble station, Pansy was one of the noblest people she'd ever met. One of the most considerate, too. And loyal. And trustworthy. Oh, and she mustn't forget to add astoundingly perceptive and sensitive to others' feelings also.

By the time Sophie had recorded and tallied those, and all the maid's other excellent assets as well, she had to admit that they totaled a most worthy person—a person far worthier than herself and her tonnish acquaintances.

Feeling wonderfully blessed to have been gifted with such a friend, Sophie gave Pansy a quick hug. "Thank you," she whispered.

"Huh?" Pansy frowned, visibly puzzled by both her words and action. "Wot are you thankin' me fer?"

"For calling me your chum, that's what. I'm honored you think me worthy of your friendship."

The other girl eyed her suspiciously. "You been scrubbin' with the Pixie's special soap again?"

Sophie shook her head, laughing at the question. "No, no. Nothing like that. It's just that I suddenly realized what you mean to me and how glad I am that we're friends."

"I'm happy, too, but—gom! Why'd someone like you be 'onored to be chums with the likes o' me? Yer quality while I'm—"

"Kind, generous, and thoughtful, exactly the sort of person everyone wishes for in a friend," she interjected.

When the girl merely gaped at her, clearly at a loss as to what to make of her words, she elaborated. "We're really not so very different, Pansy. Well, except for that you're much nicer than I." She paused to grin. "Anyway, what I'm trying to say is that the way we look and speak, and the station to which we were born have nothing whatsoever to do with who we are. Beneath my fine ways and your freckles, we're much the same. Just two woman struggling to make our way in the world and hoping to find a bit of happiness."

Pansy considered the concept, her forehead creasing in her concentration. At length she nodded. "I surpose wot you says makes some sense, tho' I still can't 'elp thinkin' that yer better fer talkin' like you do and knowin' the fancy stuff you know."

"And I can't help thinking that you're better for being so good and for knowing ever so many sensible things," Sophie countered, and she meant it.

Pansy sighed, her face growing pensive as she gazed down at her disastrous bonnet. "If I knew 'bout sensible stuff, I'd know about makin' bonnets proper."

"And since when, pray tell, is bonnet making considered sensible stuff?" When her friend merely gazed at her, Sophie grinned and stated, "Bonnets, especially lavishly trimmed affairs like this, most definitely fall into the realm of fancy stuff. That means that fashioning them is more suited to my skills than yours. And since we've agreed to share our heads, well, then it falls to me to fashion this one." Nodding to further reinforce her words, Sophie lifted the forlorn hat from Pansy's hands and examined it.

After several moments, during which she poked and prodded it, she looked up and concluded, "With a bit of work, I shall be able to make this into something quite becoming and elegant."

Pansy's face brightened. "Then, I'll 'ave a new bonnet for church tomorrow?"

"Oh, no. It shall take me at least a week to finish it."

"Oh." The girl looked as disappointed as if she'd declared the hat hopeless.

For a long moment Sophie thoughtfully studied her crestfallen face, then set the bonnet aside. Taking both her friend's hands in hers, she quietly inquired, "Is tomorrow in some way special?"

Pansy nodded. "Ezra's give me reason to believe that he'll be askin' me to marry 'im tomorrow. O' course, we can't get married fer at least two years, not till 'e can afford to rent 'is own farm."

"But you shall be engaged, and that is just as important," Sophie declared, genuinely thrilled for her friend. "How very wonderful. I'm so happy for you."

The girl looked anything but happy for herself. "It is 'portant, the most 'portant day o' my life, well, exceptin' my weddin' day, o' course. That's why I 'ad my 'eart set on 'avin' a fine new bonnet. I wanted to look as special as the day."

Sophie returned her woeful gaze for a beat, then grinned. "You, Miss Pansy Blum, shall have a fine new bonnet."

"But—"

"Just you wait and see. You shall look so wonderfully special tomorrow that your Mr. Shipley will have trouble choking his proposal past his admiration for you." Feeling happier than she had in a great while, Sophie waltzed to the trunk at the end of their bed and retrieved her valise.

Ready to burst with excitement, she extracted her best bonnet and presented it with a flourish.

"Oh! Oh!" Pansy gasped, rushing forward for a closer look. "Oh!" She skidded to a stop next to Sophie, flapping her hands in excitement as she peered at the hat. "Oh! I ain't nivver seen nothing so fine in all my life."

Sophie gazed at the modish creation, nodding her agreement. Fashioned of sapphire velvet and opulently trimmed with white lace frills, pale blue satin pleats, and a dramatic sweep of plumes, it was beyond exquisite. A millinery masterpiece. True, one of the plumes was a bit bent from being hit by the wagon, but aside from that it was as pristine as the day she'd removed it from its box.

Remembering all the envious glances cast its way during the Season, she held it out to Pansy. "You shall look like a princess in this. I can't wait to see your Mr. Shipley's face when he sees you." When the girl made no move to take it, she glanced up and frowned. "You don't like it?"

Pansy shook her head over and over again, her gaze riveted to the bonnet. "Like it? Oh, law'! It's the purtiest thing I ever seen. But"—she looked up, her expression one of wistful uncertainty—"you sure you want me to wear it? It must've cost a fortune."

Sophie laughed and dropped it atop the girl's head. "Yes, I'm sure. But only if you promise to wear the complimenting shawl." Laughing again, this time at her friend's look of slack-jaw ecstasy, she fished a richly embroidered length of blue cashmere from the valise and draped it over her companion's shoulders.

For a long moment the girl remained motionless, staring at the wrap as if mesmerized, then she uttered a hoarse cry and flew to the mirror. Turning this way and that, she examined herself from all angles. "Gom! Oh, gom!" she babbled over and over again.

Her heart gladdening at her friend's delight, Sophie went to join her in admiring her reflection. Reaching over to smooth one of the plumes, she murmured, "You look radiant, Pansy. The very picture of a bride-to-be." And she did. With her eyes glowing like topaz stars and her cheeks pink with excitement, the little laundry maid was nothing short of beautiful.

"Oh, Sophie!" Pansy fiercely embraced her. " 'Ow can I ever thank you? Nobody nivver done nothing like this fer me before."

Sophie gave her a fond squeeze in return. "No thanks are necessary. I'm thrilled I could help."

"Well, if I can ever 'elp you with anything—anything a-tall!—yer to ask me. Ye 'ear? You ask."

"You've already helped me more than I can ever repay."

Pansy shot her a mulish look. "I ain't done much. Not enough fer this."

Though she disagreed, Sophie could see that the girl was set on returning the favor, so she nodded. "All right, then. I shall let you know the second I need—" She broke off, remembering Miss Mayhew's gown. "Come to think of it, I do need your help." Praying that the maid could indeed aid her, she fetched the gown and explained her problem.

"Got a few bosom friends, 'as she?" Pansy murmured, taking the primrose and azure garment from her.

Sophie watched anxiously as she turned it inside out and examined it. "Is there anything we can do to get rid of them?"

"Well, washin' 'd be best," the girl admitted, squinting at a shoulder seam. "But seein' as 'ow we ain't got time fer that, I suppose we'll jist 'ave to pop 'em."

"Pop them?" she echoed, shuddering at the thought catching and squashing each louse.

Pansy giggled, clearly amused by her expression. "It ain't a-tall like it sounds. You pop 'em with 'eat."

"Heat? And, er, how do you do that?" she inquired, wishing it weren't necessary to ask.

"Easy as blowin' yer nose. You jist take a lit candle and run it close to the fabric. The 'eat makes the crums pop." She grinned and made a noise to simulate the sound. "O' course you gotta take care not to scorch the dress, 'specially 'round the seams. Scorch 'em even the wee-est bit, and they'll give way. Saw it 'appen to our neighbor, Mrs. Wormby. Sleeve fell right off 'er dress while she were wearin' it."

By now she'd finished scrutinizing the garment. "This ain't too bad. There's no spots or stains, and the crums ain't as thick as they could be. My guess is that Miss Mayhew ain't worn it more'n once. It'll look good 'nough when I'm done poppin' it."

Though Sophie was sorely tempted to let Pansy "pop" the gown for her, she couldn't. Not if she was to prove the Beast wrong. Knowing Lord Hateful and his infuriating way of marking her every move, he'd somehow find out the instant she shirked her duty. Not about to give him yet another reason to gloat, she muttered, "Just show me how it's done, and I'll do it myself."

"But I want to do it fer you, to 'elp you like you 'elped me," Pansy protested.

She forced herself to smile, though doing so proved a herculean effort. "Don't you see? You shall be helping me by teaching me one of your sensible skills. In order for me to learn it correctly, I must practice. And who knows when I shall ever get another chance to 'pop crums'?"

Chapter 14

Sophie had done an excellent job, Nicholas reluctantly allowed, glancing at the girl on his arm. Indeed, so improved were both her fragrance and appearance, that he might not have recognized Miss Mayhew at all had it not been for the noise she'd emitted when she'd walked down the stairs.

Cringing at the memory of that braying giggle, Nicholas wished that Sophie were as adept at voice instruction as she was at primping. Miss Mayhew's dreadful vocalization, not to mention her appalling choice of conversation, quite spoiled the effect of her improved appearance.

Oh, well. He sighed, trying to smile at his companion's lively but nauseating discourse on fish gutting. He supposed there was only so much a person could do to improve another, especially when allowed but a few hours to work their magic. And in all fairness, he must concede that Sophie had done more with the girl in those few hours than he'd have believed possible had she had a month.

Filled with sudden, grudging respect for his nemesis, Nicholas guided Miss Mayhew through the ancient lych-gate and down the churchyard path. As he led her through the forest of tombstones, he found himself admiring the splendid results of Sophie's endeavor.

Gone was the girl's smelly, tattered gown, deposed for a clean, carnation-scented one in becoming shades of yellow and blue. Her flaxen hair, which he'd thought impossible, had been washed and coiled and coaxed about her face in a shimmering frame of curls. As he gazed at that face, now so creamy and fine, he silently applauded Sophie's skill with powder and paint. Why, to look at Miss Mayhew's complexion one would never suspect her fondness for the sun. His respect rose another notch at that feat alone.

Nodding and smiling at the girl's choice of gutting knives, Nicholas focused on the chip bonnet atop her head. It belonged to Sophie. He'd recognized the yellow and white confection the instant he saw it, recalling as clearly as if it were yesterday how lovely she'd looked in it at Lady Sainsberry's picnic.

For a long moment he stared at the hat, haunted by the memory of that day. Again, he heard the music of Sophie's laughter, so sweet and seductive; again, he saw the radiance of her smile and felt the warmth of her questing hands when she caught him in a game of blindman's buff.

Again, he experienced the desperate yearning to make her his.

Vexed and frustrated, Nicholas ripped his gaze away, cursing his stubborn desire. What the hell was he doing, wallowing so in such memories? He despised the chit, damn it. How many times must he remind himself of that fact? He despised her with a vehemence that should render all thought and memory of her repugnant.

Hating himself for his weakness, he turned his attention to the girl on his arm, determined to lose himself in her stammering conversation. After several moments of listening, he deduced that she spoke of the production of silk fishing lines.

"Then you s-s-soak the w-worms in p-pickle of vinegar and w-w-water for s-several h-h-hours," she explained, visibly enamored by her topic. "After you take them out, you h-hold them at each end and t-tear them in h-h-half." She pantomimed a vicious ripping action. "You'll s-see two s-s-silk s-sacs inside. P-pull them out and s-s-stretch them until they're long enough for a line."

As she launched into a starry-eyed narrative on the drying and preparation of the rendered fibers, he was abruptly distracted by the sound of an all-too-familiar laugh. Despite his efforts to ignore it and the woman who'd issued it, he found himself stealing a peek over his shoulder.

Like the good abigail she'd proved to be, Sophie walked several paces behind her charge. Unlike most abigails, however, she was squired by two visibly infatuated footmen. Strangely disturbed by the scene, he sought to place her companions, his eyes narrowing as he watched them vie for her favor.

That was Charles, the second footman, on her right, and . . . Terence? Yes, Terence, the fourth footman at her left. His eyes narrowed a fraction more as he noted the way they looked at her.

There was something about Charles's covetous gaze and Terence's love-struck gape that set his teeth on edge. His eyes little more than slits now, he turned his attention to the object of their ogling. Like Miss Mayhew's bonnet, he at once placed her fetching gown. She'd worn it the first time he'd taken her walking in the park. As she had then, she looked ravishing in it now. And again he was captivated, utterly and blissfully captivated.

Her skin blushed like a peach against the gown's lush coral hue; a ripe, succulent peach that tempted the lips and promised heaven in every taste. As for its cut and fit . . . ah! Perfection! Absolute perfection in how it cleverly revealed nothing and hinted at everything: long, shapely legs . . . feminine hips . . . a slender torso . . . and full, succulent . . .

Nicholas blinked, appalled to find himself gaping at Sophie's breasts. Mortified, he tore his gaze away and returned it to his companion, praying that she hadn't noticed his shameful faux pas.

She hadn't. Miss Mayhew was squinting in the opposite direction, waving her arm like a drunk hailing a cab.

Thankful for that small mercy, he followed the direction of her wildly flapping arm. On the pleasant tree-strewn green to the right of the imposing medieval church, stood his father, the viscount, and several of the more prominent members of the local gentry. His father was signaling him to escort Miss Mayhew over. Grateful for the diversion, he promptly did as directed.

As the marquess introduced the girl about, speaking of her in the most glowing and exaggerated of terms, Nicholas noticed that three footmen and a valet from a neighboring house had joined Charles and Terence in wooing Sophie. As for Sophie, she held court beneath a tree several yards away, clearly enjoying their attention.

And why not? he brooded, his mood darkening. All six men had the pretty, unblemished sort of faces she favored. To his supreme discomfort he was filled with a sudden, irrational urge to pummel those faces and mar their pleasing perfection. Especially that of Charles Dibbs. The way the footman groped Sophie's arm and stared at her breasts . . .

His hands balled into fists. If rumors were true, and he was certain they were, the knave had fathered eleven of the score of by-blows running about the village. That he clearly intended Sophie to round it to an even dozen made it all the harder for him to restrain his violence.

Exactly why he cared what she did, and with whom, he didn't know. Indeed, the notion of the high-and-mighty Miss Barrington unwed and carrying a footman's babe should amuse him to no end.

But he wasn't amused, not in the least. Not when he thought of the cur kneeling between her thighs and sharing her first rapture. That pleasure should have been his, blast it! He'd earned it. He'd wooed and courted her, he'd offered her marriage. And he'd be damned if he'd stand by and let that scoundrel take what he'd failed to win.

As he glared at the bastard, wishing that looks could kill, the "Sophie Adoration Society" was approached by a pretty girl whom he instantly recognized as Fancy, the chambermaid. By the scowl on her face, she looked primed to commit murder.

"Charles Dibbs!" she bellowed, stopping just outside the group.

The footman looked up from Sophie, annoyance written on every line of his face. "What do you want, Fancy?" he growled.

"Whadda I want? Whadda I want!" She crossed her arms across her chest, her foot tapping furiously as she fixed him with a blistering glare. "What I want is to know why you dinna walk me to church like you promised. I waited and waited in the bleedin' garden, just like you said, and you nivver came."

He eyed her coldly for several beats, then shrugged one shoulder. "I forgot." Shrugging again, he shifted his attention back to Sophie, dismissing the episode as too insignificant to warrant either explanation or apology.

Fancy, however, wasn't about to be put off so easily. Expelling a crude noise of disbelief, she hissed, "Seems to be that you're always *forgittin'* me these days. You talk all lovey-like, beggin' me to meet you and makin' all sorts of promises if I do, then you go sniffin' after her"—she jabbed her finger at Sophie—"and forgit to come. The only time you pay me any mind a-tall anymore is when you want somethin' she ain't likely to give you."

Charles heaved a long-suffering sigh and rolled his eyes, as if enduring the greatest of trials. Then he slanted his companions a smug, sidelong glance, and smirked. Three of the four footmen guffawed and clapped his back, enjoying his mute mockery of Fancy and her complaint. The remaining footman, Terence, and the valet exchanged frowns, while Sophie stared at him as if he'd just sprouted horns.

Despite his reluctance to do so, Nicholas couldn't help wonder at her expression. Could it be that she'd already succumbed to the bastard's charms and was distressed to discover that he trifled with another? He was certain that such was the case in the next instant when she breathlessly exclaimed, "Oh, Charles. How could you toy so with Fancy's affections?"

The footman waved aside her protest with an impatient flick of his wrist. "I did no such thing. We had a brief dalliance, that is all. I can assure you that it meant nothing whatsoever."

Fancy squawked, visibly outraged.

He spared her his regard long enough to rake her length, then looked back at Sophie, adding, "In truth, my dear Miss Barton, it meant less than nothing. Females of her ilk throw themselves at me all the time. I simply took what she offered and moved on when I grew bored."

Sophie gasped at his admission.

Fancy squawked again. "It weren't like that a-tall, and you know it weren't," she shrieked, stalking toward him. The wall of uneasy-looking footmen parted at her approach. "I nivver throwed myself at you. Nivver! I were a good girl when I came to Hawksbury. It were you that came pantin' after me, moanin' hows you loved me and promisin' to marry me if I gave you what you wanted."

"Really, Fancy." Charles made a *tsk*ing sound. "Why would I bother chasing after you when I have so many women clamoring for my attention?"

" 'Cuz I weren't a piece of stuff, that's why. You said so yourself." She came to a stop in front of him, her gaze spitting venom as she glared at him. "You said you loved me 'cuz I were a good girl, and wheedled me into givin' you what I were savin' for my husband. You said you'd marry me if I let you have it."

He snorted. "Why in blazes would I marry the likes of you? I told you that I plan to buy a commission in the army someday, and elevate my station to that of gentleman."

Fancy sniffed. "So? I don't see what that's got to do with us gittin' married."

He eyed her with open contempt. "Then, you are stupider than I thought." Ignoring her indignant squeal, he ruthlessly continued, "As a gentleman, I shall be afforded opportunities to make my fortune, which I, of course, fully intend to take. Once I am wealthy, I will naturally want to enter society. In order to do so, I shall require a refined and genteel wife"—he cast a meaningful glance at Sophie—"preferably one of noble birth. You, Fancy Jenkins, are a slattern and thus do not meet my requirements."

Rather than look relieved by the bastard's hint at a proposal, Sophie appeared stunned, and not with delight. Nicholas found her reaction baffling to the extreme. If she had feelings for Charles, as he suspected, she should be pleased to learn of his honorable intentions. True, he was only a footman, but ruined as she was, his offer was the best she could expect. Surely the chit knew that.

He shrugged. Oh, well. Whatever it was that disturbed her, it couldn't be the man's churlish treatment of Fancy. Not after the vicious manner in which she'd spurned him. If anything, Charles's coldhearted conduct should show her how eminently suited they were to each other. Why—

"Colin?" A gloved hand waved before his eyes.

Nicholas blinked twice, then looked at his father, who shook his head. "Best to let the servants sort things out among themselves. Isn't that so?" The marquess peered at his companions for confirmation, who instantly dipped their heads and gave it.

Sir John Gibbes, an elderly knight, continued bobbing his bald head like a puppet with a loose string. "Right you are, Beresford. Bad thing to meddle in the affairs of inferiors. Very bad indeed. Causes resentment."

"And problems," interjected Sir Basil Coutts, a crusty baronet of at least eighty. "Makes them act above themselves to pay them personal notice."

"B-besides, s-s-servants don't know anything ab-b-out fishing," Miss Mayhew chimed in.

Before Nicholas could figure out exactly what fishing had to do with settling quarrels, the church bells rang, summoning the milling congregation to worship.

His father offered Miss Mayhew his arm. "May I have the pleasure, my dear?" She brayed a grating response and accepted. Giving her small hand a fatherly pat, he nodded to his companions and inquired, "Shall we proceed, gentlemen?" to which they again dipped their heads to the affirmative.

All except for Nicholas, that is. He couldn't help stealing another peek at the group beneath the tree. As he did so, he saw Fancy make what he recognized as an ancient curse sign at Charles, and heard her spit, "Quimsticker! I hope you cop a dose of dripsy-stick and piss fire." Despite the fury of both her words and tone, he heard heartbreak in her voice.

As she turned on her heels, Charles grabbed her arm

and jerked her back around. His handsome face ugly with rage, he viciously cuffed her across the cheek. "Don't you ever speak to me like that again, you slut. Do you hear me? Never!" Slapping her again, he hurled her to the ground.

Nicholas growled and started toward them, enraged beyond all reason by the scene. Letting the servants sort things out among themselves was one thing; standing by while a footman abused a chambermaid half his size was quite another.

"Lyndhurst." Someone latched onto his arm, halting him.

He shot that someone an impatient look. It was Sir John Gibbes who frowned and shook his head. "Trouble, boy. You're asking for nothing but trouble."

"I'll chance it," he bit out, pulling his arm free. Without sparing the old knight so much as a parting nod, he marched over to the embattled servants. As he did so, he saw that Terence stood toe-to-toe with Charles, his hands clenched into fists and his youthful face contorted with wrath. From what he could discern from their hissing exchange, the younger man was intent on defending Fancy's honor.

Nicholas admired Terence's bravado, for despite his manly height, he was little more than a boy, a fact readily evidenced by his smooth cheeks and spindly build. That he would champion the maid against the physically mature Charles displayed a gallantry that was as laudable as it was foolhardy.

Coming to a stop opposite the squared-off pair, he barked, "Charles! Terence!"

Both men swung around at the sound of his voice and instantly snapped to attention. Murmuring, "My lord," in unison, they sketched stiff bows. The other footmen and valet hastily followed suit, while Sophie gaped at Fancy, who lay weeping on the ground.

Firmly controlling his urge to throttle Charles, Nicholas snapped his fingers at the neighboring servants. Accepting the gesture as the dismissal it was, they scampered off toward the church, visibly relieved to be excused from the brewing conflict.

When they were well out of earshot, Nicholas fixed the object of his ire with his implacable gaze, and ground out, "I am, by all accounts, considered a tolerant man. Like all men, however, there are limits to my forbearance. You, Charles, have exceeded those limits with your ungentlemanly conduct."

"Ungentlemanly conduct?" Charles echoed, visibly taken aback. "Excuse me, my lord. But I don't know what you mean."

That the man obviously thought it acceptable to abuse women incensed Nicholas almost to the point of eruption. Shaking from the effort it took to contain his fury, he growled, "Then, listen and know, Mr. Dibbs: I cannot and will not suffer the presence of a man disposed toward striking women. Because you have proved yourself to be such a man, I hereby dismiss you from your duties. You shall return to Hawksbury this instant and pack your bags. I want you gone before I return from church."

It took several moments for Charles to fully absorb the impact of his words. When he did, his eyes narrowed and he countered, "Begging your pardon, my lord. But I am in your father's employ, not yours. It is he, not you, who must determine whether or not I am to be sacked." By his tone, it was clear that he expected a different ruling from the marquess.

Nicholas regarded him coolly for several moments, then gave a brusque nod. "As you wish. We shall take the matter up with my father after church."

The triumph in the footman's eyes was unmistakable. Dipping his head in victorious assent, he murmured, "Thank you, my lord. If there is nothing else you require, I would like to be excused."

"But of course."

The man sketched a formal bow, then started to saunter off. He'd taken only a few steps when Nicholas stopped him. "Charles?"

The footman paused, but didn't turn to face him. "My lord?"

"Before you go, I feel it only fair to warn you of my father's harsh views on striking women."

This time Charles did turn, a smug smile tugging at his lips. "Thank you, my lord. But I am certain his views will soften once he hears of Fancy's insolence. Your father is a reasonable man."

Nicholas returned his smile in kind, ignoring the barbed insinuation of his last remark. "I am glad you find him so, though I doubt the servant he dismissed last year for a similar offense would agree."

The footman shrugged. "I am certain that he will rule differently after hearing my defense. If he doesn't"—another shrug—"what will I have lost in trying?"

"Perhaps your livelihood."

Yet another shrug. "I shall find another place easily enough."

"I said livelihood, not place." Nicholas's smile broadened a fraction. "You see, Charles, not only did my father dismiss the servant, he saw him shunned from every respectable house in England. Last I heard the poor bastard was employed at one of the less—*ahem!*— savory taverns near the docks. They say he's taken to drink to ease the misery of his lot."

Charles paled a shade at his words, but otherwise showed no outward sign of alarm. It was while viewing his military-perfect stoicism that Nicholas hit upon a fitting punishment for his crime. Resisting his impulse to grin, he added, "I want you to know that while I agree with the man's dismissal, I do not believe that he deserved to be ruined."

The footman stared at him, momentarily speechless. Then he cleared his throat and croaked, "Are you saying that my references will remain unsullied if I accept your dismissal here and now?" His hoarse voice held a note of hope.

"I said that the man was undeserving of ruin, not that he should have been allowed to remain in service."

Charles frowned. "What you're saying makes no sense. A servant banned from service has no livelihood, and thus faces sure ruin."

"There are other livelihoods, you know."

"And exactly which one of them would you suggest I pursue? My only experience is in service."

"I was thinking of one that would keep you away from women and hopefully cure your unfortunate tendency to strike them."

The other man eyed him suspiciously. "You aren't suggesting that I be shipped off to Italy or Spain to become a monk, are you?"

Nicholas laughed aloud, amused by the question. "No. Somehow, I can't quite imagine you a monk." He shook his head at the ludicrous picture of the rakish footman in rough robes with tonsured hair. "No. I was thinking more along the lines of the military."

"The . . . military?" Charles more choked than uttered the words.

"The military," he confirmed. "It so happens that I have a powerful friend in the army who owes me a rather large favor. What I propose to do is to call that favor due by asking him to grant you a commission. I shall, of course, inform him of your boorish conduct and charge him with the duty of mending your ways."

As he expected, the footman was thrilled beyond ecstasy by his proposal. "My lord! Why, this is more than I—"

Nicholas cut him off with an abrupt hand motion. "I must warn you that your rank will not be high, an ensign at best. I shall also require you to sign a contract promising to stay in the military for not less than five years. After that time you may either remain in the army or sell the commission for your own profit. It matters not to me what you do. If, however, you leave before the end of the fifth year, the rights to the commission shall revert to me, and you must go about life as best you can."

"Oh! My lord, this is just too wonderful—"

Again, he cut him off. "Do we have a bargain?"

"Yes . . . yes! And thank you, my lord. Thank you! I shall be forever in your debt."

"Fine. Then, go pack your bags. I shall have the papers drawn up immediately so that you may leave for London this evening." He didn't have to give the command twice. "Young fool," he muttered, watching the footman disappear among the tombstones. "I'd bet my

title that he won't be smiling after a week under El-
lum's command."

"Pardon, my lord?" This was from Terence.

Nicholas slanted him a wry look. "Captain Ralph El-
lum's men refer to him as the Ball Crusher. He also
happens to hold women in the highest esteem. Need
I elaborate?"

Terence chuckled and shook his head. "Bravo, my
lord!"

"Then, Charles shall be punished?" Sophie exclaimed.

Nicholas shot her an irritated look. Her question
clearly indicated that she thought him as lacking in judgment—as in everything else. Provoked at her for holding
such an opinion and at himself for caring, he snapped,
"Of course he shall. What did you expect me to do?
Reward him?"

Her cheeks flushed the soft crimson of his mother's
prized amaryllis, and as always, she promptly looked
away from his face. "No . . . well, yes. I mean, I thought
that you'd rewarded him. I mean, not deliberately,
but . . ." She shook her head as if trying to jar her foot
from her mouth. "What I'm trying to say . . ."

"I believe Miss Barton is trying to inform you that
Charles has always dreamed of owning a commission,
and that she thought you had inadvertently rewarded
him by granting him one," Terence cut in. "Begging
your pardon, my lord, but I shared her belief. I realize
now that I should have known better and humbly apologize for my thoughts. Sophie, on the other hand, has
been at the manor but a short time and is thus unaware
of your superior—"

Nicholas silenced him with a wave. "No apology necessary. I quite understand." Kneeling beside the weeping
Fancy, who sat using the hem of her skirt as a handkerchief, he added, "It seems that we now lack a second
footman, Terence. What say you to the position?"

"Me? Second footman?" the young man gasped.

Nicholas nodded. "By your willingness to champion
Fancy, you have shown yourself worthy of the advance-
ment. I can assure you that my father will agree when

he hears of your gallantry. Therefore, you have only to say yes to attain the position."

"Y-yes, my lord! And thank you. I would be honored."

"Good. Then, you shall begin your duties by informing my father that I have been detained and shall be along shortly."

"Very good, my lord." Looking ready to burst with excitement, Terence sketched a quick bow and dashed off.

That matter settled, Nicholas focused his attention on the sobbing chambermaid. Pulling his handkerchief from his pocket, he murmured, "Are you hurt, Fancy? Do you need a surgeon?"

Her face still buried in her hem, she shook her head.

Nicholas leaned a fraction nearer, trying to catch a glimpse of her face. Servants, he'd learned, were loath to acknowledge their injuries and ailments, especially to their employers. And with good reason. Sacking a servant for an infirmity was a common, if inhumane practice, one which both he and his parents disdained. Yet, despite their reputation for charity, some servants still remained fearful. Thus, it often fell to the Somervilles to divine their employees ills and see to their treatment.

Aware that this might be one of those instances, he gently countered, "I'm sure you're as fit as you say. Still, I would rest much easier if you would allow me to examine your face." When she sniffled and lowered her hem enough to eye him warily, he smiled and added, "In truth, you will be granting me an immense favor by letting me do so."

Her tear-drenched eyes widened. "Huh? How"

"By saving me from your mob of admirers, that's how."

Her eyes were so wide now, they looked ready to pop from her head. "What mob of admirers?" Another sniffle.

"Why, the ones who shall no doubt rise up and tear me limb for limb should I allow your beauty to be marred through neglect."

She gaped at him dumbfounded for several beats, then

giggled and dropped her hem. "Git on, now, my lord. You're teasin' me."

His smile broadened as he cupped her chin in his palm and tipped her tear-streaked face into the sunlight. "Me? Never! I speak only the truth. You have only to notice the way men watch you to see that it is so." Pleased by her grinning response, he quickly examined her face. Aside from a bruise blossoming on her left cheek, she appeared unharmed.

Relieved, he smiled and released her. "There seems to be no serious damage, though your left cheek is turning a rather interesting shade of purple."

Fancy sniffled and gingerly prodded the area.

"Never fear, Miss Jenkins," he said, handing her his handkerchief. "The bruise shall be healed in plenty of time for you to dazzle your admirers at the Midsummer's feast."

Rather than look pleased, as he'd expected, she burst into tears again. Utterly bewildered, he glanced at Sophie for help. She was staring at him in a most peculiar manner. It took but a second for him to realize that she stared at his face, and another for him to become thoroughly discomfited by her scrutiny. What had prompted her sudden fascination, he didn't know, but he had an uneasy feeling that he wouldn't like the reason were he to discover it.

More self-conscious than he'd ever been in his life, he ducked his head, instinctively hiding his disfigurement. Praying that he sounded calmer than he felt, he said the first thing he thought of. "I'm sorry, Fancy. I only meant to cheer you."

The chambermaid shook her head. "You ain't to blame, my lord. I am. I bragged to everyone—*sniffle!*—how Charlie loved me and how he was gonna announce our engagement at the feast." She paused to blow her nose, loudly. Wiping it as if trying to rub it off her face, she exclaimed, "And it were true! He said he loved me and wanna'd to git engaged. When people hear that he was only jollyin' me to git under my skirt—" She broke off, weeping in earnest.

"There, there, now, Fancy. Everything will be fine,

you shall see." He awkwardly patted her arm. "The only thing anyone will think is that Charles is a bastard, and that they are glad he's gone. The gladdest of all shall be your mob of admirers. I shan't be a whit surprised if they clamor at the door day and night, pleading for the privilege to court you." Damnation! He hated it when women cried. It always made him feel slightly guilty, as if he should have been able to do something to prevent their distress.

To his dismay, she wept harder. "No man ain't nivver gonna want me . . . well, exceptin' for a quick game of hide the quimstick. Charlie's right. I ain't nothin'—"

Nicholas seized her shoulders and silenced her with a shake. "Don't say such things." Hearing her pain, so raw and familiar, clawed his own festering wounds, making him suffer for her with a keenness that almost brought him to tears. Suddenly desperate to ease her torment, and his, he tightened his grasp on her heaving shoulders and gave her another shake. "Look at me, girl."

When she continued to hang her head, sobbing and wailing as if her life were over, he shook her again, this time with a force that made her drop his handkerchief. "I told you to look at me, damn it! I want to be sure that you listen to what I'm about to say."

The instant she obeyed, he regretted his command. Looking in her eyes was like gazing in the mirror, their depths reflecting the same shattered doubt and bruised self-esteem that haunted his own. The sight wrenched his gut.

Oblivious now to everything but their mutual pain, he stabbed his gaze into hers and growled, "I know how it feels to be publicly spurned, Fancy. Believe me, I know. I'm intimately acquainted with what you're suffering. It's devastating, that's the only word for the feeling; devastating in that it cuts to the core of your being and eats at your soul. You feel inadequate, and undesirable, and helpless." His voice dropped to a ragged whisper, "Worst of all, you doubt yourself and wonder if you are truly as unworthy of love as the other person says."

There was a gasp, but not from Fancy. Sophie. He'd been so caught up in his rush of emotions that he'd

forgotten she was there. Nicholas gritted his teeth.
Bloody hell. She couldn't help but to know that it was
she who had so thoroughly crushed him. No doubt she
delighted in his words and now gloated over her success.
To his deepening chagrin, she ejected an unintelligible
utterance—a smothered laugh, perhaps?—and moved
nearer.

Well, he'd be damned if he'd let her keep the upper
hand. Nicholas refocused his attention on the chambermaid, actually seeing her for the first time since beginning his fevered discourse. She'd ceased weeping and
stared at him in a manner that could only be described
as shocked.

Forcing his lips into a tight smile, he hissed, "Never
let anyone destroy you like that, Fancy. Never! A person
vicious enough to deliberately wound another possesses
neither the depth of character nor the clarity of mind to
form an accurate judgment, thus rendering their opinion
worthless. Moreover, it is he who is inadequate and unworthy of love, not you. His lack of sensibility makes
him so."

"Lord Lyndhurst is right, Fancy. About everything,"
Sophie quietly interjected.

Had Nicholas not been sitting, he'd have tumbled over
in his astonishment. The last thing he'd expected Sophie
to do was agree. Perplexed, he dropped his hands from
Fancy's shoulders, stealing a glance at Sophie as he did
so.

She still stared at him, but in a way that was thoughtful and rather sad. Had she been anyone else, he'd have
said that she looked contrite. But, of course, the shallow
Miss Barrington was incapable of such noble
emotions . . .

Wasn't she? More confused than ever, he looked
away.

"Why'd you care what I think or feel, Miss Hoity-
Toity?" Fancy scoffed, blowing her nose with hurricane
force. "You don't like me, and you ain't nivver had no
bones in lettin' me know it."

There was a beat of silence, then Sophie sighed.
"You're right. I don't like you any more than you like

me, nor am I trying to pretend otherwise now. I agree with his lordship because what he says is true."

Fancy sniffed. "Sure you do. Next you'll be tryin' to tell me that you dinna agree with what Charlie said about me."

"As a matter of fact, I don't."

Another sniff. "Could've suckered me."

Nicholas heard the whisper of grass and the faint rustle of muslin as Sophie moved nearer to where he and the maid sat. "See here, Fancy. I admit that I haven't been exactly cordial, but, then, neither have you. You've shown me nothing but contempt since the very first moment we met. Why, I wasn't at Hawksbury more than five minutes before you started flinging barbs."

"That's 'cuz you was lookin' down your nose at me like I weren't no better 'n yesterday's spit slop."

"Which is the very same way you looked at me," Sophie returned in a reasonable tone.

"That's a fib! I ain't the one that started the trouble between us." Fancy turned at the waist and jabbed an accusing finger at her foe. "It were you. You and your I'm-the-daughter-of-a-bleedin'-baron airs. And don't you go sayin' that you don't put on airs, 'cuz you do. You know you do!"

"I never claimed not to put on airs. I do, which I admit has contributed a great deal toward perpetuating our silly feud. I still maintain, however, that it was your airs, not mine, that first sparked our enmity."

"Ha! That proves that you're lyin', 'cuz I don't put on airs."

"Don't you?"

"No! I ain't the one that's always queenin' around and actin' like I'm too good for everyone else."

More whispering of grass and rustling of skirts, then Sophie's dusty hem appeared at Fancy's other side. "If you don't queen around, then what would you call the way you constantly lord both your superior position and service skills over me? And what about the way you're always ridiculing me, and how you never miss a chance to tell everyone how silly and useless you find me? If you're not acting like you're too good for me, then what, pray tell, are you doing?"

Fancy shrugged one shoulder. "Why'da you give a pig's arse what the likes o' me thinks or says? You're a lady, and I'm just a chambermaid. No one pays me no mind."

Nicholas stole a glance at Sophie's face, interested to hear her response. Though he was loath to admit it, he found her handling of Fancy's animosity rather admirable. He smiled wryly at that thought. Imagine. Him, admiring Miss Barrington for something other than her looks. Amazing.

As he watched, Sophie sat next to Fancy. Solemnly returning the other woman's gaze, she murmured, "I care because I'm a person, just like you. And don't all people want to be liked and accepted by their peers?"

Fancy made a vulgar noise. "Peers? My arse! We ain't peers. You're quality and you nivver let me, or anyone else, forget it. Not with the way you're always showin' off your fine ways and puttin' us all to shame with your pretty talk."

Sophie seemed to consider her retort for a moment, then nodded. "You're right, we're not peers. Not if you use birth and breeding as a measure. But if you strip away the standards set forth by society, you'll see that beneath our differences of speech, manner, and appearance, that we are much alike. You yourself showed me that just now."

The genuine humility in her voice sparked a startling ember of warmth in Nicholas's chest; an ember that caught and kindled his heart when she looked at him and added, "As did his lordship." Her soft gray gaze met his, and she smiled a sweet, rather wistful smile. "Thank you, my lord," she whispered.

Utterly nonplussed, he tipped his damaged cheek from her sight and jerked his head in acknowledgment. To his growing discomfiture she didn't look away, but continued to gaze at his face and smile.

"How'd we show you?"

Sophie gave him one last, lingering look, then shifted her attention to Fancy, a blessing for which he fervently thanked God. Her expression sober, she replied, "When I saw your devastation at Charles's betrayal, I saw myself. When his lordship described his pain, he described my own. You see, I, too, have been spurned."

"Bugger my uncle! You?" the chambermaid squealed, gaping as if she'd just confessed to dancing naked in the town square.

Sophie smiled and nodded. "Yes. Me. And when I saw that we all hurt in the same way and over the same things, I realized that we shared a common bond. That bond is that we're all people with feelings. I also learned how badly a carelessly uttered word, or a thoughtless action can wound a person."

Damn it. She was looking at him again, but this time she wasn't smiling. She regarded him gravely, her beautiful eyes shadowed by what? Remorse? Before he could decide for certain, a fierce hubbub arose in the distance, drawing all three gazes.

Flying from the church, shrieking at the top of her lungs and shedding pieces of her gown as she ran, was Miss Mayhew. Hot on her heels was the viscount. The rest of the congregation poured out behind them, though his father and Reverend Martin were the only ones giving chase.

"Boyne, Mayfly. We'll go to River Boyne immediately and appeal to the salmon of knowledge. He'll know how to appease the fishing god," he heard Brumbly bellow.

"S-sacrilege! I'm guilty of sacrilege!" The last of Miss Mayhew's skirt panels fell away, revealing a pair of long, puffy trousers that looked to be made of canvas. Another of Brumbly's inventions, no doubt. "S-see?" she keened. Another sign. Aquaticus will never forgive me. Never! "Oh! I should have guessed something dreadful w-would happen if I washed away my angling aroma." Her stuttering had all but vanished in her distress.

Like the good host he was trained to be, Nicholas nodded to the women at his side, then jumped to his feet and joined the pursuit. Pacing his gait to his father's, he jogged at his side, shouting, "What happened?"

The marquess panted several times, then replied, "It was the damnedest thing I ever saw. Miss Mayhew stood up for a prayer and her—*Huff! Puff!*—gown dropped apart at the seams. She and Brumbly are sure it's a sign of anger from the fish god, or some such Mayhew madness." His father wheezed out a chuckle. "Who knows? Maybe there's something to this fish god rot after all. Can't imagine what else—*Puff!*—would do that to the poor girl's gown."

What indeed? Nicholas shifted his gaze from the retreating back of the fleet-footed Miss Mayhew, who wailed something about a lucky fishing bonnet, to where Sophie now stood. She was flanked on the left by a woman—Rose? Daisy? No, Pansy—who wore yet another of her bonnets. Both women had their hands pressed to their mouths as if in horror.

He grinned. What indeed.

Chapter 15

It was a day of sunshine and fragrant breezes, the rare, perfect kind that thrilled the heart and made a person rejoice in being alive. Smiling her pleasure, Sophie paused inside the garden gate, reveling in the pageantry around her.

Painted from the rich, bold palette of late spring and gilded by the afternoon sun, the Hawksbury gardens stretched into an endless panorama of dreamlike splendor. Before her stood a walk of cherry trees, their branches twining and arching overhead in a flowering canopy of fragile pink lace. To her left lay a rose-covered arbor; to her right a sunken garden, its topiary walls bordered in tulips and forget-me-nots. As far as the eye could see swept wonder after wonder.

Certain that the Garden of Eden couldn't have been more of a paradise, Sophie started down the cherry-tree walk toward the graceful crescent of forcing houses in the distance. Lady Beresford had expressed a desire for a special variety of strawberries called Francesca's Delight, and she had been sent to fetch them.

Of course she was thrilled with the assignment, for not only did it allow her a stroll in the garden, it granted her a few moments of leisure to ponder the curious twist her life had taken since Sunday. Exactly where that twist was taking her, she didn't know, but wherever it was, it was a vast improvement over where she'd been. Especially in regard to her position.

As she stopped to await a pair of peacocks to strut from the path, she puzzled over her new duties. Though no one had mentioned a change in her station, most of her time of late had been spent doing the tasks of a lady's maid that Miss Stewart was no longer able to perform.

Hence, her days were spent mending and maintaining her ladyship's wardrobe, fetching cures from the stillroom, selecting books from the library, bringing the marquess refreshment when he visited his wife, and running dozens of other errands to ensure her mistress's comfort. While she enjoyed her new position, there was one chore she found unnerving to the extreme: reading aloud.

Oh, it wasn't the reading itself that disturbed her. Skilled as she was at dramatization, she was no stranger to performing in company. No. Her disquiet stemmed from her ladyship's far too avid curiosity in her person. Exactly what had prompted the woman's sudden interest in her, she couldn't say. All she knew was that more times than not the selected reading material ended up tossed aside while her ladyship grilled her on every facet of her life.

Of course Sophie couldn't help but to reveal a bit about herself and her once lofty position in society in replying. Aware as she was of that fact, she tried to evade the woman's questions. Her ladyship, however, was a slyboots, and somehow always managed to loosen her tongue. Thus, more times than not, she ended up spilling the very details she sought to conceal. To say that the situation was disturbing was a vast understatement.

With the peacocks now out of her way and pecking at the hollyhocks bordering the path, Sophie picked up her skirts and resumed her errand. As she did so, she glanced down at the crisp, blue-sprigged muslin in her hand.

One of the best things about her new duties was that they required her to dress in a manner fit for Somerville eyes. That meant that she now wore one of the modest yet reasonably becoming gowns issued to all female servants who waited upon the family. And wait upon them she did, constantly it seemed, all except for the one member she desperately wished to see.

Lyndhurst.

Since witnessing his courtly tolerance of Miss
Mayhew's gaucheness, and the charming gallantry with
which he'd consoled Fancy, a mere servant, she'd devel-
oped the most curious feelings for him, ones oddly reminiscent of a schoolgirl crush. Why, the man she'd seen
on Sunday wasn't at all the utterly insufferable aristocrat
she'd jilted. Indeed, had she not known for a fact that
that man was he, she'd have thought him a complete
stranger.

An exceedingly exciting and intriguing stranger.

A compelling handsome stranger.

Lyndhurst? Handsome? Shaking her head in amazement, she passed the last of the cherry trees and stepped
onto an arched Palladian bridge. The last thing in the
world she'd expected to admire about his lordship was
his looks. Yet, as she'd watched him smile and tease
away Fancy's tears, she'd gazed past his scar and discovered an unexpected beauty in his face.

Granted, he wasn't beautiful in a conventional sense,
not like Julian and Quentin with their angelic prettiness.
No. His beauty lay in his warm smile, the intelligence in
his eyes, and the thoughtfulness of his expression. As
for his actual features, well, they were roughly hewn ver-
sions of his stunning brother's finely chiseled ones.

Thus, Lyndhurst's jaw was squarer than Quentin's, his
cheekbones higher, and his nose a hint more aquiline.
Then, there was his mouth. She couldn't help but to
smile her admiration. While it resembled that of his
brother, sensually shaped and generously full, his lips
were firm rather than soft and pouting. Add his thick,
straight eyebrows, sun-bronzed skin, and of course, those
marvelous dark eyes, and even she, the most discriminat-
ing of women, had to admit that his lordship was attractive in a bold, aggressively masculine way.

Shaking her head again, Sophie leaned over the stone
bridge parapet and stared at the stream below, watching
as trout after trout broke the surface to feast upon the
floating mayflies.

In a matter of moments his lordship had gone from
being an ugly, overbearing beast to an exceedingly fasci-
nating man; a man who'd shown himself to have the

same feelings, needs, and desires as everyone else. More eye-opening yet was the vulnerability he'd revealed by hiding his damaged cheek every time she looked his way. That he, a man of such vast power and daunting confidence, could be rendered self-conscious by a carelessly uttered insult revealed a sensitivity that was as surprising as it was touching.

It was that startling new view of him that made her long to see him. Somehow she couldn't quite reconcile herself to the fact that he wasn't the beast she'd assumed him to be. Indeed, she was convinced that she'd been suffering from some sort of perception-altering malaise last Sunday, and that she had only to see him again to confirm that fact. Unfortunately, she hadn't seen hide or hair of him since the disaster with Miss Mayhew's gown.

Cringing at the memory of the episode, she continued on her way.

Never in her life had she experienced such horror as she had when Miss Mayhew dashed from the church in her molting gown. Why, she'd wanted to die right then and there in her embarrassment for the girl. The only thing that saved her from doing so was her relief that her charge had insisted on wearing her queer inflatable "Buoyancy Breeches" and "Water Suspension Waistcoat," as the viscount called her inventions, instead of the filmy undergarments she'd tried to coax her into donning. Were it not for those waxed sailcloth oddities, the girl would have been left next to naked.

Just remembering the debacle and knowing that it was she who'd caused it was enough to make Sophie long to weep. Though she'd exercised the utmost of care while "popping the crums," it was apparent that she'd still managed to scorch the seams and thus caused them to split. Talk about feeling wretched!

Indeed, she'd felt so terrible that instead of feigning innocence, or concocting an excuse, or looking for a way to blame another, as was her usual way of dealing with such blunders, she'd chased after Miss Mayhew to confess her guilt and beg forgiveness.

As she'd run down the churchyard path, she'd naturally envisioned the worst sort of responses to her con-

fession: a merciless—but well-deserved—castigation
from the marquess, a blistering denouncement from the
viscount, and hysterical recriminations from Miss
Mayhew. As for Lyndhurst, well, she no longer knew
what to expect from him.

Emitting a frustrated noise, Sophie skirted the topiary
tableau of Sir George and the dragon, which marked the
entrance of the castle maze, and descended the six shallow stairs to the upper grand parterre terrace. At any
rate, when she'd finally caught her quarry, she'd witnessed the queerest scene.

The viscount and Miss Mayhew, both of whose faces
were inordinately red, stood with their arms in the air,
hands palm-to-palm, writhing like hooked worms as they
chanted some sort of gibberish. To their left, their expressions almost comical in their bewilderment, where
Lyndhurst and his father. As for Reverend Martin, he
was slowly backing away, muttering something about
heathens. It wasn't until she'd come to a stop and lis-
tened to the Mayhews words that she realized that they
prayed to some sort of fishing god. A moment later she
understood why.

From what she could determine from their garbled
speech, they attributed the destruction of Miss Mayhew's
gown to a fishing god named Aquaticus, certain that it
was his punishment for her washing away her sacred
angling aroma. By the fervor with which they keened, it
was clear that they were terrified of his wrath.

Made all the more wretched by their terror, she'd at
once blurted out her confession. As she launched into
her apology, her tongue tripping over the words in her
haste, the viscount had shaken his head and flatly refused to credit her guilt.

Never once pausing from his writhing, he then went
on to explain how Aquaticus would have prevented the
seams from being seared had "Mayfly" not desecrated
his gift of angling aroma. Since, however, she'd done so
by bathing, and in water profaned by forbidden carnation oil no less, the mishap could only be a sign of the
mighty fish god's wrath.

Rendered speechless by his addlepated logic, she'd

looked to Lyndhurst and the marquess for help. The
former simply shrugged and averted his cheek, while the
latter shook his head. Both looked rather amused by the
Mayhews display of pagan piety. As for the good reverend, well, he was long gone. No doubt he'd returned to
the church to warn what was left of the congregation
about the evils of heathenism and deviant worship.

As she'd stood there, glancing between the two parties, uncertain what to do or say, the glossy burgundy
and gold Somerville barouche had pulled to a stop before the gate. Babbling something about seeking advice
from an Irish salmon, Brumbly had all but tossed his
still-chanting daughter into the vehicle. When he'd
scrambled in behind her, Lyndhurst and his father sighed
in unison and followed suit.

It was then, as Lyndhurst climbed into the carriage,
that he met her gaze and said the most cryptic thing, "I
shall deal with Mother." And that was the last time she
saw him. Exactly what he'd meant, she didn't know. All
she knew was that by evening her life had began its
curious turn. She was just about to ponder that turn
when she spied a man hunched over a flower bed several
yards away.

Good. Someone to help her with the strawberries.
Though she couldn't tell which of the army of gardeners
he was, for his upper body was hidden by a stone pedestal, it was apparent by the abundance of dust streaking
his breeches that his position was quite low.

Picking up her skirts, she hurried toward him hollering, "You there, gardener! I need your help." So what
if it was considered vulgar for a lady to shout? She
wasn't a lady at the moment, she was a servant, and
servants had no compunction whatsoever about raising
their voices to each other.

A second after the words left her mouth, the man
reared up and sat back on his heels.

She gasped and skidded to a stop a scant yard from
where he sat. Oh, heavens! The man was no gardener,
he was Lyndhurst.

And he was just as handsome as she'd imagined on
Sunday.

For a beat or two she gaped at him, too stunned to do anything else. Then her wits returned and she looked away, blushing. Ready to melt beneath the searing heat of her embarrassment, she cast her gaze to the ground, desperately praying for it to open up and swallow her. Of course it remained willfully closed. Blast! Now what?

Well, unless she wished him to think her even more ill-bred than he already did, she must apologize for yelling at him. Not quite certain how to begin, she stole a glance at him from beneath her lowered lashes, trying to gauge his mood.

He sat staring at her through narrowed eyes, clearly awaiting either an explanation or an apology. Judging from the harsh set of his lips, he was in no humor to accept, either.

What was left of her composure fled. Though her feet itched to follow suit, she firmly ignored their prompting. Well, what did she expect, anyway? After the wretched way she'd treated him, she had no right to expect, nor did she deserve, anything but his enmity. And enmity was all she'd ever get, unless . . .

Unless she did something to mend the rift between them. That notion brought her up short. Did she truly wish to right matters between them? She looked at him again.

Her heart skipped a beat. Yes, she did. More than anything in the world. And the first step to doing so was to apologize. Thus resolved, she tendered the first of the hundred or so apologies she owed him. "Please f-forgive me for shouting at you so, my lord. It was a most . . . uh . . . improper display for which I humbly apologize. You see, um, I've never seen a . . . a . . . nobleman grubbing in the dirt before and thought that you were a . . . ur . . . g-g-gardener."

She wanted to die the instant the words left her mouth. If she hadn't offended him with her hollering, she most certainly had with her apology. Grubbing in the dirt indeed! And as if that rag-mannered slip didn't reflect badly enough upon her, she'd stammered like a green girl at court. Oh, double blast! Now he could add tongue-tied

hussy next to the dozens of other unflattering terms that
no doubt preceded her name in his mind.

For what seemed like forever thereafter, a very tense,
very miserable forever during which Sophie didn't dare
look at Lyndhurst, no one spoke. Just when she was
certain that she'd muddled things past all prayer, he
chuckled. At a loss as to what to make of his curious
response, Sophie ventured a glance at him.

He nodded and murmured, "Apology accepted, Miss
Barton." The smile that accompanied the words effectively banished all thought, highlighting his faint dimples.

And, oh! What charming dimples they were . . . even
more so than his brother's more pronounced ones. For
unlike Quentin, who clearly understood the power of his
dimples and used them with wicked calculation, Lyndhurst displayed his, seemingly unaware of their stunning effect.

And she was most definitely stunned. So much so that
she openly gaped at them, enthralled by how very dashing his scar looked bracketing the left one.

As she admired the cheek that had once so repulsed
her, his smile faltered, then faded, and he averted his
face. She, too, looked away, though what she truly
longed to do was cradle that damaged cheek in her palm
and tell him what a goose she was to have ever found
it ugly. Instead she followed his lead and retreated into
silence, doubtful if he'd either welcome or believe her
apology.

One eternity passed, then another, and yet another.
Still no one spoke. Just when Sophie was about to excuse herself, certain that he wished to be rid of her, he
murmured, "So you've never seen a nobleman grub in
the dirt, you say?"

She felt herself blush at his paraphrasing of her clumsy
words. Wondering if he made sport of her slip, she
peeked at his face. Though he still tipped his cheek from
her view, his expression was one of strained humor, as
if he sought to ease their tension with wit and was uncertain if the ploy would succeed.

What he succeeded in doing was touching her heart.
That he, the rich-and-mighty Earl of Lyndhurst, was as

uncomfortable in her company as she was in his made her chest ache with tenderness. Wanting nothing more at that moment than to reassure him, she laughed and replied, "No, my lord. I haven't. Do you do it often?"

He visibly relaxed. "Every chance I get." A wide grin. "As you've probably ascertained by now, I have a passion for gardening, which, I can assure you, is considered a perfectly lordly pastime among members of the ton. Or haven't you heard?"

His grin was infectious, and she smiled in response. "How could I not know after listening to the endless boasts of this lord or that about his latest rare tree or flower acquisition? What took me aback was finding you . . ." She gestured helplessly as she grappled for an elegant way to phrase his decidedly inelegant activity.

"Grubbing in the dirt?" he supplied with a chuckle.

She flushed, which seemed only to deepen his amusement. "I was going to say working the earth, but yes, grubbing in the dirt shall suffice. None of the gentlemen I know would think of soiling their hands with the actual labor of gardening."

His smile faded then, and he grew rather sober.

Certain that he'd perceived her last remark as a veiled insult, she hastily added, "Not that I see anything wrong with grub—ur, working the earth, mind you."

He stared at her gravely for several beats, then heaved a sigh. "I'm afraid, my dear, that you've stumbled upon the dark Somerville secret . . . our madness, some call it, and rightly so."

"Madness?" she squeaked, taken aback by his unexpected disclosure.

"Madness," he echoed in a funereal tone. "You see, Miss Barrington, every Somerville heir—me, my father, his father before him, and so on down the line—has been born with an insane desire to dig in the dirt and make things grow. My father always says that Somerville blood isn't blue, but green."

Sophie returned his solemn gaze for a second, not quite certain how to respond. Then she saw the gleam in his eyes and realized that he teased her. Giggling, as much at her own gullibility as at his jest, she exclaimed,

"Such a lot of gammon, my lord. A madness to dig in the dirt. Really!"

His laughter mingled with hers for a moment, then their gazes met, and held, and they both fell silent again, overcome by the unexpected intimacy of the moment.

It was Lyndhurst who looked away first.

Feeling suddenly awkward and flustered, Sophie blurted out the first thing that came to mind. "Tell me, Lord Lyndhurst, have you a particular fondness for"— she glanced at the flowers he'd been tending—"daisies?" She shifted back to his face only to look back down at the flowers in dismay. Daisies? Oh, heavens! Could it be? Was he a daisy man after all?

Oddly enough, rather than alarm her, as it had before, she found the notion of teasing his bare flesh with one of the delicate yellow and white flowers rather . . . thrilling.

Thrilling? Oh, dear! Appalled with herself, Sophie tore her gaze from the flowers, and forced herself to look at the statue atop the pedestal next to Lyndhurst.

Her eyes almost popped from their sockets. The statue was of a Greek god; one with a beautifully sculpted physique and a graphically detailed—

Heavens! Wherever was his fig leaf? Utterly shocked, she gaped at his flagrantly brandished endowments, too stunned to look away. When her wits finally returned, she found herself too fascinated to do so. Feeling oddly warm and flushed, she let her gaze rove over the statue's splendid form, glorying in every detail.

Oh—oh! But he had excellent shoulders . . .

Just like Lyndhurst.

And his chest! M-m-m, superb. So very broad and muscular . . .

Like Lyndhurst's.

As for his lower torso . . . she couldn't help smiling her approval of the god's trim waist and taut, rippling belly. Perfect.

Precisely how she suspected Lyndhurst's must be.

Then, there were those strong, sinewy thighs . . . why, Lydia would go into raptures over those thighs . . .

Like she always did when she viewed Lyndhurst's.

Which brought her to his . . .

Once again, she stared at his intriguing masculinity. H-m-m. She'd never really considered what Lyndhurst might look like down there. Why would she? She'd never seen a man's penis before, well, not in the flesh, thus she'd had no reason to take an interest in, much less speculate upon, the organ.

"Sophie? Is something amiss with the statue?"

Sophie wrenched her gaze from the god, beyond mortification. Oh, heavens! He'd caught her gawking. She swallowed hard, though her throat was as dry as burned toast. Question was, had he noticed what she gawked at?

She considered for a beat, then sighed. Of course he had. How could he not. Her scrutiny wasn't what anyone would call discreet.

Or maidenly.

Or modest.

Or . . .

Suddenly desperate to flee, to hide from her humiliation and her shameful new interest in Lyndhurst's body, she somehow managed to stammer, "S-strawberries. Her ladyship s-sent me for, ur, strawberries. I . . . um . . . mustn't keep her w-waiting any longer."

"Ah. Then, I take it that Mother is better this morning?" His voice was politely neutral as if nothing in the world were amiss.

H-m-m. Could it be that he hadn't noticed her brazen perusal after all? Nervously biting the inside of her lip, Sophie sneaked a glance at his face.

If he had noticed, he certainly didn't show it. Indeed, his expression was every bit as impassive as his voice. Deciding that he'd been too preoccupied with his daisies to note her faux pas, she smiled her relief and replied, "It appears so. She has expressed a strong craving for strawberries in clotted cream."

He laughed. The sight of his strong white teeth flanked by those engaging dimples stirred the oddest sensation within her, rather like that she'd experienced when Julian kissed her.

Only better.

Oh, heavens!

"If Mother is demanding strawberries and clotted

cream, she is most definitely on the mend. We shall know for certain when she requests a pot of chocolate with cinnamon for breakfast.''

Bedeviled almost beyond speech by a queer tingling in her belly, Sophie uncomfortably shifted her weight from one foot to the other, praying that her voice remained steady as she replied, "In that instance, you shall be glad to hear that she not only requested the chocolate, she drank the whole pot. She also ate an egg, half a trout, and two slices of toast with jam and butter.''

He laughed again.

The sensation quickened.

Oh, my!''

Still smiling, he pulled a rag from the bucket of gardening tools by his side and wiped his hands. "Well, I can't say that I'm surprised to hear of her improvement. I felt quite certain that you'd have a curative effect on her.''

Curative effect? Sophie gaped at him, stunned by the meaning behind his words. "Are you saying that it is you who had me assigned to assist Miss Stewart?''

He nodded and tossed the rag aside. "With my mother's permission, of course.''

"B-but why?'' She continued to stare at his face as he rose, her head tipping back as he reached the uppermost inches of his towering height. "After the terrible disaster with Miss Mayhew's gown, I'm surprised that you would allow me anywhere near your mother, especially in her fragile state of health.''

He grinned as if she'd said something immensely amusing. "Your intentions were good. My mother agreed with me on that point. We also agreed that it would be far safer for all concerned if your duties were limited to those more suited to your ladylike skills. Since Miss Stewart has been in need of an assistant for some time now, well''—he shrugged—"welcome to life upstairs, Miss Barton.''

Beyond bafflement now, she opened her mouth to again ask him why. Why he'd granted her mercy in the matter of Miss Mayhew? Why he had taken her part when presenting her case to his mother? Most importantly, why he'd delivered her from her drudgery? None of his actions made a whit of sense. Not when his sole reason for keeping her at Hawksbury was to shame and humble her.

Before she could form the words, however, he began to stretch. The unconscious grace of his motions drew her attention to his body, which in turn diverted her mind from her questions to his apparel. To say that she liked the way he looked in his work clothes would be a sweeping understatement.

Exercising the discretion she'd failed to practice on the statue, Sophie made a show of securing her bonnet, all the while admiring his appearance.

Magnificent. That was the word for him. She must have been all about in the head to have ever thought him otherwise. True, he was taller than most men she knew. And yes, more muscular. But rather than detract from his appeal, his size served only to make him all the more alluring . . . all the more earthy and masculine . . . especially dressed as he was.

A tingle of excitement rippled through her as she covertly studied his apparel. Though he wore the clothing of a common laborer: a rough shirt of indeterminate color, coarse yet snug brown breeches, thick black stockings and muddy clogs, there was nothing the least bit common about his appearance. Indeed, he looked every bit as lordly now as he did standing amid the crush of the ton bedecked in formal finery.

Only there was much more of his lordliness displayed by his current attire, and she was definitely enjoying the superior view. Why, she'd never even seen him without his coat or waistcoat, much less stripped of both with his shirt open and his chest exposed.

The sight of his chest, so tan and sculpted to a perfection that put the statue to shame, made her shiver despite the fact that she felt warm enough to wilt.

"Sophie?"

"H-m-m?" She more purred than uttered the response.

"I asked if you would like me to assist you with the strawberries?"

"Strawberries?" she echoed absently, wondering how his chest hair would feel should she rub her cheek against it. Would it tickle her with its crispness? Or ca-

ress her with its silkiness? She had just decided that it
would most probably tickle, when he reached out and
laid his hand against her cheek. Without thinking, she
nuzzled against it, closing her eyes in her contentment.

"Sophie?"

"M-m-m?"

"You're not about to faint are you?"

"Um . . . hm-m what?" Oh, but she liked the feel of
his hand, so big and strong and lightly callused.

"I asked if you felt faint from the sun?"

"Uh . . . no. Why?"

"Because your face is flushed, and you're breathing
rather hard." His hand moved from her cheek to her
forehead. "You feel a bit warm, too."

Flushed? Warm? Whatever was he going on about? It
wasn't until she opened her eyes and saw his frown that
her senses returned and she understood.

Talk about feeling warm! Her face felt on fire when
she realized what she'd done. Why . . . why, she'd behaved like a lovelorn dollymop the way she'd cooed and
sighed, and practically thrown herself at him. Oh! Oh!
What he must think of her!

What Nicholas thought was that he had to get her out
of the sun and fast, a thought that firmed to resolution
as her color deepened to an even more alarming shade
of crimson. Feeling helpless, as he always did when faced
with female frailty, he looked around for help.

Of course there was no one near. There never was
when he worked in the garden. It was an unspoken rule,
one passed down through the generations of Hawksbury
gardeners: never disturb a Somerville while he com-
muned with nature. Apparently a few of his ancestors
had taken violent exception to being interrupted.

Frantic now, he glanced at the manor, mentally gauging
the distance. Then he looked back at Sophie's face, which,
if such a thing were possible, was even redder, and calculated her chances of reaching it before swooning.

Were she a racehorse, he'd have given her twenty to
one odds . . . a risky gamble by any standards, and not
one he was willing to take. Not in this instance. If she
fainted before reaching the house, he'd have to carry

her the remainder of the way. Well, unless she turned purple and stopped breathing, then he'd be forced to tend to her where she dropped.

Just the thought of opening her gown and loosening her stays was enough to make him grab her arm and pull her toward the nearest source of shade: the forcing houses. Oh, it wasn't that he found the prospect of undressing her unpleasant, quite the contrary. The notion of holding the luscious Miss Barrington in his arms and discovering if what lay beneath all that muslin was as fine as he suspected—

Stop it! Stop mooning this instant, you fool! he chided himself. Just because the chit is being agreeable doesn't mean that things have changed. She's still the same traitorous baggage who betrayed you in London. If you're wise, you'll view her improvement with caution and question the motive for her sudden congeniality.

Problem was, he'd never been wise when it came to Miss Barrington. It now appeared that he never would be. For while he truly longed to despise her, and heaven only knew she deserved his contempt, he found it impossible to hate her when she behaved as she did now. Indeed, so disarmed was he by her flustered charm and stammering humility, that he felt powerfully compelled to forgive her her every transgression . . .

Which was exactly how he'd felt on Sunday when she'd chased after the Mayhews and confessed her guilt in the gown disaster. She'd been so contrite, so genuinely concerned for Miss Mayhew that he'd been moved to take her part when his father reported the catastrophe to his mother. It was during that same lapse in his wrath that he'd pointed out her ineptitude for household chores and had suggested that she be given work more suited to her talents. Hence, she now assisted Miss Stewart.

"My lord! Please! I can't run anymore. I—*huff! gasp!*—have a stitch in my side."

Nicholas stopped, frowning, as she yanked her arm from his grip and clutched at her side. "What?"

"I said I can't run anymore," she puffed out.

Run? He blinked several times, trying to orientate himself to his surroundings. When he did, he saw that they stood but a few yards from the forcing house stairs. Good Lord! They must have indeed been running, and exceeding fast at that, to have covered so much ground in such a brief time. Why, in her current weakened condition, it was nothing short of a miracle that Sophie hadn't toppled into a swoon two grottos and a knot garden ago.

The knowledge that he, a man who prided himself on his gallantry, had forced an ailing woman to dash, made Nicholas feel like the world's worst cad. Deeply shamed by his thoughtlessness, he murmured, "I'm sorry. I didn't mean to make you run. Truly, I didn't. I forgot myself in my rush to get you out of the sun."

She continued to massage her side, eyeing him as if he'd lost his mind. "But why? Whatever made you so eager to get me out of the sun? I said I felt fine."

"Yes, but you didn't look fine," he pointed out, skeptically. "Indeed, I can't recall ever seeing you breathe so hard or turn such a distressing shade of red."

"Oh. That." The hue in question flooded her face again. "I—I'm sorry I alarmed you. I was flushed and a bit agitated in my—uh—eagerness to fetch her ladyship her strawberries. It's almost teatime, you know, and I didn't want her to suffer the disappointment of having her tray arrive without them."

The logic of her explanation—not to mention the delightful earnestness with which it was uttered—instantly dissolved the last of his reservations.

"I truly am sorry for alarming you," she repeated, gazing at him solemnly.

He smiled down at her upturned face. "I'll tell you what, Sophie. You forgive me for making you run, and I shall forgive you for alarming me."

She returned his gaze gravely for several beats, as if considering his proposal. Then she laughed, a lilting, mirthful sound that was quite unlike the forced giggle with which she'd responded to his humor in the past. "All right, my lord. Done. But only if you direct me to the Francesca's Delight strawberries."

He chuckled and sketched a bow, suddenly feeling more lighthearted than he'd felt in many a year. "Your servant, madam," he murmured, presenting his arm with a courtly flourish.

She took it, grinning like an imp. "Speaking of servants, my lord, there is one more condition to winning my forgiveness."

"Which is?" he quizzed, more enchanted by her grin than by all her tonnishly correct simpers combined.

"You must promise not to think the worst of me for shouting at you earlier. It is the way of the servants to shout at one another to draw each other's attention. Since I am now a servant and I mistook you for a gardener, well—"

"There is no need to apologize or to explain," he interjected, surprised and yes, touched, that she cared for his opinion of her. "I'm perfectly aware of the servants penchant for shouting."

"You are?" She couldn't have looked more astonished if he'd ordered her boiled in oil for her infraction.

He nodded as he escorted her up the stone stairs to the main forcing house entrance. "Of course I am. I would have to be deaf not to be. Why, I heard Fancy shouting for Edith to help her turn my mattress this very morning, and I was at the opposite end of the hall at the time."

Sophie sighed, as if greatly pained. "I told Fancy not to shout like that, not if she's serious about becoming a lady's maid. She promised to watch her tongue."

"I take it that you and Fancy are on better terms these days?" he inquired, ushering her through the tall glass-paned door.

"Much better, thanks to you." She paused to smile her gratitude, a smile so breathtakingly lovely that his heart danced an odd little jig in response. "Fancy and I had a long talk Sunday night, and do you know what?"

"No, what?"

"We found that we rather like each other. She seems truly sincere in her desire to become a lady's maid, and has asked my help in refining her person. She wishes to be polished enough to take Miss Stewart's place when she finally marries John. Of course I promised to help her, though I must admit that it's proved a challenge thus far. She can't read a word and, well, you've heard the way she speaks. I must constantly remind her not to drop her *g*'s or say the word bloody."

Nicholas couldn't help chuckling at her comical expression of distaste as she uttered the word *bloody*. "If I remember correctly, there are several good reading and grammar primers in the schoolroom. You have my permission to use them or anything else you find there that might aid you in your endeavors," he said, leading her from the exotically tiled palm court, which served as an entry hall for the forcing pavilions, and into the first of the seven adjoining buildings.

"Why . . . thank you," she sputtered, looking genuinely surprised by his offer. "Having the proper books shall make my task ever so much easier. The only ones we have in the servants hall are a dreadful novel called *Pamela,* and the Bible, neither of which—oh!" She stopped short, gaping at her surroundings in awe.

Nicholas followed her gaze with his own, his chest swelling with pride, as it always did when he viewed Hawksbury's impressive collection of rare trees and plants.

To his right loomed a row of prized banana trees, to his left a dense stand of fig trees. Both sides boasted tracts of pineapples, trellises of passion fruit vines, and colorful expanses of tropical flowers. Before him, stretching on as far as the eye could see, was hothouse after magnificent hothouse, each sheltering fruit, vegetables, and flowers beneath their curving glass ceilings.

"Oh—oh!" she softly exclaimed. "I'm in paradise."

"I take it you approve?" he said, pleased by her enthrallment.

"I more than approve, I—" She shook her head, clearly at a loss for words.

"I love it, too. I always have. My father used to bring me here when I was a babe and let me play among the foliage. Indeed, one of my mother's favorite tales involves me crawling off and getting lost among the mangosteen trees in the East Indian Pavilion."

"Well, I can't say that I blame you. I wouldn't mind being lost in here myself," she murmured, cranking her head first this way, then that, as if trying to take in all the wonders at once.

Nicholas chuckled. "I spend so much time out here when I visit, that my mother has accused me of trying to do so again. Indeed, this is the first place John looks every time she sends him to find me."

"I'll remember that if she ever sends me instead." She almost sighed the words as she closed her eyes and tipped back her head, deeply inhaling the air. "Oh, but it smells glorious in here."

So beautiful, so very artless and dreamily content did she look in that pose, that he was struck speechless by the picture she made. He was also struck by a powerful urge to kiss her. Tempted beyond reason, he inched his face nearer to hers, his gaze hungrily riveted to her mouth.

Oh, how he longed to claim those lips with his, to sweep her into his embrace and show her the untamed passion that raged beneath his civilized facade. He yearned to plunder the warm honeyed depths of her mouth with his tongue, and hear her moan of surrender as she melted against him. He—

"My lord?" called a masculine voice.

His head snapped up, his forehead narrowly missed colliding with Sophie's as she, too, came to attention. In the next instant his senses returned, and he realized what he'd almost done. To say that he was mortified didn't begin to describe the depth of his shame. That he'd almost stolen a kiss from a woman he knew found him physically repulsive, well—he shuddered to think of how she might have reacted had he succeeded.

Cursing himself for his lapse and praying that Sophie hadn't noticed it, Nicholas turned toward the advancing footman. "Yes? What is it, John?"

John sketched an elegant bow. "It's the Duchess of Windford and her daughter, Lady Helene, my lord. They have arrived."

"They have?" He frowned, trying to pull his mind from his near embarrassment to the business at hand. "I thought they were to arrive tomorrow?"

John nodded. "So did the rest of the household, my lord. It seems, however, that the marchioness mistakenly wrote the seventeenth instead of the eighteenth when she made out the invitation." He shrugged. "And, well, today is the seventeenth."

Though Nicholas was tempted to curse aloud, he bridled the urge and replied, "Tell my mother that I shall be along shortly."

"Very good, my lord." Another bow and the footman was gone."

The next few moments passed in silence as Nicholas grappled for something to say. Exactly what one said to a woman from whom he had almost stolen a kiss, he didn't know. He'd never been in such a position before. Utterly at a loss, he looked everywhere but at Sophie, and rather inanely muttered, "Well, I suppose I should prepare myself to meet Lady Helene."

"Yes, I suppose so."

Damn it. He had to say something more. He couldn't just walk off and leave her standing there like that. Even if she hadn't noticed his amorous advance, he had to say something to bring closure to the episode . . . if not for her sake, then for his own.

Closure? H-m-m. Yes. Remembering their errand, he said, "You'll find the strawberries you seek in the third pavilion. Wait there, and I shall send a gardener to assist you." Oh, bloody hell! He hadn't meant that last to come out like an order.

"Thank you, my lord. I shall do that."

He lingered a moment more, wondering how to proceed. Then he decided it best to retreat before he did or said anything else stupid. Thus he nodded and turned on his heels. As he did so, he couldn't resist stealing a final peek at Sophie.

She caught him and smiled. So soft, so genuinely sweet and full of fondness was that smile, that he suddenly felt like the most desirable man in England. That smile won his forgiveness . . .

And his heart.

Chapter 16

"And then Lady Helene say—"

"*Said*," Sophie corrected, looking up from the lace she was repairing on the marchioness's night rail.

"Said. Lady Helene *said*." Fancy nodded her comprehension, then scrunched her face into a caricature of their guest's supercilious expression and mimicked, "You there, girl." She scowled and snapped her fingers at Sophie and Pansy, who sat beside her in the airy servants hall, doing their respective mending. "Look at this bedsheet. Just look at it! A crease."

Three more finger snaps, this time directed at an imaginary bed. "I cannot sleep on that crease. I simply cannot! It shall rub my skin quite raw." An imperious wave of the hand. "Take it away! Take it away this very instant and see that it is properly pressed." She resumed her normal expression and tone to add, "It were her own—"

"*Was*," Sophie interjected.

"It *was* her own fault that the sheet were—uh—*was* wrinkled. She spent half the bleedin' afternoon wallowin'—"

"Fancy—"

"I know. I know." A sheepish grin of apology. "Sorry. I'm not surposta say bleedin'."

"You're not *supposed* to say bleeding. Also pigs *wallow*, and ladies *lounge*."

"It looked like wallowing to me," Fancy retorted, frowning at the pillowcase she was mending. "You should have saw—*seen* her rolling around on the bed

with that ugly little rat of a dog of hers. Why, you'd
have thought that—"

"*Thought.*"

"*Thought.* You'd have *thought* that rat dog were—*was*
her lover the way she was hugging and kissin'—kissing
it on its mucky mouth, and making those queer boo-
by . . . boo-by . . . Mingy noises she's always makin'—
making to it."

"No!" Pansy looked up from the stocking she was
examining, her face a mask of horror. "She don't *really*
kiss *it* on the mouth?" Like many of the servants, Pansy
was unconvinced that Lady Helene's odd-looking pet
was a dog. Thus, she had designated the animal an *it*.

Fancy nodded. "Square on the lips, like this." She
demonstrated an exaggerated kiss, complete with loud,
wet smooching noises. "And she don't—ur—*doesn't*
wipe the drool off its face first, either. She kisses it, muck
and all."

Pansy looked as nauseated as Sophie felt. "Gar! I 'ope
she washes 'er face 'fore she kisses 'is lordship. Yeech!"

Sophie froze mid-stitch, stricken by the notion of
Lyndhurst kissing Lady Helene . . . or anyone else for
that matter. Well, anyone but herself.

Fancy shrugged one shoulder. "I wouldn't worry over
much on his lordship's account. I doubt there's been any
billin' and cooin' goin' on between them two."

"An *exchange of affections* sounds more genteel than
billing and cooing, Fancy. And it's *those* two, not *them*
two." Though she knew that she should discourage such
talk, and perhaps even chide the pair for their unseemly
speculation, Sophie couldn't resist asking, "What makes
you think that his lordship hasn't kissed Lady Helene?
She is lovely, and he seems quite taken with her."

As much as it pained her to admit the last, it was true.
Not only was her ladyship a beauty in the purest sense
of the word, Lyndhurst seemed exceedingly appreciative
of that fact. Indeed, he'd spent so much time dancing
attendance upon her the last few days, that you'd have
thought they were pinned together. To say that Sophie
was miserable about it was akin to saying that the devil
was a naughty fellow: a huge understatement.

"Taken with her?" Fancy sniffed. "Shows what you know about his lordship."

"Oh? And what, pray tell, makes you such an authority on him?" she retorted. The instant the words left her mouth, she was struck with a most wretched suspicion. Could he and Fancy . . .

Apparently her face reflected her thoughts, for Fancy drew back, frowning. "You think that me and his lordship—" she broke off, shaking her head over and over again.

Pansy, too, shook her head. "Fancy . . . and Lord Lyndhurst?" She and Fancy exchanged an incredulous look then threw back their heads and howled with laughter.

Sophie glanced from one woman to the other, growing more chagrined by the moment. "I don't see what is so very funny. It isn't exactly unheard of for a nobleman to dally with his maids."

"It is if the nobleman you're talkin' about is Lord Lyndhurst. Why just the thought of him—" Fancy made a choking noise and succumbed to another fit of hilarity.

"Talking, you mustn't drop your *g*'s," Sophie snapped. "And what is so ludicrous about the notion of his lordship turning a serving girl's head? In case you haven't noticed, he is a charming and handsome man." She could have bitten off her tongue the instant she uttered that last. A few more remarks like that, and everyone would know of her feelings for him.

"Oh, 'e's turned their 'eads right 'nough," Pansy chortled.

Fancy nodded. "It's true. Plenty o'—*of* servant girls have thrown themselfs at him over the years. But his lordship, well, he gives them a pretty speech on how he don't bed women he don't—*doesn't* have feelings for, and how he's got too much respect for them to treat 'em like whores. Of course, he don't—*doesn't* say whore. He's too much of a gentleman for that kind of language."

"They offer themsel*ves*, not themsel*fs*. And he *has* too much respect, not he's *got* too much respect," Sophie muttered, feeling like the world's biggest goose. Whatever could she have been thinking? Of course Lyndhurst didn't trifle with the maids. He was a fine, honorable man . . . a gallant through and through. Hardly the sort of man to use a woman for a casual game of . . . *daisies*.

For a long while thereafter the women stitched in silence. Though Sophie tried to lose herself in her work and forget about Lyndhurst, she couldn't. She simply couldn't stop wondering about him and Lady Helene. Was he indeed taken with her, as she suspected? Or was Fancy correct in believing otherwise?

She pondered a moment, then stole a glance at the chambermaid. There had been something in her voice when she'd dismissed the notion of a romantic attachment, a sort of knowing incredulity that implied a secret insight into the relationship. Could it be that she'd seen or heard something to make her privy to such information? Dare she ask?

After what felt like a century, when she could bear the suspense no longer, she cleared her throat and said, "Fancy? What makes you think that his lordship doesn't care for Lady Helene?"

Fancy shrugged. "He's being too much of a gentleman."

Sophie frowned at her cryptic response. "Excuse me?"

"He's being too much of a gentleman." Fancy paused to thread her needle, then added, "A man, no matter how much of a gentleman he is, can't help lookin'— looking at a woman in an ungentlemanly way if he's got feelings for her. Know what I mean?"

Sophie considered that for a beat, remembering the hunger with which the gentlemen of the ton had eyed her during the Season, then slowly nodded.

"Well, if you ask me, it's good that 'is lordship don't like 'er," Pansy piped in, drawing a stocking over her darning egg.

"Why?" Oh, blast! There she went again, encouraging the very talk she should be discouraging.

" 'Cuz then 'e'd marry 'er, 'n' we'd all 'ave to look fer new places. Ain't no one downstairs that wants 'er fer a mistress."

"Especially Cook," Fancy interjected with a snicker.

Pansy tittered. "Gor, Sophie! You should o' see'd the row in the kitchen when Lady 'Elene tol' Cook that she's gotta make Chinese food for *it. It* comes all the way from China, you know, 'n' 'll only eat Chinese food. Or so Lady 'Elene says. Any 'ow, I thought Cook'd split a gut fer certain when she 'eard."

"Can you imagine?" Fancy snorted. "Who'd—"

"Fancy—"

Fancy shot her an apologetic look. "Sorry. I know: Ladies don't snort." She shook her head. "Still, I were— *was* shocked to hear that rat dog came from China. Who in their right wits'd—uh, *would* bring back something that ugly?"

"Ming-Ming wasn't brought back," Sophie replied, placing one last stitch in the lace she was repairing. "She was a gift to the king from a Chinese envoy who visited the court last year."

Pansy looked up, frowning. "If *it* was a gift to the king, 'ow come Lady 'Elene's got 'er?"

"Would you keep rat dog if someone gave her to you?" Fancy retorted.

Sophie smiled. "The king gave her to Lord Windford as a reward for him translating some Chinese documents into English. Lord Windford, in turn, gave her to his daughter."

"Think him giving rat dog away had something to do with how she yaps and pisses every time she gets fraught?"

"*Fouled,* Fancy. One mustn't utter such words as—" Sophie gestured helplessly, unable to repeat the vulgarity in question. "Well, you know which word I mean. Also *when* she gets *excited* sounds better than *every time* she gets *fraught*. And please, do try to get in the habit of referring to Ming-Ming simply as a dog. I shudder to think of what Lady Helene might do if she hears you referring to her little darling as rat dog or"—Sophie glanced from Fancy to Pansy—"*it,* for that matter."

"Well, *it* don't look like no dog I nivver seen," Pansy muttered. "Don't look much like a rat, neither, 'cept that she's got short legs." She shook her head. "Rats got pointy faces. *Its* face's mushed in, like it got 'it with a glossing iron.' "

"Either that, or run through the mangler," Fancy quipped.

The three women looked at each other, then burst out laughing in unison. Lady Helene's dog truly was a terror and a trial to the servants . . . as was her ladyship. Indeed, both dog and girl seemed to loathe everyone at Hawksbury, save the Somervilles, of course, and treated them accordingly.

Clutching her sides as if they ached, Pansy gasped out between giggles, " 'Ave you seen 'ow *it* acts 'round Lord Lyndhurst? Ye'd think that 'e was a stud and she was a bitch in 'eat the way she whimpers 'n rubs against 'is leg."

Fancy guffawed. "His poor lordship. Can you imagine his weddin'—wedding night if he marries Lady Helene? I'll bet pounds to pence that she insists that the bleedin'—uh—dreadful beast sleeps—sleep?" She paused to consider, then nodded. "Sleep. I'll just bet that she insists that the dog sleep with them."

Sophie pricked herself with her needle as she indeed imagined it. The vision of Lady Helene, bridal bouquet of daisies in hand, doing her wifely duty with Lyndhurst stabbed at her heart.

"Aye! I can see it," Pansy tittered, her cheeks growing very pink. "Lady 'Elene'll lay there all stiff and Friday-faced while 'is lordship fights to keep *it* from sniffin' at 'is man's parts."

"Pansy!" Sophie exclaimed, genuinely shocked, while her companions burst into bawdy laughter. She was about to lecture them on the unseemliness of mentioning Lyndhurst's unmentionable parts, when the door swung open.

It was Miss Stewart, looking uncharacteristically harried. "Ah. Good. You're here, Sophie," she exclaimed, hurrying into the room. "Lady Helene has requested your presence."

"Lady Helene?" she echoed, frowning. Whatever could her ladyship want with her? Why, she wasn't even aware that the girl had noticed her, much less knew her name.

"Lady Helene," Miss Stewart confirmed. "She observed your elegant ways when she visited the marchioness's sickbed, and has now decided that you, and only you, are fit to look after Ming-Ming while she takes tea at Hennington House."

"Gor! Glad I ain't elegant," Pansy muttered.

At that moment Sophie wished that she weren't, either. Praying that it was all a hideous mistake, she countered, "But her ladyship takes Ming-Ming everywhere. Can't she take her to Hennington as well?"

Miss Stewart shook her head. "It seems that there was an—*ahem!*—incident involving Ming-Ming and Lord Hennington's prize hunting hound the last time Lady Helene visited. As a result, his lordship has requested that Ming-Ming be left at Hawksbury."

"Oh." Sophie cast her companions a pained look, who returned it with one of boundless sympathy. "Well, then what about her abigail? Surely Mademoiselle Loring would be more suited to the task than I? At least Ming-Ming knows her."

Miss Stewart again shook her head. "She is to accompany her mistress to Hennington."

"But her mother—"

"Is suffering a megrim. And since both the marquess and Lord Lyndhurst are in Exeter on business"—the lady's maid shrugged—"well, as you can see, that leaves only mademoiselle."

She did see, just as she saw that she had no choice but to play nanny to the ill-tempered dog if she wished to retain her new position. The mere thought of returning to the drudgery of her former duties was enough to make her ask, "When would her ladyship like to see me?"

"In a quarter of an hour. You are to meet her in the blue drawing room to take charge of Ming-Ming and receive instructions for her care." Apparently Sophie looked as miserable as she felt, for Miss Stewart's expression grew suddenly apologetic, and she added, "I'm sorry, dear. Truly I am. I know that the dog is a bit of a trial, but, well, it's just for a few hours."

"Yes. Just for a few hours. I'm certain I can endure the beast for that long," she murmured, glancing first to Fancy, then Pansy for help in convincing herself.

Both looked doubtful.

"And under no circumstances are you to walk Ming-Ming in the garden. Those horrid gravel and sand paths quite ruin her feet. Makes them impossibly rough," Lady Helene directed, admiring the picture she and her pet made in the drawing room mirror.

Sophie nodded, hard-pressed not to giggle. Dog and girl wore matching caps; costly scarlet velvet caps with pearl-embroidered borders and curling white ostrich feathers. While the creation looked quite elegant on her ladyship, it served only to emphasize the gargoyle-like ugliness of the dog's broad, flat face . . . a fact to which her mistress was clearly oblivious.

Indeed her expression was nothing short of fawning as she pressed her beautiful face to Ming-Ming's monstrous one, cooing, "Mama's pretty little boo-by has the tenderest feet in all of England. Yes, she does! Yes, she does! Boo-by . . . boo-by . . . Mingy . . . Mingy . . . boo-by . . . boo-by . . ."

Sophie watched with repulsed fascination as the girl kissed the dog's mouth, producing a series of loud smacking noises, exactly as Fancy demonstrated.

Ming-Ming rolled her bulbous brown eyes, whimpering and slobbering in ecstatic response.

The girl kissed her again, this time crooning between noisy smooches, "Mama loves her little boo-by . . . boo-by . . . boo-by . . ."

"Ahem!" Mademoiselle Loring, her French abigail, cleared her throat, obviously trying to gain her mistress's notice.

Lady Helene ignored her. "Mingy Ming-Ming is the sweetest, most beautiful boo-by . . . boo-by . . ."

The abigail tried again. *"Ahem!"*

"Boo-by in the whole world," the girl continued.

Mademoiselle sighed. Like all the servants in Lady

Helene's entourage, the abigail, her ladyship's sixth in as many months it was rumored, bore an air of long-suffering martyrdom. Indeed, she reminded Sophie of a painting she'd seen of Joan of Arc being burned at the stake, especially at that moment as she cleared her throat a third time and murmured, "Pardon, my lady. But we must leave now if we are to be at Hennington House on time."

Lady Helene froze, breaking off mid-boo-by. After a beat, one during which Sophie could feel the abigail's tension, she slowly turned. "Did I speak to you, made-moiselle?" she inquired, her tone chilly enough to frost hell.

The abigail bowed her head, shaking it to the negative.

"Well?" Her ladyship snapped her long white fingers at the woman. "When I ask you a question, I expect you to answer. I repeat: Did I speak to you?" Three more finger snaps.

Mademoiselle flinched as if struck. "No, my lady."

"The rule?" *Snap!-Snap!* "Repeat the rule."

"A servant must never speak unless first addressed by her master or mistress," the woman choked out.

"Correct." *Snap!-Snap!-Snap!* "See that you don't forget it in the future."

"Yes, my lady."

"As for you, girl." Lady Helene shifted her icy gaze from her cowed abigail to Sophie. "Repeat my instructions for Ming-Ming's care. I want to make certain that you understood me."

Understood her? Ha! She understood her perfectly. She'd met dozens of her kind in the ton. Lady Helene was a spoiled, utterly detestable little tyrant whose greatest pleasure in life was bullying the servants and making everyone around her miserable.

"Well?" *Snap!-Snap!-Snap!*

Sophie stifled her tart retort. Oh, what she wouldn't give to be the Toast of the ton again, if only for that moment. What a pleasure it would be to put the chit in her place and make *her* jump when *she* snapped for fear of being cut by the ton. Since, however, such was not the case, and she didn't wish to spend the remainder of her time at Hawksbury scrubbing the spit—

"I am to take Ming-Ming for a walk promptly at three o'clock and for exactly one-half hour," she dutifully recited. "We are to walk in the southeast Hawksbury park, but only in the centermost section. Before allowing her down on the grass, I must remove my shoes and walk about the area to make certain that it is free of brambles or anything else that might damage her paws."

"Feet." *Snap!* "Ming-Ming has feet, animals have paws."

Chamber pots. Remember the chamber pots. That reminder instantly squelched her urge to inquire as to the sort of creature her ladyship fancied Ming-Ming to be, and made her murmur instead, "Feet, yes. Please do forgive me."

The tyrant nodded. "Continue."

"Ming-Ming is prone to colds. Therefore, if the grass feels even the least bit damp, I am to walk her in the conservatory. After her walk I'm to brush her one hundred strokes, no more, no less, then tuck her into the cradle next to your bed for a nap."

"And if she refuses to sleep?"

"I'm to rock her and sing 'Ding Dong Bell.'" A vivid memory of the meat press and how disgusting it was to clean prevented her from rolling her eyes at the absurdity of that particular order.

"I do hope you sing on key," Lady Helene murmured, surveying her critically. "My poor darling simply cannot abide off-key singing. She howls quite dreadfully in protest."

Oh, wonderful! It just so happened that she wasn't musically inclined. Indeed, her music instructor had pronounced her singing quite impossible; Lydia had declared him kind in doing so. Sensing that her ladyship would take the news rather badly, she curved her lips into an agreeable, but noncommittal smile, and prayed, *Please, God, please let the dog fall right to sleep.*

"Good." The girl nodded, interpreting her smile as one of reassurance. "Now. I shall do everything in my power to return in time to give Mingy her dinner. Dining with strangers quite spoils her digestion. However, should I be delayed, you are to feed her—when?" *Snap!-Snap!*

"Promptly at six-thirty."

"And what must you do before she eats?" *Snap!*

"Give her a spoonful of ginger tonic to stimulate her digestion."

Snap! "When?"

"At six-ten, not a moment earlier or later."

"And if her dinner gives her wind?" *Snap!-Snap!*

"I'm to dose her with two measures of peppermint oil."

Snap!-Snap!-Snap! "And?"

Remember the slop buckets. "Massage her belly."

Lo and behold, the tyrant smiled. "Yes. Good. Very good indeed." She nodded, this time with an approval that made her ebony curls bob. "I see that I was wise to demand your services."

Nodding again, she glanced down at the fluffy white monstrosity in her arms. Her expression that of a mother viewing a beloved child, she crooned, "Mama must go now, Mingy darling." *Smooch!-Smooch!* "You be a good boo-by . . . boo-by . . . boo-by—*Smooch!*—and Mama shall be back before you know it." After kissing the dog thrice more, she held it out for Sophie to take.

Sophie pasted a wan smile on her face and reached for it.

G-r-r-r! The evil beast growled and snapped at her hands.

She jerked away, narrowly missing being bitten by its tiny, but alarmingly sharp-looking teeth.

Lady Helene scowled. "Do stop being skittish. Can't you see that you're upsetting the poor darling?"

The beleaguered mademoiselle, who now stood behind her mistress, nodded at Sophie and pantomimed a series of actions that suggested distracting the dog with one hand while grasping it from behind with the other.

Smiling her gratitude, Sophie did as demonstrated. First she extended her left hand to the dog.

G-r-r! Yap! Yap! Yap! It snapped and snarled at it.

Then she slipped her right one behind it and swiftly scooped it up into her arms.

Yip! Yip! Whine. It thrashed its head and nipped the air several times, then sank its teeth into the ruffle edging her fichu. *G-r-r-r!* It chewed and tore at the delicate fabric, making the most horrendous slobbering noises as it did so.

"Well?" *Snap!-Snap!-Snap!*

Sophie sighed and looked at Lady Helene.

She snapped her fingers again, this time to indicate the furiously gnawing animal. "Can't you see that she's anxious, girl?" When Sophie merely stared at her, not daring to reply for fear of speaking her mind, the chit made a disdainful noise and said, "Don't tell me that you have already forgotten what I told you about soothing Ming-Ming's nerves?"

At a loss Sophie shot mademoiselle a pleading look, who in turn pretended to rock a baby, her lips moving mutely.

She groaned inwardly. Not that. Anything but that.

Snap! "Well?"

Miserably she glanced down at the dog, which continued to snarl and savage her now ruined fichu. Wanting to die on the spot, she slowly began to rock it, crooning, "Boo-by . . . boo-by . . ."

Chapter 17

"Here, Mingy! Here, boo-by . . . boo-by!" Sophie called, crawling on her hands and knees beside the yew hedge.

Wretched little cur! It had to be in the hedge, it just had to be. She'd seen it dash in there with her own two eyes . . . right after it had bitten her ankle and tripped her with its leash. Granted, she'd been flat on the ground at the time, and everything around her had been fuzzy through the galaxy of stars shooting about her head, but what else could the white blur with its streak of scarlet have been, if not the dog dragging its red leather leash? A comet?

Her palms itching to strangle the beast, Sophie called again, then sat back on her heels to listen for telltale rustling among the foliage. Nothing. Silence.

Blast! She resumed her crawling, alternately calling and listening until she'd completed a full circuit around the four yew walls that enclosed the small park. Still nothing.

Alarmed now, she hurried through the gate, certain that the animal had burrowed out the opposite side. Her heart in her throat, she walked the entire outer perimeter, more croaking than calling the dog in her anxiety as she went. Again nothing. Wherever had the wicked beast gone?

Her alarm exploding into panic, she turned from the hedge and scanned the landscape around her. To her right lay the Hawksbury stables; to her left the marquess's favorite fishing lake. Before her, beyond a lush green fairway, was an ancient, densely wooded deer park. Behind her, past the hedges and stretching on for what looked like forever, was a meadow abloom with valerian, cinquefoil, and lady's-smock.

Nowhere in sight was Ming-Ming.

At wit's end she looked around her again, trying to decide where to search first. Was the dog in the lakeside pavilion, nibbling on a forgotten picnic delicacy? Or had it seen a hare and chased after it into the deer park? Ming-Ming did, after all, have a most vexing habit of attacking anything that moved. Indeed, according to Robin, one of the four stable boys, she particularly delighted in weaving between horses legs and nipping at their fetlocks.

That recollection made her cast a speculative gaze at the elegant brick stables. A beat later, she sighed and looked away again. Several of the grooms knew of her errand, having commented on the dog as she'd passed by on her way to the park. If it turned up there, they were sure to send someone to find her.

That left only the meadow. She spared the flat tract of grassland a brief glance, then dismissed it as well. She could see for what must be miles, and nothing moved. Ming-Ming had to have run in one of the other directions. The question was, which one?

After a moment of deliberation, she decided to start at the lake. No sense in wasting the hours it would take to search the deer park woods when she might find the dog in the minutes it would take to search the picnic pavilion. Thus, she was off.

But Ming-Ming wasn't anywhere near the lake.

Or in the woods.

And there was still no sign of her in the meadow.

On the verge of tears now, Sophie rushed toward her last bastion of hope: the stables. Perhaps, just perhaps, the grooms had come looking for her while she was in the woods, and had thus been unable to find her. Praying that such was the case, she ran into the stable yard, calling between pants, "Dicky? Conrad? Joseph?"

No reply.

Fighting to catch her breath, she frantically looked about her. Though she saw no sign of the grooms, she noticed that the door at the end of the far building stood ajar. Certain that the men were within, preoccupied, she hoped, with the dog, she hurried across the courtyard.

"Excuse me? Is anyone here?" she called, stepping through the door. She paused a few feet inside, peering down the wide corridor of brass and mahogany box stalls, awaiting an answer.

Two whinnies, four nickers, and a snort from a fierce-looking stallion on her left were her only responses. Nothing more.

She called again, this time louder. Still no reply—well, nothing human. With tears of frustration and worry welling up in her eyes, she turned to leave, only to stop short in the next instant. The grooms weren't here, but maybe, just maybe . . .

Her nerves stretched to the point of snapping, she called, "Here, Ming-Ming! Here, boo-by . . . boo-by . . . boo-by! Mingy? Here . . ."

"Gorblimey! That wee divvil ain't loose in 'ere, are it?" exclaimed a youthful voice behind her.

Sophie swung around to find Robin, the twelve-year-old stable boy, standing on the threshold, his freckled face screwed up in horror. Her heart sank to an all-time low at his words. "Then Ming-Ming isn't here," she murmured. The utterance was a statement to herself, not a question to the boy.

Robin, however, took it for the latter. "O' course she ain't 'ere. What'd that bugbear be doin' out 'ere?"

She dismissed his question with a shake of her head. "Could someone else have seen her, one of the grooms or under-coachmen, perhaps, and not told you?" Please, God. Make him say yes.

"Nay. It's Thursday. Ain't nothin' 'appens on Thursday that I don't know 'bout."

"Are you certain?" she squeaked past the lump in her throat.

"Aye. Thursday's the day I 'elp 'xercise 'n' wash the 'orses. I work wit' the grooms, the coachmen, too. I jist left 'em. They're all 'cross the way in the foalin' box. 'Er ladyship's prize mare, Lily, be givin' birth." He cocked his head, eyeing her curiously. "Why ye askin' after divvil dog? Ye ain't lost 'er, 'ave ye?"

"Yes. I-I'm afraid I have," she whispered, bowing her head to hide her tears.

"Gor! I'd 'ate to be in yer shoes when Lady 'Elene 'ears," he exclaimed as she turned and walked out the door.

Sophie hated being in her own shoes. What the girl would do when she heard, she didn't know, but it was bound to be awful.

Weeping with all the despair she felt inside, she ran through the stable-yard gate and down the road that led to the house. So caught up in her misery was she, that she didn't see the approaching horse until it was almost upon her.

"Whoa!" The rider reined sharply.

Neigh! The enormous stallion reared, skittishly dancing back on its hind legs.

"Lyndhurst!" Sophie gasped, instantly recognizing both man and beast.

"Whoa! There, now, Tityus! Easy, boy!" his lordship commanded, fighting hard to control the startled animal. *Neigh!-Whinny!* The horse bucked, almost unseating him, but he held firm. "Easy, Tityus! Whoa!" The stallion snorted and pranced several more times, then began to calm beneath his master's skillful handling. When he stood completely at ease, Lyndhurst shot her a furious look. "Bloody hell, woman! What were you trying to do? Kill yourself?"

Sophie returned his glittering gaze for a beat, morbidly viewing his words as a lost opportunity. Then she burst into tears anew and blubbered, "What would it have mattered anyway? All I ever do is make a muddle of things! Oh, why didn't you just run me down and end my wretched life!"

He was off his horse in a flash, grasping her upper arms. "Good God, Sophie! What has happened?"

She shook her head, too choked with anguish to reply.

For a long moment he simply looked at her, as if at a loss as to what to do or say, then he released her arms and drew his handkerchief from his pocket. Pressing it into her hand, he murmured, "Don't tell me that you were bitten by another bogle?" When she didn't reply, he smiled gently and added, "If you were, please be assured that the bite of a Hawksbury bogle is quite free of poison or any other deleterious effects."

So kind, so genuinely warm and full of concern were both his expression and voice that Sophie impulsively threw herself against him. Burying her face into his shirt frills, she wept in earnest.

He stiffened briefly, as if shocked by her action, then slowly wrapped his arms around her.

She nuzzled yet closer. The feel of him, so warm and solid, gave her the oddest sensation that she'd found something for which she'd searched forever; something that she never wanted to lose.

She felt safe . . . wanted . . . loved.

Her desperate longing for the feeling to be fact and the devastating knowledge that it could never be, made her weep harder.

"Hush, now, Sophie. Don't cry," he crooned, tightening her into his embrace. "Everything will be fine. I promise."

She shook her head, wanting to believe his promise, but too aware of the impossibility of it to do so.

He made a soothing little noise beneath his breath. "There, there, now. Nothing can be so dreadful as all that."

"Yes, it can," she wailed.

"You weren't cursed by gypsies, were you?"

She shook her head.

"Did Cook's old black cat, Abecrombie, cross your path?"

Another head shake.

"No?" A beat of silence, then, "Don't tell me that you did something to tempt fate and forgot to knock on wood afterward?"

Despite her distress, Sophie couldn't help smiling at his endearing attempt to cheer her. Touched, she looked up and croaked, "Fancy is right, my lord. You are a tease." *Sniffle!*

He grinned. "True, but please be good enough to re-

frain from telling anyone. It would never do for the
world to know that the Earl of Lyndhurst isn't at all the
staid, dignified fellow they all believe him to be."

"You could tease every girl in England in such a manner, my lord, and the only thing anyone could ever ac-
cuse you of being is charming." And handsome, she
added to herself, her gaze worshiping the contours of
his face.

Instead of looking pleased by her words, as she'd
hoped, he looked rather discomfited. In the next instant
his smile faded, and he tipped his disfigured cheek from
her sight. Dropping his arms from around her, he
stepped back saying, "But enough of such nonsense. If
you will be good enough to tell me what has you in a
stew, I shall do my best to help you."

Grieved over the death of their unexpected intimacy,
Sophie merely gazed at him, wondering at his change of
demeanor. Most men she knew preened like peacocks
when called charming. Could it be that he was different
from other men in that he neither liked nor wanted compliments? Or was it just her compliments he disdained?

It had to be the latter, she grimly decided, remembering how he'd smiled when Lady Helene had compli-
mented his mother on having an attractive son. The
thought that he still detested her so, despite the new-
found ease between them, started her weeping anew.

"Well?" he bit out.

"It's just that—" It was on the tip of her tongue to
tell him of her feelings, to spill forth all her pain, regret,
and longing. To beg his forgiveness for everything. But
she couldn't, she didn't dare, not after the terrible way
he'd responded to her compliment.

Thus, she swallowed her emotions and instead confessed, "It's Ming-Ming. I've lost her. She ran away
while I was walking her in the park. I looked and looked,
but—" She broke off shaking her head, once again over-
whelmed by the gravity of her predicament.

He looked almost amused by her plight.

Her dismay deepened, if such a thing were possible.
He must harbor an even deeper resentment than she
suspected to look so.

Smiling in a way that confirmed her awful suspicion, he turned and strode back to his horse. After stroking the animal's neck and whispering something in his ear, he opened his saddlebag and extracted a sleepy-looking Ming-Ming.

Holding the yawning dog up for her inspection, he explained, "I found her on the road by the gatehouse. She probably burrowed under the hedge at the north side of the lake and wandered down the manor lane."

Rather than be relieved, as Nicholas expected, Sophie wept harder. Perplexed, he looked first at the dog, which slobbered and gazed back at him from beneath its silly cap, then at Sophie, who sobbed as if faced with the world's greatest tragedy. Emitting a noise that perfectly expressed his aggravation, he snapped, "Would you please be so kind as to tell me what is wrong now?"

"She's dirty and tangled—and look at her hat! The plume is ruined. Lady Helene shall murder me for certain when she sees her."

Nicholas opened his mouth to dispute her ladyship's murderous tendencies, then closed it again when he remembered who it was they discussed. While Helene most probably wouldn't kill Sophie, she was bound to make more of the incident than it merited. Indeed, judging from her hysterics when she'd caught him teaching the dog to fetch a stick, she'd no doubt demand Sophie's dismissal were she to see her pet in its current state. Not that he'd oblige her, of course. But why become entangled in a coil that was so simple to avoid?

Amazed that Sophie hadn't thought of the solution herself, he moved toward her saying, "Her ladyship will never be the wiser if you bathe the animal before she returns."

She shook her head, sniffling loudly. "I can't. Ming-Ming won't let me. She hates me."

As if to prove her claim, Ming-Ming growled and bared her teeth at Sophie as he came to a stop before her.

"See?" She gestured to the animal.

It growled again and lunged at her hand, its tiny jaw snapping open and closed as it tried to bite her.

"I see," he replied, eyeing the dog with annoyance. Like her beautiful, spoiled mistress, Ming-Ming seemed to have an ugly intolerance for servants. And since he had no intention of allowing Sophie to be abused by either, he added, "I guess there is only one way out of this coil."

"Which—*sniffle*—is?"

"Since Ming-Ming and I are on the best of terms, I shall bathe her while you mend the hat."

She froze amid blowing her nose, peering at him over the top of his handkerchief as if he'd just made a particularly addled suggestion. "You? Bathe Ming-Ming?"

He couldn't help smiling at her consternation. "Just because I'm an earl doesn't mean that I'm opposed to soiling my hands." His smile broadened into a grin. "Have you forgotten my fondness for grubbing in the dirt?"

She wiped her nose, blushing a most delightful shade of pink as she did so. "No, but—"

"Fine. Then, it's settled. I shall wash, and you shall mend." With that interjection, Nicholas strode back to his horse and gathered up its reins. Glancing over his shoulder, he inquired, "Shall we retire to the stables, Miss Barton? We will find everything we need to wash the dog there."

She returned his gaze for a beat, then nodded.

For a long while thereafter they walked in companionable silence; he leading his horse with one hand while cradling the drowsing dog in his opposite arm; she walking beside him, stealing glances at him as if she had something on her mind.

It wasn't until they were almost to the stables that she revealed her thoughts. Looking everywhere but at him, she blurted out, "I'm sorry if I offended you by calling you charming. It was meant as a compliment."

Of all the things Nicholas suspected she might be thinking, this wasn't one of them. Indeed, so surprised was he, that he stopped short to stare at her. He hadn't been offended by her compliment, he was disappointed; disappointed that it had been nothing more than light, meaningless banter. He'd have so loved to believe that she truly found him charming, that she felt the same attraction for him that he felt for her.

Solemnly returning his gaze, she vowed, "I promise that I shall never again refer to you as charming, though I fear you shall most probably have to endure other women calling you so." She bowed her head and began picking at the edge of her shredded fichu. "Of course, perhaps you shan't mind it so much if it is said by someone else. I can't blame you for not wanting my compliments."

Not want her compliments? Dear God! Was it possible? Could she really think him charming? Calling himself every kind of fool for daring to hope, he murmured, "I'm not so different from other men, Sophie. I very much desire compliments from beautiful women such as yourself, provided that those compliments are sincere."

She looked up quickly with a rather startled expression. "But I was sincere. Whatever made you believe otherwise?"

"Perhaps it had something to do with the way you so sincerely pronounced me stiff and dull just last month." Try though he might, he was unable to keep the bitterness from his voice.

"I-I see." She bowed her head again, but not before he saw her face. If ever a woman looked contrite, it was Sophia Barrington. "To be honest, I did think you tedious. Intolerably so. But that was because I never bothered to listen to you. I was too—too—distracted—by your s-scar to notice anything else about you."

He smiled sardonically at her use of the word *distracted*. If she were indeed being honest, she'd have said repulsed.

"I was a fool, the worst kind of one to have dismissed you in such an unjust manner," she continued. "I see that now. I have also discovered that you are a most charming man and that—that I like you very much."

When he didn't immediately respond to her declaration, she looked up and earnestly added, "I shan't blame you at all if you never forgive me for treating you as I did. I know that I shall never forgive myself. I do want you to know, however, regardless of what you choose to do, that I am deeply sorry for everything and that I now think you the most splendid man in all of England. Not that I expect my opinion matters to you."

Little did she know that at that moment it meant the world to him, especially the one she'd just expressed. True, she hadn't said that she no longer found his scar repulsive, nor had she indicated desire for him. Yet she had said that she liked him. Yes, and she'd called him the most splendid man in England. Surely she wouldn't have said such a thing if she found his person offensive?

Would she?

Uncertain what to believe, Nicholas reluctantly met her gaze, hoping to read the truth in her eyes, yet terrified of what it might say. What he saw made his heart miss a beat.

There was anxiety and uncertainty and a look of appeal, as if she humbly begged his forgiveness and expected to be rebuffed. That she so clearly wished to make amends brought a smile to his lips. More than willing to grant her her wish, he exclaimed, "I like you, too, Miss Barrington, and gratefully accept your apology."

At that moment, as he watched her face light with a smile more radiant than the sun, moon, and stars combined, he realized that it was true. He didn't just desire Sophie as a man desires a beautiful woman, he liked her as a person.

He liked her for her honesty in the Mayhew disaster and respected the bravery it took for her to express it. He also admired the spirit with which she bore her servitude. Then there was the kindness she showed the other servants. How could he not like a girl who not only accepted, but befriended and cherished people who most in her class considered beneath their notice?

In truth, she surprised him daily by revealing new and praiseworthy facets of herself; ones that gave him reason not just to like her, but to love her. And love her he did, he realized.

Wanting nothing more than to take her in his arms and tell her of his feelings, Nicholas ripped his gaze from her glowing face and murmured, "We had best be off to the stables. Ming-Ming must be bathed soon if she's to dry before Helene returns."

"Yes, of course . . . and thank you, my lord."

He nodded stiffly and resumed walking, not daring to look at her for fear of losing control and kissing her against her will. As for Sophie, she fell into stride beside him, wishing that she were in his arms again.

Thus they continued the rest of the way in silence, each aching for the other, neither daring to voice their desire. Once at the stables, both were too caught up in their bustle to prepare the dog's bath to exchange more than a few hurried words.

It wasn't until everything was ready and they were alone in the saddle room—he in his shirtsleeves, sitting on the floor brushing the brambles from the dog's long coat, she seated on a clean saddle blanket nearby, trying without either hope or success to repair the animal's cap—that they again conversed.

It was Sophie who spoke first. "My lord—"

"Nicholas," he interjected, without looking up.

"Excuse me?"

"Nicholas. Please call me Nicholas. Or if you prefer, Colin."

"I couldn't. It wouldn't be proper."

"It is perfectly proper if I ask you to do so. Unless, of course, you don't wish to address me by my given name?" He looked up then to cast her a quizzical look.

Sophie felt herself blush, curiously warm and self-conscious beneath his gaze. "I would very much like to do so, but I'm a servant now and subject to certain rules. One of those rules is that I use proper forms of address. Mrs. Pixton would have my head if she heard me call you Nicholas."

"Then, you must call me by my name only when you're certain that you're out of earshot of the other servants. Cook has called me Colin since I was no bigger than, well"—he nodded down at the dog—"Ming-Ming, and the Pixie has never been the wiser."

Sophie couldn't help smiling at his referring to the housekeeper as the Pixie. "I see that the servant's secret nickname for Mrs. Pixton isn't such a secret after all."

He smiled back. "Who told you it's a secret?"

"I just assumed it was. I mean"—she shrugged—"no one ever addresses her so to her face."

"No one except Quentin. He created the name, you know."

"No, I didn't know. How did he come to do so?"

Ming-Ming whimpered then, objecting to her lack of attention.

His expression wry, Nicholas dipped down and whispered something to the dog, something that made it wag its tail. After giving its ear a friendly tweak, an action which would no doubt have given Lady Helene apoplexy had she witnessed it, he eased the animal into the tub of water next to him. To Sophie's surprise, Ming-Ming didn't emit so much as a yip of protest.

As he briskly worked the mud from her coat, he explained, "Quentin first called Mrs. Pixton 'Pixie' when he was about, oh, he couldn't have been beyond one at the time. He was quite taken with her and would toddle after her at every opportunity."

"Perhaps it was her hair that attracted him," Sophie commented, resuming her efforts to fix the plume. "I've noticed that your brother has a particular fondness for women with red hair."

"Perhaps. Or it could be that his preference stems from the kindness Mrs. Pixton showed him as a child. Whichever is the case, hers was one of the first names he said, or at least attempted to say. Since he was too young to form the words correctly, it came out as Pixie. She's been his Pixie ever since."

"In view of that fact, I suppose she doesn't mind the nickname, not coming from him," she murmured, trying to coax the bedraggled feather to curl in the proper direction. Blasted thing! Why must it be so obstinate?

"Mind?" He chuckled as he lifted Ming-Ming from the water to examine her paws. "She adores it, as she does him. Everyone at Hawksbury adores Quent. He is quite the favorite around here." The statement was uttered without the slightest hint of rancor one would expect to hear in the voice of a person acknowledging their sibling as the favored child.

Surprised by his neutral tone, especially in light of his brother's role in propagating his recent disgrace, Sophie inquired, "What about you, my—ur—Nicholas? How do you feel about Quentin?"

He shrugged as he set the wet dog before him. "I love him."

"You do?" She stared at him, unable to believe her ears.

"Yes. Very much."

"But—" She shook her head over and over again. "How can you love someone who so clearly loathes you? Especially after the way he trumpeted your shame to the ton and gloated over your humiliation? I know he's your brother, but—"

"To love is to forgive," he interjected quietly. "And as I said, I love Quentin. Oh, I admit that I was furious with him for spreading the scandal. I am, after all, no saint. But then I remembered how very close we once were and the jolly times we had together, and I couldn't stay angry with him for long." He paused to pluck a bramble from Ming-Ming's clean but matted fur, smiling wryly as he did so. "Of course, just because my wrath has cooled doesn't mean that I shan't dress him down the next time I see him."

Sophie watched as he began towel drying the dog, wondering what had set the brothers at odds. Though she longed to ask, wanting to know everything about the man before her, she was reluctant to do so. To make such an inquiry would be to pry into his private affairs, and simply being at peace with him gave her no license to take such liberties. Still, if she were to ever truly know him . . .

"What happened to make Quentin dislike you so?" she blurted out before she completely lost her nerve.

When he continued to dry the dog, refraining from response, she was certain that she'd angered him. As she opened her mouth to apologize, he replied, "Quentin grew up, that is what happened. He learned what it means to be the second son and became resentful that I, by virtue of being born first, shall inherit everything."

"Well, I suppose I can understand his resentment, but

why hate you?" she said, aching at the pain in his voice. "You didn't ask to be born first, nor did you make the inheritance laws."

"True, but that doesn't change the fact that I'm heir to the title and fortune he covets." He tossed aside the cloth and picked up a clean brush. "Though it grieves me to admit it, I sometimes wonder if perhaps it isn't my fault that he feels as he does."

"Your fault?" She frowned. "I can't imagine you doing anything to prompt his bitterness. Indeed, I'm certain that you were the most devoted of brothers. It isn't in your nature to be less."

He smiled wanly at her praise. "Perhaps I was a bit too devoted. In truth, I spoiled him terribly—probably worse than anyone else. Yet how could I not? I spent the first seven years of my life longing for a brother or sister, hoping as Mother delivered three babes who never lived past their first hour." He looked up then and met her gaze, his dark eyes wounded and pleading. "After suffering so much disappointment, how could I not dote on Quent?"

"Of course you couldn't help doting on him," she declared, crawling nearer to where he sat. Ming-Ming growled and showed her teeth in protest, but Sophie ignored her. "Nicholas," she murmured, laying her hand on his arm, "you did nothing but love him. Where is the wrong in that? Had I been blessed with a brother, you can wager that I'd have spoiled him until he was thoroughly rotten."

He smiled. "You'd have been a splendid big sister, Sophie. It's a shame that you never had the chance."

She felt herself blush at the warm approval in his voice. "Yes, well, at any rate, what I'm trying to say is that you mustn't despair so for Quentin. I'm certain that, like you, he remembers what you once shared and will come about in time. I'm also certain that he loves you. How could he not when you care so for him?"

He returned her gaze solemnly for a beat, then laid his hand over the one she had rested on his arm. "When did you become so very wise, Miss Barrington?"

She smiled, savoring the feel of his hand against hers.

"I'm not wise, not in the least. I simply remember my own family and how it felt to be loved. That kind of love is something one never forgets or stops craving."

"My poor Sophie." He twined his fingers through hers and gave her hand a squeeze. "You miss your parents very much, don't you?"

"Not a day goes by that I don't long to feel my mother's embrace and hear my father's laughter," she softly declared.

For a long moment he simply looked at her, his gaze soft and expression thoughtful, then he murmured, "You've never spoken much about your childhood, but I can tell from your words that it was a happy one."

"It was more than happy, it was perfect. I couldn't have asked for more wonderful parents." Her words came out a hoarse whisper.

"I would like to hear about them, if you wouldn't mind telling me." He smiled gently, as if asking to be trusted with her memories and promising to cherish them if she did. She smiled back, deciding that there was no one with whom she'd rather share them. "I would be honored to tell you, my lord."

"Nicholas," he corrected, his gaze boring into hers.

"Nicholas," she echoed, mesmerized by the tenderness she saw in his beautiful brown eyes.

G-r-r! Yip! Yip! Yip!

Both jumped, startled, and looked at Ming-Ming, who stood with her front paws braced possessively on Nicholas's knees, growling and yapping at Sophie.

"Just like her mistress," he muttered, eyeing the animal with annoyance. "She can't bear it when a man so much as glances at another woman."

Sophie grinned at his comment, secretly understanding both dog and girl's desire to monopolize his attention.

Looking as if he'd like to strangle the beast, Nicholas resumed brushing. As he worked, carefully easing the tangles from Ming-Ming's snarled coat, he reminded her, "I believe you were going to tell me about your parents."

She started at the sound of his voice, blushing as she wondered if he'd noticed her staring at him. Certain that her face was as red as it felt, she picked up the cap and bent her head over it, trying to hide her embarrassment. "Yes, of course." She gave the plume a tweak. Wonder of wonders, it finally fell into place. Grinning her victory, she inquired, "Where should I start?"

"Why don't you tell me about your mother? I'm told that she was once considered the greatest beauty in England."

"Yes. She was lovely. She had the softest, most beautiful blond hair in the world. And her eyes! Oh, you should have seen them, Nicholas. They were such an amazing shade of green. My father had his dyers concoct batch after batch of green dye, trying to capture that exact shade, but none ever came out quite right. He so wanted her to have a gown that matched her eyes."

Nicholas smiled, though he didn't look up from his task. "It sounds like he loved her a great deal."

"Oh, he did. And she him. They were constantly kissing and touching and looking at each other as if they wanted to gobble each other up." She smiled wistfully, remembering those looks. What she wouldn't give to see Nicholas look at her like that.

"How did they meet? Your father was from Leeds, I believe, and your mother from Oxfordshire."

"They met at the Michaelmas fair in Leeds. My mother was there visiting a school friend," Sophie replied, grateful for his tact. Most people used the couple's differences in station rather than their geographical ones as a basis for their speculation at the novelty of the match. "They loved each other at first glance and eloped within the fortnight. And, well, you know the rest. Everyone in the ton does. Her father disowned her for marrying him."

She smiled ruefully at that last. "I always thought it queer that he would do such a thing. The Barringtons were one of the wealthiest and most respected families in the county. Despite their lack of a title, they were every bit as noble as the Marwoods."

"Probably nobler," he countered. "It takes a far greater man to earn a fortune than to inherit one."

"That's what my mother used to say," she replied, beyond pleased by his comment.

"I imagine that they were quite pleased when you were born."

"According to my mother, my father was so thrilled that he rode through the village, shouting the news at the top of his lungs. Both told and showed me how much they loved me at least a hundred times a day."

He glanced up from the dog, smiling. "How did they show you?"

"Well, my mother baked me Shrewsbury cakes every single day, even though we had plenty of servants who could have done it for her. Her cakes were special, you see, because she baked laughter and a kiss into every bite."

Nicholas looked genuinely intrigued. "How did she do that?"

"Simple. She'd blow a kiss into the bowl, like this"—she demonstrated—"then stir. Then she'd blow another kiss and stir a bit more. She'd go on and on like that until we both collapsed into giggles. That was the laughter, you see, and we would both stir furiously to make certain that it was blended in as well."

He chuckled. "Yes, I do see." And indeed he did. He could just imagine Sophie, so small and pretty, giggling into a bowl of cake batter with a woman who looked much as she did now. It was an exceedingly pleasant picture, one that made him long to see Sophie with their daughter carrying on the charming tradition.

"And then there was Sir Nightslayer," she continued.

"Sir Nightslayer?"

She nodded, her expression a million miles away. "Sir Nightslayer was the small wooden knight my father slipped under my pillow when he tucked me into bed. I was afraid of the dark, you see, imagining it filled with all sorts of dreadful creatures just waiting to gobble me up while I slept. Sir Nightslayer was my protection against them."

"I take it that Sir Nightslayer was magical?"

"Yes. Magical. My father told me that he came to life after I fell asleep and guarded me against monsters all night long. Of course he was seven feet tall when he was alive, and quite fierce." She fell silent then, as if lost in that happier time.

Loath to disturb her reverie, Nicholas continued brushing the dog, wishing that she loved him so he could bring the happiness back to her days. And her nights. What he wouldn't give to be her real-life Sir Nightslayer, to show her that the dark held not demons, but pleasure.

"Poor Sir Nightslayer," she said on a sigh. "I wonder what became of him?"

"You lost him?"

"I left him under my pillow when I fled London. I'm afraid I quite forgot him in my rush."

Nicholas's hand tightened around the brush as he recalled the tale of her flight from London. As he'd demanded that night on the road, she'd recounted how she'd come to be in service at the manor as they rode back to Hawksbury. Even then, as much as he'd despised her, he'd been furious at her aunt and cousin for abandoning her as they had.

Now that he loved her, he wanted to strangle them. When he said as much, well, the part about strangling the Marwoods, she smiled wistfully and said, "Sometimes I think I got exactly what I deserved. I was such a vain, selfish, and altogether horrid chit."

"No one deserves to be deserted like that, no matter what they have done, and most especially not by people who are supposed to love and care for them," he protested hotly.

"Perhaps." She sighed and shook her head. "The only thing I know for certain is that you deserved far more respect and consideration than you received from me. I can't imagine why you wanted to marry me. I was such a conceited little fool."

So dejected, so very remorseful did she look, that he rushed to ease her conscience by confessing, "I wanted you because you were beautiful and because the ton had decreed you the finest of the Season's Marriage Mart offerings. The shameful truth is that while I admired you, I didn't love you. Not in the way a man should love the woman he marries. So you see, I was as much a fool as you. You couldn't see past my scar, and I couldn't see past your desirability."

Rather than be mollified, she looked positively crestfallen. Certain that she'd misunderstood his reason for telling her what he had, he elaborated, "What I'm trying to say, Sophie, is that I'm as much to blame for what happened in London as you. If I had opened my eyes and really looked at you, I'd have seen your loathing for me and never proposed. Perhaps then you might not be in your current fix."

"Perhaps. But I'd also never have opened my own eyes and discovered what a wonderful man you are," she whispered. The instant she uttered the words, she wished she could take them back. What did he care that she'd had a change of heart? It wasn't as if he were lovelorn and languishing over her. One couldn't be lovelorn if they had never loved in the first place. Embarrassed, she bowed her head and pretended to smooth the scarlet silk cap ties.

After several beats of silence, he murmured, "Sophie?"

"H-m-m?"

"If I weren't scarred, do you think you could have learned to love me?"

There was rawness in his voice, a heartbreaking inflection of hopelessness and yearning that caught her off guard and made her glance up at him. He didn't look at her, but at Ming-Ming, who lay on her side, slobbering. As he always did when in her company, he held his head at an angle, hiding his disfigurement. Her throat strangled by emotion, she choked out, "Oh, Nicholas. I—"

"No." He turned his head abruptly to face her, treating her to a full view of his scar. "Don't answer. I'm sorry. I had no right to ask you such a question."

She smiled tenderly, aching at the pain in his eyes. "I shall be pleased to answer."

"Sophie—"

"The answer is yes, my lord. I have discovered that you are a very easy man to love."

"Sophie—" He more groaned than uttered the word.

"No. I'm not finished. I have also discovered that I like your scar . . . very much." Her smile broadening, she met his gaze. He returned it unblinking, his dark eyes gleaming with hope, yet tortured with uncertainty. Desperate to prove the truth of her words, to free him from his haunting doubt, she reached out and gently touched his damaged cheek.

He closed his eyes, flinching convulsively.

Her motions slow and deliberate, she traced the length of the scar, exploring its texture. It felt smooth and cool, like a satin ribbon in the silk of his skin. When she reached the end, she cupped his entire cheek in her hand and cradled it as if it were the most precious thing on earth. And to her it was, *he* was. "Such a lovely, dashing scar," she murmured. "How did you get it?"

"Quentin cut me with a saber," he whispered hoarsely.

"What!"

"He didn't do it on purpose. He was only five at the time."

"Five! Whatever was a child that age doing with a saber?" she exclaimed, utterly shocked.

He smiled faintly, though he still didn't open his eyes. "Like all boys, he was fascinated with fencing. His favorite game was engaging in swordplay, using sticks for foils. One day, just before his sixth birthday, he decided that he was old enough for a real sword. The one he set his sights on was our grandfather's saber, which hangs over the fireplace in the armory at Somerville Castle."

"I'm surprised he could lift it," she interjected. "I picked up Uncle John's saber when I was ten, and it took almost all the strength in both arms to do so."

"He couldn't lift it, not really, which is how I got cut." His smile faded then, and he sighed. "It was I who discovered him standing on the mantel, trying to lift it from the wall. He succeeded just as I reached him. Because of the weight of the sword, he was pulled off balance, and when I moved to block his fall, the blade somehow sliced my cheek."

"Oh, Nicholas! How awful! You could have been

killed," she cried, her heart missing a beat at his peril. "I do hope Quentin was contrite."

"Very. He cried much harder than I, though I must confess that it was a long while before I could look in the mirror without weeping. It took a year for me to accept the fact that I was scarred, and two to become accustomed to the sight of it. I hadn't thought much about it in years until, well—"

He opened his eyes then and looked at her, his gaze searching as it touched hers. His voice raw with emotion, he whispered, "Is it true, Sophie? Do you no longer find my scar repulsive?"

Spurred by her need to reassure him, she slipped her hand from his cheek to his chin and drew his face to hers. Murmuring, "Would I do this to something I find repulsive?" she kissed his scar.

He groaned her name once, then his arms closed around her and he dragged her to him, crushing her so near that she was forced to straddle his lap. Gazing at her with the adoration she'd so longed to see, he swooped down and captured her mouth with his. She sighed her pleasure and pressed against him, returning his passion with a fervor that echoed his.

Oh, but his kiss was wonderful . . . rough yet tender and filled with a demand that awakened the most unimaginable feelings within her. Her whole body felt hot, as if he'd lit a fire inside her that danced beneath her skin and made her burn in places that were as shocking as they were secret. It was that heat that made her twine her legs around his waist, pressing and rubbing against his belly . . . seeking . . . though what she sought, she didn't know.

Nicholas knew, and he groaned his torment. Dear God! Did she know what she did to him? The feel of her, her long legs clinched about his waist and her womanhood surging against his belly . . .

A ragged sob escaped him. Heaven help him! It was more than he could bear. Never in his life had he desired a woman as he did Sophie; never had he felt such urgency, such unbridled need. There was no coyness in her passion, no self-consciousness or calculation. She gave it freely and joyously, with a generosity that was as innocent as it was brazen. Driven beyond all thought by her responsiveness, Nicholas deepened the kiss.

Sighing her rapture, Sophie melted against him, growing boneless with pleasure as wave after thrilling wave of new sensation washed over her. Oh, those sensations . . . the ecstasy! They kindled within her the strangest and most bewildering desires, ones that made her moan and flush and quiver all over. She sighed again and clung to him yet tighter. Ecstasy, yes . . . sheer ecstasy.

Moaning in a way that gave voice to his own desire, Nicholas eased Sophie back onto the stable floor, never once pausing in his amorous assault on her mouth. When she lay beneath him, her legs about his hips and her thinly veiled womanhood pressed against the bulge in his trousers, something inside him snapped. Sobbing at the intensity of his need, he thrust hard, convulsively rubbing and grinding his arousal against her.

"Oh, Nicholas," she moaned into his mouth, thrashing in frenzied response.

With a hoarse cry that echoed hers, Nicholas arched up and again slammed against her. She whimpered and clasped his taut buttocks, pinning his erection against her, her body stiffening as she thrilled to the resulting sensation. He reciprocated, grasping her backside to lift her to him. Shuddering and jerking with every move, he thrust against her over and over again.

Maddened by a need she didn't understand but desperately wished to relieve, Sophie wildly rubbed her sex against his pummeling one, growing more frenzied with every thrust. "Oh, Nicholas, please!" she begged, though what she begged for she didn't know. All she knew was that she would die if she didn't get it. "Nicholas, please—"

Yap!-Yap!-Yap!

Neigh!-Whinny!

Thump!

A man's bellow, "Bloody hell!"

A woman's shriek, "Boo-by!"

Nicholas and Sophie froze, then looked at each other in horror. "Ming-Ming!"

Chapter 18

Nicholas came to a skidding halt on the threshold of the stable door, a curse escaping him as he viewed the scene before him. Bedlam. The scene in the stable yard was utter bedlam. Beside him, he heard Sophie gasp as she, too, observed the spectacle.

Clompity-clomp! Clompity-clomp! His father's gray stallion raced around the twilight-shadowed yard, its long silver mane and tail streaming like mist off a ghost.

Yap! Yap! Ming-Ming chased after it, her short legs pumping furiously as she barked and snapped at its hind fetlocks.

Neigh! Whinny!

G-r-r. Tiny canine teeth sank into horseflesh.

The gray screamed and kicked.

Ming-Ming skittered aside, just barely escaping having her skull crushed by the horse's flailing hoofs.

"Boo-by!" Helene shrieked, dashing headlong into the fray. Mindless of everything but her need to rescue her pet, she lunged at the animals, screeching at the top of her lungs.

As for his father, he sat in the center of the yard where he'd been thrown, shaking his head as if trying to restore his wits.

"Father!" Nicholas shouted, rushing to him.

"I'm fine," he muttered, "but I most probably shan't be able to say the same for Helene if you don't take her in hand."

Nicholas followed his grimacing father's gaze to Helene, who had caught onto the horse's tail and now ran

behind it, tugging hard and commanding it to stop. As
he watched, the animal bucked, sending her tumbling
onto her backside. Terrified that she'd be trampled, he
plunged into the melee and narrowly missed being run
down himself as he scooped her up and pulled her
against him.

"Boo-by!" she screeched, struggling in his grasp.

G-r-r! Yap! The dog weaved between the gray's legs,
avoiding its hooves with a canniness that was nothing
short of amazing.

U-o-mph! Helene elbowed Nicholas in the belly.
Tightening his grip to further immobilize her, he
shouted, "What the hell were you trying to do? Kill
yourself and the animals?"

"But my boo-by!" she wailed.

As he hauled her screaming and kicking form to
safety, four grooms, two stable boys, and Oliver, the
head coachman, poured from the stables. His father,
over whom Sophie now fussed, shouted to them, "Forget
the horse! Get that damn dog. Gilbert will calm down
once you get that demon off his heels."

"Demon! How dare you!" Helene shrieked, impo-
tently slapping at Nicholas's restraining arms. When he
refused to release her, she flung back her head and
glared up at him. "Well, don't just stand there like a
dolt, Lyndhurst! Do something! If you were any sort of
man at all, you would rescue Ming-Ming."

"Ming-Ming doesn't appear to want rescuing, and I
would be less than a man if I let you get your silly head
smashed in," he retorted, watching as the dog bit a
groom who sought to contain it. "However, if you promise to stay put and not do anything so foolish as grab
the horse's tail again, I shall do what I can. Gilbert is a
valuable bit of cattle, and I would hate to see him
injured."

"Gilbert? Who cares about that evil horse. It's my
Mingy who's in danger!"

"It's your Mingy who is the danger," he growled, re-
leasing her. Determined to tell his mother exactly what
he thought of her matchmaking when this was over,
Nicholas stalked across the yard. After pausing to in-

quire after his father, who appeared to be enjoying Sophie's ministrations, he moved to where the grooms swarmed about the animals, coaxing and commanding both in turn.

Motioning the men away, he shouted, "Ming-Ming! Here, girl!" punctuating his command with finger snaps.

The animal paused mid-nip to glance in his direction.

He snapped his fingers again and dropped into a crouch. "Come on, Ming-Ming!" He snapped and pointed to the ground near his feet.

G-r-r! She latched onto the gray's rear fetlock, where she clung with leechlike tenacity. The poor stallion screamed and reared, forcing the grooms to fling themselves flat against the stable wall to avoid being struck by its hoofs.

Helene screeched as if she were being murdered. Expecting to see her charging across the yard, Nicholas glanced behind him. Blessings of blessings, mademoiselle was there, restraining her.

"Release me this instant!" Helene was shrieking, bucking with a violence that rivaled that of the stallion. When the abigail refused to comply, she threatened, "If you do not unhand me, I shall dismiss you. Do you hear me?" Still, the maid held firm.

Shaking his head, Nicholas turned back to the animals. The horse was now lathered and foaming at the mouth. Exhausted from its panic, it slipped on the cobblestones and fell forward, its front legs buckling beneath it. To Nicholas's immense relief, it instantly bound up again.

Growing desperate now, he looked around him, grappling for a way to stop the madness before the animals destroyed each other. It was then that his gaze fell upon a stick laying nearby. Remembering how Ming-Ming had enjoyed their short-lived game of fetch, he seized it and shouted, "Ming-Ming! Here, girl!"

Again, she looked at him. He waved the stick. She yapped and wagged her plumelike tail. Praying that she remembered the game, he shouted, "Fetch, Ming-Ming. Fetch!" and flung the stick as far from the horse as he could.

The dog froze, its stubby legs stiff and drool streaming

from its mouth, then it yipped and dashed after the stick. He dashed after it, tackling it just as it tackled the stick.

"Boo-by! Oh, my poor boo-by!" he heard Helene wail.

Ming-Ming growled her protest at his rough treatment and promptly sank her teeth into his forearm.

Nicholas gritted his own teeth against the pain, hard-pressed not to murder the dog where they stood. Indeed, he might have done exactly that had Helene not rushed to him, sobbing her pet's name.

"Oh, boo-by . . . boo-by . . . boo-by." She snatched the furry white leech, which was still attached to his arm, and yanked it away, ignoring the way its teeth tore his flesh as she did so.

As Nicholas stood clutching his bleeding arm, watching with distaste as she kissed its slavering mouth, Sophie and his father approached. His father, he noted, favored his left leg and was leaning heavily on Sophie, who scolded him for rising too soon.

Despite the pain in his arm, he smiled. Only Sophie would dare to chastise his father, and his father would only allow a servant as comely and sweetly earnest as she to get away with doing so. As they stopped beside him, Helene rounded on Sophie.

"You!" She furiously snapped her fingers at Sophie. "Stoo-pid . . . stoo-pid girl! This is all your fault." *Snap!-Snap!* "Explain yourself this very instant!"

Sophie cast Nicholas a helpless look, who returned it with a faint smile. Before he could speak up in her defense, however, his father boomed, "Come, now, Helene. Time enough to discuss this matter later, after you've calmed yourself."

"I assure you that I am perfectly calm," she retorted, clearly resenting his intrusion.

"Nonsense, girl. You look as if you could do for a glass of brandy. Indeed, I daresay we could all do for one." His father paused to smile at Sophie. "You, too, my dear. What say you to joining us?"

"What!" Helene's face turned an exceedingly unflattering shade of purple. "How dare you invite her"—

Snap!-Snap! at Sophie—"to join us? Need I remind you who I am?"

Nicholas gazed at her, not even bothering to disguise his dislike. "I can assure you that we are perfectly aware of your exalted station, Helene. You have been exceedingly vigilant in pointing it out at every opportunity."

Her dark eyes narrowed. "Indeed? Well, then, in that instance, I can only assume that the invitation was meant as an insult."

"Insult? Poppycock!" his father exclaimed. "Sophie is a lady born and bred. In case you haven't heard, her father is a baron."

"Oh?" Helene's full red lips twisted into a sneer as she transferred her gaze to Sophie. "Tell me, Miss . . . Barton, is it?"

Sophie nodded. To her credit she remained unperturbed.

"Yes . . . Barton." Helene studied her face for a beat, as if trying to place it, then dropped her gaze to sweep her length. As she did so, her expression turned positively frigid.

And no wonder, Nicholas thought, noting her appearance as well. Not only was her gown askew, her hair had come down and her lips were swollen in a way that bespoke of ravishment.

Certain that he looked the part of the ravisher, he glanced at himself. Bloody hell! As if it weren't damning enough that he wore neither coat nor waistcoat, his shirt was half pulled out and his trousers were awry, probably from Sophie grasping his buttocks. Then, there were those telltale scruffs on his boots—

"Tell me, Miss Barton," Helene purred. "Exactly which baron's by-blow are you?"

Something inside Nicholas snapped when he heard Sophie gasp and saw the color drain from her face. It was his fault that she was in such a state, and he'd be damned if he'd let her suffer for it. Eyeing Helene coldly, he bit out, "I can assure you, *my lady,* that Miss Barton's birth is every bit as legitimate as yours."

"Perhaps even more so," his father injected.

"What!" Helene spat, rounding on him. "How dare

you imply such a foul and wicked thing. You, sir, are even less of a gentleman than your"—she gestured wildly at Nicholas—"whoremongering son!"

Despite his fury with the girl, Nicholas couldn't help but pity her when he saw his father's expression. Had it been he who he glared at in such a manner, he'd have jumped on his horse and ridden hell-bent for London. In truth, he would rather face the devil than his father when he was in such a mood.

"Unless you wish to pursue our present conversation, my dear, the conclusion of which I assure you shan't be to your liking, I suggest that you return to your rooms and calm yourself." Despite his mild tone, the threat in his father's voice was unmistakable.

Unfortunately for Helene, she was either too stupid to detect it, or too arrogant to heed it. Casting him a look that clearly conveyed her contempt for him and anything he might say, she snapped, "I assure *you* that both my birth and my parents' morals are above reproach . . . something which cannot be said for some people." She uttered that last while gazing pointedly at Sophie.

"Are you so very certain?" his father drawled.

"Utterly."

"In that case, you shan't mind if I inquire as to the date of your birth?"

"Of course not. I was born September 23, 1789."

"And your parents were wed . . . when?"

"A year or so before, I suppose." She shrugged. "I never thought to ask."

"Then, I suggest you do so."

"Why ever would I—" Her eyes widened in sudden understanding. To her credit, she instantly regained herself and countered, "Even if it turns out that I was a six-month babe, what does it matter? It simply proves that my parents loved each other too much to await the reading of the banns. Just because you cannot understand such a love, my lord, does not make it wrong."

"Try a three-month babe," he shot back, "and your father never even set eyes on your mother until a month before their wedding. He was rather desperate for funds, you see, and your mother happened to be a very wealthy widow in need of a husband."

She gasped. "I don't believe it . . . I shan't believe it! Next you shall try to tell me that I'm the by-blow of a commoner."

"Oh, you were sired by a nobleman, though which one is anyone's guess." His father seemed to consider the matter, then shrugged and shook his head. "Your mother enjoyed the, er, consolation of so many gentlemen during her bereavement for her first husband."

If looks could kill, his father would be dead from the one Helene shot him. "You are a truly vile man," she hissed. "And I refuse to remain beneath your roof a second longer than it takes to pack my bags. No doubt my mother shall be eager to leave as well when I tell her of your filthy lies."

"No doubt," his father uttered dryly.

Casting both Nicholas and Sophie a venomous look, Helene crushed Ming-Ming to her heaving breast and turned on her heels. Furiously snapping her fingers, she commanded, "Come along, mademoiselle. You must pack my bags immediately."

Mademoiselle shrugged. "You sacked me. Pack them yourself."

"How could you, Harry?" the marchioness berated, glaring at her husband. "Suzanne is my oldest and dearest friend. Whatever possessed you to say such dreadful things to her daughter?"

The marquess shrugged unrepentantly. "I didn't say anything that wasn't true."

"True?" She sniffed. "Fiddlesticks! Those old rumors about Suzanne being a wanton are nothing but rubbish. She was—"

"Seduced by an unscrupulous rogue during her bereavement," he finished for her. "Yes, I know. So she claims."

"Well, I for one believe her, and do not hold any part of the unfortunate affair against her. The poor dear was distraught over the death of her husband, and the scoundrel took advantage of her heartbroken state. She confided everything to me when she found herself with child."

"Everything but her seducer's name." He shook his head. "Don't you find it even the least bit queer that she refused to name him? Most women would be eager to expose such a man for the knave he is."

"Well, Suzanne isn't like most women. She's a dear through and through. She refused to tell out of pity for his wife." A sigh. "Sweet, noble Suzanne. Always thinking of everyone but herself."

The marquess couldn't help snorting at his wife's misguided view of the woman. "Saint Suzanne didn't name Helene's father because she didn't know who he was."

She snorted back. "Rumors. Spiteful rumors. I shall never believe that gammon about her taking a dozen lovers the month her husband died."

"Believe it. I could name at least that many men who had her during the first week. Could have had her myself had I been so inclined." Though he hated to shatter his wife's illusions about her so-called friend, it was high time she learned the truth.

"What!" She stared at him in stunned disbelief. "Surely you're not suggesting that she made a play for you?"

He chuckled, trying to soften the blow with levity. "Why so surprised? You always say that I'm the handsomest man in England."

"You are. Of course, you are. You always shall be. But"—she shook her head—"I simply cannot imagine Suzanne doing something so very loathsome as to try to steal you from me."

"Oh, she didn't want to steal me, she simply wished to borrow me for a night or two. Since you two used to share everything from secrets to trinkets, she no doubt decided that you wouldn't mind sharing me as well."

"No. Oh no!"

"I'm afraid so, my dear. Worst yet, she tried to share me again just last night. She was most concerned about the state of my manly needs, what with you ailing and all."

"Oh, Harry. Why didn't you tell me the first time she

made advances?" she exclaimed, looking every bit as ill as she wished everyone to believe her to be.

"Because I love you and didn't wish to break your heart," he replied, rising from his chair to move to the bed. Smiling all the love he felt inside, he lay down beside her and pulled her into his embrace. Gently stroking her hair, he murmured, "The one thing I try to avoid at all costs is breaking your heart."

She nuzzled against his shoulder, the very place she'd laid her head every night for the past thirty-two years. "You, Harry, are the dearest and most considerate man in the world."

"Don't forget handsomest," he teased.

She smiled. "That goes without saying. Still"—her smile faded and she grew solemn again—"I do wish you'd never said anything to poor Helene."

It was all he could do to keep from grimacing at her referral to the horrid little termagant as poor. Struggling to keep the distaste from his voice, he said, "I rather think that I did the girl a favor. At least now she shall be prepared for the rumors she will undoubtedly hear during her Season."

"I suppose." She sighed. "Poor girl. I do hope the rumors don't spoil her chances to make a good match. She's such a winning creature. Indeed, I found her so agreeable that I'd have welcomed her into the family, in spite of her mother's faults."

"Not I," he declared, shuddering at the thought of Colin shackled to such a shrew. "I'd have forbidden the match under threat of disinheritance."

His wife lifted her head from his shoulder to glare at him. "Why, Harry Somerville! Don't tell me that you would hold Suzanne's sins against her daughter?"

"Come, come, now, Fanny," he murmured, kissing the end of her nose. "You know me better than that. I shall gladly give my blessing to Colin to wed whomever he pleases, provided that I'm convinced she will make him happy."

"And what makes you so certain that he wouldn't be happy with Helene? As I said, I found her perfectly charming."

"Well, I found her insufferable. Can't recall the last time I met such an ill-natured chit." He shook his head. "No. Helene would never do for Colin. The man who marries her shall spend his life plagued with misery and servant problems."

"Servant problems?" She frowned. "Whatever are you going on about now, Harry?"

"You would know exactly what I meant had you put aside your deathbed charade and actually spent time with the chit."

"For your information, I truly am ailing," she exclaimed indignantly. "And please do stop being cryptic. I still have no idea what you meant by your last remark."

"Fine. Then, I shall put it bluntly: There isn't a servant at Hawksbury who'd have remained in our employ had Colin married Helene. She behaved most abominably toward them, insulting and criticizing them at every turn. Why, she even went so far as to slap little Agnes, the under-housemaid, and all the poor girl did was wish her ladyship a good day." He shook his head grimly. "I say good riddance. And if we never see either her or her mother again, well, hurrah!"

"Hurrah, indeed," she agreed, relaxing back against his shoulder. After a beat she sighed. "Ah, well. There is always Lady Julianna. She and her mother are to arrive in three days. Perhaps she shall prove more suited to Colin."

It took his every effort not to grin. "I wouldn't throw too much hope in that direction if I were you."

She made a frustrated noise. "If you know something, please do just say it. Your riddles are making my head ache."

"Do you want me to be blunt again?" he inquired playfully.

"Present it anyway you wish, just tell me."

"All right, then. Colin shan't be suited to Lady Julianna because his heart is already engaged."

"What!" Her head popped up again, and she peered at him as if he'd lost his wits.

He grinned. "It's true, Fan. Our Colin is in love."

"Who? When?" She punched the shoulder she'd just

vacated. "Oh, but you are the most provoking man! Do tell me the gel's name."

"Bluntly?"

"Harry!" She punched him again.

He chuckled. "It's our own Miss Barton."

Instead of being stunned, as he expected, she looked thoughtful. "Then, Helene's accusations are true? Colin and Sophie were dallying in the stable?"

"Judging from their appearances, I would say yes."

She pondered a few moments, then nodded. "Come to think of it, it makes sense. He was rather vehement in his defense of the girl over the Mayhew affair. And he can look at nothing but her every time he visits me." She nodded again. "I do believe you are right."

"And what would you think of such a match?"

"I've always thought Sophie lovely and charming, you know that. Indeed, I have even considered promoting such a match myself. What gave me pause is the fact that we know nothing about her family. She never speaks of them, and what information I have managed to pry from her is out of keeping with her tale."

He frowned. "In what way?"

"Well, for one, she knows much too much about the ton to have never had a Season, as she claims. I also noted that what few gowns she owns are of first-rate materials and all the kick in style. One does not find such garments in Durham." She shook her head. "My guess is that Miss Barton isn't who she claims to be."

"My thought exactly," he countered, his smile returning.

"In that instance, I am certain that you agree that we cannot allow a match until we know who she is and how she came to be here. For all we know, she's a murderess running from the law."

The marquess's smile broadened into a grin. "Oh, I can assure you that she's no murderess."

It was his wife's turn to frown. "What makes you so certain?"

He chuckled. "Come, come, now, Fan. Surely you have some inkling as to our Sophie's identity? I've had one for quite some time now." In truth, after watching his son's demeanor toward the girl change from frigid hostility to heated captivation, he had more than a mere inkling.

She grunted. "There you go with the riddles."

"You want it blunt again?"

She punched his arm.

Taking that punch as an affirmative response, he gleefully replied, "My guess is that Miss Sophie Barton is in truth Sophia Barrington. And from all appearances, she and Colin have settled their differences."

Chapter 19

"Thank goodness. You haven't left yet, Terry," Sophie exclaimed, rushing into the kitchen.

The footman looked up from the shopping list in his hand, smiling. "I was just about to do so now. Is there something you or the marchioness need from Exeter?"

She paused a beat, plagued by second thoughts, then nodded and pulled a letter from her pocket. "I need you to deliver this note, that is, if it isn't too much trouble." She rather hoped it would be.

But of course it wasn't. Taking the letter, as she'd known he would do, he replied, "Nothing you could ask me to do could ever be too much trouble."

She smiled faintly at his gallant response, though smiling was the last thing she felt like doing. The note was to her uncle, who was due to return home any day now, informing him of her whereabouts and begging him to rescue her. It was a note that grieved her to write and devastated her to send, for she now loved Nicholas with an intensity that made her soul cry out with longing.

That love was the reason she must leave Hawksbury, and soon, before she did something reckless that could only result in heartbreak and a score of hopeless quandaries for the both of them. For she knew, as surely as she knew they could never wed, that the next time their passion exploded, they wouldn't stop at a mere kiss.

Desperate to escape the kitchen before the tears flooding her eyes fell, Sophie turned and hurried to the door. She was on the threshold when Cook paused from chastising Meg, one of the kitchen maids, to shout, "Aren't you forgetting something, Miss Barton?"

"Pardon?" she forced past the lump in her throat.

"Her ladyship's luncheon tray." The woman gestured to the sideboard next to the door, where the meal trays were always set.

Today, Sophie noted, it held three. Apparently Nicholas and his father were too busy preparing for their houseguests' imminent arrival to dine together, as they usually did.

The lump in her throat swelled at the thought of the coming company and the purpose of their visit. If Nicholas found Lady Julianna agreeable, he would most probably marry her.

Well, he has to wed someone, someday, she ruthlessly told herself, blinking back her tears, *a suitable, well-bred someone who can stand beside him in the ton and be a credit to the Somerville name.* It was a fact she had to accept, no matter how much it hurt, just as she must accept the hopelessness of her lot and get on with her life as best she could.

Drearily contemplating the emptiness of that life without Nicholas, she picked up the marchioness's tray. As she did so, she noticed that his tray, the one with apple cider instead of tea, lacked the tarts the other two held. She frowned. How very odd that Cook would be so careless, especially in preparing Nicholas's tray.

Like everyone in the house, Sophie knew of Cook's fondness for Nicholas, and she often found herself smiling at the lengths to which the woman went to please him. Indeed, not a morning passed that she didn't bake him a special treat; one made from fruit, since fruit was his weakness. This morning she'd baked the apricot-and-pineapple tarts that now graced the other trays.

Certain that the omission was an oversight, she turned to inform Cook. The woman still scolded Meg. All too familiar with the dangers of interrupting her when she was thus engaged, she decided to take matters into her own hands. She might not be able to love Nicholas as she wished, but she could most certainly see that he got his tarts.

Wistfully picturing his smile as he tasted the treat, she selected the plumpest and most perfect tart from each of the other trays, and placed them on his plate. Satisfied, she again picked up her ladyship's tray. As she did so, Julius, the third footman, appeared to claim Nicholas's meal. After exchanging brief greetings, each rushed off to their respective destination.

Meanwhile, at the other end of the kitchen, Cook continued to berate Meg, gesturing furiously at the basis for the scolding: a plate of tarts. "Now, then. Do you understand?" she inquired, glaring at the thin, red-faced girl before her.

The maid nodded so emphatically that her cap tumbled from her head. "Aye, ma'am. Lord Lyndhurst ain't to have nothin' with pineapple 'cause it makes him itchy and gives him spots."

"Among other unpleasantness, yes," Cook murmured, grimacing at the thought of those other effects. His poor lordship. It was a good thing she'd caught Meg putting the tarts on his tray.

"Beggin' yer pardon, ma'am," Meg murmured, bending down to retrieve her cap. "But wouldn't his lordship have tasted the pineapple 'n' not ett them tarts?"

She shook her head. "Not with the apricot. Pineapple and apricot are a wretched mix, can't taste one fruit for the other."

"If'n it's so wretched, how come you used it?"

"Because it's her ladyship's favorite, and she requested it." Sighing over the hopelessness of her mistress's palate, she waved the girl away. "Well, don't just stand there. Cut a slice of the pear pie cooling at the window, and put it on his lordship's tray."

The girl hastened away to do her bidding, only to return moments later, wringing her apron. "Oh, law! Julius already taked his lordship's tray."

Cook grunted her irritation. "Well, there's no help for it now. Just set the pie on the sideboard. No doubt his lordship will note the lack of a sweet and send Julius back to fetch it."

* * *

Nicholas, however, was too preoccupied to notice anything on his tray. What occupied his mind was Sophie.

Never had a woman captivated him as she did, never had one confounded him so. One minute she was in his arms, her body pliant and her lips yielding, the next she avoided him as if he were the deadliest of plagues. Indeed, all he'd seen of her in the last three days was a blur of blue gown as she dashed from his sight.

Trying to make sense of her actions, Nicholas absently plucked a tart from his tray and took a bite. As he chewed, he wondered if his kisses had prompted her sudden avoidance. Could it be that she'd found them unpleasant and sought to escape suffering more?

He polished off the tart as he considered. Well, he'd never had any complaints about his kisses before. In fact, once experiencing them, women usually seemed eager for more.

Then again, he'd never kissed a woman as he had Sophie. With her he'd been swept away by passion, letting his desire rather than his head guide him as it had done in the past. Could it be that his abandon had made him too rough? Too eager and demanding? Could he have frightened her with the savagery of his need?

He smiled ruefully at that last. Hell, he'd frightened himself with the intensity of his own need. There had been something shockingly primal in it, something deep and desperate—a hunger that went beyond the urgency of his flesh and made him yearn to love all of her . . . heart, soul, and mind.

As confused by his own behavior as he was by hers, he picked up the second tart and nibbled on a corner. As the sweet, syrupy filling flowed over his tongue, he become aware of an odd tingling in his mouth. The unpleasant familiarity of the sensation made him pull the pastry from his mouth and eye it with alarm. The last time his mouth had felt like this was when he'd unwittingly eaten the pineapple garnish on the ham at the Kingsdale *soirée*. Talk about a miserable night!

Shuddering at the memory, he tossed aside the tart and hastily gulped down his entire glass of cider. To his everlasting relief the tingling instantly subsided. It was then, after his momentary panic had passed, that his senses returned. And his senses told him that there couldn't possibly be pineapple in the tarts. Not only had he not tasted it, Cook would never allow it to be served to him, knowing as she did how it affected him.

His mind thus eased, he returned to his problem with Sophie and his theory that he'd either frightened or disgusted her with his passion. After brief but serious contemplation, he dismissed it. Neither reason made any sense. Not when he remembered how she had kissed him back. The way she'd grasped his buttocks and moaned for more bespoke of an ardor that matched his. It was remembering her abandon that made him hit upon another idea: Could it be that she was ashamed of her own conduct and thus too embarrassed to face him?

He reached down and scratched his side as he considered. Embarrassment would certainly explain the way she bolted every time she saw him. Then again—he scratched his neck—one couldn't always count on logic when trying to fathom the workings of the female mind. As all men knew, there was no rhyme or reason to the way women thought. As for the way they acted . . .

Wanting to howl his frustration, Nicholas gave his neck another scratch, vaguely noting as he did so that his tongue had begun to tingle again. This time, however, he was too absorbed in his problem with Sophie to pay his discomfort much mind.

After several moments of deliberation and a furious bout of scratching, he came to the conclusion that there was only one way to solve it: He must chase her down and simply ask point-blank why she was avoiding him. Whether or not she would give him a satisfactory answer . . .

Scrape!-Scrape!-Scrape!—at the door.

Annoyed by the interruption, he barked, "Enter!"

It was the majordomo, his face flushed and his breathing labored, as if he'd been running.

"Well? What is it, Dickson?" he growled, rubbing at his neck. The blasted thing itched. Jessup must have shaved him too closely this morning.

After panting several times, the man gasped out, "A

thousand pardons, my lord. But Lady Chadwick's out-rider has arrived—*puff!*—and reports that her ladyship's coach is but moments behind him."

Nicholas rubbed his neck again, none too pleased by the news. Not even trying to mask his irritation, he muttered, "Thank you, Dickson. I shall go outside to welcome them."

The man bowed. "Very good, my lord." Then rushed off to resume his post.

Testily imagining the horrors that awaited him, Nicholas clawed at his belly through his clothing, trying to assuage its sudden itching. No relief. The maddening sensation simply increased. Grimacing, he tried pinching and slapping the area. The discomfort persisted. Oh, bloody hell. The laundresses must have overstarched his shirt.

Firmly ignoring his urge to remove the offending garment, he stalked from the library, scratching assorted body parts as he went. By the time he reached the entry hall, he felt hot and cold in turn, and itched all over.

As he miserably awaited Dickson to open the door, he again speculated upon the tarts. Could Cook have filled them with some exotic new fruit that didn't agree with him?

"My lord! They are here! The coach has pulled up to the steps," the majordomo exclaimed, growing flushed again.

Wanting nothing more than to strip off his clothes and dive into a cool bath, Nicholas stepped onto the stoop, praying for the coming greetings to be brief. Staunchly curbing his impulse to scratch his backside, he proceeded down the steps, determined to do his gentlemanly duty and assist the ladies from the coach.

The first person to emerge was an older woman in a stylish yet dignified lavender and black ensemble. Deducing from the colors that she was in half-mourning and thus the widowed marchioness, he sketched a courtly bow. "Lady Chadwick, I presume?" he murmured, offering his hand.

She accepted with a lovely smile. "And you must be Lord Lyndhurst. My, my! Your mother claimed you to be a most dashing and handsome fellow in her letter, but I must say that she hardly did you justice."

Nicholas returned her smile, liking her immediately. Not only was she gracious and charming, she was quite attractive. If her daughter was anything like her, she would have no trouble making a suitable match, despite the scandalous circumstances of her father's death. Secretly thinking Chadwick a dolt for dying over a dollymop when he had such a wife, he handed her down. His hands clenching against his urge to scratch his belly again, he then turned back to the vehicle and awaited her daughter's appearance.

The next to emerge was a pinch-faced woman who was introduced as Miss Benning, Lady Julianna's abigail. As he assisted her as well, he couldn't help but to wonder at the physic case she carried. By the size of it, she looked to be on a mission to cure the entire country . . .

Or one extremely ill patient. Could the girl have sickened on the journey? Suddenly concerned, he peered into the coach.

Darkness. He saw nothing but darkness. The windows were closed and the shades drawn. He frowned. Good God. It must be devilishly hot in there, what with the heat of the day. Whatever could the women have been thinking? Certain that the girl had either fainted or suffocated, Nicholas glanced back at the marchioness.

She scowled at the vehicle as if greatly annoyed. "Do come along, Julianna," she exclaimed, her voice perfectly matching her expression. "I assure you that the air here is most healthful."

There was a faint rustling from within, then, "Are you quite certain? You know how susceptible I am to contagion."

"Quite," Lady Chadwick replied, while Nicholas shot Miss Benning a quizzical look.

The woman smiled rather wanly. "Lady Julianna has an, ur, inordinate concern for her health, my lord."

He scratched beneath his chin as he grimly absorbed that disheartening bit of news. Damnation. He hoped she wasn't one of those tiresome females who chattered constantly about ailments and whose sole interest in life

was collecting the latest cures. Such women made Miss
Mayhew's discourses on fish gutting and Lady Helene's
prattle about Ming-Ming's digestion seem positively
scintillating.

Miserably bracing himself for the worst, he dropped
his hand back to his side. Whatever the case, he wished
the girl would get out of the coach so he could go to his
rooms and attend to his itching. Not only was it spreading, it intensified with every passing second. As he balled
his hands against his bedeviling urge to scratch his groin,
Lady Julianna appeared at the door. The sight of her
made him momentarily forget his discomfort.

After her fuss about contagion, he'd expected her to
be one of those thin, pallid creatures whose preferred
activity was swooning. But this girl! Why, she looked fit
enough to live to be a hundred. Not only that, she was
beautiful. Indeed, had Quentin been in residence, he'd
have instantly fallen slave to her glorious red-gold hair
and voluptuous figure. Suddenly remembering his manners, Nicholas stepped forward and offered her his hand.

She shuddered and shrank away. "No . . . please. I-
I—"

"Oh, for heaven's sake, Julianna," Lady Chadwick
snapped. "Do take his lordship's hand and greet him
properly."

She shot her mother a mulish look. "I shall do no
such thing. His lordship is recently from town, and everyone knows that London abounds with contagion this
time of year. Indeed"—her lovely jade-colored eyes widened as she glanced back at Nicholas—"he could have
some dreadful disease and not even know it yet."

As Nicholas opened his mouth to protest his health,
he heard the pounding of footsteps on the stairs behind
him and his father boom, "Lady Chadwick! Lady Julianna! Welcome to Hawksbury."

He smiled his relief. Good. Let him deal with the
chit's nonsense. He'd had quite enough of her. Besides,
his bowels had begun to gurgle in a way that always
boded ill.

"My dear Lord Beresford," Lady Chadwick exclaimed, beaming as he kissed her hand. "I simply can-

not tell you how very wonderful it is to see you again. I do hope your wife's health has improved?"

"What? What? What?" Lady Julianna squawked, sounding for all the world like a hen laying an egg. "His wife is ill?"

"Hush, girl," her mother chided. "Her ladyship's ailment presents no threat to you. Now, do get down from the coach so we can go inside and freshen up."

Yes, please do come down, Nicholas silently pleaded, gritting his teeth as his bowels gave a violent spasm. When the spasm was followed by an excruciating cramp, he knew what was about to happen and gazed rather desperately up at the front door. It might as well have been atop the Alps for all the chance he had of reaching it without embarrassing himself.

"No! I can't—I shan't go in that house! Not if there is illness within," the girl was shrilling.

"You shall do as I say and do it now, or I shall slap you," her mother growled, clearly at the end of her patience.

"Then, you must slap me, for I refuse to go anywhere near that—that—pest house!—or them." She pointed an accusing finger at Nicholas and his father. "If her ladyship is ill, then both the manor and everyone within must be swarming with contagion."

"Fiddle-faddle, girl," her mother shot back. "Anyone can see that Lyndhurst and Beresford are perfectly fit."

The instant the words left her mouth, Nicholas was struck with a cramp so vicious that he moaned aloud and doubled over. Grasping his belly in agony, he sank to the steps, groaning, "Help me into the house, Father. Now."

"Colin?" His father was at his side in a flash, peering anxiously at his face. "Good God, boy. Whatever is wrong? You look like death himself." He leaned a fraction nearer, his eyes suddenly narrowing. "Heavens. I do believe you have spots."

"Spots?" A shriek. "It's the pox! The pox, I tell you! We must get away from here this instant!" Lady Julianna wailed, diving back into the coach. Her abigail squeaked and rushed in after her.

His father sighed. "You might as well take your daughter home, Lady Chadwick. I fear that an audience with God himself wouldn't lure her into the house after this."

Her sigh echoed his. "Yes. I believe you are correct, my lord."

As she launched into a barrage of what sounded like well-rehearsed apologies, Lord Beresford slipped his arm around Nicholas and helped him to his feet. Firmly bracing him against his solid form, he murmured, "Easy there, now, boy. Everything shall be fine. Do you wish me to send Julius for the surgeon?"

Nicholas grasped onto his father as yet another cramp twisted his bowels. Fervently praying that he would make it in time, he gritted out, "Just get me to the privy . . . now."

"This looks to be a fine article on perfumed waters," Sophie said, glancing from the magazine in her hands to Lady Beresford's face. To her consternation the woman was staring again, and with the sly, knowing expression that always unnerved her. Commanding herself, as she always did, to ignore both the look and her disquiet, she smiled and added, "Would you like me to read it aloud?"

Her ladyship returned her smile. "You know, Sophie, you are an exceedingly fine-looking gel. I imagine that you had a great many suitors in—Durham, was it?"

Sophie gazed at her in dismay, hard-pressed not to frown at her question. The last thing in the world she wished to discuss was courtship and romance. Indeed, she doubted she could do so without bursting into tears. Her impossible love for Nicholas made the subject far too painful to address.

Thus, she looked down at her hands and murmured, "Yes, Durham. And no, I had no suitors. Our estate was in a remote area, and I seldom saw anyone save my father and the servants." There. That response left her ladyship with nowhere to go, hence nipping the conversation in the bud.

Her ladyship, however, merely scoffed, "Come, come,

now. Do not try to tell me that you have never had feelings for a man. You did go to school in Bath, after all, which means that you had to have encountered a few gentlemen. Indeed, I have yet to meet a Bath miss who didn't develop at least one crush while there."

As Sophie grappled for an appropriate reply, the marquess burst into the room, clearly in a lather.

"Harry? Whatever is wrong?" the marchioness cried.

"It's Colin. The most wretched thing has happened to Colin!"

Sophie and her mistress gasped in unison. "Oh, please—please! Do tell me that he is all right," Sophie begged. The instant the words left her mouth, she blushed and added, "You have all been so kind to me. I would hate for anything to happen to a member of your family."

The dreaded look was back on her ladyship's face, and she resumed staring. Her gaze never wavering from Sophie's face, she snapped, "Well? Don't keep us on pins and needles, Harry. What has happened to Colin?"

"He ate a pineapple-apricot tart," he replied, his voice as grim as if he reported that he'd been shot dead.

Her ladyship's gaze instantly darted from Sophie to her husband, horror written on every line of her face. "What? But how could such a thing happen? Cook knows better than to serve him anything with pineapple. She's seen how ill it makes him."

"Pineapple makes him ill?" Sophie squeaked, suddenly feeling sick herself.

"Wickedly so," his lordship retorted. Turning his attention back to his wife, he explained, "The tarts were on Colin's luncheon tray, though no one seems to know how they got there. Cook and Meg both swear they weren't there when it left the kitchen. Julius swears they were." He shook his head. "Worse yet, he sickened while greeting Lady Chadwick and her daughter."

"My poor darling. How very wretched for him," her ladyship murmured. "I do hope our guests understood?"

The marquess snorted. "No. They didn't. Well, at least the chit didn't, which is just as well. She's almost as eccentric as Brumbly's—"

"Oh, to Hades with the gel," his wife interjected, gesturing her impatience. "Where is Colin?"

"In his rooms. Mrs. Pixton dosed him with one of her remedies and prepared a special bath to soothe his spots. Last I saw of him, George was helping him into the tub."

"My poor baby. I must go to him immediately," she declared, sitting up and tossing aside the covers. "A mother's place is by her son's side when he is ill."

"Oh, no! No, my lady. You mustn't leave your bed," Sophie cried, rushing forward to stop her. "You must remember your health." After poisoning Nicholas, the least she could do was take care of his mother for him.

The marchioness waved her away. "Pshaw, gel. I feel fine. Go fetch me a dressing gown. The purple cashmere shall do nicely."

"But you can't . . . you mustn't! You might have a relapse, or worse," she protested, casting a desperate look at the marquess.

He merely shrugged. "Mark this day on your calendar, my dear. You have just witnessed a miracle worthy of being recorded in the annals of medicine."

"But—"

He shook his head. "She shall be fine. I promise. Go ahead and do as she says. I daresay that Colin could do with a bit of mothering just now."

Sophie returned his gaze for a beat, then swallowed hard and bowed her head to hide her burgeoning tears. "Yes, my lord. As you wish," she choked out. Oh, what she wouldn't give to be able to go to Nicholas as well. She would—

She would no doubt do something stupid and kill him. That is, if she hadn't done so already.

Chapter 20

The rest of the afternoon crawled by like an eternity as Sophie awaited the marchioness to return with word of Nicholas. When afternoon dimmed to dusk, and dusk faded to night, she began to fear the worse. Nicholas must be very bad off indeed for his mother to remain by his side so long.

Tense to the point of shattering, she moved restlessly about her ladyship's rooms, straightening, mending, and rearranging everything in sight to pass the time. She even organized all her mistress's hats according to color, the lots of which she then arranged in alphabetical order determined by the first letter of their trim.

Therefore, Provence roses came before Scotch heath, and Brussels lace before marabout. It was only when she came to a morning cap trimmed with blue satin ribbons and a cluster of daisies that she paused in her frenetic activity.

The sight of those daisies, so jaunty yet delicate, struck at her aching heart, making her weep at their poignant reminder of all she wished to share with Nicholas, but couldn't.

Oh, how she longed to hold him again, to feel his strong arms about her and his warm body close to hers. She yearned to hear his voice, so hoarse and rough with desire, so raw with tenderness as he moaned her name. And his kiss!

She sighed and closed her eyes, imagining the feel of his lips against hers, dreaming of the taste of his mouth. So caught up in her wishful fantasy was she, that she still stood before the clothespress, fondling the daisies and envisioning loving Nicholas when Miss Stewart entered the room a long while later.

"Goodness, child! Whatever are you doing up?" the woman exclaimed, frowning at the sight of her. "It's after midnight."

Midnight? Oh, dear. Nicholas must be even worse off than she suspected. Much worse . . . perhaps even dying. That tormenting thought started her tears anew. Wanting nothing more than to beg news of him, she bowed her head to hide her distress and somehow managed to reply, "I had several chores I wanted to complete before retiring."

Apparently her voice reflected her distress, for Miss Stewart was by her side in a twinkling. Ducking her head to peer at her face, she murmured, "Why, you're crying. Whatever is wrong?"

So kind, so very compassionate did she look, that Sophie dropped the hat and threw herself into her embrace, weeping in earnest.

"There, there, now, dear," the lady's maid crooned, patting her heaving back. "Nothing can be so bad as all that."

"B-but it is, w-worse even," she sobbed.

The other woman sighed. "Well, it shan't do any good weeping about it. Indeed, you shall just make yourself ill, which will only make matters worse." She gave Sophie's back several more pats. "My suggestion is that you calm down and tell me what is wrong. Who knows? Perhaps I can help. Even if I can't, it might make you feel better to talk about your troubles."

Sophie continued to cling to her, considering her suggestion. If anyone would listen and not pass judgment, it was Miss Stewart. She was also one of the few people she could trust to be discreet. Thus she raised her head to meet the other woman's gaze and whispered, "I think I murdered Lord Lyndhurst."

Rather than look shocked, as she expected, Miss Stewart merely frowned. "Murdered him?" She shook her head, visibly perplexed. "Whatever are you talking about? His lordship isn't dead. I saw him myself not ten minutes ago."

"Well, he may not be dead yet, but he probably shall be before morning. Oh, Miss Stewart! I didn't mean to poison him, truly I didn't! I only wanted to make certain that he had a sweet with his luncheon."

The lady's maid stared at her blankly for several moments, then a look of dawning rose on her face. "Are you saying that it was you who put the tarts on his lordship's tray?"

Sophie nodded, wishing that someone would shoot her and put her out of her misery. Her voice broken with grief, she croaked, "I saw that he didn't have a sweet on his tray when I fetched her ladyship's luncheon, s-so I gave him one tart from each of the other trays. I thought, well"—she sniffled and shook her head—"his lordship has been so kind to me that I simply couldn't bear the thought of him not having a sweet. He does so love his fruit. Instead I killed him." That last was uttered on a moan.

"Oh, Sophie. You silly, silly, child," Miss Stewart exclaimed, giving her a hug. "You haven't killed him. Indeed, he shall be up and about tomorrow . . . the day after at the latest. This sort of thing has happened before, and he always survives."

"But I feel so wretched. I—"

"Hush, now," the other woman interjected, hugging her again. "You had no way of knowing that pineapple makes him ill. What you did, you did out of kindness. I'm certain that her ladyship will agree when you tell her."

"Tell . . . her ladyship?" Sophie echoed in alarm.

Miss Stewart nodded. "Of course you must tell her. Our poor mistress wonders how those tarts came to be on her son's tray, and worries about a reoccurrence of the mishap. If you tell her exactly what you told me and promise not to repeat the mistake, you shall take an enormous load off her mind. You will also ease your own by getting it off your conscience."

Sophie returned her companion's bespectacled gaze, pondering her words. Then she reluctantly nodded.

"Yes, I suppose I must confess, though where I shall find the courage, I cannot say."

"I suspect that you will find it the same place you found the courage to admit fault in the Mayhew disaster." Picking up the daisy cap Sophie had dropped, she directed, "Now, off to bed with you. You can finish"—she glanced into the clothespress—"well, whatever it is you're doing with the hats in the morning."

Though Sophie was far from tired, she obeyed.

Like the afternoon before it, the night proved endless. Sleepless with anxiety over her coming confession, she tossed and turned until Pansy was forced to seek her rest in Fancy's bed. By morning she was so exhausted from fretting that she could barely drag herself from bed. But drag she did, and the first place she dragged was to her ladyship's rooms. Best to get the dreaded interview over as soon as possible.

Once there she was greeted at the door by Miss Stewart, who informed her that her ladyship had just gone to bed after a night of tending Nicholas, and wasn't to be disturbed until later. Disappointed yet at the same time relieved, Sophie wandered downstairs for breakfast, then passed the day helping Pansy mend the family linen. It wasn't until evening that she again mustered the courage to face the marchioness.

But her ladyship wasn't in her rooms, she had gone to visit Nicholas. Determined not to spend another night in torment, she resumed her task of arranging hats and awaited her mistress's return. She had just reached the white hat *r*'s—red ribbon and rose ruching respectively—when she heard the bedchamber door open. Her stomach aflutter, she reluctantly went into the adjoining room.

It was Lady Beresford, at last. When she caught sight of Sophie, she smiled and exclaimed, "Why, Sophie. I didn't expect to find you here. Why ever aren't you downstairs having your dinner?"

Her courage fleeing like rats before a cat, she blurted out, "I need to speak with you, my lady."

"Surely it is something that can wait until after you

have dined? A young gel like you needs nourishment to keep up her strength."

Sophie shook her head, feeling all the worse at her ladyship's fond tone. "If I wait until later, I most probably shan't have the courage to say what I must."

The marchioness frowned, but not unkindly. "As you wish, but you must promise to seek nourishment and rest afterward. You look terribly pale and tired this evening."

"I am tired," she admitted miserably. "I was awake all night worrying about your son and stewing about what I must tell you."

"But of course you were worried about him," her ladyship muttered beneath her breath.

Sophie creased her brow at her odd response, but didn't ponder its meaning. She was far too busy searching for a way to begin her confession. Finally deciding on directness, she bowed her head and said, "It was I who put the tarts on Lord Lyndhurst's tray."

"Indeed?" The word was uttered softly and without the slightest inflection.

She nodded, swallowing the growing lump in her throat as she did so. "I knew nothing of his problem with pineapple. Truly I didn't. I simply saw that there was no sweet on his luncheon tray and took it upon myself to remedy the situation. I know how he loves fruit, so I thought he would enjoy the tarts."

When her ladyship didn't immediately reply, she hastened to add, "I know it isn't enough to say that I'm sorry, but I am. Wretchedly so. When I think of how ill I made poor Nic—uh—Lord Lyndhurst, I-I—" Her voice faltered, strangled by her remorse.

As she struggled to regain her speech, she heard the rustle of silk, then felt her ladyship's hand on her shoulder. "Sophie—"

"Please forgive me, my lady," she whispered, her voice raw and bleeding with emotion. "I speak the truth when I say that I would sooner hurt myself than you or your family. You have all been so kind to me and—and—" Again her voice failed her, this time overpowered by a wrenching sob. Before she knew what was

happening, tears spilled forth and she shattered beneath
the weight of her anguish.

"Sophie. Look at me," her ladyship softly commanded, giving her shoulder a squeeze.

When she didn't obey, too caught up in her heartache
to do so, the woman clasped her chin and lifted her
face for her. Forcing her to meet her gaze, she said,
"I understand that what happened was an unfortunate
mistake, and of course I forgive you. Anyone can see
that you are genuinely sorry. However, it isn't my forgiveness you should be seeking, but my son's. It is he
who suffered from your mistake."

Sophie froze, taken aback by her suggestion. After a
beat she smiled. "There is nothing I would rather do
than apologize to his lordship," she fervently whispered,
and it was true. There was nothing she wanted more
than to see Nicholas and assure herself that he was truly
all right.

"Well, in that instance, you shall find him in the forcing house."

"The forcing house?" Sophie echoed in dismay. She
had assumed that she would meet him somewhere in the
manor, somewhere less private than the forcing house
was likely to be at this hour.

The marchioness nodded. "He was restless from sleeping the day away and insisted on checking on a new
strawberry plant he is cultivating."

Sophie smiled weakly and returned her nod, though,
in truth, she had no intention of going to him. She dare
not be alone with him. She simply hadn't the strength
to resist her desire for him.

As if sensing her reluctance, her ladyship said, "It is
dark outside. Would you like me to send John with
you?"

John? Perfect! Nothing was likely to happen with the
footman present. Relieved, Sophie looked at her mistress to accept.

The woman stared at her again in that queer, unsettling way.

*   *   *

"Why don't I wait for you here?" John said, halting in the center of the brightly lit palm court.

Sophie tightened her grip on his arm, alarmed by his suggestion. "No . . . please. Don't make me face him alone."

The footman smiled. "What is this? A case of the nerves?"

"Yes," she admitted quietly.

He patted the hand on his arm. "I can assure you, my dear, that there is no need for it. His lordship is a most kind and understanding man. I am certain that he will forgive you for putting those tarts on his tray once you explain your reasons."

"I-I suppose you are right," she reluctantly admitted. Everyone in the household knew Nicholas to be of a fair nature, thus making it impossible for her to argue John's logic.

"Of course I'm right. Just as I'm right in saying that it's best to get these things over quickly." Nodding his encouragement, he pulled his arm from her grasp and nudged her toward the pavilions.

"But I-I—" she sputtered, scrambling for a new excuse to keep him by her side. Suddenly remembering Nicholas's tale of being lost among the mangosteen trees, she finished, "As much as it shames me to admit it, it isn't fear of his lordship that makes me wish your company, but my dreadful sense of direction. I'm afraid that I shall become hopelessly lost in here while searching for him, and never find my way out again."

The footman chuckled. "Well, as far as I know, no one has ever become permanently lost in here. However, since I do not wish you to be the first, I shall naturally escort you." He offered her his arm again. "Shall we?"

Almost weak with relief, she took it. With John by her side, she had only to apologize to Nicholas and accept his forgiveness, and that would be that. There would be no seductive sense of intimacy between them, no sizzle of excitement in the air, and not a single word or look to inflame their burgeoning desire. There would be nothing but safe formality.

As they made their way through pavilion after fragrant pavilion, her relief firmed into confidence . . .

Confidence that splintered the instant she spied Nicholas. So pale yet heartbreakingly handsome did he look as he examined the fruit on a small bush, that she was forced to grip John's arm with both hands to keep herself from running to him and throwing herself into his embrace.

"John. Sophie," he greeted, looking up with a smile.

Oh, heavenel His dimples showed, his lovely, tempting dimples. Unbidden, the memory of the feel of his cheek, so warm and smooth beneath her lips as she kissed his scar, sprang to mind, and she was possessed by a sudden, almost irresistible urge to explore those dimples in a like manner. Just the thought of doing so made her knees go weak with pleasure.

"My lord." John bowed as best he could with her attached to his arm. "Please pardon our intrusion, but Miss Barton has a matter she wishes to discuss with you."

"Does she indeed?" Nicholas's gaze was on her face now, his dark eyes glowing with sensual fire as they slowly bore into hers. Their impact was instantaneous, and she gasped aloud as a salvo of heat exploded within her. Holding her helpless captive with his gaze, he murmured, "You may leave us, John."

Leave them? Her mind screamed in protest, while her heart cried yes. As for her mouth, it became caught betwixt the battle of nays and yeahs, and simply refused to work.

"As you wish, my lord."

Sophie felt a tug on her clutching hands as John bowed. That tug broke the spell of Nicholas's gaze and promptly restored her senses. With the return of her senses came her panic.

Apparently she looked as frightened as she felt, for John smiled gently and said, "Everything will be fine, child. I promise." A reassuring pat on the cheek. "I shall wait for you in the palm court to escort you back to the house."

"No need to wait," Nicholas interjected. "I will see to Miss Barton."

"No!" she gasped, before she could stop herself. Instantly regaining herself, she hastily added, "You are exceedingly kind, my lord, but I do not wish to trouble you."

"It is no trouble, I assure you," he countered, a faint frown creasing his brow. "I was about to return to the manor when you appeared."

"Very good, my lord." John bowed again, giving the arm she clasped a meaningful tug in the process.

Seeing no other choice, she released it.

Within moments he was gone.

There followed a long, tense silence during which she looked everywhere but at Nicholas. Finally he sighed and said, "I believe you wish to speak with me?" His voice was utterly bland, as if they spoke in the presence of his mother.

Surprised, she glanced at his face. It was as neutral as his voice. So neutral, in fact, that she wondered if she had imagined the heat in his gaze. Had it, perhaps, been nothing but a wishful illusion created by her infatuation for him?

She was certain that such was the case in the next moment when he frowned and snapped, "Well?"

Rather than be relieved by his lack of desire, Sophie felt strangely bereft. Almost crushed. Could it be that their kiss had meant nothing to him after all? Devastated by that possibility, she bowed her head and said, "I—I put the tarts on your tray." Her voice quivered as if she were on the verge of tears, which she was.

"Indeed?"

She nodded, a tear seeping from the corner of her eye as she did so. "They looked so lovely, and well, I know how you love fruit. I didn't know that"—a broken sob escaped her—"that the pineapple would make you ill."

"Sophie." The word was uttered softly, edged with . . . Tenderness? She sniffled. Blasted imagination.

She heard the scrape of his leather mules against the floor as he moved nearer, then he commanded, "Look at me, Sophie." When she didn't obey, he added, "Please?"

There was something in his voice as he whispered that last word, a queer huskiness, that made her do as he asked. The instant her tear-blurred gaze touched his face, he smiled and said, "Thank you for the tarts."

Her eyes widened at his unexpected response, allowing several more tears to escape. "But—but, I don't understand," she choked out, wondering if he could be sicker than anyone realized. "Everyone said that the tarts made you terribly ill."

"They did."

"Then, why are you thanking me?" It was all she could do not to step forward and lay her hand on his cheek. He had to be fevered to be saying such things.

"I'm thanking you because you care enough about me to want to please me. That was the reason you gave me the tarts, wasn't it?" The warmth was back in his eyes.

She nodded, not quite certain what to make of that warmth. Was it due to fever or fondness?

His smile broadened, again displaying his dimples. "Ah. And here I have been thinking that you no longer like me."

"What?" Fever. It had to be fever. "Whatever would put such a notion in your head?"

"It could have something to do with the way you run the other direction every time you see me. I was beginning to think that I had either offended or repulsed you with my kisses."

"What!" She practically shouted the word in her surprise. After the way she had responded to him, how could he possibly believe such a thing? "You most certainly didn't offend me."

His smile faltered a bit. "I see. Then, I repulsed you."

"Of course not." Frowning, she moved toward him. "Are you quite sure that you have fully recovered from the pineapple?" She laid her hand against his scarred cheek. It felt cool.

"The pineapple, yes. Your kisses, no. Don't you know what your kisses do to me?" he whispered, again capturing her gaze with his.

So intense, so naked with tender emotion were his eyes, that the fragile wall of her resistance crumbled and she softly confessed, "Yes. I do know, because they do the same thing to me. In truth, it frightens me how much I desire you."

"My sweet, innocent, Sophie," he murmured, pulling her into his embrace. "Desire is to be savored, not feared,"

"Perhaps, but I can't help being a bit afraid. These feelings are so new . . . so strange," she replied, resting her chin on his chest to continue staring into his expressive eyes.

Smiling tenderly, he lowered his face and rested his forehead against hers. Returning her adoring gaze in kind, he whispered, "Don't you know that I would never hurt you?"

"Yes." She more sighed than uttered the word.

"Then, trust me."

"I do." And it was true, she did trust him. He was a man of honor, a true gentleman. As such, he was no more likely to use a woman for a casual game of daisies than the pope. Emboldened by her faith, she stood on her tiptoes and coiled her arms around his neck, declaring, "I not only trust you, Nicholas Somerville, I love you." With that, she pressed her mouth to his.

He groaned once, then returned her kiss, his lips first caressing, then nibbling, now molding and shaping hers. The resulting sensation made her tingle all over, and she moaned in fevered response.

He, too, moaned and pulled her nearer. Settling his mouth more firmly on hers, he slid his tongue between her lips and lightly traced their inner shape. Once, twice, then again and again, he traced them, delving deeper with every pass. At last his tongue slipped all the way into her mouth and twined with hers.

Sighing, she clung more tightly to his neck, her knees growing weak as she tasted him as she'd never before tasted a man. When she was certain that she would faint from the pleasure of it, he pulled his mouth from hers.

For a long moment he simply looked at her, his eyes dark and hungry, his breath harsh and ragged. Then he groaned and buried his face into her neck. Hoarsely whispering her name, he kissed her there as well.

"Nicholas! Oh, Nicholas!" she cried, grasping his head to urge him on.

And on he went, lower and lower, kissing over her collarbone and down the slope of her cleavage. She arched and moaned, thrilling to his every move. And still he dipped lower, stopping only when he came to the neckline of her gown. Whispering her name again, he outlined the shape of it with his tongue, tickling her sensitized flesh until her breasts tingled and ached.

Oh, how she wanted him to touch them, to strip away her clothes and fondle them. Maddened by her need, she pulled his arms from around her and guided his hands to caress them.

Sobbing his own need, Nicholas did as directed. God, but she was magnificent in her passion, so responsive, so honest and unbridled in her desire. Never had a woman aroused him as she did, never had one so tested his control. And yet—yet—

For all that he felt ready to burst from his urgency, he had no wish to take her quickly. No. He wanted to savor the taste and feel of her, to love her slowly and thoroughly. If it took him forever to do so, all the better. For what he felt for her went way beyond lust for her flesh, splendid though that flesh was. What he felt was deeper and truer, it was a feeling he knew would last for all eternity.

Sophie, however, wasn't feeling nearly so patient. His every kiss, every caress fanned her excitement, making her throb in an unspeakable yet thrilling manner. Giddy from the new sensations and eager to experience more, she arched and rubbed against him, gasping when she felt his answering hardness.

Eyes wide, she leaned back to stare at that hardness. Alas, it was concealed by the folds of his gold velvet dressing gown. Curious beyond propriety, she reached down and gently poked the area.

His hips jerked, as if he sought to escape her touch, and a strangled groan issued from his throat. Bewildered by his response, she glanced at his face, searching for an explanation. His eyes were closed, and he looked exceedingly uncomfortable. Could it be that men didn't like to be touched with anything but daisies?

Certain that that was the case, Sophie gazed about her. Surely one of the pavilions grew daisies? But which one? The forcing houses went on forever. Seeing no choice but to ask, she cleared her throat and murmured, "Er—Nicholas?"

He grunted.

Taking that grunt as a signal to proceed, she shyly inquired, "Where would I find—uh d daisies?"

His eyes flew open, and he frowned. "Daisies? Whatever do you want with daisies?"

She felt herself blush. "You know—ah—unless you p-prefer feathers or custard?"

"Feathers? Custard?" His frown deepened. "Whatever are you talking about?"

Her face burning, she repeated what Lydia's brother had told her about sexual acts. He looked more amazed with every passing second. When she had finished, she looked down at the floor and timidly inquired, "What sort of man are you, my lord?"

There was a long pause of silence, as if he considered her question, then he chuckled. "None of those sorts, though I must admit that licking custard from a cup between your breasts does sound rather interesting." He chuckled again. "The sort of man I am, however, is the kind who likes to make up the game as he goes along. Naturally, I wish you to help me do so since you are playing it with me."

It was her turn to frown. "I don't understand."

He tightened her in his embrace again and kissed her puckered forehead. "In other words, the goal of our game is to please each other and ourselves in whatever manner we choose."

"Does that mean we can touch each other?"

"Most definitely."

He saw her steal a downward peek. "Anywhere we wish?"

"Anywhere and everywhere," he replied, grinning at her charming curiosity. "My body is yours to explore, and yours mine. And if either of us wants the other to do something to us, we have only to ask."

She tipped her head back to meet his gaze, her face radiant in her delight. "Oh, I must say that I far prefer your game."

"As do I," he growled, reclaiming her mouth with his.

This time, however, it was she who kissed him, her lips and tongue greedy as she explored and tasted every inch of his mouth. Helplessly inflamed by her probings, he grasped her buttocks and ground his arousal against her belly. She cried out and thrust back in uninhibited response.

"I feel so—queer," she whispered, dragging her lips from his. "I ache in the oddest places. I—I—" She squirmed against him, making it perfectly clear where her discomfort lay. "I—oh!" She wriggled again. "Nicholas—please help me. I—I—"

"Shh. Hush, now, love," he murmured, stopping her plea with a kiss. "Of course I shall help you, just as you shall help me. I feel exactly as you do, you know."

She looked up at him, her beautiful gray eyes troubled. "I want to help you, truly I do, but I don't know how."

He smiled down at her, his hands going to her hair to release it from its pins. "Never fear, love. I shall show you how."

"But—oh, Nicholas! You know what a mess I make of everything. What if I make matters worse instead of better? You have already suffered so from my stupidity."

"You shan't make a mess of it," he assured her, entranced by the beauty of her hair as it tumbled down her back. This was the first time he'd seen it down, and it was every bit as glorious as he'd imagined. Gently finger combing its golden length, he added, "You also shan't make matters worse. I promise."

She nodded, though her eyes were still filled with uncertainty. "In that instance, w-what should I do next? I mean"—she shook her head—"what would feel good to you?"

He eyed her thoughtfully, then replied, "It would give me great pleasure to look at your body."

She flushed a most delightful shade of rose. "You want me to—to—remove my—uh—clothes?"

"No. I want to remove them myself, but only if you wish me to do so."

Her color deepened, and she bashfully looked away. "I—I wish it very much."

His hands trembling with anticipation, Nicholas reached around to the back of her gown and rather clumsily unbuttoned the buttons. When the garment lay at her feet, he quickly divested her of her corset. Pausing only long enough to kiss her blushing cheek, he pulled her thin cambric chemise over her head. It was then, and only then, that he stepped back to look at her.

She stood before him naked from the waist up, her lower body covered by drawers and long pink stockings. Nicholas couldn't help smiling at her drawers. Of course she wore them. Such garments were worn only by the most modish women, and even in her reduced circumstances she remained *au courant*.

It wasn't her drawers, however, that arrested his attention, interesting though they were with her woman's triangle shadowed beneath them. No. What enthralled him was her form. She was exquisite, a visual feast of slender lines and lush curves.

Never in his life had he seen such breasts as hers, ripe yet firm and succulently round. And her waist! It was so small, flaring into such lusciously rounded hips, that he wondered at her need for a corset. If she were his, he'd toss them away so he would have the pleasure of feeling her delectable body every time he hugged her.

If she were his. His heart raced at the thought of having such sweetness and beauty in his arms every day for the rest of his life. As his gaze moved over her, relishing the flawless texture and blushed cream hue of her skin, his thought firmed into resolution. He would have her . . . for all eternity if she would have him.

"Nicholas? Is something wrong?" Sophie inquired, her voice tinged with alarm. "Don't you like my body."

"Like it?" he groaned. "I adore it. You, Miss Barrington, are the most beautiful creature on earth. It leaves me breathless just looking at you."

She sighed her relief, making her breasts heave in a most tantalizing manner. Smiling timidly, she softly inquired, "Would you mind if I l-look at your body, too?"

He smiled back and held out his arms. "Be my guest."

Worrying her lower lip with her teeth, she slowly unbuttoned his dressing gown. When she finished, he shrugged it off and tossed it onto the worktable behind them. He then turned back to her to allow her to continue.

Quivering as much from excitement as from apprehension, she reached up to unknot his neck cloth. The wicked thing refused to cooperate. No matter what she did, it became more and more tangled. Just when she was ready to scream her frustration, Nicholas removed it for her. "Damn complicated, these knots," he declared, flinging it next to his dressing gown. "Took me years to master them."

Sophie smiled at his obvious attempt to save her feelings. Her heart swelling with tenderness at his thoughtfulness, she unbuttoned his shirt. When he pulled it over his head to bare his torso, she could only stare in stunned awe.

He was perfect, more perfect than she'd ever imagined. So perfect, in fact, that she couldn't resist touching his muscular chest to see if it were as hard as it looked.

It was, and as she'd imagined that day in the garden, the sprinkling of dark hair there was crisp rather than soft. Delighting in the way that crispness tickled her hands, she thoroughly explored the sculpted contours of his chest, then smoothed down his ribs, marveling at the way they tapered into his lean waist.

As she moved inward to trace the ridges of his flat belly, she breathlessly whispered, "Oh, Nicholas. You are so magnificent that I can scarcely believe you are made of flesh and blood."

He moaned and pulled her into his embrace. "I am indeed flesh and blood, my love . . . flesh that trembles beneath your touch, and blood that sings with desire to possess you."

"Then, possess me," she murmured, standing on her tiptoes to kiss him.

His only reply was a feverish groan as he scooped her up in his arms. Pausing a beat to glance about, he finally set her atop the worktable, her backside pillowed by his dressing gown.

For a long moment thereafter he simply looked at her, his gaze hot and hungry. Then a hoarse cry tore from his throat, and he cupped her breasts in his hands. His breath harsh and rasping, he circled her nipples with his thumbs, producing the most exquisite sensations. She moaned her bliss and arched up, thrusting the hardened peaks beneath his fingers.

For several rapturous moments he teased them, flicking and tweaking them in turn, then he leaned down and took them in his mouth. Time froze in a burst of ecstasy as he suckled them, sometimes licking, other times nipping and kissing. No matter what he did, it sent surge after electrifying surge of sensation vibrating through her.

Where those vibrations terminated was deep and low, bedeviling her unmentionable place in a way that made her squirm and groan. Mindless of everything but her need, she grasped his hand and wantonly pressed it between her legs.

Nicholas lifted his head from her breasts to stare at where she held his hand, then he growled and stripped her lower body bare. After laying her back on the table, he parted her swollen flesh, lightly tracing its length as he did so.

She gasped and strained her thighs apart. When he separated her farther to expose and caress her hardened core, she thrashed her hips, screaming her pleasure. For a long while he stimulated her thus, stroking, teasing, and tickling her, then he knelt down and kissed her intimately.

Over and over again he took her to the edge, only to pull back at the last moment. She arched against his mouth, sobbing and begging for release. When she lay wet and trembling before him, he stood up and stripped off his trousers.

"Oh, my! Just look at you," she whispered, rising to her elbows to stare at his sex. Slanting him a shy glance, she stammered, "May I t-touch you?"

At his nod she grasped him. He emitted a strangled sob and jumped. Certain that she had again done something in her ignorance to hurt him, she released him, murmuring, "I'm sorry."

"For what?" He stammered between gritted teeth.

"For hurting you. I didn't mean to do so. I—I just wanted to feel you."

There was a pause, then he softly commanded, "Look at me, Sophie." When she did, she saw that he smiled. "You didn't hurt me. I like you touching me."

"But you jumped," she protested, staring at his handsome face in bewilderment.

"You jumped when I touched you intimately, too. Don't you remember?"

She nodded.

"And did you do so because I hurt you?"

She shook her head. "No. No! What you did felt wonderful."

"Well, that is exactly how it is with me. I move from pleasure, not from pain. Do you see?"

She did see, and smiled. Thus assured, she again took him in her hand.

Nicholas, however, instantly regretted his encouragement. The feel of her fingers, gentle yet eager, as they touched and explored his inflamed length proved far more stimulating than he'd expected. So stimulating, that within moments he was forced to pull from her hands, certain that he'd lose himself if she continued.

"Nicholas?" she whispered, her eyes again wide and worried.

He shook his head at her silent query. "No, my love. You did nothing wrong. What you did was very right, and I promise that next time I shall let you explore me to your heart's content. Right now, however, it is time for us to release each other." After thoroughly kissing her, he again teased her woman's flesh.

When he was certain she was ready to receive him, he moved between her thighs and rubbed his tip over her. She cried out and opened yet wider. Lightly stroking her feminine bud to ease the pain of penetration, he slowly entered her.

Her head shot up at the feel of him, and she exclaimed, "Nicholas! Whatever are you doing?" all while staring at their joining flesh.

"Why, I'm entering you, of course," he murmured, leaning down to kiss her lips.

Her eyes widened. "You're what!"

"Entering you," he repeated. "Surely you know that that is how things are done between a man and a woman?"

She shook her head, her face troubled as she continued to stare at his sex. "But—but—it won't fit."

"Of course it will. Women have babies every day, and a baby is much larger than I shall ever be."

"Yes, well, I hear that it hurts dreadfully to have even the tiniest of babies," she retorted, squirming to remove him.

He smiled gently and drew her up into his embrace. "Unfortunately, I can't promise that this won't hurt the first time. It shall. But the pain will soon pass, and you shall enjoy the experience immensely. I promise."

She frowned, clearly not at all reassured.

He kissed the tip of her nose. "Trust me?"

She gazed at him for a beat, then bit her lip and nodded.

"Good, then try to relax. It will be much easier if you are relaxed." Though she still looked frightened, she leaned back again, calming only when he had again prepared her.

"Now, just relax, love. And remember: You have only to tell me to stop and withdraw, and I shall do so immediately." With that, he eased into her. Though she gasped at the feel of him, she voiced no protest. He entered a fraction more, pausing to stimulate her when she tensed.

Inch by slow inch he moved deeper until he felt the barrier of her maidenhood, then he stopped and gathered her into his arms. Hugging her close, he thrust sharply and broke through. She sobbed and buried her face against his chest.

Expecting her to demand his withdrawal, Nicholas sat perfectly still, stroking her hair. To his surprise, she instead moved her hips, as if adjusting to his size. After a few moments of such squirming, she nodded.

"Are you certain, love?" he murmured, fearful of causing her more pain.

She looked up and smiled. "Yes. It doesn't hurt so much now."

"Do you promise to tell me if the pain worsens?" he said, searching her face for signs of discomfort. There was none.

"I promise." With that vow, she again moved her hips, making him groan at the resulting friction. "Now, please do continue. I find that I like the feel of you inside me."

In one smooth motion he filled her completely. She wrapped her legs about his hips, urging him on. Ardently he complied, thrusting time and again. Soon she found his rhythm and moved with him.

As one now they continued on, thrusting and arching in perfect harmony, their pleasure swelling with every blissful stroke. And when they finally reached their climax, they did so together, shuddering in unison as they found heaven in each other's arms.

"Nicholas! Oh, Nicholas," she gasped as they gently floated back to earth. "Will it always be like this?"

He laid his scarred cheek against her forehead, sighing his contentment. "For all eternity, my love."

Sophie should have been exhausted when she entered the kitchen the next morning, beyond exhaustion really, for she and Nicholas had remained together, laughing and talking and making love until just before dawn. Yet she wasn't tired, not in the least. Indeed she'd never felt so wonderful in her entire life, or so very alive, for Nicholas loved her.

Oh, he hadn't uttered the exact words, but she knew it was so. It had to be. How could he have shared what he'd shared with her last night if he didn't love her? Besides, he'd promised her an eternity of bliss, and a man didn't pledge his eternity to a woman he didn't love. Not a man as good and honorable as Nicholas.

Smiling with all the joy she felt inside, Sophie gaily greeted the staff as she waltzed to the sideboard to collect her ladyship's breakfast tray. She had just picked it up when she heard Cook holler to Meg, "No need to fix Lord Lyndhurst a tray this morning."

Sophie grinned to herself. No doubt he was exhausted and still slept.

"He left for London earlier," Cook continued.

"London?" Sophie exclaimed, her heart freezing in her chest.

Cook nodded without looking up from the carrot she chopped. "It was the queerest thing. His lordship stormed downstairs just after dawn, announcing that he was off to London and demanding that his horse be saddled. Queerer yet, he rode off without a single word to anyone as to when, or even if, he intends to return." She shook her head. "It was like he was running away from something."

Chapter 21

"Your shoulders are sagging again," the marchioness complained, frowning at Sophie. "You are supposed to be Diana, goddess of the moon, remember? And I can assure you that moon goddesses do not slouch. So shoulders up. Up! Up!" She jerked her pencil in an upward motion to illustrate her point.

Sophie murmured an apology and did as instructed. Her ladyship, she'd discovered, had an inordinate fondness for sketching, and ever since her miraculous recovery two weeks earlier she'd insisted that Sophie pose for her every day. Today they worked in the garden before a temple folly with waterfall stairs.

"Let me see, now. What was I saying?" her ladyship muttered, critically eyeing the sketchbook before her. "Oh, yes. I remember." She nodded and added a slashing stroke to the drawing. "I was telling you about the horse race Colin won when he was nine."

Sophie smiled wanly. The woman also had a predilection for talking about Nicholas. Indeed, she'd spoken of little else since he'd left, chatting about everything from his first steps to his latest gardening experiments. It was apparent that she loved and missed him a great deal.

As did Sophie herself.

"Turn your head a little to the left. I want to get your lovely profile."

Sophie complied.

"Just a bit more." The marchioness waved her pencil again. "Yes. There. Perfect. Now, hold that pose." Nodding her satisfaction, she resumed her sketching and her motherly prattle.

Sophie resumed brooding over Nicholas. For almost two weeks now she'd been trying to think of a reason for him leaving as he had. And though she'd thought of dozens of them, only one truly fit his actions, the one she was loath to believe: He regretted their rendezvous in the forcing house and had rushed off to escape her, and the demands he feared she would make. Trouble was, while the explanation fit his actions, it didn't fit the man.

Or at least not the man she thought him to be. A flash of doubt, jagged and painful, ripped through her. Could it be that she was wrong about him? That he wasn't as good and honorable as she believed?

As it always did when she thought that traitorous thought, her mind screamed a resounding no. She couldn't be wrong, she simply couldn't be! Nicholas was exactly as he appeared: kind, good, wise, honorable, gallant, and everything else fine a man could be. Just because he'd gone away as he had, abruptly and mysteriously, gave her no reason to doubt him. Why, there must be a hundred excellent reasons for him doing so that she just hadn't thought of yet.

Maybe even two hundred.

"Sophie. Your shoulders, dear. Your shoulders."

Sophie stiffened both her shoulders and her faith. Nicholas had asked her to trust him and—blast everything! She would. She would continue to do so until he did something to prove himself unworthy of it.

She smiled faintly at that last. Deep in her heart she knew that she would never find him unworthy of her trust, or anything else. Not even if they remained together the eternity he had promised her.

"Oh, botheration!" her ladyship exclaimed.

Sophie hastily squared her shoulders a fraction more and murmured, "I am sorry, my lady. I shall try not to slouch again."

"You are perfect as you are. It's my confounded pencil." The marchioness held up the culprit to reveal its broken lead. "It is my last sharp one."

Sophie was just about to offer to sharpen it when she spied a man over her mistress's shoulder, hurrying toward them. It didn't take a second glance for her to recognize his lustrous mahogany curls and elegant form.

Lord Quentin.

A black chill swept through her. He would recognize her for certain and expose her to his parents.

Strangely enough, that prospect more saddened than frightened her. She had grown exceedingly fond of the jolly marquess and his lovely marchioness, and it would break her heart to lose their goodwill. But lose it she would when Quentin revealed her identity, for how could they not despise her for what she had done to Nicholas? As to what they would do, well, that was less clear.

The marchioness turned at the sound of his footsteps. "Why, Quentin! My darling boy! What a lovely surprise!" She stood up and held out her arms to him, letting her sketchbook tumble to the grass in the process.

Sophie immediately knelt down to retrieve it, hoping to escape Quentin's notice. As an afterthought she shoved the bonnet she had dangling over her arm like a basket back atop her head. There! If she kept her head tipped just so, the brim would hide her face. Hopefully, Quentin would assume her to be just another servant and ignore her.

As she picked up the book and pretended to smooth its pages, she stole an anxious glance at the pair before her. The marchioness had Quentin in her embrace, kissing and fussing over him as if he were five years old. As for Quentin, he was at his most charming, dimpling and fussing back like the most doting of sons. Both appeared quite absorbed in the other.

Good. She bowed her head over the book again. With luck her ladyship would forget all about her and take him back to the house, leaving her behind unnoticed. Exactly what she would do then, she didn't know, but she would think of something.

As usual, luck abandoned her. After several long moments, she heard the rustle of grass. A second later a pair of gleaming boots appeared before her. "And who do we have here, Mother?" Quentin drawled. "Can't say that I recognize the figure."

"No. I am sure you do not, and I shall thank you not to make such personal remarks about the servants," her ladyship replied in a censorious tone. "Especially this particular servant. This is Miss Sophie Barton, Miss Stewart's assistant, and a gentlewoman."

"Indeed?" He more purred than said the word, sending a chill down Sophie's spine. "In that instance, please do allow me to help you up Miss Barton." A gloved hand appeared before her eyes.

Seeing no other choice, Sophie took it and slowly rose, keeping her head bowed in one last desperate attempt to avoid the inevitable. When she was on her feet, she murmured, "Thank you, my lord," and tried to pull her hand from his.

He held tight. "I do hope I didn't offend you with my indelicate remark just now. If I did, please accept my apologies."

"I assure you that you didn't offend me in the least," she replied, again trying to reclaim her hand.

Again, he refused to relinquish it. Instead he moved nearer and whispered, "In that case, I hope you shan't take offense at me telling you that you have a particularly fine figure, one that I wouldn't be at all displeased to find in my bed some night."

"My lord!" she gasped, looking up in her shock.

He, too, gasped.

For a long moment they stared at each other: he, in stunned recognition, she, in terror. Then he smiled slowly.

A suffocating sensation tightened Sophie's throat. Here it came.

To her surprise, he merely kissed her hand and said, "It is a pleasure to make your acquaintance, Miss Barton." Smiling blandly, he tucked her hand in the crook of his arm and turned back to his mother. "I see that I shall have the privilege of escorting two beautiful ladies back to the house."

"Indeed you shall," the marchioness replied, accepting

his other arm. Sophie couldn't help but to notice that she wore that queer expression again.

Like the afternoon of the pineapple tragedy, the stroll back to the house seemed interminable. Indeed, Sophie was certain she would shatter from tension as she awaited Quentin to reveal his game. Whatever he played at, she knew she wasn't going to like the rules, just as she knew that she hadn't a prayer of winning. Better that he denounce her here and now, and end her suffering.

But he gave no sign of doing any such thing. Indeed, he was at his most charming, taking care to include her in the conversation and forcing her to feign laughter at his witty stories. So tortured was she, that by the time they reached the manor she was ready to denounce herself and be done with it.

"My lady, I just sent John to the garden to find you," Dickson exclaimed, opening the door at their approach. He paused a beat to bow, then added, "Cook has a need to consult with you immediately. A problem with the menu, I believe."

The marchioness nodded. "Thank you, Dickson. Please tell her that I shall speak with her in the library this very instant." She handed Sophie her bonnet and gloves, then turned to Quentin.

As she gave him a kiss and a promise for her undivided attention that evening, Sophie escaped up the stairs. Her first instinct was to flee. To run as fast and far away from Hawksbury as possible. Yet there was a part of her that resisted, telling her that Nicholas would return any day now and handle matters.

But what if he didn't return in time? She had no idea how long Quentin would keep his counsel, but she had a feeling that it wouldn't be long. Not unless she consented to join whatever game he played. She had just reached her ladyship's chamber door when someone grabbed her shoulder.

"Well, well. Miss Sophia Barrington. Fancy meeting you here."

Quentin! Panic raced through her veins like quicksilver. So preoccupied was she with her thoughts, that she hadn't heard his approach. Firmly bridling her urge to run, she slowly turned to face him. "What do you want, Quentin?" she whispered, far too distraught to bother with pleasantries.

"The same thing you are giving my brother, of course." The insinuation in his voice was unmistakable.

Pointedly ignoring it, she retorted, "I do not know what you mean."

"Come, come, now, pretty Sophie. Surely you don't think me such a dolt as to believe that Nicholas has granted you sanctuary here out of the goodness of his heart?" He inched nearer. "Good old Colin might be a fine and noble gentleman, but he isn't a particularly forgiving one."

She took a step backward. "Then, you do not know your brother very well, my lord. He is fine, noble, *and* exceedingly forgiving. You would do well to heed his example."

He stepped forward. "Oh. But that is exactly what I wish to do. And I promise that you shall find me just as noble and far finer in bed than you do my brother. Indeed, though I may not be as oafishly large as he, I can assure you that I am counted to be a giant among men— a superbly skilled giant, if you take my meaning."

She did take it, but she had no intention of letting him know that she understood. "You speak in riddles, my lord," she snapped, "riddles to which I have no interest in learning the answers. Now please do go about your business and allow me to go about mine. I have no time for such nonsense."

As she started to turn away, hoping without faith that he would let her go, he grasped her shoulders and pinned her against the door. Pressing his face to hers, he spat, "You don't care for riddles? Fine, then I shall speak plainly. I know that my brother has had his way with you. Everyone in London knows it. Why, I saw dearest Colin at our club just last week, and do you know what he was doing?"

When she refused to reply, he snarled, "He was bandying about how he wooed, won, seduced, and then spurned you. Quite a fitting revenge after the way you jilted him, eh?"

"No! I don't believe you!" she cried, her very soul weeping with anguish at his words. It couldn't be true! Nicholas would never do such a thing.

Yet if it weren't true, how did Quentin know that Nicholas had wooed and won her? Grief such as she had never known welled up in her throat at the answer. As much as she hated to admit it, the explanation suited Nicholas's actions perfectly. All of them.

"Believe it, it is true," he shot back.

"Why are you doing this Quentin?" she whispered, her voice trembling with repressed tears.

"Because I fancy you, and wish you to warm my bed. You are quite lovely, you know." He smiled an undeniably sensual smile as he reached out and lightly fingered a curl.

"And if I refuse?"

"Why, then, I shall tell my parents who you are and personally escort you back to London to face your creditors. I can promise you that no one will stop me from doing so. In case you haven't noticed, dear mother and father quite dote on their beloved heir." He all but spat that last.

To her surprise, he released her then and took a step back. "I shall leave you now, my dearest Miss Barrington, to go about the business to which you are so eager to attend, and to think about what I have said. I will expect you in my chamber no later than midnight." With that, he sketched a bow and stalked away.

She watched him go, despair clinging to her like mist on the moors. There was nothing for her to think about. She must leave. Now. Before she shattered completely and was unable to do so.

Quentin lounged on the drawing room settee, a glass of Madeira in hand, listening to his mother recount Nicholas's recent brush with a pineapple tart. As she described his suffering in detail, he made a note to remember the fruit's effect on his darling brother and use the information to his own advantage. How very amusing it would be to watch the exalted Earl of Lyndhurst break out in spots and lose his bowels before the entire ton.

Not as amusing, of course, as the expression on his face would be when he learned that he'd stolen Miss Barrington from him.

It was all Quentin could do not to rub his hands together in his glee. How his brother could be such a looby as to forgive the chit after what she had done to him, he didn't know. How he could actually love her was beyond the grasp of his wildest imaginings.

But love her he did. And despite the fact that he would most probably be looked upon as the worst sort of nodcock for doing so, he also intended to marry her. He'd overheard Nicholas tell his equally priggish best friend, Lord Huntley, of his plans to do so while at White's just last week. Not that his plans were any great secret. There were rumors flying fast and furious all over Town about him paying Miss Barrington's debts as a wedding gift to her.

Quentin smiled scornfully. He had no doubt that the rumors were true. It was just the sort of thing his brother would do for the woman he loved. It would also make what he was about to do all the more gratifying. Nicholas's pockets would be thousands of pounds lighter with nothing to show for his investment but heartbreak and embarrassment.

As for himself, he would have the pleasure of telling the ton that his perfect, privileged brother had once again made a fool of himself over Miss Barrington. How sweet it would be to reveal yet more tarnish on Nicholas's seemingly flawless armor. Almost as sweet as the way it would discredit him in his parents' eyes. In his mind they esteemed him far beyond his desert, and it was high time they realized that he wasn't at all the nonpareil they blindly assumed him to be.

He out and out grinned as he thought of what they would do and say when they discovered that the Lord of all Goodness and Light had actually planned to marry the very chit who had disgraced him. If anything could make them realize their mistake in revering him so, it was that. When he then explained how he had seduced

Miss Barrington to save poor Colin from making a dreadful mistake, they were bound to transfer some of that adoration to him.

"Why, Quentin! How can you smile so? I hardly find your brother's tongue swelling up and almost choking him amusing," his mother chided.

Quentin instantly sobered. "Nor do I. I was simply marveling at his fortitude in enduring his trial so bravely." No doubt Lord Paragon hadn't uttered so much as a cross word during his ordeal.

"Yes. He was very brave," she agreed, her face glowing with pride, as it always did when she spoke of her precious firstborn. "Poor dear didn't complain even once, though he had every reason in the world to do so."

Of course he didn't, damn him.

Before they could resume their discussion of Nicholas's virtues, there was a scratch at the door.

The marquess looked up from the newspaper he read and directed, "Enter."

It was Dickson, an exceedingly agitated Dickson. "My lady. My lords." He bowed. "I am afraid that I have the most distressing news. We have been robbed!"

Quentin saw his parents' gazes dart to him. "Don't look at me. I didn't do it," he protested, genuinely insulted. Just because he had once made off with a valuable Chinese vase to pay his tailor bill was no reason to automatically suspect him this time. Besides, the vase incident had taken place over six months ago . . . a veritable lifetime. It was high time they forgave and forgot.

"Well, you cannot blame us for being suspicious," his father retorted, eyeing him dubiously. "The only time you ever grace us with your presence is when you are in need of funds."

Which was the case this time as well, though finding Miss Barrington here had quite erased the purpose from his mind. He'd naturally assumed that Nicholas had tucked her away in Scotland or some other remote place until he had cleared her debts and paved the way for their marriage. Thus, it had come as an enormous shock finding her beneath his parent's roof . . .

A shock, a boon, and a blessing. The boon, of course, was his chance to discredit Nicholas in his parents' eyes; the blessing was that Miss Barrington had so readily believed his tale about his brother seducing her for revenge. Admittedly, he had taken a chance in assuming that Lord Virtue had bedded her. He was, after all, just the sort of man to wait for a trip to the altar before taking his beloved's maidenhead. That he had obviously not waited, at least judging from the chit's devastated expression, made him feel a niggle of grudging respect for the old boy.

"Oh, no, my lord. The thief most definitely wasn't Lord Quentin," Dickson was saying. "The theft occurred in the kitchen."

"I can't imagine there being much worth stealing there," the marquess mused thoughtfully.

The majordomo nodded. "On most days you would be quite right, my lord. Today, however, the silver was brought down for its monthly polishing. It was at a point between the time the footmen finished the polishing and carried it back up to the safe that the crime was committed. It—"

"What exactly was stolen?" the marchioness interrupted.

"Two spoons and a salt cellar, my lady."

She frowned. "I simply cannot imagine any of the servants stealing from us. Did you question everyone?"

He looked uncomfortably at his feet. "Everyone but Miss Barton. She is nowhere to be found."

"Well, I am quite certain that she isn't our culprit," she retorted, her frown deepening.

Quentin, too, frowned, instantly understanding her absence. Stupid little bitch. So she thought to evade him, did she? Well, they would just see about that. Clearing his throat, he said, "I wouldn't be so very certain of that if I were you, Mother."

"Indeed?" The way she looked at him, eyes narrowed and lips pursed, you would think that he, in contesting her, had committed a sin every bit as grave as theft.

He nodded. Well, her expression would change quickly enough once he'd said his piece. "As much as it grieves me to tell you this, Sophie isn't Miss Barton, but Miss Barrington, the very chit who jilted and humiliated Colin. I didn't mention it right off because I wasn't quite certain how to tell you. You seem rather fond of the girl."

The look his parents exchanged wasn't so much surprised as it was odd. "Even if that is true, what makes you think that she is the thief?" This was from his father.

"In case you haven't heard, she fled London to avoid debtors prison."

"Indeed?" his mother murmured.

He nodded. "Yes. And she is so certain that you will turn her over to the authorities if you find out who she is, that she begged me not to reveal her identity to you. Knowing how distressed you are over what she did to Colin and that you would wish to know of her deception, I naturally refused."

He paused to nod again. "My guess is that she stole the silver to purchase transportation to take her as far from here as possible, thus saving herself from your wrath."

Another strange glance between his parents.

"Do you wish me to have the grooms search for her?" Dickson inquired, looking rather down in the mouth. It was apparent that he, too, liked the girl.

"Well—" His father stared at his mother. "I suppose we have no choice. If the girl is a thief, she must be brought to justice."

"I suppose so," she agreed with a sigh. "Please do send the grooms, Dickson. She can't have gone far."

Quentin bowed his head to hide his smile. Not only was Nicholas's intended a liar and a jilt, she was a thief as well. Perfect.

"Mr. Renton, the parish constable," Dickson announced.

The constable! Sophie stared at the hulking, grim-faced man the majordomo ushered into the drawing room, her insides coiling with fear. This had to be a nightmare, it simply had to be! Only in a nightmare could her life be so wretched and continue to get progressively worse with every passing second.

Fighting to keep her panic at bay, she closed her eyes. She would count to twenty and then awake. When she did so, she would find herself safe in her bed with Nicholas still at Hawksbury and in love with her.

One . . . two . . .

As she counted, she heard the marchioness exclaim, "The constable? Who the devil summoned the constable?"

Seven . . . eight . . . nine . . .

"I did, Mother. Considering the circumstances, I thought it for the best."

Fourteen . . . Quentin, of course. The demon of her dream . . . fifteen . . . sixteen . . .

"Really, Quentin! I hardly think it was necessary to send for the constable," her ladyship chided. "Your father and I are perfectly capable of dealing with our own servant problems."

Twenty! Sophie pinched herself for good measure, then opened her eyes. She still sat in the blue drawing room, and the constable still stood a scant ten feet away, looking, if possible, even more menacing than before.

"Pardon, my lady, but thievery is everyone's problem," the man objected, his voice every bit as ominous as his appearance. "If a thief's crimes are ignored or too easily dismissed, they will be repeated again and again, each time to a greater magnitude." He shook his white-wigged head. "As I always say: Pardon the theft of bread today, and you create the highwayman of tomorrow."

"I hardly think Miss Barrington likely to take to highway robbery," the marquess commented dryly. "Besides, my wife and I have serious doubts as to her guilt."

"Yes. There isn't the slightest bit of evidence of her guilt," her ladyship chimed in.

Her husband nodded. "There you have it, Mr. Renton. As you can see, we have no need of your services." He signaled the majordomo. "Please do accept my most humble apologies on behalf of my son for inconveniencing you so, sir. Dickson shall show you out."

The constable frowned. "A thousand pardons, my

lord. Be the girl innocent or no, the fact remains that
there is a thief in your house. As parish constable, it is
my duty to find and apprehend him."

"Yes. Besides, Miss Barrington is hardly without guilt.
There still remains an outstanding warrant for her arrest
in London." Quentin, naturally.

"A warrant you say?" The constable's beady blue eyes
shifted to Sophie. Of course they held no mercy. "Is this
the felon?" He jabbed an accusing finger in her
direction.

Quentin's gaze, too, was on Sophie, spiteful and trium
phant. Forbidding herself to show her fear, she returned
it with as much disdain as she could muster. Oh, how
could she have ever thought those violet eyes beautiful?

As they dueled with their glares, he replied, "That,
sir, is Miss Sophia Barrington, one of the most notorious
and despised women in all of London. Not only is she
guilty of defrauding the entire ton, she racked up enormous debts during the Season and then fled the city
when her game was discovered."

Despite her best efforts to remain brave, she shrank
back in her chair in terror. On the verge of hysteria now,
she gazed first at the marchioness, then the marquess,
mutely pleading for help. The couple exchanged a peculiar look, then Lord Beresford smiled—a smile that
turned into a frown as Quentin added, "She is indeed
a felon."

"Have you proof of her guilt, brother?" a voice rang
out.

Sophie's heart stilled in her chest as she recognized
that voice, that deep, lovely . . . beloved voice.

Nicholas.

Not quite certain what to feel or think, she followed
the sound of his voice to where he stood in the open
door. It was apparent from his hat and greatcoat that he
had only just arrived.

With the majordomo dogging his steps, clearly anxious
to relieve him of his outer garments, he stalked into the
room. "Damn you, Quentin," he spat. "What sort of
mischief are you about this time?"

"I could ask the same of you, Colin." This was from Lady Beresford.

Nicholas glared at his brother for several more beats, his handsome face a mask of fury, then he slowly turned to the marchioness. "Please do explain yourself, Mother."

"I think it is perfectly obvious. You allowed Miss Barrington, the same Miss Barrington who publicly shamed you, to take refuge beneath our roof without offering so much as a clue to anyone as to her true identity. You then proceeded to champion her at every turn, and finally coaxed me into allowing her to serve as my personal maid." So disapproving was her expression, that had Nicholas not been a grown man, she'd have no doubt taken him over her knee and spanked him until he was unable to sit for a week.

As it was, she wagged her finger, finishing in a most severe tone, "And as if that in itself isn't quite enough, you fly off to London to do heaven only knows what, without a single by-your-leave to either your father or I. Worst yet, you remain there for nigh on a fortnight without bothering to send a note to relieve my worried mind."

Rather than look chastened, Nicholas simply looked more irate. "Surely you know me better than to suspect me of knavery?"

"Of course we do, my boy," his father exclaimed, starting to rise. "We—"

"We had no idea what to make of your sudden, irrational behavior," her ladyship cut in, shooting her husband a quelling look. He shrugged and sat back down again.

The constable cleared his throat. "It seems that I intrude on family business. Therefore, I shall take the girl and be off to allow you to discuss your affairs in private."

"Yes. Please do take her," Quentin said, smirking at his brother.

Sophie, too, gazed at Nicholas, her heart crying out in anguish. All she wanted was a sign: a look, gesture, or a word. Anything to show her that he indeed cared for

her, that Quentin had lied. Even if he was unable to
save her from prison, and she doubted he could, just
knowing that he loved her would make her life worth
living. It would be a light in the darkness of her future.

Before anyone could respond, however, John charged
through the open door, hauling a sobbing Pansy in his
wake. Miss Stewart followed on his heels, looking uncharacteristically distraught.

"My lords. My lady." He bowed as best he could with
the laundry maid struggling in his arms. "I have found
our thief."

"Pansy? Oh, no. It cannot be," Sophie exclaimed,
springing to her feet to go to her friend.

Mr. Renton was by her in a flash, roughly shoving her
back down again. "You! Stay where you are!" he
bellowed.

"And you, keep your hands off her," Nicholas
growled, his long coat swishing furiously around his legs
as he advanced toward the man. "There is a strict rule
at Hawksbury against manhandling women, regardless
of the circumstances."

"Hawksbury? Hell, that rule applies to the entire parish," his father boomed, marching over to join forces
with his son.

The constable looked from lord to wrathful lord, visibly taken aback by their ire.

"Why do you care how he treats the chit, Colin?"
Quentin baited. "After the way she humiliated you, I
should think that you would want nothing more than to
see her get her just rewards."

Nicholas transferred his wrathful gaze to him. "Unlike
yourself, brother, I have the capacity to forgive." He
more spat than uttered the words.

An ugly expression contorted Quentin's beautiful face.
"Ah, yes. Of course. Let us not forget that we are in
the presence of Saint Colin, Lord of Perfection."

Rather than be further incensed by the taunt, Nicholas
looked suddenly weary. "Quentin—"

"*Ahem!*" John cleared his throat, interrupting whatever it was he might have said. When every pair of eyes

in the room was upon the footman, he inquired, "Pardon. But what about Pansy?"

Nicholas and his father glanced at each other, then the marquess inquired, "How do you know that she is the thief?"

"Because we caught her with the stolen property."

"But I were putting it back. 'Onest I were!" Pansy exclaimed, glancing wildly about the room.

"Is that true?" the marchioness queried, standing as well.

It was Miss Stewart who replied, "Yes. It is true, my lady. She apparently didn't see John and I sitting before the fire when she entered the kitchen. Thus, we saw her remove the spoons and salt cellar from her apron, and place them on Cook's worktable." She glanced at Pansy, her lips curving into the kindest of smiles. "Would you like to tell her ladyship your reason for taking them?"

When the girl merely hung her head, sniffling loudly, the lady's maid prompted, "It's all right, dear. I am certain that her ladyship will understand." She uttered that last while shooting the marchioness a pleading look, who nodded in response.

Though Pansy continued to hang her head and sniffle, she slowly choked out, "I needed blunt t' get married. I'm 'xpecting a babe, you see, an' Ezra 'n' me can't afferd to get buckled. Not till we got money to rent a farm. We been saving and saving, and we'd 'ave 'ad 'nough in a year, but that ain't soon 'nough."

"I see," her ladyship murmured. "And did this Ezra know of your plans to steal the silver?"

Pansy's head came up in a flash. "Oh, nay! Nay, my lady! There ain't a no more 'onest man than my Ezra. 'E'd nivver want me to do nothing wrong. It were all my doing."

The marquess and marchioness exchanged a frown.

"I can see that you were indeed desperate, Pansy," Nicholas said, both his tone and expression compassionate. "What I don't understand is why you returned the silver."

Pansy looked at Sophie, tears streaming down her pale cheeks. "I 'eard that the constable 'ad come to take

Sophie away fer the crime, 'n' I couldn't bear to let that 'appen. Sophie's my friend, my best friend. There ain't nutting I wouldn't do fer 'er."

"Well. That settles that," Mr. Renton declared, moving toward Pansy. "The stolen property has been returned, and the thief has confessed. All that remains is for me to arrest her."

"No!" Sophie gasped, coming to her feet again. Rushing across the room, she threw her arms around her friend, exclaiming, "You cannot arrest her! Since she returned the property, she cannot be accused of truly stealing it." Her gaze found Nicholas's, and she pleaded, "Surely a wise man like yourself, Lord Lyndhurst, can see the truth of my words?"

He nodded and smiled. It was a gentle smile, full of wisdom and warmth, the same smile that never failed to melt her heart. "Miss Barrington is indeed correct. There has been no real crime committed. Please release Pansy this instant, John."

John immediately complied, looking relieved to do so.

"But, my lord! You can't just dismiss this incident," the constable protested. "This girl indeed stole from your family. That she decided to return the property and confess most certainly doesn't excuse her crime."

"She did something far more important than just return the silver. She proved her loyalty to the Somerville family," Nicholas retorted.

"She proved her loyalty to Miss Barrington, not our family," Quentin sneered.

The marchioness shot him an exasperated look. "Do be quiet, Quentin. I have had quite enough of your spiteful harping."

"You are wrong, brother," Nicholas replied, quietly. His gaze was on Sophie again, his eyes gleaming and his expression tender. "Pansy indeed displayed loyalty for a Somerville."

"Just like your father. Always speaking in riddles," his mother complained. "Do just say what you mean."

"I mean that I wish Miss Barrington to be Mrs. Nicholas Somerville, the Countess of Lyndhurst," he smiled faintly, "if you will have me, Sophie. I truly meant it when I promised you my eternity. I love you."

Sophie gaped at him, barely able to believe her ears. He loved and wanted to marry her. Her worst nightmare had just turned into her fondest dream.

His smile broadened then, displaying the dimples she so adored.

And she ran to him, her heart ready to burst with joy. "Oh, Nicholas! Yes! Of course I will marry you. I love you, too."

He caught her as she rushed into his arms and swept her up into a kiss that expressed everything in his heart.

"It's about time you declared yourself, boy," the marquess remarked. "Thought I was going to have to save the girl myself."

"What!" Sophie and Nicholas exclaimed in unison, though they remained firmly in each other's arms.

The marchioness nodded. "Your father saw your feelings for the gel first, and guessed her identity. When he told me, I must say that I was a bit shocked. And with good reason. Even you must admit that it is beyond unbelievable that you could love Miss Barrington after all that has happened." She shook her head, as if still amazed. "You both must sit down and tell me how such a thing came to pass someday. It is certain to be a most lively tale . . . a fine one to tell my grandchildren."

"Then, you have no objection to our marriage?"

She made an impatient noise. "Of course not. All your father and I ever wished for you is that you be happy. Your father made me see that Miss Barrington shall make you so. Besides, I like the gel. Best model I ever had, even if she slouches." She winked at Sophie. "How about giving your future mother-in-law a hug?"

"And your father-in-law as well," the marquess added, moving to stand beside his wife.

As she joyfully did so, Mr. Renton cleared his throat. "This is all very touching, but there is still the matter of the warrant for Miss Barrington's arrest."

Nicholas looked away from his bride-to-be long enough to glance at the majordomo. "Would you please bring the packet I brought from London, Dickson?"

The man presented him with a flat black leather case. "I anticipated your need and already fetched it, my lord."

"Remind me to raise your wages, Dickson," the marquess said.

Dickson grinned. "Very good, my lord."

Nicholas shuffled through the case, then drew out several papers. Handing them to the constable, he said, "These rescind the warrant. I am certain that you shall find everything in order." With that, he moved to Sophie, who stood encircled by his father's arm, and handed her the case. "The rest of this is for you, my love."

Sophie examined the contents, her eyes widening when she realized what it was she looked at. It was receipt after receipt, all marked paid in full. "Oh, Nicholas. You settled my debts," she exclaimed, breathless in her gratitude.

"I saw no choice if I wish to show off my bride to the ton next Season. It would be ever so tiresome to constantly fight off the sheriffs," he teased, opening his arms to embrace her again.

She eyed him rather solemnly. "I doubt the ton shall accept me after all that has happened."

"Nonsense, my dear!" the marchioness interjected. "The ton wouldn't dare cut a Somerville. Harry and I shall be there to make certain that they don't try."

"And I shall be by your side, beaming with pride," Nicholas declared. "Now, how about another kiss for your future husband."

She was back in his arms in a twinkling. As they kissed, Dickson led Mr. Renton from the room, while Quentin snorted his disdain and stalked off.

Oblivious to everything but their love for each other, Nicholas pulled his lips from Sophie's and rested his forehead against hers. Gazing deeply into her eyes, he murmured, "What would you like for a wedding gift, my love?"

She smiled and stole another kiss. "You have already done so much for me, it hardly seems right that I ask for more."

"It is a husband's duty to spoil his wife," he teased, stealing one back. "So what shall it be? Jewelry? A house in London? Anything. You have only to ask."

She considered for a beat, then said, "Actually, there are two things I want."

"Ah. I see that I am about to saddle myself with a greedy wife," he countered with a mock groan.

She shook her head. "Never. Just grant me these two wishes, and I promise that I shall never ask you for another thing."

"I shall be delighted to grant you both your wishes, and a great many more. Ask away."

She did as directed, dropping a kiss to his lips after each request. "I want Pansy and Ezra to have their farm, not to rent, but to own. And I want Fancy for my lady's maid."

As Nicholas opened his mouth to reply, a gravelly voice boomed, "Unhand the gel this instant, Lyndhurst."

Sophie's gaze flew in the direction from which the voice had come. There, standing in the door, was a thin, stooped figure in a cherry-red greatcoat and an exceedingly tall top hat. Remembering the stir a similar coat had caused at her parents' funeral, she gasped, "Uncle Arthur?"

"Of course. Who were you expecting? Wellington?" he retorted, hobbling into the room with the aid of a cane.

"No. It's just that—"

"I said to unhand her, boy," he cut in, pounding his cane against the parquet floor for emphasis. "I still ain't decided whether or not I'm going to let you marry her."

Nicholas shot Sophie a pained look and did as directed, muttering, "I should have left him in Bath."

"You brought him here?" she exclaimed.

He nodded. "Of course. He is your guardian now, and it is only right that I ask his permission to marry you."

"But how—" She made a helpless hand gesture.

He grinned. "You mentioned him that night on the road when you explained your presence at Hawksbury. Remember?"

"Yes. I'm just surprised you remembered."

"Not remember that you're Bomphrey's great-niece?" He chuckled. "Arthur, here, has been a family friend for years. Indeed, he and my grandfather were the best of friends."

"And a worse grouse hunter I never saw. Always worried that he'd shoot my hounds by mistake," grumbled her uncle, tottering nearer. When he reached the center of the room, he pounded the floor with his cane again and commanded, "Well, don't just stand there gaping, gel. Come and give your old uncle a kiss."

When she had dutifully hugged him and kissed his withered cheek, he wrapped his arm possessively around her waist and rasped, "Now, about this marriage business. Before I give my consent, I want to know why you two want to wed?"

"I already told you why: We are in love," Nicholas replied, his eyes gleaming with adoration as they met hers.

"Yes, but do you love each other enough to spend a lifetime together?" her uncle shot back.

Nicholas took a step forward, holding his arms out to Sophie as he did so. She pulled herself from her uncle's grasp and ran to him. As he crushed her into his embrace, he huskily replied, "Enough for all eternity."

"Yes. Eternity," she whispered, staring up into his beloved face.

And in their hearts they knew it was true.

☐LAIRD OF THE WIND 0-451-40768-7/$5.99

In medieval Scotland, the warrior known as Border Hawk seizes the castle belonging to the father of the beautiful Isabel Scott, famous throughout the Lowlands for her gift of prophecy. During the battle, Isabel is injured while fighting alongside her men and placed under Border Hawk's protection. As the border wars rage on, the warrior and prophetess engage in a more intimate conflict, discovering their love for the Scottish borderlands is surpassed only by their love for each other.

Also available:

☐THE ANGEL KNIGHT	0-451-40662-1/$5.50
☐THE BLACK THORNE'S ROSE	0-451-40544-7/$4.99
☐LADY MIRACLE	0-451-40766-0/$5.99
☐THE RAVEN'S MOON	0-451-18868-3/$5.99
☐THE RAVEN'S WISH	0-451-40545-5/$4.99

Prices slightly higher in Canada

Payable in U.S. funds only. No cash/COD accepted. Postage & handling: U.S./CAN. $2.75 for one book, $1.00 for each additional, not to exceed $6.75; Int'l $5.00 for one book, $1.00 each additional. We accept Visa, Amex, MC ($10.00 min.), checks ($15.00 fee for returned checks) and money orders. Call 800-788-6262 or 201-933-9292, fax 201-896-8569; refer to ad #TOPHR1

Penguin Putnam Inc.	Bill my: ☐Visa ☐MasterCard ☐Amex _____ (expires)
P.O. Box 12289, Dept. B	Card#_____
Newark, NJ 07101-5289	Signature_____

Please allow 4-6 weeks for delivery.
Foreign and Canadian delivery 6-8 weeks.

Bill to:

Name_____
Address_____City_____
State/ZIP_____
Daytime Phone #_____

Ship to:

Name_____	Book Total	$_____
Address_____	Applicable Sales Tax	$_____
City_____	Postage & Handling	$_____
State/ZIP_____	Total Amount Due	$_____

This offer subject to change without notice.